# THE COMPANION

# THE COMPANION

## LESLEY THOMSON

HEAD
of ZEUS

*An Aries Book*

First published in the UK in 2022 by Head of Zeus Ltd,
part of Bloomsbury Publishing Plc

9 7 5 3 1 2 4 6 8

A catalogue record for this book is available from
the British Library.

ISBN (HB): 9781801109260
ISBN (XTPB): 9781801109277
ISBN (E): 9781801109246

Typeset by Divaddict Publishing Solutions Ltd

Printed and bound in Great Britain by
CPI Group (UK) Ltd, Croydon CR0 4YY

Head of Zeus Ltd
First Floor East
5–8 Hardwick Street
London EC1R 4RG

WWW.HEADOFZEUS.COM

*For Philippa Brewster who set me on this road.*
*Thank you, dear friend.*

All day within the dreamy house,
The doors upon their hinges creak'd;
The blue fly sung in the pane; the mouse
Behind the mouldering wainscot shriek'd,
Or from the crevice peer'd about.
Old faces glimmer'd thro' the doors,
Old footsteps trod the upper floors,
Old voices called her from without.
She only said, 'My life is dreary,
He cometh not,' she said;
She said, 'I am aweary, aweary,
I would that I were dead.'

"Mariana", Stanza 6, by Alfred, Lord Tennyson

# I

'Boys' day out. Let's do it.' Bouncing on his heels, James Ritchie rubbed his hands.

'You haven't shaved and you're late.' Opening the front door only inches, Anna Petty groused, 'Wilbur's been ready over twenty minutes.'

'It's a beard. Hey, cut me slack, Anna.' James saw himself as a punctual person who was inexplicably never on time. Today he'd stopped to, as he called it, farm Facebook. A 'like' here, a laughing emoji there to show the good guy he was. He'd been gratified to see that his post on the page for old pupils of his school – *Who remembers that music teacher Mr Braid who chucked board rubbers at the boys for looking out the window?* – had garnered eleven comments and twenty likes. Ridiculous how happy it had made him, if only for a few minutes. He'd checked to see if Anna had liked it – loved it – she hadn't.

Lots of forty- and fifty-something men had been hit on the head by the rubber's wooden grip. A woman had posted that Mr Braid 'sadly passed in 1994 of a brain tumour which might explain his unpredictability.' 'A brain tumour without a brain? How's that work?' James finger-typed, infuriated by the sanctimonious tone of this Susan Parker. She'd apparently started at school the year he'd left, what did she know? He'd heard Anna's voice in his head saying how James always had to be smarter, cooler and nastier and deleted it. To bolster his dipping mood, James had scrolled through his friends, last count 403. That's when he saw that Anna had unfollowed him.

Now, he told Anna, 'Mr Braid, you know, the music teacher with the bad skin? He died of a brain tumour.'

'How do you know?'

'I saw it on Facebook.'

'Sorry, did we tear you away from social media for a day out with your son?'

*Crap.*

'You're not my friend any more. Why's that?' James couldn't help himself.

'Jamie, don't let's do this now.' Anna touched his arm.

Anna had cited James's hours of tweeting and facebooking as one reason for wanting a divorce. *'There are three of us in the marriage; ooh, silly me for forgetting. I mean four and counting...'*

Twenty minutes past eleven on Saturday and Anna wore make-up, a short tweed skirt topped with a Fair Isle polo-neck, undyed blonde hair carefully twined into a careless bun. James's beard was spur of the moment, he hadn't washed or shaved. His hair, grey since his twenties, was finger-raked. He'd slept in his shirt.

'Are we going?' The dark patches under Wilbur Ritchie's eyes were more typical of a depressed sleep-deprived adult than a nine-year-old boy. His parents, thrashing through the thorns and tangles of their own lives, were blind to the toll it was taking on their son.

'*Let's go fly a kite...*' Singing the Mary Poppins song in a rich baritone, workman's flat cap at an angle, James was Dick van Dyke. Anna covered her smile with a hand, James had always been able to make her laugh.

'Don't let him near the cliff, a man went off there flying a kite.' The day before when James had rung to propose the trip and Anna had objected, she'd agreed not to mention the tragedy – some years before – in front of Wilbur. 'It's a common accident.'

'Mum, come with us.' Wilbur became animated.

'It's just us, remember?' James said. Then, because he too wanted Anna to come, 'You can if you want.'

'I'm going shopping. When you're back tomorrow, we'll have roast chicken for tea, your *favourite*. A treat even though it's a school night.' Anna was showing James she knew what Wilbur loved. The hectic outings, go-karting, paintballing, kite-flying, were for James, not his son.

Wilbur pecked his mother on the cheek. He wouldn't let his dad see he wanted to stay with his mum. 'Mummy', when it was just them. Heart heavy, Wilbur trotted to his father's Toyota Aygo – the flashy Qashqai a casualty of their separation – and numbly strapped himself in the front seat.

'He loves this stuff. Spoiling him with food will make him fat.' James spun on his heel.

Anna Petty waved at Wilbur, the wan face like something out of *Turn of the Screw* burned into her memory. The image would alter over time, from brave little soldier to scared eyes to abject terror until Anna came to believe Wilbur had mouthed *Help* through the glass and would blame herself for staying behind.

'If you had, you'd be dead too,' people said.

# 2

*Freddy*

'...Lord God, Lamb of God, you take away
the sins of the world, have mercy on us.
Lord God, Lamb of God, you take away
the sins of the world, have mercy on us.
Lord God, Lamb of God, you take away
the sins of the world, grant us peace...'

Freddy Power dropped her voice to a whisper to better hear
Rex, sitting next to her in the pew, recite the Communion Rite
after Father Pete, robe swishing, had raised the host, showing
it to each of his communicants. A retired defence counsel,
Rex Lomax's voice conjured liquid chocolate; the crack in his
timbre must easily have swayed many a jury to let a criminal
walk. Just seventy, in a powder-blue suit, Rex still had it.

Brought up a Catholic, but lapsed after she left the convent
school twenty or so years ago, Freddy had been attending
Mass at Our Lady of Sorrows for three months. Her reason
for returning was because, Freddy had told herself, Rex's
regular driver had retired and Rex would have to get a taxi.

On the spur of the moment, as she was stowing Rex's weekly fish order in his freezer, Freddy had offered to take him.

She was not, she had insisted to Toni, returning to God.

Taking Rex to Mass had prompted a gear change in Rex and Freddy's acquaintanceship. Until then Freddy Power had been Rex Lomax's mobile fishmonger. Their exchanges were limited to the weather, how Rex might cook his fish, a run on smoked salmon due to a recipe on *MasterChef*. They hadn't discussed each other's lives. With much to hide, Freddy was grateful, although Rex knew the Powers had owned a fish processing factory on Newhaven Harbour, but then, everyone knew. It was also common knowledge that one of Freddy's brothers was in prison and the other had drowned at sea, but Rex never referred to this. However, last year, when Power Fisheries – the name retained because it carried currency – was destroyed in an electrical fire weeks after it was sold, Rex had expressed his sympathy. Freddy had made light of it – she could get her produce from Newhaven's other fishery. She didn't say this suited her because, although Fred Power senior had been dead decades, for her, his presence had still darkened the business.

Freddy knew that Rex's wife Emily had died in a car crash five years ago, on the lane near Blacklock House soon after the Lomaxes had moved there. Freddy had been told that by Garry Haslem, another resident of Blacklock House, while he was humming and hah-ing over which fish to buy. 'Poor Emily's Citroën shoots off the road, hits a tree and... boom.' Garry never pulled punches. 'After that, Rexy lost his mojo, poor bugger.'

Whatever mojo Rex Lomax had lost, Freddy supposed he'd found it because driving him to and from Our Lady of

Sorrows on Sundays, Rex had become chatty. He told Freddy Emily had been his soulmate, she'd kept him on the straight and narrow and wasn't afraid to tell him when he was wrong. 'We all need that, don't we?'

Freddy, plucking up courage to try a dating app, wondered if she should put that she wanted to meet a woman who would tell her when she was wrong. Sarah had been good at that and Freddy had *not* needed it. When Freddy had come out to her family, her father had not only told her she was wrong, he'd called her 'a freak of nature' and kicked her out. Since his death when she was twenty, Freddy had been free to be herself and to love women. *If she could meet the right one.*

Last week, Rex had said the lawyer in him was still tortured by unanswered questions. The police had found nothing wrong with Emily's car. The afternoon of the fatal accident the roads were dry, thin cloud had filtered dazzle from the low winter sun. In short, there had been excellent visibility. Emily didn't drink and wasn't on medication. Before impact, she had not suffered a brain bleed nor had a cardiac arrest. Rex used medico-legal language, his inner lawyer having scoured the reports on Emily's death. Freddy felt for him; beyond asking God why he allowed terrible things to happen, Freddy herself had no unanswered questions.

The first time they'd gone to Mass, Freddy had cancelled brunch with Toni, her best friend since convent school. With no more faith now than she'd had then, Toni had objected to being 'blown out' for God. She warned Freddy that if Rex was a father figure, 'He'll likely turn out as rubbish as your actual dad. Whatever, I don't like him taking advantage of your lovely nature. He can afford to live in Buckingham Palace,

surely he can afford a cab to go and confess his sins.' Freddy
had explained that she loved the drive through country lanes
and villages while *not* selling fish.

Father Pete's voice lulling her, Freddy's mind drifted again
as it occurred to her that Toni was envious of her friendship
with Rex. No, that couldn't be. Nicky Kemp – who had died
when they were kids – was everyone's favourite dad, certainly
Freddy's. More likely Toni – Detective Inspector Antonia
Kemp now – was looking out for Freddy. They were each
other's *person*.

One day at Blacklock House, leaning on the fish van, Garry
Haslem had hoarsely whispered that Rex had Parkinson's.
Freddy had seen an occasional tremor in Rex's hand. He no
longer came down for his fish, instead Freddy delivered it to
his flat. She was caught out by how sad Garry's news made
her feel.

Today must be a good day. Rex had given the first reading,
standing straight at the lectern. Looking nearer sixty than
seventy he still resembled the younger handsome Rex in
the wedding photograph of decades ago, displayed on his
mantelpiece.

While Rex was reading, Freddy had glanced down and
spotted something under the pew in front. Twisting, she'd
scrabbled up not a coin, but a devotional medallion.

*Follow the footprints of the Lord. They will lead you
through troubled times and brighten your life.*

Freddy's mother had kept a St Benedict medallion in her
purse. *Vade Retro Satana.* Satan Be Gone. Once, when they
were kids, Freddy's brother Andy had asked Reenie if Satan

was one of the pets lodged in Reenie Power's small animal hotel, a garden shed housing rabbits, gerbils and the like. Overhearing, Fred Power had smacked Andy on the head for being blasphemous. Neither Andy nor Freddy understood the word nor dared ask. Freddy did know a St Benedict medal wasn't a talisman to ward off evil, but a reminder that you served God, yet from that day she'd prayed for *Vade Retro Fred Power*. A prayer answered unexpectedly when, at his surprise sixtieth birthday party, her dad's surprise was a fatal heart attack.

Sweeping her too-long fringe away from her eyes, Freddy caught Jesus gazing down from the altar and crossed herself.

*Follow the footprints of the Lord. They will lead you through troubled times and brighten your life.*

After her mum's death, Freddy had found her St Benedict medallion in her purse. Despite considering herself 'lapsed', Freddy carried it in her own purse, comforted by knowing it was there.

'*...but only say the word...*'

'and my soul shall be healed.' Freddy hurried out the end of the response to the invitation to communion. On a whim, she turned to Rex and pressed the medal, warmed by her grip, into his palm. He examined it and reddened. *She'd embarrassed him.*

'How lovely, Freddy.' Rex's face broadened into a smile. 'How lovely of you.'

*Thank God.* Freddy felt Rex tense when Father Pete had spoken Emily's name at the start of Mass. Now Rex knew Freddy was there for him. Moments later she nearly gasped out loud. *She'd given Rex stolen goods.*

Suppose the owner came looking for their medallion? She

9

could not claim it was the thought that counted. She should have handed it in to Father Pete.

*'The Body of Christ.'*

Suffused with guilt, Freddy choked out, 'Amen.' She scrambled from the pew and pattered after Rex up the aisle to Father Pete. When it was her turn, she crossed her arms over her chest as a sign she wouldn't take communion.

As Father Pete anointed her forehead, his eyes rested on hers. He never put pressure on Freddy to re-join the church. Until she did, she couldn't take communion.

*Thou shall not steal... and then pass off your ill-gotten gains as a present.*

Watching parishioners mill around Rex in the shadow of an imposing statue of Mary, Freddy enjoyed seeing him the centre of attention. Although Rex had left Newhaven to 'downsize' in an apartment in Blacklock House, he and Emily had lived in the town for decades, with Rex commuting to London when he was a QC. As Rex once joked, he had a triple-A pass to Our Lady of Sorrows.

The milling parishioners were a varied group made up of many generations of Newhaven families, some who had known Freddy as a child and retirees in genteel poverty fleeing from London to eke out their capital. One such elderly woman, possessed of a BBC Home Service accent and steely determination, had established herself as the go-to reader to rival Rex. Not that Rex cared, it was Freddy who competed on his behalf.

As Rex circulated, a hand occasionally steadying him, people making way for him as if he was a visiting dignitary, Freddy glimpsed the man whose heavyweight criminal cases had bankrolled a staunch defence of poorer clients. Garry had told her Rex's nickname was ProBono Lomax. Rex and Sarah were entirely different: Rex motivated by justice for all, Sarah by a dollar sign.

'I won't be needing you next week.' Rex clipped on his seat belt and, pulling a face as if in pain, stretched out his legs; a short man, the footwell of the fish van had ample space.

'What? Why not?' Freddy braked more sharply than necessary at the junction to the ring road.

'I'm getting a *companion*.' Rex laughed.

'Have you met someone?' Freddy trod carefully.

'Goodness *no*, not that sort of companion. Emily was *irreplaceable*.' Pulling at the seat belt, Rex smoothed his jacket. 'This companion will literally keep me company. Someone with whom to pass time, engage in desultory conversation, take me shopping or go for me. Take me out. And, pertinently, take me to Mass. A glorified factotum.'

'*Wow.*' Freddy felt strangely upset. Unreasonable, since she had no wish to be Rex's – *anyone's* – companion. Being single was preferable. She kept her voice light. 'When is she coming?'

'*He* is coming tomorrow.' Rex lowered the window and tilted his face to the breeze off the River Ouse as they crossed the swing bridge. 'Easy assumption. The nineteenth- and early twentieth-century image is of spinsters consigned to unwinding a ball of wool for their employer on the deck of a ship and condemned to cribbage night after night. My companion is more of a witness, if you like.'

'Like an alibi?'

'Hah, if you like.' Rex slapped his leg. 'Actually, to *see* me. Loneliness is not conversing with another person from one day to the next. Having no one to tell about your day. Having no day to tell anyone about. A companion will witness my daily doings. He will make sounds in another room, turn on a tap, put on the kettle. He will break the silence that feels like the grave.'

'I didn't know you were lonely.' She should have guessed.

'We all have that capacity, Freddy.' Rex looked briefly sad.

'I suppose...' Freddy had avoided naming the feeling that some evenings would cloak her. After her mother's death, Freddy had reversed her decision to keep the animal hotel. Out all day in the fish van, she couldn't provide the service which pet owners received from her mum. But with no rabbits, parrots or hamsters to feed and entertain, her house was silent. *As the grave.*

'Won't you miss your privacy?' Freddy prized privacy over company.

'I shall still have that,' Rex said.

As the sun dipped in the west, the Dieppe ferry approaching the harbour might have been plying through molten gold. Freddy turned off the coast road towards the A27.

'It's a mutual contract.' Rex explained that Cuckoo's Nest matched those needing cheap lodgings with elderly people who had spare rooms. In exchange, a lodger undertook light tasks for the elderly owner.

'Your lodgings are hardly cheap.' Freddy pictured the stately home nestling in the Sussex Downs.

'Cheap as in economically affordable. This lad works for some charity helpline and, unlikely to get a council place, will never afford more than a room in a house. This allows him to live in style.'

Why should this companion live in style? Freddy believed you cut your cloth according to your means. Was this man taking advantage of Rex? This notion reminded her that Toni's concerns about Rex were that Freddy would be exploited. Freddy was feeling the same about Rex.

'So, that was our last Mass.' Freddy made it sound a cheery thing.

'Wish me luck with a new chapter of my life, Freddy.' Rex patted Freddy's arm.

'Absolutely. You don't need luck.' Freddy tried to sound sincere. At Mass she'd asked to be freed from sins and every evil and here she was resenting that she'd been ousted by a companion. 'Has the companion got a car? Or will you be going by taxi?'

'I've bought a car.' Rex's right hand trembled, he covered it with his left. 'I told Cuckoo's Nest to find a companion who can drive. Actually, Freddy, could we go to the Waitrose in Lewes? I think champagne's in order for when he comes, don't you? It's a new chapter.'

'No. I mean yes.' Merging onto the A27, the Hail Mary popped into Freddy's head:

...Holy Mary, mother of God,
pray for us sinners now,
and at the hour of our death.
Amen.

Was a new chapter always good?

# 3

## Toni

Missing her Sunday lie-in, Detective Inspector Toni Kemp parked her beloved Jeep Wrangler opposite a snack-shack on the promenade beside the crime investigation trucks – one marked *Dog Section* – and made for two tents erected above the shoreline. A growing crowd was cordoned at a distance, and the beach was busy with forensic-suited figures and uniformed officers combing the shingle.

'A dog walker found the man, or rather her dog did.' DS Malcolm Lane came to meet her. 'The boy was washed up later.'

They tramped along duckboards to the tent which billowed in a breeze too slight to offer relief from the sun which at just after nine was already warm. The sea was as calm as glass. In the brilliant sunshine, the Rampion Windmills appeared to vanish and reappear.

'The woman had trouble pulling the dog off, he thought he'd found breakfast.' Deadpan as ever, Malcolm bent and adjusted an overshoe.

'Father and son, I was told?' Toni hoped she'd been told wrong. They didn't like dead children.

'James Ritchie, aged thirty-eight, driving instructor. Wilbur, nine. Ritchie, separated from wife. Renting flat in Whitehawk.' When he was upset, Malcolm was telegrammatic. 'Anna Ritchie shares family home in Queen's Park, Brighton with Wilbur. We think James and Wilbur were flying a kite. There's a massive one stuck on a ledge halfway down the cliff.'

'How come Anna Ritchie hasn't reported her family missing?' Toni knew Sheena had broken the news to the victims' wife and mother.

'James Ritchie was having Wilbur for the weekend, he would have returned him this evening. Anna Ritchie told Sheena she was annoyed Wilbur hadn't rung last night, knowing his dad wouldn't have reminded him. No love lost, Sheena says.' Malcolm mussed his Cromwellian haircut.

'Or love is well and truly lost. Alibi?' Although Toni had not dealt with a mother killing her partner and child, never say never.

'Sheena said Anna didn't appear upset when they broke the news.'

'A clever murderer could feign shock.' After a rocky start when DC Sheena Britton had transferred from Police Scotland to Sussex Police and Toni suspected her of waiting to trip her up, Toni had grown to respect her. Sheena was integral to her team.

'It's Dr Clovis on duty.'

'One thing to go right.' Toni shook her head. Minnie Clovis was one of her favourite colleagues. Extremely knowledgeable and equally willing to share her knowledge.

They stepped inside the nearest tent.

The man's body lay across a knoll, his shirt and shorts sodden and stained pink where seawater had rinsed off his blood. His fair skin was recently sunburnt to red and shrivelled from being in the sea. Both feet were bare and covered in tiny cuts.

'Good to see you, Minnie.' Toni didn't say it was a shame it wasn't in happier circumstances. Apart from occasional evening drinks, these were the circumstances in which they met.

'You too.' Dr Minnie Clovis stood back from the body for the photographer to take pictures. 'This is not pretty.'

'Was he pulled off Seaford Head by the kite? Wouldn't be the first time.' Toni saw a frayed string wound around James Ritchie's wrist.

'Sixteen stab wounds. The one in the jugular would have been fatal.'

'Murder?' Toni exclaimed. Malcolm's expression reflected her own horror.

'First stab wound in the jugular caused the victim to lose consciousness. Fifteen stab wounds after that, the majority gratuitous.' Dressed in the boots she wore on walking holidays for the seriously fit and De Walt trousers, the brand matching the victim's shorts, Dr Clovis began packing her case.

'Overkill,' Toni said. When wounds, unnecessary to ensure death, were inflicted to gratify the killer.

'One cut was not enough to achieve satisfaction,' Malcolm voiced it.

'As for whether James knew his killer or the killer chose a random stranger – two random strangers – that's for you, Toni.'

'Have you examined the boy?' Toni's mind was busy. The ferocious attack suggested involvement with the victim. Most victims are murdered by people close to them. Anna Ritchie didn't have an alibi…

'Yes, and again, the number and fierceness of the wounds suggests loss of control, if only momentarily. I'd say he or she was skilled. All the wounds are from behind, but the attacker reached around to their front.'

'Broad time of death?' Toni pulled a face at her nice try. With many variables, pathologists did not commit themselves to strict windows of opportunity.

'Both bodies have been here overnight. It rained the day before yesterday. That sunburn is recent, there's no peeling. Along with seawater effect and tide tables, we know they arrived at Seaford Head yesterday lunchtime.' Minnie Clovis shook her head. 'You could have told me that.'

'It sounds better coming from you.' Toni grinned. She knew the only certainty was that day followed night.

'We know the Ritchies headed to Seaford Head mid-morning yesterday,' Malcolm said. 'James picked Wilbur up at eleven thirty and they stopped at a Tesco garage for an egg and cress sandwich, a wrap with duck in hoisin sauce, and four tins of Coke Zero. They're on CCTV. We've found a Toyota Aygo with dual control by the Martello Tower. They must have eaten before going to Seaford Head. There's only two tins of Coke in the carrier bag on the back seat of Ritchie's car. Anna Ritchie told Sheena James booked a meal in a fish and chip restaurant in the town for six p.m.'

'For now, let's assume they were killed between twelve p.m. and six p.m. when they didn't arrive for the meal,' Toni said. 'We need to talk to Anna.'

Toni gazed at the murdered man. Despite twenty years in the police, the reality of brutal death never failed to move her. Some victims looked as if they were sleeping, which was both harder and easier. Harder, because they would never wake up, and a fraction easier because a peaceful expression allowed Toni to kid herself that, in their last moments, the victim hadn't been frightened out of their wits.

After hours in the sea and then on the beach, James Ritchie was beginning to lose his humanity. Had he been killed first or seen his son die? First, or surely he'd have tried to stop him.

'Are there defence wounds?' Toni asked.

'None.' Dr Clovis swung her bag onto her shoulder.

Toni's father had been murdered when she was a teenager. He was stabbed by the milkman over a disputed order of gold top. Even now, years later, Toni hadn't found a way to tell this to anyone asking about her family that didn't come over like a bad joke. *My dad was murdered by the milkman.* Not that anyone ever laughed.

Her dad's murder had taught Toni it was not just how you lived, but also how you died that mattered. Those who were murdered were for ever linked to the manner of their death. In effect, they were murdered twice. James Ritchie and his son Wilbur were brutally killed during the quintessential childhood pursuit of flying a kite. It could have been a lasting memory which Wilbur told his own kids or did with them. As his family split apart, perhaps James had intended it as bonding time with his son. Instead, their lives had been extinguished one sunny Saturday on a cliff top overlooking the English Channel. Whatever James and Wilbur had done with their lives to that point, this was now their story.

'Any info on why the Ritchies were separated?' Toni looked at Malcolm.

'Sheena has left it to us to ask the questions.'

'Good call.' No harm leaving an interval between breaking very bad news and asking awkward questions.

When the police had arrived at the Kemp family home on that morning in the dim and distant past that was yet like yesterday, Toni's mum argued with them. *'No, my husband's upstairs getting ready for work...'* No one realised Nicky Kemp had gone out in his pyjamas to tackle the milkman who had ignored their notes cancelling the gold top. Toni had raced up to the bedroom. His dressing gown was on the floor. Every room was empty. A detective even then, the girl pieced together action from the trailing garment, one arm inside out, and a slipper on the landing. Nicky Kemp had abandoned putting on his dressing gown and, unable to find his other slipper, dumped the one he wore. If he didn't hurry the milk float would be in the next street. Somehow, Toni's belief that her dad was upstairs shaving increased her shock at his murder. Toni had rerun this scenario many times since. It always ended with her dad reaching the doorstep too late for the milkman.

Nicky Kemp died in stripy M&S pyjamas at the hands of a milkman who was having a breakdown because his wife was leaving him.

Unlike Anna Ritchie, Katy Kemp had had her girls. Toni and her younger sister Amy moved around her, keeping the house clean and the family fed until she returned to them. Even though Katy Kemp had remarried, when she had moved to America she left some of herself behind with Nicky. If Anna Ritchie hadn't murdered her estranged husband and her son, then, Toni knew, a chunk of her would always be missing.

'How is it possible to kill two active people in broad daylight in a popular seaside spot?' Toni watched Dr Minnie Clovis lug her rucksack off along the promenade. 'There must have been witnesses. A picture of a dad and his boy with a kite is so cute it could be put to music, someone must have clocked them.'

'It's not like we can do door-to-door.' Malcolm was scanning the shoreline. Seaford was free of the beach shops, games arcades and amusement rides typical of seaside resorts. Aside from a long line of pastel-coloured beach huts and the refreshment shack, from Seaford Head to the ruined village of Tide Mills and Newhaven, the shoreline was a tapering stretch of uninterrupted shingle.

'We've got officers along the beach and in the town. The briefing should generate responses,' Malcolm said.

'Yeah, but what responses? Fake confessions, callers sorry they didn't see a thing. Chief Super Worrier snapping at our heels to find the killer because the chief constable has the media snapping at hers.' Toni didn't have to say that the pressure was on. But it helped. 'Let's go and rule out Anna Ritchie. I doubt she's our killer.'

The Ritchies lived in an Edwardian double-fronted villa with laburnum growing up the brick frontage that Toni associated with storybooks like E. Nesbit's *Five Children and It*.

When Anna Ritchie flung open the stained-glass panelled door and ushered them in, Toni was annoyed to find the woman was alone. Sheena had told Toni Anna had a friend coming so Toni had asked Sheena to get access to James Ritchie's flat in Whitehawk – a less salubrious part of Brighton than Queen's Park. Anna told them she'd lied about the friend: *'I don't need babysitting.'*

'How long had you and your husband been separated, Mrs

Ritchie?' Toni settled into an armchair similar to one in her nana's flat long ago. Nana would have been aghast at the Warhol-soup-inspired antimacassars. Otherwise, the room was a bizarre mix of dour Victorian – brocade curtains, oak bookcases, flock wallpaper – and a child's playroom. A rug was decorated like Twister and two pouffes like giant dice, or vice-versa. Toni guessed it was what happened when the whole family got a say in the décor.

'Petty, not Ritchie. Call me Anna.' Anna Petty stayed standing, perhaps hoping it was a flying visit. Bronze highlights in her long, curly blonde hair glinted in the sunlight. Her cotton dress and walking sandals – mauve like the house – suggested Anna had been ready for another summer's day. 'I kicked Jamie out two months ago.'

'Do sit Mrs— Anna.' Toni indicated a mauve velvet sofa, tossed with primary-coloured cushions, in the bay window. 'I'm sorry, but for us to catch whoever did this terrible thing, we have to learn as much as possible about you, James and Wilbur.' Toni avoided saying 'murder', she wanted Anna Petty articulate.

'Thing? You mean you're trying to find out if I murdered my son.'

'Did you?' Toni asked.

'No.' With obvious reluctance, tugging down her dress, knees and the toes of her sandals together, Anna perched on the sofa, the vulnerable pose unlike her uncompromising manner.

'What was the reason you and James separated?' Toni said.

'Where shall I start?' Anna bashed at a cushion then, as if in apology, smoothed the material. 'Jamie left doors open, letting in draughts, because I wanted them shut. I'd have to interrupt what I was doing and *slam* them shut. Then he'd return and leave them open again.' Anna bashed the cushion once more. 'Never cleaned the bath or picked up his clothes. Only emptied or filled the dishwasher when it suited and never in time for the next meal. After he'd drunk too much, he fell asleep. I'd leave him on the sofa.'

'Did James have a dependency on alcohol?' Toni knew the door and bath thing would drive her mad. She would remind Freddy, who was considering dating, that there was a lot in favour of living alone.

'Dependent? Wilbur and I couldn't depend on *Jamie*.'

'Did James ever say he felt depressed?' Toni knew it was one reason some fathers killed children. Except Minnie Clovis was adamant James's wounds were not self-inflicted. Minnie had also said the first wound was to James's throat, meaning he'd have lost consciousness and couldn't have stabbed himself again and again. Overkill had to be murder.

'After his affair he claimed he was depressed.' Anna slumped back on the sofa. 'So was I.'

'James had an affair?' Toni was surprised that reason hadn't come before James's failure to shut doors or stack the dishwasher.

'Yes.' Frowning, as if at her reflection, Anna patted at her hair.

'Was it someone you knew?' Now they were getting somewhere. She saw Malcolm discreetly take out his notebook.

'No idea. It's not relevant, she didn't kill them, if that's where you're going.'

It wasn't only where Toni was going. Hopefully the woman's number would be on James Ritchie's phone.

'James wanted to start again. I said no.' Her outrage dissipated, Anna Petty spoke dully.

'Would you like a cup of tea?' Toni said. 'It's not a cliché for nothing. It's something to hold and sip, and with sugar for shock.'

Anna Petty didn't respond, but Malcolm was on his feet and out of the room in a flash. Distantly, Toni noted that the ceiling, from which hung a thirties' glass lampshade, catered for Malcolm's beanpole height. James Ritchie had been tall.

'...he called himself my anchor, he never said that meant we'd be snagged on a sunken shipwreck out at sea.'

Freddy Power would be at home with the marine image. Toni heard the creak of a stair. Waiting for the kettle to boil, Malcolm was doing a recce. Fortunately, Anna was on a roll.

'His mother called me the home-wrecker because I made him leave. I couldn't tell her the truth about her precious boy. When I was crying, Wilbur told me that, on James's weekends, he "looked after Daddy too when he cried". I had my sister pleading for me to "give Jamie another chance".'

'It must have been frustrating.' Toni felt for the little boy who, she suspected, had propped up both his parents.

'...no one took my side; even my best friend cooked him a vat of stew, she said she had to remain neutral for Wilbur. My friends – gay and straight – fancied James. 'Sake. You discover who your friends are when your life is ripped apart.'

'Is that what happened – your life was ripped apart?' Harking back to the sister's plea to Anna, Toni went on, 'Did you consider giving James another chance?'

'No, Sergeant, I did *not*.' *Inspector*, but Toni could live with that.

'I wanted – *still want* – what we promised each other. A supportive team, a gorgeous child, fantastic holidays – Peru, Sydney, the Amazon – and to grow old in this house.' Anna's face spasmed as, again, she allowed in the terrible facts. 'I was going to give James another chance. For Wilbur's sake if nothing else, but I didn't want James to see me as a pushover, that he could do that and I wouldn't mind.'

'Is there anyone who didn't take James's side?' Toni knew people lived as if they or their loved ones would be alive tomorrow. Her dad's death had taught her there wasn't always time to fall out and not make up until you felt like it.

'No one. As his mother kept saying, James was adored right from a baby. I told her it doesn't do a boy good to treat him like a paragon of virtue.' Anna bashed the cushion again. 'Being a single mum is no joke. School run, lunch boxes, homework.'

'I brought sugar, and the tea is not too hot.' Malcolm was fussing to divert Anna from calculating that in the time he'd been away, he could have baked a cake. And as the Super-Dad he was, Malcolm asked, 'James didn't help?'

'He did the fun bits.' Anna sounded defeated. 'Does Nicola know?'

'James's mother? Not yet. We only have her number, do you have her address.' Fully prepared to be rebuffed, Toni was relieved when Anna Petty pulled out an already-opened Filofax from under one of the cushions and passed it to her.

'I was going to call her when you arrived.'

'What did you do instead of going with James and Wilbur?' Toni handed the Filofax to Malcolm.

'I was here, but I can't prove it. I didn't spend the evening with a friend or make a fuss in a public space which witnesses will remember.'

'What did you do yesterday?' Malcolm rephrased the question.

'After they left, I cleaned Wilbur's bedroom.' Anna pulled a lock of hair to her mouth, perhaps thinking of sucking it then, realising it wasn't a good look, let it go. 'I binge-watched *Grey's Anatomy*, had a takeaway Chinese – duck pancakes, sweet and sour veg and egg-fried rice – followed by a large tub of Rocky Road ice-cream.' She hugged the cushion to her chest. 'Comfort food. Then I went to bed. It's vile when Wilbur's not here...'

'Which restaurant did you order from?' The duck pancake – unless after triangulating Anna's mobile, it showed her in Seaford yesterday – could be Anna's alibi. That Anna herself didn't seem to realise this was in her favour.

They were interrupted by the arrival of the family liaison officer, an older woman called Marie who Toni hadn't met before. Listening to her explain her role to Anna, Toni considered how she'd have welcomed a woman like Marie, but the service had come in a couple of years after Nicky Kemp's murder.

'Have you any questions, Anna?' Marie asked.

'Why do I need you?' Anna sat upright. 'I don't have a family.'

# 4

## Martha

'Hey, that's Dedmans Heath. It's where Sally Robinson insists they go for family picnics every week. Fancy an outing next Sunday? We could drop in on the perfect family.' Taking her hand off the steering wheel Martha gestured at an expanse of gorse and bracken stretching away to the left of the winding lane.

'I do not and you shouldn't go. Listen to this...' Long legs jammed under the dashboard, Timothy Mew read aloud from his phone: 'Last time one of the apartments came up for sale – in fact Rex's – this was the estate agent's description: "...one of six luxury dwellings, this apartment offers a private terrace overlooking an exquisitely designed garden, ornamented with a marble fountain. The estate boasts a tennis court and acres of rolling parkland stocked with deer and other wildlife..."'

'You will be shooting deers?' Martha Merry encouraged her fifteen-year-old Fiesta up a steep hill.

'*Deer.*' As he often did, Timothy corrected Martha. 'Of course not.'

'Sounds too good to be true.' Martha tooted her horn on a

sharp bend. 'Timothy, you spend your days being nice to old people on the Silversage helpline, don't you want a break?'

'It's not the same, and anyway, now I've got a vacancy for an elderly person.' Timothy had been lodging with a couple in their eighties who had moved in with their daughter.

'You've got a *vacancy* for a stately home, you mean,' Martha retorted. 'Know what, your grandparents showering you with praise for the slightest achievement did you no good. It's made you think you're better than you are.'

'Are we not all better than we are?' Timothy examined his hands.

'You know what I mean. Be careful.'

Martha Merry and Timothy Mew had been erstwhile friends for ten years. Erstwhile, because their friendship was rooted in geography and hair. They lived near each other in Newhaven and Martha, a hairstylist, shaved Timothy's hair to exactly the right degree and fashioned his chin-strap beard. Over time, habit and a tacit exchange had fused the bond. Timothy advised on Martha's ultimately fraught affairs, and Martha didn't charge for wielding her scissors. Friendships based on mutual devotion have fared worse.

'What about when the old woman in the house threw her supper on the carpet, you said you'd kill her,' Martha recalled cheerfully.

'A turn of phrase.' Timothy's pleasant features briefly darkened.

'So, when this Rex chucks his porridge at you, that's OK?'

'I'm not his carer.'

'Timothy, you could stay sleeping on my sofa until you're sorted.' Martha went serious. 'You won't have to shop for me or play dominoes and do some crummy jigsaw every evening.'

'I won't have to do that there.'

'Then why did you buy that weirdy-wonder game from the hospice shop?'

'As an ice-breaker. I'm not much of a conversationalist.' Timothy tweaked at his newly trimmed beard.

'You're going to be a companion, not a dinner party host.'

'I stayed on your sofa for a week and we nearly killed each other.'

Martha pulled up to towering iron gates.

'Jesus, Timothy, this is creepy. Seriously, it's not too late to change your mind.'

In the shadow of a high wall, the little black Fiesta was dwarfed. Two pillars were topped with carved lions, each with a differently accusatory expression. But for the car's throaty idling, it was silent. The Fiesta's occupants sat as still as the lions.

Timothy got out and, tramping across to one of the pillars, he punched a keypad under a sign.

*Blacklock House*
*Private*

The wrought-iron gates jerked open with a proverbial creak.

At forty-four, Martha Merry was eleven years older than Timothy Mew and although she referred to him as her toy-boy, presumed Timothy was gay. Her evidence being that during their long friendship, Timothy had been single.

'Sally Robinson was in Waitrose this morning doing the "family shop".' Martha shoved the gearstick forward.

'Will you stop grazing her Facebook, it's self-torture, never mind stalking.' Timothy took off his spectacles, a discreet transparent grey accentuating shaped eyebrows which Martha suspected Timothy got 'done', and not by her.

'I'm a friend.'

'You're what?' The William Morris patterned silk with which Timothy was cleaning his glasses was typical of his airs and graces. Perhaps this Blacklock House would suit him.

'It's not stalking. Sally's Facebook page is public and she accepted my request. I'm her two hundredth friend.' Martha avoided a pothole on a drive fringed with hawthorn and ash trees.

'Won't Tristan be angry, you nosing on his wife's Facebook? I doubt he wants you and Sally to be besties.' Timothy struggled to put on his glasses as the Fiesta bumped along the uneven ground.

'I'll get Tristan so riled he'll tell *Mrs Robinson* about us.' Martha was grim-faced. 'Months of false promises, I've had *enough.*'

'Maybe Mrs R knows about his affairs and her perfect family thing on Facebook is two fingers up to his mistresses.'

'*Mistress.* There's only me. And I'm *not* his mistress. She uses Facebook like PR to promote the Robinson brand. None of it's true. They don't even have sex. If Tristan doesn't leave her...' Martha scowled at Timothy as if it was Tristan beside her. '*I'll...*'

'You'll do nothing, is what you should do,' Timothy said pleasantly.

'We'll see.'

This was an example of their dynamic – Martha ignored Timothy's advice while, because Timothy divulged nothing about his life, not knowing if he took his own advice.

The Fiesta tooled up a slight incline. Below, nestling amidst trees, was Blacklock House, roof bristling with chimneys and turrets silhouetted against the summer-blue sky. To one side of the house was a glimpse of Dedmans Wood, apostrophe lost long ago, on the other a high beech hedge.

'Now do you see why this is worth it?' Timothy beamed. '*I belong here.*'

Since the Norman Conquest Blacklock House had been rebuilt twice, the present iteration was Georgian. When, in the 1950s, the tenth Earl Blacklock died without issue, the title passed to a several-times-removed cousin in America. He had retained the title and, converting the house into six apartments, sold them. Because he too died childless, the earldom, like the apostrophe in Dedman's, was defunct.

'Don't we all.' Martha, who lived in a flat above Head Case, her hair salon, couldn't hide her envy. She knew she had herself to blame. When a client for whom Martha was doing grey highlights had shown her an article in a magazine about Cuckoo's Nest, more as a joke, Martha had told Timothy about it. On the website he'd found an advert:

*Elderly gentleman residing in idyllic Sussex countryside amidst ancient woodland and tranquil waters needs a live-in companion for fifteen hours a week to accompany him on outings and undertake light housekeeping...*

Timothy applied and got the job.

'You've only met Rex Lomax once, what if he's a total mare?'

'When the Cuckoo's Nest lady left us to have lunch, we

struck up a real rapport. Rex has a great sense of humour and he trusts me.'

'GSOH, *that* old chestnut,' Martha said meanly. 'He trusts you? Silly him.'

'After the brasserie, we passed bric-a-brac outside a house, clothes and what-not. Rex spotted a jigsaw of a cottage called Happily Ever After. He said, "Not *so* happy, since they're junking it."'

'Dennis Nilsen probably had a laugh with his victims before he washed them down the drain.' Martha clambered out of the car. Literally joined at the hip to what she called the Tristan-phone, Martha unclipped it from her waistband. 'No signal. I can't tell if Tristan's texted.'

'He won't have.' Timothy sounded weary.

'Suppose you're running away and can't call for help?' Martha was beginning to understand the ramifications of Timothy moving to the middle of nowhere. No spontaneous coffees or late-night wine sessions.

'*God's* sake, Martha, I won't want to run away and if I did, it would hardly be a drama, Rex is old, he won't be haring down the drive after me.' Timothy looked exasperated.

'Isn't a companion someone who empties people's bank accounts and alters wills?' Timothy's new home had deprived Martha of her own companion. 'Remember that woman you told me about on Silversage who married her lodger? Next thing he'd transferred her house into his name and sold it.'

'Do you see me doing that?' Timothy enquired softly.

'Absolutely.' Martha curled a lip to indicate her own sense of humour.

'Silversage gave Cuckoo's Nest a glowing reference for me.'

'I'd say, "He's lovely, but lock up the valuables."' Making to gather back her hair, Martha forgot she'd had it cut; thinking of her new wedge style, she brightened. Tristan hadn't seen it yet. This notion was swiftly followed by a spark of fury that she cared what Tristan thought. 'Will you stand being at someone's beck and call just to live in Downton Abbey? Be gad, sir, you'll need a new wardrobe – green wellies, a gun, changes for dinner.'

'You're jealous.'

'Yes, that's it.' Martha laughed it off.

Timothy had told her that his parents had died within days of each other, his mother of cancer, his father in a car crash on the way to the hospital. Taken into his grandparents' Newhaven council flat, his grandmother had died when he was twenty and after his grandfather's death, Timothy had had to move out. This was soon after Martha had met Timothy. After that he had lodged with the couple who had – Martha had liked the metaphor – tossed Timothy the cuckoo out of their nest, to live with their actual child. Martha suspected the daughter had got antsy that the couple might leave Timothy their house. Martha had occasionally wondered if, given that he'd done light housekeeping – and not so light – if that was what Timothy had hoped. In a rare moment of indiscretion, Timothy once had confided to Martha that, as a child, unhappy with his life, he'd fantasised that he belonged with a rich family who lived in a stately home.

*A stately home exactly like Blacklock House.*

'Not much for thirty-three years.' Timothy put his case down on gravel.

'Possessions weigh you down.'

'Says you who orders off Amazon on a daily basis.' Timothy arched his back in a stretch. 'Will you miss me?'

'What kind of question is that?' Martha snorted. 'You're only up the road.'

'Distance means nothing, this is an entirely other world,' Timothy said in answer.

'It's on a bus route and anyway, I'll come and fetch you,' Martha said. 'What about you, will you miss me?'

'No.' Timothy appeared to be counting off the windows on his fingers. Martha could see he'd run out of fingers.

'I lied.' Martha bumped a fist on the other. 'OK, so introduce me to your new landlord.'

'Best not to confuse him and anyway, you'd better escape from this dead zone in case Tristan texts.' Timothy stroked his beard as if it were a pet.

'You just said Tristan wouldn't text.'

A cavalry's fanfare made Martha and Timothy turn round. In a spray of gravel, a van pulled up behind Martha's Fiesta.

Freddy's Fresh Fish. White lettering inside the image of a mermaid. Without acknowledging them the driver, a woman in royal blue overalls and yellow wellingtons, jumped out and hoisted up the back hatch. She revealed an undulating bed of crushed ice on which lay rows of glassy-eyed fish delineated by pink crabsticks.

'You waiting for me?' The woman shot them a smile.

'Not especially.' Martha approved of the woman's short and shaggy hair, while noting it needed shaping. She nodded at the Fiesta. 'Am I in your way?'

'No.' The woman was busying with her fish.

'Timothy's moving in. I brought him—' Martha knew the longer they chatted, the longer she could stay. Her incentive for bringing Timothy was to nose around his new home.

'Kilo of prawns, Freddy-Freds.'

A man in cream linen trousers, billowing lime-green shirt escaping from the waistband, silvery hair glossy and styled with product, came running down broad steps from the house. Seeing Timothy and Martha, he did an exaggerated double-take. '*Sorry*, guys, *après vous.*'

'I don't want fish.' Timothy's tone implied he never would.

'Timothy's moving in with Rex,' Martha tried again. 'Cool place you have here. I was saying Timothy has landed on his feet. I brought him because he doesn't have a car. Are you Rex?'

'No.' Timothy dropped his voice. '*I said*, Rex has impaired mobility.'

'"Impaired mobility". Is that something you do in bed?' The man gave a rackety laugh and did an 'O' shape with his mouth. 'OK, dude, so I'm thinking you're the "companion"? There was me picturing a Girl Friday type-thing. I had one of those until it got fussy about what it did.'

'It?' Martha raised her eyebrows. As with many of her middle-aged male clients, once baby-faced gorgeous, although sun and age had etched his face with wrinkles, Garry Haslem would expect to be considered irresistible still. Indeed, Martha thought him both attractive and revolting, a combination which had proved disastrous for her.

'Good one.' Garry gave a gust of laughter.

'Timothy will work for fifteen hours a week, take Rex shopping, he has to play games – cards, dominoes and what have you – basically keep him company.'

'It's not working. I have a job,' Timothy corrected Martha, but she was looking at the fishmonger.

'I guess Timothy will be buying old Rex's fish.'

'Rex likes me to deliver his order,' Freddy the fishmonger said. 'Here are your prawns, Garry.'

'How can you take boysie shopping without your own wheels?' Eyes on Martha, Garry took the bag of prawns. 'He won't get behind a wheel since his missus crashed her car into a tree.'

'He's bought a Jaguar which I will drive.' Timothy nibbled his moustache. 'It's brand-new.'

'*Wowzah.* Why haven't I seen that in the carriage house?' A shadow passed across Garry's face – Martha supposed he liked to be kept in the loop. *A carriage house?*

'We're collecting it tomorrow.' Timothy plunged his hands in his jacket pockets like Prince Charles.

'Ah, that's awful about his wife. You never said,' Martha told Timothy.

'Not much to tell.' Timothy shrugged, embarrassed.

'They had a domestic and his missus stormed out then Rex caught Parkinson's Disease. Shock, I reckon.' Garry transferred the prawns and shook Timothy's hand. 'Garry Haslem. With two Rs. Mine's the biggest apartment in this gaffe. Any problems, come to me.'

'I'm Martha, Timothy's friend.' Martha wondered what 'any problems' might be.

'Martha has to go,' Timothy announced.

'Not on my account, I hope.' Garry's grin would be the pride of his dentist.

'Thank *God*, I *dreaded* I'd missed you, Fred-er-ee-cah. Your hooter should be *maarch* much *lider*.' An elderly woman of indeterminate age swayed chaotically down the steps, fingers patting the balustrade. Cotton and tulle flapped in patterned layers – long shirt over shorter shirt, trailing skirt from which peeped bright pink Crocs.

'*Incoming*,' Garry warned. 'Still with us, you sleek old puss?'

'That's really quite ru—' Martha caught Timothy's frown. *Not her business.*

'Lady Dorothy was born in my lounge. She moulders across the hall now.' Haslem slapped a Gold Amex card onto Freddy's card reader. 'Get a hearing trumpet, Bunteee, Freddy's horn carries from Lewes.'

'I'm sorry if you didn't—' Freddy looked worried.

'You're all right,' Garry reassured her. 'Bunty has to have a pop at me.'

'Bunty to my *friends*, Garry with two Rs.' Bunty lurched towards the van and clamped a bony hand onto Timothy's shoulder, getting her balance.

'Your friends are dead and buried, if I don't call you Bunty, you'll forget who you are.' Addressing Timothy confidentially, Garry bellowed in his ear, 'Watch out, Timmy – Lady Penelope has companions for canapés.'

'Sticks and stones, Two Rs.' Bunty was clutching Timothy so tightly, she'd pulled his jacket askew. Martha knew this would be torture, Timothy had a horror of being touched.

'I have your huss, Lady Erskine.' Seemingly unperturbed by the insults flying, Freddy spoke clearly.

'*Ghastly.* Huss is rubber with a spine. Darling poppet, amidst your delightful spread, have you lemon sole?' Bobbing inches from the array of fish, Lady Dorothy Erskine might be a heron preparing to dive.

'Sole is pricy this week, the catch was down.' Freddy tucked a bag marked 'Lady B' on a shelf beneath the display and waited.

'Despite what Chummy says, I'm not a pauper. I'll have three and settle next week.'

'Is that the Twelfth of Never, your Buntyness?' Garry trilled in imitation. 'Freddy *dahl-ling*, call in the debt before she croaks.'

Martha was shocked at Garry Haslem's incredible lack of manners, but Lady Bunty only seemed more energised with each insult. Treating Timothy like a lamp-post, she dipped and twirled like a young girl.

The attention of the group was diverted by the thud of the front door. A middle-aged man, comb-over slipping and holding a wallet, trailed behind a woman astonishing in a blue satin skirt suit and matching high heels and sculpted Margaret Thatcher hair.

'We are not in the queue.' Martha snatched up Timothy's case. Not a kindness, it was her passport to Blacklock House.

'Six scallops please, Freddy dear.' The woman indicated the wallet. 'Card, Martyn.' Slowly, as if reluctant, Martyn fished about until he found a black First Direct bank card. He waited until Freddy had bagged the scallops and prepared the card reader.

'Card declined.' Doubtless Garry saving Freddy any awkwardness was unintentional.

'Not that one,' the woman hissed.

'It's the only one, Sylvia.' Martyn flung her a look of venom. 'Remember?'

'Pay next week.' Freddy gave Sylvia the scallops.

'You'll go bankrupt, that way.' Garry made a sucking sound with his teeth.

'I'll transfer the sum to your bank,' Sylvia said.

Bidding a general goodbye, Martyn and Sylvia returned to the house.

Martha darted a look at Timothy – would he like her to get

him the hell out of there? Stuck in idyllic surroundings with horrible neighbours was a simple recipe for nightmare.

As if to emphasise the idyllic bit, after the thud of the heavy front door, from high up in the sky a skylark twittered. From over the Downs came the toot of a steam engine from the reclaimed railway line, puffs of white smoke curdling on the horizon.

Freddy produced a polystyrene box from beneath the counter. Lady Bunty, swinging her bag of lemon sole, was ripping heads off geraniums in a pot by the steps. Timothy appeared transfixed by the ruined flowers scattered on the ground.

Garry broke the silence. 'OK, peeps, what about this axe-wielding maniac we've got roaming free? Lucky you're here, boysie, built like a truck, you'll guard Rex.' He kicked at the gravel. 'Freddy love, you see anything suspicious on your rounds?'

'All the time,' Freddy quipped. 'Customers living alone can't trust their neighbours. One woman even told me she didn't trust her son.'

'Don't trust your neighbours *ever*.' Garry read from his phone, '"Boy and dad slain by maniac. James Ritchie and his son Wilbur were innocently flying a kite on Seaford Head last Saturday afternoon when they went over the cliff."' Haslem looked up. 'Not being funny, but Saturday there wasn't a breath of wind, they wouldn't have got the stupid kite off the ground.' He resumed, '"When police beat the tide to retrieve the bodies, they found James and Wilbur's throats had been cut." I mean, who does that?'

'You tell me.' Glaring at Garry as she twirled a snapped-off geranium head, Bunty said, 'Methinks perhaps, a cut-purse from the sewers of London.'

'They're appealing for witnesses. Anyone acting strangely, whatever that looks like.' Haslem ignored the elderly woman. 'No bets on the dad killing Wilbur – wasn't that a pig? – to stop his ex getting custody.'

'The angle was wrong for self-infliction,' Timothy said.

'How do you know?' Martha asked.

'I already read it.' He tried to reach for his case, but seeming not to see, Martha edged towards the steps.

'I'd have a kid to get one like Wilbur.' Garry held up his phone with a photograph of a boy grinning, dark hair rumpled as if from sleep. 'Reminds me of me, although I'd give him a sensible name.'

'If Wilbur was yours, he'd still be dead. More so, indeed.' Holding the geranium head in the palm of her hand, Lady Dorothy had the air – and the look – of a fortune teller. 'Wilbur Ritchie does look a sweet poppet.'

'No child is sweet,' Timothy suddenly said. 'Think of *Lord of the Flies*.'

'The wife could have done it,' Garry said. 'Makes you think.'

'Anything that does that is a godsend.' Bunty blew on the geranium head and it fell heavily onto the gravel.

'Love you too, Bunty.' Garry trotted up the steps, the image of effortlessness spoiled by a misstep at the door.

'That man is his own worst enemy,' Bunty said enigmatically and, trampling on the decapitated geraniums, bag of lemon sole gyrating like a diviner, she lurched away around the side of the house.

'Do you come here every week?' Martha felt no one had paid proper attention to Freddy.

'Usually on Tuesdays.' Freddy said.

'I should eat more fish,' Martha ventured.

'Fish is good for you.' Obviously, a mantra.

'I'll have one of those, please.' Martha pointed at the display.

'Smoked haddock?' Well might Freddy sound doubtful, Martha had no idea what she'd do with it. 'Dyed or undyed?'

'What? Oh, dyed, I guess,' Martha said. 'In my business we call it colour. I'm a hairstylist. So, a smoked haddock with highlights please.'

'Undyed is better, I think.' Freddy smiled. 'Kedgeree is nice.'

'Good idea,' Martha agreed. Juggling her debit card with the suitcase she left the fish bag on the Fiesta's bonnet, and hastened after Freddy to the front door where Timothy wrested the case from her.

'I'm coming anyway.' Martha was surprised when Timothy acquiesced. Perhaps he was having second thoughts about being Lord of the Manor.

'I have a code for the door.' Timothy was consulting his instructions.

'Tradesman's entry works.' Freddy hit a button marked X and led the way inside.

'Meaning, anyone can get in?' Martha asked.

'Yes,' Freddy said as if this notion was new.

'Oh no, have I missed you, Freddy?' A man in a 1982 *Serious Moonlight* Bowie tour T-shirt and jeans came running down a wide staircase.

'If you don't mind waiting, Patrick, I won't be long,' Freddy said.

'Are you the companion?' Before Martha could say she was not, Patrick was shaking her hand. 'Patrick, I live with the servants, in the attic.'

'Martha, but the companion is Timothy.' Martha gestured behind her.

'Hi.' Patrick nodded at Timothy without enthusiasm and went out. Holding the door he called back, 'The ingredients for a fish pie when you're down, Freddy.'

A staircase, oak treads mellowed to gold and enriched by sunlight from a glass dome above, was carpeted with a pale blue runner inset with cream lozenge shapes. The stairwell was supported by twelve slender iron pillars painted cream with yellow filigree set equidistant on four sides.

Martha stopped under two crossed swords with a breastplate at their axis hung on the landing. She imagined the soldiers slain by the swords centuries ago. *Slain*, she recalled Garry reading out. Boy and dad *slain*...

'That's one hell of a skylight.'

The staircase split off left and right. Timothy and Martha followed Freddy up the left side where both flights of stairs met at a gallery lit by three recessed windows that overlooked the drive. Martha imagined the young Bunty nestled in one of the recesses reading or watching the comings and goings.

'Cupula.' Timothy corrected her.

'Didn't that Patrick bloke mention he lived with the servants in the attic? Maybe Rex is there too,' Martha needled. Timothy would not like the association with the lower orders even if dead.

Timothy read Cuckoo's Nest's instructions. '"Mr Lomax occupies the apartment on the first floor in the west wing of the house."'

'Follow me.' Carrying the tray of fish Freddy walked straight at the left-hand wall, turned abruptly right and vanished.

'It's an architectural conceit,' Timothy said. 'It's designed to disguise the entrance.'

Martha said, 'Just makes it hard to find.'

Freddy was halfway down a passage lined with gilt-framed hunting scenes. At the end was a door. She pressed a button fashioned in burnished gold metal and far off a bell sounded.

'Rex is excited about having a "companion".' Freddy's back was to them. 'I gather you'll be taking him to Mass. I'll see you there.'

'I don't go to church,' Timothy said. 'You'll see me dead first.'

As if Timothy was joking, Freddy the fishmonger laughed.

# 5

*Martha*

Rex invited Martha to have lunch on his terrace where a table
under an umbrella had been set with two glasses and various
bowls of nibbles – olives, Japanese rice crackers and pretzels.
As they approached it, like a magician, Rex produced a third
glass from his jacket pocket.

'Had Timothy told me you were coming I would have set a
place for you.' He smiled at Martha.

'He didn't know.' Martha felt bound to defend Timothy
although Rex didn't sound annoyed. 'I'm afraid I gatecrashed.'

'No such thing, my companion's friend is mine too,' Rex
said.

Below a balustrade was a lawn with a marble fountain. On
the right, beyond the lawn, was Dedmans Wood that in turn
gave onto the heath. A rickety summer house, paint peeling
and windows dark with grime, was on the edge of trees that
now shaded it from the sun. A wrought-iron table and chairs
had been placed in the shade of a twisted willow tree.

On a Lutyens-style bench beside a path leading around
from the side of the house lay a bag and a book, spine up.

This was, Martha considered, the perk of a communal garden over a public park – you could leave stuff without fear that the neighbours would nick it. Or could you?

Rex filled their glasses with Veuve Clicquot and returned the bottle to an ice bucket.

Screened by her Ray-Bans, Martha gave Rex the thrice-over. Silver, glossy hair – not a wig – swept from his forehead. Wire-rimmed spectacles hooked into his shirt gave the impression that he'd just put down the kind of book not expected to be read by 99.9 per cent of the population. Perhaps the one on the bench, except the bag, light blue canvas, didn't fit with Rex's tailored look. He was about her own height – five four – Timothy's six foot towered over them both. Timothy had said Rex was about seventy, but he looked younger.

Conversation took off. From perky fish banter prompted by the fishmonger's visit and Timothy's tactful anecdotes about elderly people he supported on the helpline, Rex could think Timothy loved fish and the older generation. Martha knew he was unnerved by the dead eyes and scales and although Timothy had claimed he had a vacancy for an elderly person, with his impatience and need to be in charge, how long before he made the role redundant?

'This is a stunning place, how long have you lived here?' Martha asked Rex.

'Five years. My wife Emily and I came here to retire.'

'How lovely.' Martha caught Timothy's warning glare and recalled that Emily Lomax had died in a car crash. Used to bereaved clients, Martha wasn't fazed by mention of death, but did hate putting her foot in it.

'Blacklock House has all the hallmarks of an idyllic home.'

Rex winced as he stretched his legs to the side of the table. *All the hallmarks*. What did that mean?

Used to clients confiding in her, Martha was disappointed that Rex had not. Feeling vaguely competitive for Rex's attention she said, 'I was friends with Timothy for ten years. You could say he was a companion.'

'We didn't see each other that often, did we?' Timothy said.

'Lucky me to have you. However, Martha,' Rex refilled her glass, 'you must visit as often as you like.'

'I will, thanks, Rex.' Martha knew Timothy would be possessive about his new life. The champagne making her recalcitrant, she resolved Blacklock House could be her life too. Considerably cheered, she declared a hitherto unproven fact, 'Timothy *loves* to help others.'

'An exaggeration.' Perhaps realising his response was counter to the expectations of a companion, Timothy qualified, 'We all like to help others.'

'Not true,' Rex said. 'As a defence QC, I witnessed many examples of those out only for themselves. Me too, if I'm honest.'

'Why not? You've earned it.' Timothy laughed, nervously, Martha thought. What if Rex was selfish? Through the French doors the chandelier, in what Rex had called the drawing room, shone in a shaft of sunlight. The elegant room was hung with paintings of country landscapes and lined with books. A large desk at one end called to mind the Oval Office in *The West Wing*. Martha felt envy, cold as an icicle. This beat a flat above a hair salon in Newhaven. Why should Timothy have it?

Rex raised his glass. 'To new friends and old.'

'Absolutely.' Timothy tipped his glass to Rex and then to

Martha. Their eyes locked. In that moment, Martha saw that their friendship was predicated on circumstance and habit. When they had described it to Rex, they had both spoken in the past tense.

The silence was shattered by a scream.

'That's King Tut, you'll get used to him.'

A cliché in the picturesque scene, a peacock, fanned feathers swaying, pranced from below the terrace and strutted towards the fountain. Timothy's lips were pursed – Timothy would *not* get used to King Tut.

Leaving Blacklock House, the glow of Rex's welcome wore off. It wasn't feasible for Martha to take Rex up on his invitation to visit whenever she liked. Rex was being polite and Martha hadn't popped in on Timothy when he lived in Newhaven. Vaguely aware that the car behind her on the drive when she left also took the Newhaven turn-off, Martha was struck with dread. *Rex should not fill Timothy's vacancy for an elderly person.*

# 6

*Toni*

'You'll never guess.' Sheena slammed down the receiver, her cheeks red perhaps with excitement but more likely because, even with the windows open and the blinds on the sunny side pulled down, the room was like an oven. 'Ritchie didn't have an affair, he was seeing sex workers.'

'Why didn't Anna Petty tell us that?' Chewing a bite of an already melting Snickers bar, Toni covered her mouth. 'She said she didn't know the woman.'

'James probably didn't give Anna names.' Malcolm was populating the board with the victims' images, arrows linking the facts so far. *Method of murder, crime scene/deposition sites, likely time of death...* or, Toni brooded, precious little.

'Did Anna know, I wonder?' Toni locked eyes with the grinning Wilbur Ritchie. *Had that little boy watched his father die?*

'James was registered with an escort agency called Your Companion. We dealt with it before when Emma Smith, the sex worker, was murdered a couple of years back. Not that Emma was with them, she was on the streets.'

In the silence the detectives in the room relived their effort to get media interest in Emma's case, a mother of two found strangled and dumped in a skip.

Toni had been proud of her team's unerring drive to find Emma's killer.

In the minds of many remained the view 'she'd been asking for it'. How had James Ritchie viewed the woman whose services he bought? Toni could envisage forgiving an affair, but that? Not her job to judge. Anna Petty had judged. Had she done more than chuck her husband out of the family home?

'…the proprietor, Jacinda Brunell, said Ritchie always asked for a woman called Belinda Storey.' Sheena shouldered her bag. 'I'm seeing Storey now, although Jacinda said she was working all yesterday.'

'Good work, Sheena.' Toni nodded as Sheena left. 'I'll check out what Anna knew.'

'No love lost towards Mrs Ritchie senior, I noticed.' Malcolm came away from the board. 'Anna rang her mother-in-law before we got to Mrs Ritchie. Nasty to hear over the phone that your son and grandson have been murdered.'

'I feel empathy wasn't Anna's strong point.' Toni guessed that her mother, Katy Kemp, charging around like an untrained horse, had seemed like a lunatic to the officers who had informed her family about her dad.

'Anna's phone says she left a message on The Yummy Zone's machine at five p.m. That's a takeaway in Kemp Town. They have confirmed it. They've sent me a file from the driver's head-cam. Her meal was delivered at six fifteen p.m.' Darren Mason was a young constable who, talent spotting, Toni had plucked from uniform the year before. For obvious reasons, he had landed the nickname Chisel.

'A head-cam. Bless surveillance,' Toni said without conviction. She resented Google demanding a review of a pub, garden centre or whatever she'd visited, perhaps for five minutes, but hadn't managed to turn the feature off.

'Not an alibi,' Malcolm said. 'Anna could have killed her family earlier in the day. Whoever it was gained their trust, there were no defence wounds or skin under fingertips.'

'I don't see her killing her son,' Toni said.

'I've contacted the head at Wilbur's primary school. She's holding an assembly to announce the murders and is bringing in counsellors. I'll go along, it's possible kids in Wilbur's class and his teacher might know something.' Malcolm didn't sound hopeful.

'Nothing from the briefing or the PM; we need a break because if it's a stranger— *Freddy*.' Leaping up, Toni yelled out of the window at a van with a mermaid logo that was about to join the ring road. She didn't hear Malcolm finish her sentence.

'...then there could be another murder.'

# 7

*Freddy*

Freddy couldn't work out where the voice came from – she checked her mirrors, no one on the pavements, nothing on the road behind. Then she saw Toni waving from a top window in the old police station. Freddy reversed up Fort Road and pulled forward onto the opposite pavement. Not legal, but she reasoned that she'd been stopped by a police officer.

'What are you doing there? Aren't you based in Brighton?' she asked when Toni jogged out to her, half a chocolate bar in one hand.

'We've taken over a room for these murders.'

'I was going to suggest we did that brunch next Sunday; Rex has got someone else to take him to Mass. Guess you're tied up for the foreseeable.'

'You've guessed it right. Unless we've got an arrest by then it'll be for ever before I get to go out to play.' Leaning on the window sill on the passenger side, Toni chomped on the rest of the Snickers.

'Did you nick that?' Freddy hadn't meant to ask, but Rex

getting a companion and two no-shows for large orders had made her short-tempered.

'What? *No.*' Toni looked outraged.

'Any nearer to finding who did it?'

The question was meant as a change from a touchy subject, but made things worse. Toni snapped, 'Not one iota. I'd rather sell fish. A man murders two people in broad daylight on a Saturday afternoon and absolutely no one sees it. Or no one's willing to come forward. You'd think it was a professional hit, we've got nothing. Someone knows something, he must surely have been splattered with blood.' She made a dismissive motion. 'Enough of me, how come you can see me on Sunday anyway? Has Reg given you the sack?'

'Rex. It's sort of the sack, he's got a companion.'

'A sex worker?'

'No. *God* no. Why would you say that?'

'One-track mind. James Ritchie, the dad who was murdered, used an escort agency called Your Companion. Now forget I told you.'

'I deliver fish to them. Or rather to Jacinda.'

'Definitely forget I told you.' Toni grimaced. 'So, Rex doesn't want to see you?'

'I only saw Rex to take him to Mass. It's fine. I've got Sunday mornings back.'

'Just as mine are snatched away.' Toni slapped the van window sill. 'I'd better get back to it.'

'If you turn up late one night with a bottle of Jack Daniel's, I'll let you in.' Freddy grinned.

'You're on.' Toni said something else that Freddy didn't catch.

'What?' Freddy pulled out onto the road.

'*I did nick it.*'

As Freddy joined the ring road, she felt a flicker of dread. If Toni was shoplifting again, that meant things were very serious indeed.

# 8

*Martha*

Can't get away tonight, it's Ben's parents' evening, forgot ☹

'Sorry about that, I'm expecting a call.' Martha slipped the Tristan-phone, one of the two burners Tristan had bought so they could secretly text, into her nylon tunic and, snatching a foil from the trolley, slathered it with paste. She didn't need to text in secret, she had nothing to hide. *Nor would Tristan if he left his wife.*

'Mike blown you off again?' Cheryl Sanders met Martha's eyes in the mirror. 'Or as they say nowadays, ghosted you.'

'Mike? Oh. Yes. *No,*' Martha said. Cheryl was referring to the month before when Tristan had cancelled their sneaky week in the New Forest. Martha had cleared her appointments and packed her bag and he'd left her high and dry. 'He'll be in touch eventually.'

While Martha soaked up her client's problems, she saved her own for Timothy. But upset by Tristan bailing out at the last minute, Martha told Cheryl Sanders everything. She was having a relationship – not an affair – with a married father of two who planned to leave his wife. Just not yet. Martha changed Tristan to Mike as a less memorable name, but had forgotten it. Cheryl had not.

'He will ghost you, darlin'. Men like that never leave their wives except for twenty-somethings. What's his excuse this time?' Turning the bottles and pots so their labels faced out, Cheryl snapped a picture of them with her phone. She always bought her products online for less than Martha could afford to sell them.

'Meeting at his kids' school. His wife is family-orientated.' Folding on the last foil Martha led Cheryl to the infra-red drier at the rear of the salon.

'Don't be fooled, he needs his family, the George Foreman BBQ, a Kubota self-propelling lawn mower – boys don't easily give up their toys and the cosy hearth. At least he does the school stuff. My Harry always had to work late, he never made parents' evenings.' Cheryl ignored the magazines Martha placed next to her. *Hello!*, *Elle*, *The World of Interiors*, *Angling Times*. 'He'd never have dared play away.'

'Tris— Mike's different. You can't help who you fall in love with.' Tristan did have a self-propelling lawn mower, he'd complained Sally insisted on it. Was Martha being an idiot?

'You are too good for a two-timing B-word.' Cheryl liked to be the older wiser woman. 'You don't need me to tell you that a man who cheats on one wife will cheat on another.'

'Hello.'

In the reflection of the mirrored wall Martha saw a man bypassing Joanne in reception. His hair was too long for the shape of his face and looked as if he'd hacked it with pinking shears.

'Excuse me, Cheryl.' Relieved to escape, Martha hastened to the front of the salon.

'Good evening, sir.' Martha injected warmth into her voice. 'I'm sorry, we have no spaces today, we're closing shortly. We could find you a slot tomorrow?'

Martha avoided using Joanne's name; she protected her young staff from dodgy members of the public. Although the man, with unremarkable looks and soulful brown eyes, didn't look threatening. He reached for her hand.

'Patrick. We met this morning. When you dropped Rex's companion at Blacklock House? You were going up the stairs with Freddy the Fish. I was coming down.'

'Oh, right.' The man in the attic with the servants.

'"Of all the salons in all the world..."' Patrick drawled. 'I don't often get a haircut, that's probably obvious, but I had an appointment in Newhaven and on the spur of the moment, ducked in here. It'll stop Dorothy, this old lady who thinks she owns the place, calling me the wild man of Blacklock.' He rolled his eyes.

'I could do it now, as it's you.' Martha held the opinion that any bloke who recognised he looked a mess should be rewarded with a tidy up.

'You're lucky,' Cheryl Sanders called from under the dryer. 'Martha doesn't put herself out for any man.'

'Carry on cooking, Cheryl,' Martha told her.

'I often am lucky.' Patrick's flirtatious expression didn't suit him.

'Please sit here, I'll be back shortly.' Martha indicated a chair by the door.

'What a sweety, and after he's been under your blades, he'll look a treat, you'll see,' Cheryl hissed from behind *Hello!*.

'No wedding ring. Be bold, love, ask Wild Man on a date. It'll teach Mike a lesson and you'll have fun at the same time.'

'I don't date clients.' *Except Tristan.*

'No need, listen to your Aunty Cheryl. I bet he asks you as soon as you've administered the snip.' From beneath the revolving infra-red saucer, Cheryl waggled a finger.

Cheryl was wrong. An hour later, Patrick, his hair given a short cut with a quiff, had left the salon. Martha packed Joanne and her assistant off for the night and cleared up the salon herself. Arranging bottles and pots beside each chair – labels turned away – sweeping up Patrick's clippings.

She glanced out of the window. As shops in the street closed – a record store which only opened sporadically, a tool-hire shop, a café optimistically called Heaven on Earth, and a betting shop – with no restaurants, the street was frequented by drunks, and the homeless pitched tents in doorways. In the mornings after Martha unlocked the grille, she collected up used condoms and needles, disposing of the latter in a sharps bin she kept under the counter. There were more cheerful places to have a salon, but Martha had a good deal with the landlord.

Timothy said it was Martha doing the landlord a favour and Martha knew he had a point. Unlike Timothy, she could not escape to a stately home. She flipped the sign to Closed and was pulling down the blind when she gave a yelp.

A man's face was pressed to the glass.

As Cheryl had predicted, Martha's haircut having transformed him from a geek with a mullet to passable-looking, she didn't immediately recognise Patrick from the attic.

'Did you forget something?' Martha wrestled open the door.

'I wondered...' Patrick coughed. 'Do you fancy a drink? Or a walk by the sea? Look at the sunset.' *Damn Cheryl.*

Martha envisaged her evening. Staring at the telly, she'd pick at last night's spag bol. Eventually she'd go on Sally Robinson's Facebook page and grind her teeth. Sally reported everything short of her perfect family's toilet habits. Martha could check if Tristan had gone to Maddie Robinson's school. Although Tristan was out, Martha would keep her phone close in case he called.

Cheryl had said Martha should go and have fun with a single man. Tristan never believed Martha when she threatened to leave him, but what if she told Tristan she'd met someone else?

'Why not?' Martha joined Patrick on the deserted street.

# 9

Timothy had been shocked when, after Martha left and Rex had given him a tour of his sumptuous labyrinthine apartment, he had shown Timothy into a poky room lit by a small casement window facing a wall of trees.

Squeezed in beside a double bed with a dark-grained headboard were a matching chest of drawers, a folded gate-leg table and a chair.

When he'd read the Cuckoo's Nest advert, Timothy Mew had known Blacklock House was, as he'd told Martha, home. Timothy had not envisaged living in a cupboard.

That evening, Rex invited Timothy to toast their first evening together. Seated either end of a vast chesterfield, they'd clinked glasses of single malt.

'I brought this.' Timothy placed a cardboard box on the coffee table.

'The Leela of Self-Knowledge.' Rex peered tentatively at the box. 'What is this?'

'I played it with my nanny.' Timothy rubbed his hands as if with anticipation.

'Snakes and ladders, isn't that for children?' Rex watched as Timothy unfolded the board.

'The original game Leela was invented in India. My grandfather had worked for the last viceroy, he brought this home.'

'You didn't play it with him?' Rex asked.

'Games were in the nursery with Nanny.' Timothy gave a firm nod.

'I see.' Rex sighed. 'So, in my dotage let's relive your childhood.'

'It's a… game of life. You learn about where you are and your onward journey.' Perhaps Timothy hadn't heard Rex's acerbic tone.

'How nice it's an heirloom, steeped in family history. Same as snakes and ladders, chuck a dice and so on?'

'Pretty much.' Timothy was reading an instruction pamphlet. 'Oh, except instead of counters, we each have some object which means something to us. Like a lucky charm or a trophy, I suppose.'

'You suppose? Aren't you an old hand at this?'

'It's a long time since I played it.' Timothy was swishing through the pamphlet.

'I'm not one for trophies although I've defended clients who kept locks of hair, a finger.' Rex widened his eyes at Timothy. 'I think one makes one's own luck, but let me see.' Pointy leather slippers padding soundlessly on the carpet, Rex left the room.

Through the open French doors an owl hooted. Glass in hand, Timothy wandered out onto the terrace. King Tut, the peacock, emerged from the direction of the summer house and, hazy in the gloaming, circled the fountain. Perhaps sensing Timothy, he stopped and fixed him with a beady stare, letting out a screech.

'*Shut up.*' Timothy leaned over the balustrade.

From the other side of the house, an owl hooted.

'Molly's wishing us goodnight.' Rex was beside Timothy.

'Molly?'

'The owl. Bunty – who you said you met when you arrived – rescued her from a trap. When she's ready, Molly will return to the wild. Not yet or she'll be food for foxes or Rendell, Barbara's cat. Or, as I privately call her, Barbara's *Familiar*.' Rex gave a low laugh as he returned to the drawing room. 'I've found a lucky charm.'

'Good.' Timothy embarked on a faltering explanation of the game.

'Each of the seventy-two squares are qualities – goodness, evil, and er... planes, rows mean something too. The sixth row means... wait...' He flipped the pages of the pamphlet. 'The Theatre of Karma. If you're bitten by the snake on square twenty-four, you've chosen Bad Company who will encourage your selfishness and ego. You go down to number seven, Conceit.'

'My *bad*. Let's see.' Rex took the instructions. 'Whoa, the first row is The Fundamentals of Being, Illusion, Greed, Anger, Delusion and, as you said, Conceit. The second row looks more fun: Fantasy, Entertainment. Except for Envy and Jealousy, and I don't fancy Purification. Didn't this scare you out of your wits when you were small, Timothy?'

'It's only a game.' Timothy gave the ghost of a smile.

'The last square is Inertia. How is that winning?' Rex hugged himself. 'I'd die rather than be inert.'

'There's no winning, when we reach square fifty-nine, the Plane of Reality, we know who we are.'

'Something tells me that by the time we've finished, I won't know who the hell I am.' Rex grimaced.

'Now for our objects.'

'Show me yours first.' Rex looked mischievous.

'It belonged to my great-grandfather.' Timothy laid a silver cufflink – two engraved ovals attached together with a fine chain – on the first square, Genesis. 'He was given it when he joined the board of the East India Company. Hence the initials, EIC.'

Rex picked up the cufflink. 'Why's this important to you?'

'It's been handed down the generations,' Timothy said.

'And I guess you'll pass it to your child?'

'I don't want children, I will be buried in the family vault with it. What is your trophy?'

'Not a trophy. A friend gave this to me. One day I'll pass it to another friend.' Rex set a pewter disc spinning on the board and slapped it to a stop. Timothy leaned forward and read out the words.

'"Follow the footprints of the Lord. They will lead you through troubled times and brighten your life." Profound.'

'I think so.' Rex flipped the disc over. On the other side were two bare footprints.

'We need to throw a six to start.' Timothy rummaged in the box. 'They're not here.'

'Dice?'

'Nothing.' Timothy held up an empty Bakelite beaker.

'Fear not.' Rex eased up and crossed to a glass-fronted cabinet, opening one of the doors and reaching inside. 'I successfully defended a casino owner accused of failing to pay up a huge win. I proved he owed nothing because the gambler had bowed out. He wanted to pay me double my fee, but I never took a reward, it makes you beholden. I did accept these.'

Rex placed a gold-tinted steel box on the table and prised open a lid held in place with magnets. In two slots lay steel dice, six dots uppermost.

'They're exquisite,' Timothy breathed. 'Surely they're worth a fortune?'

'I chose not to ask.'

'You go first.' Timothy was gazing at the little steel box.

Rex dropped one of the cubes into the beaker and rattled it before tossing it out. It skittered over the board onto the carpet.

'Does that count?'

'It's a six.' Timothy retrieved it. 'It does.'

Rex looked as if he didn't believe Timothy, but said nothing. He tapped the pewter disc along to Delusion.

'Since we need a six to get going, we're both deluded, yes?'

'It's a point on the journey.'

By the time Timothy threw a six, Rex, landing only on ladders, had submitted to Purification and climbed to twenty-three, Celestial Plane. Purification, Timothy – possibly fed up with reading out the details of each square – said, could be got through sleeplessness, celibacy and fasting.

'I do two out of three. Never slept a wink last night, I tend to nap in the afternoons.' Watching Timothy take his turn, Rex appeared delighted. 'You've made landfall on Jealousy, I hope you don't have an inner green monster, Timothy.'

'I have nothing to be jealous about.' Having finally got to

the sixteenth square, Timothy slid his cuff-link to the bottom of the snake. Number four, Greed.

'Seems you mix up your sense of fulfilment with material possessions. Greed opens you up to anger and the other first-row stuff which we know are, wait for it...' Rex held up the pamphlet, 'Illusion, Delusion, our old favourite Conceit—'

Outside, King Tut screamed.

'You seem to be lucky.' Timothy stroked his beard as Rex's four put him on Selfless Service and thence up the ladder to forty-one, Human Plane.

'It says that gives me a proper understanding of the nature of humanity. Blimey, I gained that in my twenties as a rooky defence lawyer.' Rex refilled their glasses while Timothy hit Envy and was back in the pit of the first row on Avarice.

Tap-dancing the pewter disc along to the square labelled Conscience, Rex continued its journey up to Happiness.

Timothy plonked his cuff-link on Irreligiosity and from there back to Delusion. By now neither man was reading out the meanings.

'Are you letting me win? Please don't do that,' Rex said sharply.

'No,' Timothy said.

'Did I say I'm Catholic?' Rex chattered happily. 'I am looking forward to you taking me to Mass in my new car. I've been reliant on Freddy Power, the woman who sells the fish. While going to Our Lady of Sorrows in a fish van was fitting in a biblical sense, it's not a Jaguar.'

'No, you didn't say.' Timothy revisited Avarice.

'Lordy, you'll be stealing the clothes off my back.'

'It's only a game,' Timothy said.

'Surely we must take it seriously or it's pointless?'

They played on, the only sounds being the rattling of the beaker, the tap-tap of Rex's medallion – Timothy counted in his head, then placed the cuff-link on the square – and, the peacock now quiet, the swish of trees in Dedmans Wood beyond the garden.

'I've *won*. I've attained cosmic thingy.' Rex snatched off his glasses and placed his medallion on square fifty-nine.

'It's not actually winning—'

'Timothy, I have to say, going by your profile revealed this evening, you're a match for any of my criminal clients. Should I be scared?'

'No.' Timothy folded up the Leela board.

'I'd like to assure you this dice isn't weighted,' Rex held up the steel cube, 'but remembering the chap who gave it me, I can't.'

'For future reference, dice is plural,' Timothy said. 'When there's one, it's *die*.'

## IO

'Giving the fishmonger that dud bank card played into Haslem's hands.' Dr Sylvia Burnett berated her husband over supper. 'Haslem loves the chance to humiliate us.'

'He would have found another way.' Martyn Burnett's jaw clicked when he chewed. It drove his wife to distraction.

'The man is poison,' Sylvia fumed. '*God*, I wish he was dead.'

'We agree on one thing,' Martyn remarked.

'He's like Barbara's cat playing with a bird, teasing and batting it. One knows how it ends.'

'Will you *stop*?' Martyn was pale, his face glistened with sweat.

'You disgust me,' Sylvia Burnett said.

'I love you too, darling.' Martyn manipulated the knife with the skill he once used with a scalpel, resecting a piece of soft white flesh, piercing it with the tines of his fork. Click-click went his jaw.

'I said it was a mistake moving here,' Sylvia said.

'At least two hundred times.'

'I wondered about talking to Rex.'

'Rex? What can he do?' Martyn stabbed the fish with his knife.

'He was a barrister.'

'Defending the bad, the worse and the ugly. God, Sylvia, you tell me I'm stupid. We will deal with this our way.'

'So, it's "we" now?' Sylvia's mouth twisted into a sneer.

The Burnetts continued eating in silence. Afterwards, Sylvia cleared the supper things onto a tray depicting a sepia-toned photograph of Blacklock House and carried it to the kitchen. Scowling at his wife's retreating figure, Martyn Burnett jammed the pills she had put beside his glass into his mouth and washed them down with Merlot.


That morning, skulking behind the sitting room curtain on the second floor, her cat Rendell in her arms, Barbara Major had watched Rex's companion arrive amidst the usual fuss of the fish van. Garry Haslem had fawned over a woman who'd brought the companion. *Typical.* Although also surprising, because she'd looked in her forties, which was at least twenty years too old. Apart from him asking Barbara where the bodies were buried, it was a relief to her that Garry's interest in her equalled that of a lamp-post. As per, there'd been an altercation between the doctors over money. No surprise there. Barbara believed that doctors in general, and the Burnetts in particular, disliked parting with money.

Barbara Major's sitting room was redolent with mute suffering and premature mortality. Hung on dark green walls, cheek by jowl, were Victorian prints, the most 'cheerful' being Arthur Hughes' sunny rural churchyard of a woman beside her sailor brother who lies prone on their mother's grave. There were also nocturnal depictions of drowned women taken from the Thames such as George Frederick Watts' *Found Drowned* of a woman laid out beneath a brick arch; an etching of a woman poised to leap from London Bridge by Gustave Doré; and the last in Augustus Leopold Egg's triptych of fallen women, the grim scene with the River Thames and London framed by another arch. All were uniformly tragic.

Barbara was seated at her bureau in the corner. A fire burning in the grate cast flickers of light into the cave-like interior, which was lit otherwise only by a green shaded banker's lamp set on the bureau. Rendell basked in front of the flames.

Despite the images of mourning and loss, a faint smile hovered on Barbara's thin pale lips. Dipping a fountain pen into an inkwell set into the bureau, Barbara was filling out, in italic turquoise script, a fresh card from a stack by the base of her lamp.

For *Title*, Barbara Major wrote *The Companion*. *Name* – thanks to her coming across Bunty by the tennis courts, Barbara knew the man was called Timothy, but so far, no surname.

*Description: Tall, plump, pink-cheeked, despite male pattern baldness looks between fifteen and twenty-five. Dress: country squire/fogey, tweed jacket, green cords, brown brogues. Attitude: tense.* As she gained facts, Barbara would complete the other categories. *Age, Personality, Background* and *Motivation*.

When Garry had told Barbara that '*Rexy-Boy was shipping in a fancy bit*', her respect for Rex, a retired QC, plummeted. Rex was the only resident who Barbara didn't actively dislike. He had betrayed her. This feeling deepened when from behind the curtain she'd seen that the companion was a man.

Barbara was resentful. Had she known Rex Lomax needed a help, she would have offered herself. She lived in the flat above Rex and the money would have come in handy. Why would a young man move in with a seventy-year-old pensioner in the heart of the countryside. The companion must have an ulterior motive.

The sound system in Garry Haslem's ground floor flat was playing the theme song from *Alfie*, sung by Cilla Black, on repeat. A framed portrait of Michael Caine in the role hung over a vast marble fireplace, the only original fitting Haslem kept when he had modernised the flat. Among residents who rarely agreed, it was considered that fifty-something Garry Haslem had been born behind his time. Garry belonged in the swinging sixties when women – *girls, dolly-birds* – were his for the taking.

At the same moment that Barbara Major was adding her newly opened 'case-card' to her filing system, in the flat on the east side of Blacklock House, Garry Haslem was also deliberating on why Timothy Mew had answered Rex's advert.

Garry knew too well there were predatory scum out there who lured old people into marriage or getting them to sign over power of attorney and, dead or alive, ripping them off. Rex was only seventy, but as Garry had told the neighbours, he had Parkinson's Disease and, what's more, liked a drink. If people were given a reason for increasing frailty, they didn't ask questions. Now this companion had thrown everything off course.

Humming to Cilla, Garry Haslem fried up his prawns in butter, garlic and ginger as Freddy the Fishmonger had suggested and, as he tossed them about in the pan, determined to put a bead on Timothy Mew. He knew a gold-digger at first sight.

Lady Dorothy Erskine – Bunty – occupied the flat across the hall from Garry Haslem. When Bunty's father, the tenth earl, had died, the American cousin who benefited from male-line primogeniture over her had Blacklock House divided into flats, setting aside one on the ground floor for the duration of Bunty's lifetime. Perhaps a poisoned chalice because, although Bunty had done nothing to the interior since she'd moved in, she still had to find the maintenance fees from a small state pension and a trust fund that, over the decades, had dwindled to a pittance.

That Bunty was heron-thin was partly genes and partly that her outgoings left her with little to spend on food. Fish was her weekly treat, although, as Garry Haslem had warned Freddy Power, Bunty, and the Burnetts, were running up a tab.

Tucked up in bed – high ceilings made the flat impossible to keep warm so her bed was where she spent her time – the emptied plate of lemon sole on the floor beside her, Bunty too was taken up with Rex's companion. Neither annoyed at missing out on the role nor convinced Timothy was a crook, Bunty was consumed with envy that she could not afford a companion. Especially such a charming young chappy as Timothy.

Patrick Bell's flat in the attic had the look of having been deserted in a hurry. A cupboard door hung open, a jacket and a coat lay on the carpet under a row of hooks from when

Patrick, grabbing a jacket, had pulled them off before racing out and down the stairs.

Furnished according to second-hand IKEA, the cramped roof space had an unlived-in appearance that suggested this would not change were Bell there and not, as he currently was, seated with Martha Merry in a Chinese restaurant in Newhaven.

Shadowy eaves and a long narrow corridor made it easy to conjure up the cold draughty space in which, less than a hundred years ago, the household's staff had shivered or sweltered during the few hours there before their daily toil must begin again.

Lonely and trapped in his job, Patrick Bell was perhaps less happy than the unhappiest scullery maid to occupy the attic. For this reason alone, when Patrick had heard voices on Rex's landing which meant Martha the companion's friend must be leaving, without hesitation, he snatched his jacket and raced to his car conveniently left on the drive.

Patrick Bell was the only one of the residents who had given scant thought to Timothy Mew's arrival at Blacklock House.

Patrick had couched turning up at Martha's salon as coincidence, however anyone who knew him – and few did – were aware that Patrick left nothing to chance, he worked to a plan. It had been his plan to take Martha out on what he, if not Martha, considered a 'date' and everything had, so far, gone swimmingly.

Through the thinly insulated roof came the hoot of Molly the owl. The wind was getting up, it whistled through the trees of Dedmans Wood and harassed the tiles and rafters. Tonight, Patrick Bell wasn't there to hear his demons.

# 11

## A Month Later

*Freddy*

The altarpiece was, Rex explained to Freddy Power the first time she had driven him to Mass at Our Lady of Sorrows, a life-size copy of Carlo Crivelli's *The Madonna of the Swallow* painted in 1491. The original hung in London's National Gallery. Mary held Jesus – '*a rather podgy baby*', Rex had remarked – flanked by Saints Jerome and Sebastian. Rex said he preferred the piece this had superseded, a less overwhelming work done crudely in the Renaissance style showing Jesus on his throne surrounded by saints and prophets. '*It was tacky, but well-meaning. This one makes me feel I must never err.*'

Freddy had enjoyed Rex's knowledgeable, if sometimes risqué, comments about decor and other parishioners. A month since Rex had 'sacked' her, Freddy hadn't admitted to herself that she was at Mass today in the hope of seeing Rex.

She chose the back pew on the south side of the nave where she had a good view of the congregation and was as far away from Father Pete as possible. Freddy wasn't prepared for the uprush of anger she felt when she did see Rex. He walked briskly up the aisle, then stopped suddenly, something she'd read happened with Parkinson's, then moved on again. Timothy, following behind like an acolyte, took their coats into the cry room at the left of the altar, a room where mothers with noisy babies sometimes cowered, it seemed to Freddy, as if in shame.

Unknown to Freddy, she wasn't alone in being concerned about the companion. Although she'd reassured herself that the man came from a reputable company, Freddy had checked the website and knew that Cuckoo's Nest had been in business for ten years and received glowing testimonies from Cuckoos (aka companions) and Nest Owners alike. Freddy couldn't fault the premise, but she disliked the change it had brought to her own life. Father figure or not, over the last month she had missed Rex.

It had been a mistake to come. Freddy was about to leave when the choir struck up with 'Gather the People'. More as a prop – the order of Mass was in her bones – Freddy flicked to today's Ordinary Sunday in her missal.

*Ordinary Sunday.* Freddy longed for ordinary. Rex said he applied to Cuckoo's Nest because, '*I want to hear sounds in my home made by someone other than myself.*' Freddy understood. Sundays with Rex had alleviated her loneliness. Even when Toni didn't have a big case – and Toni and her team had not yet found the killer of the boy and his father on Seaford Head – her work meant she was rarely around. Toni was also single, but she said she preferred it to the hassle of a relationship. Freddy envied Toni her contentment. Freddy's last relationship had been fraught with problems, but there had been ordinary days, shopping, garden centres, teashops and restaurants.

Freddy could have driven Rex to country pubs and brought him to Mass in his new Jaguar.

Her next thought took Freddy by surprise. Were she Rex's companion, she could give up the fish round. Except the fish round was the one good thing in her life.

The clear speech and upright demeanour of the teenaged girl giving the reading recalled Toni Kemp when they were at the convent school. Having no truck with Catholicism, to the consternation of the more devout girls Toni was often chosen for readings.

Freddy contemplated the meaning of the passage from the Book of Exodus, the provision of bread and meat to Moses's followers in the wilderness. Freddy had not eaten breakfast and the mention of bread and meat whetted her appetite. Rex often suggested they stop at a pub for brunch after Mass. Freddy hoped he might invite her along today.

'The Lord gave them bread from heaven.' Freddy trotted out the psalm's response.

Rex was doing the second reading. Were this an ordinary Sunday, she would have known. He was St Paul addressing the Ephesians, '"…you must put aside your old self, which gets corrupted by following illusory desires…"'

When Mass ended, Freddy fled the church.

Timothy was outside in the porch brandishing a bunch of keys. Freddy slipped past and along the path to Mary's Garden.

Ivy-strewn flint walls, a lawn of wild flowers bisected by a flagged path to the statue of Mary, arms outstretched in welcome. The August sunshine, at twenty to twelve, as good as overhead, cast the sliver of a shadow.

The enclosed garden had long been one of Freddy's

favourite places. A peaceful spot where she could give doubts about her faith free rein. The biggest question: how could she worship with a church that didn't allow her to be a lesbian?

'Oh, sorry.' Freddy saw she wasn't alone.

'Goodness, why, *Freddy*.' Rex had been examining the flowers growing around the base of the statue. Staggering, as he got to his feet, Freddy ran to help but too late, Rex was smacking grass from the knees of his trousers. 'What are you doing here?'

'I was—' Freddy didn't know whether Rex meant Mary's garden, so she opted for 'I was at Mass.'

'Of course.' Rex sounded approving. Freddy decided it was good Rex supposed she would have come to church regardless of bringing him. Gesturing at Mary he said, 'I needed a bit of peace. Silence.'

'Right.' Freddy felt her spirits lift. Was Rex already tiring of his companion?

'Hah, Timothy.' Rex was suddenly fulsome. 'Is it time to go?'

Martha hadn't heard the younger man approach.

'That's up to you, Rex.' Timothy gave Freddy a vague nod that suggested he hadn't recognised her from the fish van.

'I think it is. Table's booked for twenty minutes' time.' Rex steadied himself on Mary's gown then said, 'Freddy, why don't you come? Pub lunch – all the trimmings.'

A few minutes ago, this invitation was what Freddy had yearned for. She caught a cloud briefly pass over Timothy's face. *He didn't want her there.* Freddy refused.

However nice Rex was, Freddy knew she'd tire of watching telly, shopping, and whatever else. She couldn't be anyone's companion.

\* \* \*

'Where is this pub?' Timothy asked Rex as he drove him away from the church.

'Actually, Timothy,' Rex slumped in his seat, 'would you mind if we head home? A sandwich will do me, then a lie-down.'

# 12

'*Abbey-an-toe*, Kezia love.' Garry Haslem handed a tall woman, her carefully drawn make-up augmenting her death-mask resting-expression, into a cab and waved manically at the departing car. As soon as it had rounded the bend, he let his arm drop to his side.

'Another floozy bites the dust?' Bunty Erskine lurched through a gate set within a yew hedge at the side of the house, enamelled cane under her arm like a rifle, her slightly silly-looking floppy cotton sunhat failing to diminish her commanding demeanour.

'Dust to dust, Bunty-loveliness.' Garry made a show of checking his Rolex. 'Good to see you risen from your casket on this fine day. Doubtless you're on top of the effects to the mummified of exposure to air?'

'Your attempts at humour betray your origins. Let me remind you, as recently as fifty years ago I'd be deigning to communicate with you only because you had delivered my meat order. No amount of washing can cleanse you of the reek of blood and sawdust.' Bunty raked the gravel on the drive with her cane. 'As much as you're capable, thoughts on Rex's companion?'

'Weird job for a man, ask me. Surprised you ain't got one, a crumbling spinster like you.'

'As you know, I live modestly.' Bunty shot Garry a look of venom that, guffawing at his description of her, Garry didn't see.

'Rex is losing it.' Garry was suddenly serious. 'That bloke looks slippery as a snake. He's after Rex's money, no mistake.'

'Takes one to know one,' Bunty said. 'The chap seems lovely, you only have to look at him to see he's a true gentleman.'

'Oh, is that what he is?' Fiddling with the greying chest hair grizzling out of his open shirt, Garry glanced at Rex's windows on the first floor. 'Face it, Lady B, you're outnumbered by noo-voes; your lot are just stuffed corpses in the paintings we have to keep on the walls so residents can pretend they're lords of the manor.' Garry leered at the elderly woman. 'Or so you like to say.'

'You disgust me.' Bunty's voice grated.

'I'd pull this place down and stick up a *smart* apartment block, roof-top swimming pool, basement gym, proper wi-fi. *Wallop*. Less upkeep, no draughts and *no* walking dead. Hold on tight.' Garry disappeared inside the house, the door closing behind him with the thud that Lady Dorothy Erskine had known all her seventy-five years.

Setting off at her lurching pace, Bunty dotted her cane along the flagged path that encircled the tennis court divided from the side of the garden by the tall yew hedge. After several laps around the court's mesh fence, still flustered by Garry, she flopped onto a bench facing one end of the sagging net. Face to the sun, her expression of beatific contentment intended to be reminiscent of the Buddha, Bunty appeared to be asleep.

However, had he been there, Garry Haslem would have seen Lady Dorothy Erskine's eyes were open a slit. Like Miss Marple, and most women of Marple's indeterminate age, Bunty's dithering old lady persona was just that. A difference to the elderly detective was that Bunty Erskine wiled away her hours not solving crimes, but plotting their execution. A prime victim was Garry Haslem.

A shadow cut across the weed-cracked asphalt. Barbara Major, in cotton skirt and frilly-fronted blouse, was fiction's quintessential middle-aged spinster, although she had never learnt to knit.

'Careful you don't get burnt sitting there,' she called to Dorothy, perhaps to warn of her approach.

'Sit if you're sitting, Barbarella.' The eyelids remained nearly shut.

'Barbara.'

'Not counting stab wounds and festering corpses for your man?' Bunty asked.

'I needed a break from the screen. I didn't say he was a man.' Employed as researcher and typist for a crime writer, Barbara claimed expertise on the processes and procedures of key roles involved in solving murder: police, coroners, pathologists. This made her a rich source of humour to Bunty and Garry. Their cards in Barbara's filing system gave *Personality* as both narcissist and psychopath. Another source of rich material, for Garry at least, was Barbara's cat Rendell now sitting at her feet, tail coiled around his paws, green eyes fixed on Bunty.

Rex, as a retired criminal defence barrister, was always

polite, although he doubted anything that Barbara's anonymous crime writer made up was more extraordinary than his own cases.

Because the crime writer was famous, Barbara had signed a non-disclosure agreement. Having ensconced her in Blacklock House, Barbara's neighbours assumed the writer must make a decent living although Barbara herself, dressing in charity shop bargains and only buying fish every fortnight, appeared careful with money. Garry kept on at Barbara to demand a pay-rise.

Single, in her fifties, at a residents' meeting Garry had once compared Barbara's pallor to the drowned woman in the painting adorning her flat. He had tapped the side of his nose when Bunty demanded to know why he was there.

In addition to a sour complexion, Barbara Major suffered from a rash on her chest, accentuated by the foundation cream she used to disguise it. Dr Sylvia Burnett, when once collared in the hall of Blacklock House, had suggested it was stress.

'What's the murder of the moment, Miss Major?' Eyes now wide open, with a whack of the cane Bunty bid Barbara sit beside her on the bench.

'I'm looking into unusual murders.' Barbara was prepared to divulge this to Bunty because she always claimed it went in one ear and out the other.

'Aren't all murders unusual?'

'Some don't capture the reader's imagination which is, Rex told me recently, true of real-life murders too. Have you heard of Trevor Joseph Hardy?'

'Can't say I have, but he sounds like a murderer.' Bunty wrinkled her nose.

'He murdered three women between 1974 and 1976; he was called the Beast of Manchester. However, what about Peter Sutcliffe?'

'Never heard of him.' Bunty kicked her heels under the bench.

'Well, he's actually...' Perhaps suspecting Bunty of teasing her, Barbara trailed off.

'The murders of that chappy and his boy flying a kite in Seaford a few weeks ago were unusual,' Bunty allowed.

'That's a live case. My writer concentrates on cold cases, where police have stopped investigating. There's more scope for fiction.' Getting up, perhaps intending to tighten the net, Barbara tried to turn the handle, but with lack of use – no one in Blacklock House played tennis – it had rusted. 'I saw Garry Haslem talking to you. You looked upset.'

'My hide's too thick for that fool's arrows.' Bunty sucked in her lower lip. Still with all her own teeth, for a moment it looked as if she had none.

'This meeting later – I shall propose we cut the maintenance fees.' Barbara gave up on the net handle and ran her fingers over the fabric at the top, no longer white.

'I don't pay maintenance fees, dear.' Bunty's expression suggested she didn't know the meaning of the term when in fact the fees bled her dry.

'We need to be one voice.' Barbara looked impatient.

'Choir of angels,' Bunty trilled. 'Why do you care, your murdering boss pays anyway.'

'Murdering? Oh yes, droll,' Barbara snapped. 'It's the principle.'

'Blacklock House is a funny place to plant you, if I may say. Don't you need to be near a library?'

'He says the country house atmosphere is Christie-esque.'

'How does he know? He never comes here.'

'Yes, he does,' Barbara said.

'Do you sneak him in under cover of darkness?' Bunty ogled at Rendell.

'That doesn't deserve an answer.' Blotches on Barbara's cheeks suggested Bunty had hit home.

'If you say so.' As she often did, Bunty had lost interest.

'We can't let Haslem win,' Barbara said.

'Or as one of your characters would declare, "Someone will have to die."'

'They're not my characters.'

But, head tilted against the back of the bench, Dorothy appeared to have dozed off.

# 13

'She was killed here. I don't leave flowers, that's morbid and a distraction, it could cause another accident.'

In the end, after the sandwich, Rex decided against lying down and had got Timothy Mew to drive him to the tree by the side of a lane near Blacklock House where, for no apparent reason, Rex's wife had crashed five years before. The gash having healed, the tree, a two-hundred-year-old oak, with a girth measuring four metres, appeared unscathed.

'Emily was a good driver; she was, if anything, too careful. She was one of those who paused for cars coming out of side roads and pedestrians crossing. Police said she was exceeding the speed limit when she hit this tree. When I had to do speed-awareness training, not long before her accident, Emily gave me a hard time. I can hardly call her a hypocrite, although believe me, in the dead of night when I miss her most, I'm tempted.' Rex laid his hand on the gnarled trunk.

Timothy, a good listener, listened.

'People do drive too fast along here, but there's time to recover if there's another car.' Rex pointed up the lane where, partially hidden by hedge, was a sign marked P. 'That car park is rarely used. Police considered that a car had come out of the entrance and Emily was caught by surprise. It leads to Dedmans Heath, but most people park at the one off the main road where there's an ice-cream van.'

'What do you think happened?' The Silversage helpline had trained Timothy to sound interested.

'Now you're asking.' Rex puffed out his cheeks. 'Garry Haslem says someone stepped into the road and made her swerve. I have to say that tyre marks over there on the tarmac did suggest that. But no one walks here. No need – beyond that hedge, on Dedmans Heath, are plenty of footpaths.'

'Deliberately?' Timothy tried to avoid Haslem who, whistling 'Every Breath You Take' by The Police whenever they met on the stairs or by the fish van, gave him the creeps.

'He says so. I'd call it a wind-up, Haslem likes to goad his neighbours, but so far he's spared me. God knows why.' Thrashing at nettles around his feet with his stick, Rex recrossed to the car. 'Talking of the heath, let's go and get an ice cream. My shout.'

'I'm not...' Timothy didn't eat soft ice-cream – a concoction of untold horror that had little to do with cream – but he didn't need Martha to tell him it would be churlish to refuse. 'Lovely, thank you.'

Timothy regretted his manners when, once they were on a bench on the heath, his ninety-nine began to melt and trickle down his wrist and the wafer became soggy. Rex, taking dainty mouthfuls from the tub he'd ordered, was unhurried.

'It could have been suicide.' The tub emptied, Rex licked his wooden spoon clean. 'So damn selfish.'

'You don't know that's what she...' Timothy had handled

suicidally depressed callers on the helpline. Most of them lonely. 'Suicide is beyond common or garden traits like selfishness. I doubt a person can think of others in that state.'

'Leela, your Game of Knowledge, doesn't rate selfishness as common or garden.'

'It's not my— Not in daily life, it isn't. If you're contemplating killing yourself, the qualities Leela leads us through via the ladders and serpents have ceased to matter.' Timothy crammed the rest of the cornet into his mouth and swallowed it without chewing.

'Wise words, Timothy Mew.' Rex often called Timothy by his full name.

They had played Leela thirteen times in the last month, out of which Rex had won nine. Rex suggested they leave the board out so they could play whenever they wanted to.

'The police informed me one tyre was bald and investigators said the brake pads were worn. Emily's car was due a service, I forgot to take it.'

'That doesn't mean you're to blame,' Timothy said.

'No, I don't believe it does.' Rex looked surprised, as if this had not occurred to him. 'They asked me if she was unhappy. I said it was completely out of character for Emily to commit suicide.'

'Suicide is, by definition, out of character,' Timothy said.

They lapsed into silence, each man letting his gaze rove over the heath. A tract of undulating common land mapped with bracken, some leaves tipped with orange although it was still August. Vivid moss crept around reeds and grasses that grew in bogs of black brackish water. Bogs that were only treacherous to the unwary, they were at most knee-deep. The treachery being soaked boots and trousers. Groups and single people, some with dogs, strolled on swards of grass that cut through the vegetation, or meandered along animal tracks between the furze. A man, arm in arm with another man, carried an excited toddler on his shoulders. The men laughed at something that, imperiously, the girl was pointing at. A dog, a bird. She lost interest before the men had established what it was. The still air gave their voices a muffled quality.

In their telephone conversation a couple of weeks ago, Martha had told Timothy that she had a new man. Nothing serious, but it was making Tristan jealous. 'Be careful,' Timothy had warned. 'Never play with people's emotions.'

A family straggled past, the boy, perhaps seven or eight, horse-played with his dad. They tussled and chased each other, darting ahead, wrestling and bellowing. A woman followed them, taking photographs of their antics with her phone with an expression of concentration.

'Still no arrest for those murders on Seaford Head.' Rex crushed his ice-cream pot and laid it on the bench between them. 'The boy was about the same age as that kid, eight or so, wouldn't you say?'

'I'm not good with children's ages.' Timothy did not add that he was even less good with children. Even as a child he'd found them scary, rude and unpredictable. Timothy had always preferred the company of adults.

Tagging several metres behind the boy and his parents was a young woman. She wore a pink dress with drop shoulders, and her strappy sandals made her clumsy on the spongy ground of tripwire brambles and unexpected troughs and hummocks. She clutched a bright yellow phone in one hand, continually checking it, which hampered her progress.

'For God's sake, Maddie, keep up.' The woman with the

boy and the man wheeled around. Rex and Timothy uttered surprised noises that the two were connected, each revising their vague estimation downwards.

'I don't have to do what you say. I never even wanted to come.' Maddie pouted. Perhaps catching sight of the men seated metres away on the bench, her pout became self-conscious and with a gesture of impatience she flicked back her hair and made to cram her phone in her pocket.

A couple more steps and her phone fell out, falling into the bracken. Unaware, the girl stumbled after her family.

'You've dropped your phone,' Rex called after a moment.

Head down, the girl didn't respond although she was still in earshot.

'Hold on, hey,' Rex called again. 'Timothy, don't just… can you?'

With clear reluctance, Timothy got leisurely to his feet and trudged after the girl.

'Excuse me,' he called as he veered off to where the phone had been lost.

The girl turned back.

'Your phone.' Timothy ran his hands over his scalp. 'It's in there somewhere.'

Her family no longer in sight, Maddie hesitated.

'It fell somewhere over there.' Timothy pointed at the sea of bracken.

'Where?' Maddie didn't move.

'I don't know.' With effort, Timothy stomped down the bracken leaves, kicking out in every direction. 'There.'

He retrieved the phone and, crushing foliage, made his way to the girl.

'There you go.'

'Thanks.' The girl snatched it.

'You're welcome.' Timothy fixed her with a judgemental gaze. Daubed in make-up, her skirt too short, she repelled him.

'I didn't want to come,' Maddie said. 'At least you can do what you want.'

'You'll be able to do what you want, soon enough.' Assuming her nearly eighteen, Timothy dismissed her complaint. 'I had to do what my parents said until I left home.'

'Like right *now*,' the girl said. 'We do this every *freakin'* Sunday afternoon because my mum has a thing about picnics, it's tradition. I swear I'll *kill* her if she makes me come again. All so she can smear us all over *Facebook*.'

The girl marched off as if furious.

'What about the grandfather in the East India Company?' Rex had been a few paces away. 'Don't you use his cuff-link for Leela?'

'I said that to make her feel better.' Timothy scowled.

'That was kind of you.' Rex returned to the bench. 'Impossible task with a teenager.'

When they got back to the Jaguar, Rex went to the driver's side.

'Rex, you can't drive.' Timothy stepped forward.

'Old habits...' Recovering himself, Rex used the car for balance and went to the passenger side.

'Garry Haslem thinks I murdered Emily,' Rex said as they turned into the drive and saw Haslem coming out of the gate in the yew hedge that led to the garden.

'That's slander.' Timothy touched the brake.

'It's slander if there were witnesses,' Rex corrected him. 'How dare he.'

'I appreciate your confidence in me, given we hardly know each other.' Grinning, Rex rested his chin on the head of his stick. 'I guess Leela gave you a heads-up?'

'If that were the case, I wouldn't still be here.' Timothy shrugged. 'Leela hates me.'

'It's a game, remember?' Rex said. 'I'll be interested to hear your second impression of Garry after our meeting tomorrow.'

'What meeting?'

'The Residents' Committee. Never a pretty affair.' Rex's hand started to tremble, he clamped it between his knees.

'But I'm not a resident.'

'You're my companion, ergo you are a resident.' Rex gave Garry a hearty wave as the car swept around the turning circle towards the carriage house. 'When we get in, I shall have a lie-down in my bedroom. You can entertain yourself, I imagine.'

Neither of the men saw the face at a second-floor window. Pale as the moon, it remained until a bank of cloud cast premature dusk across the drive. Drawing shut the curtains, Barbara Major dunked her boil-in-the-bag cod with parsley sauce into a pan and set the dining table for one.

# 14

*Freddy*

At around the time Rex was telling Timothy he would have a lie-down in his bedroom, Freddy decided to go out on her bike. It was the first time that year she had used her bicycle and by the time she was leaving Newhaven, her thighs ached and perspiration trickled into her eyes making them sting. The long flat stretch of the Alfriston Road came as a relief, she could intermittently freewheel, letting the bike's momentum carry her forward.

It was Toni who had made Freddy haul the tarpaulin off the mountain bike she'd brought back from Liverpool. She'd used it regularly after her mum's death, but this year it had stayed propped against the shed that once housed the small animal hotel.

After her mum and then her brother had died, Freddy had lost her way. Her return to Newhaven to her mother's deathbed was meant to be fleeting. But fresh out of a relationship and fresh into reviving her friendship with Toni, Freddy had continued to run the family fish round even after, essentially, there was no family. Power Fisheries was no more and if she'd been asked who she considered her family, discounting the brother in prison, Freddy would have said Toni Kemp. Who else?

Not keen to wile away Sunday afternoon at home waiting for Monday morning, and low from seeing Rex and Timothy at Mass that morning, Freddy had wiped the spiders' webs off the bike and hurtled out of Newhaven along the Egrets' Way by the Ouse. At Southease, Freddy veered through the village and up into the Downs. She could not have said at what point she decided to go to Blacklock House. Not that she planned to visit Rex, but a target gave the ride purpose.

Standing on the pedals, blood pumping in her ears, Freddy forced herself forward. She would not get off and have to push the bike up the slope. She told herself she would die if she gave in. At last, reaching the crest, her legs trembling, Freddy slumped over the handlebars and freewheeled on the slight incline. Ahead, the lane, a grey ribbon, twisted away over the hills until it was blotted out by Dedmans Wood.

Freddy had been so intent on reaching the top without giving up she hadn't been aware of anything behind her. Realising now, she wobbled and steered to the side of the ditch to let it overtake.

Wiping her face on her sleeve, she looked around. Dazzled by the sun, she made out a black shape. It wasn't moving. Not just the sun – Freddy saw now that the headlights were on full beam. Still, it didn't try to overtake.

Annoyed now, Freddy pushed off and pedalled along the lane. As she rounded a bend she glanced over her shoulder. The car was still behind her. Drifting, as if an illusion, in the bright sunlight. Thinking to pull over into the small car park that led onto Dedmans Heath, Freddy felt suddenly afraid.

Visitors to the heath tended to go to the larger car parks with toilets. Freddy only knew about this one because she used it to rearrange her display, fill in gaps, bag excess change and bring the next deliveries to the front of the shelf. She hardly ever saw another car there. She became convinced that the car behind her would follow her into the car park, screened from the lane by tall hedges of hawthorn.

Instead of cycling past Blacklock House, Freddy swerved in through the iron gates. A flash of metal, the car accelerated past at a tremendous speed. Freddy had no time to see the colour, let alone the model or number plate.

Leaving her bike by the yew hedge, Freddy hit the tradesman's button.

'Rex is asleep,' Timothy said. 'He asked not to be disturbed.'

# 15

*A week later*

'Seriously, no *way*.' Feet tucked under, her thumbs working her phone, Maddie Robinson was curled up in the ratty armchair by the Aga. 'I'm fifteen, I can do what I like on a Sunday, *every* day.'

'Sometimes we think of others, and this is for Ben's birthday. Never mind it's family tradition.' Sally Robinson winced at the killer phrase – it was a red rag to a furious bull. Maddie, always in make-up when not in school, claimed she'd been adopted and got stuck with a nightmare family. Sally should have been familiar with the argument – thirty years ago, it had been her own. Yet she couldn't bear to leave Maddie behind. That would spoil everything. It opened the gates for Tristan to suggest they did their own thing. He'd done that once and seeing how upset it had made her had backed off. *'We're a family, don't you see?'* Now she tried to mollify her daughter. 'I've done salmon sandwiches and made you up a flask of tea of your own.'

'Of my own?' Not looking up from her phone, Maddie

rolled her eyes. 'It's not me who was eight yesterday, Mum. If it was vodka, then you're talking.'

'Do it for Ben?' Sally knew the battle was lost. Soon Ben too would want to stay behind. Then Tristan… Sally trembled on an abyss of abandonment and betrayal.

'His birthday was yesterday and besides, we go there every stupid weekend.' Perhaps remembering her encounter with the balding man on the heath the previous Sunday, Maddie added, 'I can choose to do what I like. It's not up to you. And it's all so you can post crap on Facebook. I could get you arrested for invading my privacy.'

'One day you'll appreciate me for making memories for you and Ben. And your children,' Sally said.

'I'm not having children – you lot are ruining the world.' Maddie had weaponised climate change to go into battle against her parents. It tended to work because neither of them wanted to discourage her interest in anything outside herself.

Sally Robinson was the family's archivist. The Bliss Family Robinson's Facebook page showed Maddie and her brother Ben's first days at school. Maddie, features bleached by the sun, knock-kneed and pigeon-toed in a starchy uniform. Ben, cap *Just William* askew, gap-toothed and willing. Facebook's algorithms presented Sally with anniversary photos of their birthdays, of holidays, *five/seven/four years ago today you were…* Robinsons toasting their less lucky and absent friends beside azure swimming pools in Italy, Spain, France and, for their fifteenth wedding anniversary, Sydney. The three-hundred-plus photos depicted Dickensian-style Christmas tableaux of goose and flaming plum pudding. There were family selfies in matching T-shirts – *Stripy Robinson Day*

– and in parkas – *Robinsons go to Alaska*. If the Robinsons' 202 friends felt snappish envy, it wasn't indicated in the deluge of likes/loves/lols and comments, *Go Team Robinson... Love you guys...*

Ben Robinson's eighth birthday was to be a family 'Ben-Fest'. Yet even if Sally persuaded her hormone-fuelled daughter to come on the family picnic, Maddie would refuse to be photographed. There would be nothing to say she was there.

'You can't stay in the house on your own, it's illegal.' Sally saw a chink.

'That's actually not true?' Maddie's phone made a swooshing noise as she sent off a text. 'You can't leave me overnight unsupervised, but it's OK for an afternoon. Although you can stay out all night for all I care.'

'So you can have an orgy, Mads.' Her dad grinned.

'You're both clichés.' Maddie huffed deeper into the chair. 'I've got French revision, so, if it's OK, I'll stay and do it.'

An adroit move, as at the parents' evening at the end of last term, Maddie's French teacher had told her parents that, regardless of reprimands, Maddie hadn't done one assignment since the start of the summer term. Sally had told Maddie to pull her socks up and, it seemed, Maddy had.

'She doesn't have to come.' Sally was used to Tristan breaking ranks, he liked to get down with the kids.

'It could be just me. I don't mind.' Ben liked any family outing that involved birdwatching or insect-spotting. And cake. 'I don't mind if Maddie stays.'

Sally felt despair.

Early in their relationship, before the children were born, Tristan and Sally Robinson had devoted Sunday afternoons to Tristan's widowed mother. Sally enjoyed snuggling up with Tristan by the fire while his mother prepared crumpets and warming mugs of tea in her large dilapidated house on the other side of Dedmans Heath.

Over time, her arthritis grew worse so Granny Grace, as Sally called her on Facebook, remained at home for the family route-march. Then last year, to Sally's dismay, everything changed. Granny Grace sold her house and paid for an annexe to be built onto the home of Geoff and Rachel Robinson, Tristan's younger brother and his wife.

On Facebook, Sally posted, *Granny Grace has a secure home but, selfish though it sounds, this branch of the Robinson family tree is drooping, we miss her terribly.*

As she did every week, Sally had composed 'pre-posts'. *Well folks, it's still Ben's birthday, we're taking scrumptious nosh for a picnic to end all picnics. Wish us luck!*

'We barely eat together at mealtimes. She spends hours in her room *not* doing homework. We are *doing* this.' Squirting suntan cream on her arms and smoothing it in, Sally went for firm.

'I'm not coming and you can't force me.' Maddie's yawn was a sign that the girl knew the significance of her rebellious leap. Sally saw only lethargy in the face of what was nothing short of a catastrophe.

'I'll confiscate that for a start.' Sally Robinson snatched the phone from Maddie's hand.

'*Hey.*' Maddie struggled out of the armchair and made to lunge at Sally. Her dad and brother stepped in front of her.

'OK, OK, Maddie. You've made your point,' Tristan said.

What never went on Facebook was how Madeleine Robinson's family were frightened of her temper.

A tinny gibbering sounded in Sally's coat. *Sorry, I didn't understand.* Sally had activated Cortana on Chrome. Suppressing a smirk, Ben tried to catch his mother's eye, but she was already at the door, a hamper cradled in her arms.

'You are *coming*, Madeleine. That's an end to it. I'm not wasting good food.'

'I'll have her food.' Ben trotted after Sally.

'I'll be in the car. Maddie, you have two minutes to find your shoes.' Sally loaded the hamper into a shiny Range Rover Defender.

'Give me my phone, *bitch*,' Maddie yelled from the front door.

'Maddie, don't use—' Tristan had paled.

'You'll get it back after our *family* picnic.' Loading a rucksack into the boot, Sally uttered the last words she would ever say to her daughter.

'*I hate you.*' Ignoring her father and brother's muted entreaties to *leave it* and *just come*, Maddie hurtled upstairs and locked herself in the bathroom.

Team Robinson left her behind. Hunched on the closed lavatory seat, Maddie Robinson's triumph ebbed and instead of revelling in victory, she felt miserable.

'It'll be nice with just me,' Ben chirped from the back seat as Tristan Robinson turned on the ignition.

'Yes, mate.' Tristan craned around and patted his son's knee. He checked the inside pocket of a cotton jacket which, while unnecessary for the hot afternoon, *was* necessary for secreting a burner phone on silent. A dot of Maddie's nail varnish on the cover distinguished it from his main phone. Tristan left nothing to chance.

Cruising lanes of blackthorn and dog rose with the radio

at top volume, the Robinsons tapped the beat and chorused to Shanice's 'I Love Your Smile'.

As she sang, Sally amended her Facebook post.

Today the troops are stationed at Dedmans Heath for the last event of the Ben-Fest. What a weekend, phew! Memories have been made! Blue cloudless sky, not a soul about, fabulous to spend quality—

Tristan braked hard as he turned into the car park so Sally typed instead a k instead of an l in quality and had to correct it.

Music is pumping, we're scaring the birds... I LOVE YOUR SMILE...

The argument with Maddie had made the Robinsons later than Sally had planned. The blue of the cloudless sky deepened as the sun fell beneath the top of Dedmans Wood which, as recently as the early nineteenth century, had been grazed heathland, the bracken valuable fuel. Now, as the afternoon waned and shadows lengthened, a fanciful observer might see Scots pines, chestnuts, ancient oaks creeping forward as if trammelling the oceans of furze and ling in inexorable conquest.

The Robinsons were not fanciful. While Tristan flicked flecks of dirt from his treasured Range Rover Defender Sport, Sally perched on the tailgate and changed into her 'country' trainers. Ben clipped the lead onto the collar of Teabag, the family's black King Charles Spaniel, and chased off along a path onto the heath.

'Christ, Sal, how many is this for?' Tristan heaved the hamper from the boot.

'Four. Obviously.' Sally looked suddenly sad then, getting up, said, 'Oh, and thanks for the support back there. You realise our daughter has us wrapped round her little finger.'

'I do, but know what? Ben had a point – it'll be great without her. We stand a chance of enjoying ourselves.'

'That's a terrible thing to say.'

'True though.' Tristan sucked on his teeth. 'At some stage, unless this is a personality disorder, she'll come out the other side.'

'God, I hope so.' Sally dropped her voice as people appeared from the path. Few people used the car park, and unreasonably Sally felt annoyed.

A woman in a black butler cap, jeans and a man's check shirt whacked aside branches with her elbows, followed by two greyhounds led by a boy of Ben's age and a teenaged girl. Talking at once, with gales of laughter, they piled into a grubby Audi estate and were gone.

'Those teenagers are OK spending the afternoon with their mum.' Sally was wistful.

'Maddie might have come if we let her boyfriend smoke a joint in her bedroom,' Tristan said, stuffing empty poo bags into his back pocket.

'Where was the dad, I wonder.' Sally felt briefly cheered that, unlike her kids, the boy and girl were growing up in a broken home. At least the Robinsons were a proper family. *At least Tristan was there.*

'It was an own goal to take her phone.' Pointing his key fob at the car, with votive concentration, Tristan watched the lid of the boot slowly descend.

'Everything's an own goal with her and I didn't see you dealing with her,' Sally said when they reached their favoured spot, off the main paths, a few metres from Dedmans Wood. 'She's never said she hated us before.' She laid out Tupperware boxes on the rug and began pulling off lids.

'She said she hated *you*,' Ben corrected his mother and reached over, grabbing a chicken drumstick and swirling it in a pot of mayo.

'She didn't mean it,' Tristan said. Silence while all three reflected that Maddie had meant it.

'Napkin, Ben.' Sally flapped a wad of kitchen towel at her son and resumed her post.

We ate all Ben's favourite food, fried chicken, mini burgers, doughnuts. Don't tell anyone, but Tristan, Maddie and I love it too. We brought home an empty hamper!

Sitting cross-legged, Tristan tied Teabag's lead to his ankle, keeping it short to prevent the dog from reaching the food, and popped a can of Coke.

'Fall to, troops.' Giving the family rallying cry, Sally tossed down her phone and slathered a mini-burger with tomato sauce.

It was Ben's job to fix Sally's phone to the selfie-stick-cum-tripod for the photos. Setting aside the remains of their picnic, Sally pulled her husband and son to her and pressed the widget.

'I like your smile,' Sally sang. A couple more lines and she posted it.

In the last of the sunshine, Ben tore off to explore the heath with Teabag, Tristan dozed and moving her rug a couple of metres from the food to get the last of the sun, Sally settled down to *Middlemarch*, an annual read.

When he awoke twenty minutes later, muttering about having a pee, Tristan made for the woods twenty metres away.

The atmosphere of Dedmans Wood, worming tree roots, vertical lines of trunks mesmeric to the unwary, was subterranean. Occasional shafts of light penetrated the canopy of branches and leaves like moments of revelation. The silence was of sound, rustling, clicks and snaps of secret lives above and below the loam carpet.

Tristan's call went to voicemail. He had told Sally he would look for Ben. He stumbled deeper into the wood. As if in a church he felt loath to call or to whistle.

Tristan lost what path there had been and in unhooking his jacket from a bramble, stumbled into a hole, the entrance to a badger sett, landing on the knee he'd fractured last year playing squash.

Struggling up, wincing at the pain, Tristan felt sudden warmth around his neck, liquid gushing down his chest, soaking his shirt.

'Did you find him?' Sally asked her husband without lowering her book.

'Yes.' A whisper. 'And now I've found *you*.'

# 16

*Martha*

Half an hour after Freddy had passed that way, Martha, having tried every car park on Dedmans Heath, was giving up when she saw a car park sign. She bumped her Fiesta into a space shaded by overgrown hawthorn and blackberry bushes. The concrete surface was cracked by weeds and nettles. At first it looked empty, but turning her car around, Martha saw the Range Rover, an enemy tank, crouched in a corner. Black and monstrous.

When she had left her flat, Martha had been buoyed by her quest. Tristan could never see her on Sunday afternoons, he could not bail from the ritual family picnic. *Any other time but that.* Martha had been out with Patrick Bell from Blacklock House a few times, but he bored her. A boredom that felt too great a price to pay for winding Tristan up.

Once the idea was formed, Martha was fired up by the scent of the chase. Now that she was there, faced with the Range Rover, Martha's feeling of adventure converted to anger. Tristan said he found it unbearable leaving Martha and going home to Sally, he hated waking up beside her in bed, sitting opposite her at meal tables. Martha hated that she had believed him.

But now, walking around the huge black car, teeth clenched, she asked herself that if Tristan felt that, how could he swan off with his family every Sunday for tea and cake on a stupid rug? Surely, he could cancel? He was a grown man, he could do what he wanted.

*Was a family picnic what Tristan wanted?*

The Range Rover wasn't the only car. A black Fiesta, the bonnet hidden beneath the overarching branches of a blackberry bush, was parked in the other corner to Tristan's car. Covered in bird's mess and dirt, it seemed abandoned. It looked ancient, but noticing the number plate, Martha was sobered to see it was the same age as her own car, which had belonged to her mum who, after the first stroke, had passed it to Martha along with the hair salon. Martha had loved her mum; people used to say they looked like sisters until the stroke when Tracy Merry gained a decade and stopped colouring her hair. Driving the fifteen-year-old Fiesta and working in the salon her mum had opened thirty years earlier gave Martha the sense that although she'd died ten years ago, her mum was still around. Not sentimental, yet every year on Mother's Day, Martha put up a picture of Tracy Merry above her chair in the salon. Many of her older customers – including the advice-giving Cheryl – had been her mum's. Her mum had bought the Fiesta brand new. Now, the same vintage Fiesta had been dumped in a car park to rust. Time moved on.

Once, when she and Tristan were rowing on the River Ouse, he'd said, 'Don't waste this time moaning about Sally, be in the now.' Martha had lost it – *be in the now* – and she threatened to trash one of their family outings. 'That'll spice up Sally's Facebook page.'

At first Martha had teased Tristan when he complained he was under Sally's thumb; she had supported Sally. *Being chained to your wife is a worn-out stereotype.* She'd even mocked him when he said he was in love with her and would leave his wife. Timothy had suggested that Martha was scared of commitment, that if Tristan did break up his marriage, Martha would run a mile. Not true, Martha had protested. And it wasn't true. She had begun to imagine a life with Tristan, even having the kids at weekends.

One year had morphed into three and Tristan was still with Sally. His declarations of love were less frequent, but the stream of complaints about Sally and the kids had, if anything, increased. Martha no longer voiced sisterly concern for Mrs Robinson. Sally was the enemy who Martha had not needed to meet for her to declare war.

Today, as he did every Sunday, when Tristan texted, he'd been *dragooned into the picnic with the troops.* Martha was clear: Tristan had a choice and he hadn't chosen her.

She'd laid it on thick about Patrick. How she'd seen him when she'd brought Timothy to Blacklock House and a few hours later he'd appeared in her salon. Tristan had said, *Sounds like he's stalking you.*

Since he'd moved into Blacklock House, Timothy seemed to have changed his tune. After years of telling her to leave Tristan and find a man without baggage, when they had spoken Timothy warned her off Patrick. *'You don't know anything about him.'* Martha had asked Timothy to find out about him, *'strike up chat at the fish van'.* Timothy, seemingly only free to talk in the afternoons when Rex Lomax was having a lie-down, refused. He wouldn't get involved. *'He's my neighbour.'* Since then, on the rare occasions that Martha called, she got Timothy's voicemail.

When she had said she was busy that Sunday, Patrick had asked her to the Blacklock House residents' meeting the next evening. Torn between irritation that this was Patrick's idea of a date and the option of waiting for Tristan to call, Martha had eventually agreed. She'd meet Rex again and check out Timothy's new neighbours, and Rex might invite her in afterwards.

Martha did feel a bit bad that she was using Patrick to get at Tristan. Neither Tracy Merry nor Cheryl Sanders would have approved. She had to admit to liking that Patrick asked about her day and about the salon. He loved the idea of it being handed down from her mum. He even asked about the customers, *'Are they all as seedy as me?'* *'None of my customers are seedy.'* Meanly, she had left Patrick to decide if he was included in this or was the seedy exception. Tristan never asked about the salon – *'a haircut is a haircut'* – he was unsentimental: after they had started seeing each other, he'd found a new hairdresser. Tristan wouldn't tell her who, *'in case you stalk me'*. Timothy said Tristan was ashamed of going out with a hairdresser and had suggested he was sleeping with the new hairdresser too. Timothy, too, could be mean.

Martha felt her body thrill as if with electricity. She glanced about, although in such a neglected place, there would be no CCTV. If Tristan did call – he had promised to try – she'd let it go to voicemail.

On their first night out, Patrick had been obsessed with the murders at Seaford Head. How the police assumed suicide, then, beating the incoming tide, had retrieved the bodies and discovered most of the wounds were not caused by hitting the cliff side on the way down. Father and son had not jumped to their deaths, they had been stabbed. Patrick had gone on that the killer couldn't have expected to fool the pathologist. Even if the bodies had been washed out to sea and found further up or down the coast weeks later, blade injuries to the bones would have revealed what happened.

'You don't know that,' Martha had argued for the sake of it. The subject had made her uncomfortable.

'I bet he wanted the police to know it was murder,' Patrick had said. He was still saying it. Every time they met, he gave her an update on the investigation. From the way he talked you'd think he was the detective running the case. Tristan said Patrick's interest in the murders was creepy. *'What if he's the killer?'*

Martha said that was nonsense, Patrick wouldn't hurt a fly. *How did she know that?*

'How can you possibly know that?' Tristan had scoffed. When he fretted that Seaford Head wasn't far from Barcombe and Sally never locked the doors, Martha had put down the phone. Newhaven was a lot closer to Seaford Head but that hadn't occurred to Tristan. She couldn't complain about Tristan to Patrick, he didn't know Tristan existed.

Martha circled the Range Rover, trying to see in through the blacked-out rear windows.

Patrick was interested in her. She'd told him she was an only child and about her mother's stroke. The result of a one-night stand, she didn't know her father. He told Martha he'd grown up in London and had been an accountant for a friend's company but it hadn't worked out. Patrick didn't say if the friend was a man or a woman. Martha guessed a woman. He too was an orphan, or as good as. His parents emigrated to Sydney as soon as he'd done his accountancy exams. His mother had since died and his father had remarried. 'We exchange Christmas cards, or we did until I moved without telling him my new address.' Patrick had laughed. Martha, until then not properly listening, thought it sad. He'd told her that the attic flat in Blacklock House had made him a pauper. When Martha suggested Patrick sell the flat, for the first time, he had looked capable of killing a fly.

Tristan never talked about his family. Martha didn't count Sally and his kids. Tristan never talked about his parents, his childhood. Martha knew he had a brother called Geoff because Geoff had featured in a post on Sally's Facebook page.

One of the excuses that Tristan gave for staying was that without him Sally would be destitute. The kids would lose their house. Martha had reminded him what Sally's English degree at the University of Brighton had cost. He could stop paying out for her. Martha had seethed over Facebook pictures of Sally in cap and gown (fifty-five comments, ninety-nine likes). *Hoorah for the Prof, We're proud of you Sal, Brain-Box Sally rides again!* Martha plumbed the messages for the meta-meaning. Surely Sally's success hadn't made the friends so happy? Who could seriously feel 'overjoyed' by Sally Robinson's perfect family? As a friend, Martha had been poised to contribute to the incontinent adulation: *Love you, Sal.* Tristan had told her that he never looked at Sally's page. Then yesterday, scrolling down, Martha had found, *So very proud of my darlingest wife! Tris x*

That did it. She had stabbed out the message with her forefinger: *When you start job hunting, they'll snap you up* ☺

As if determined to torture herself, Martha opened her phone and swiped to Facebook.

Today the troops are stationed at Dedmans Heath for the last event of the Ben-Fest. What a weekend, phew! Memories have been made! Blue cloudless sky, not a soul about, fabulous to spend quality—

A red mist descended. Later, Martha had trouble recalling what happened next.

# 17

*Freddy*

'The front door was open,' Freddy said, before it occurred that she didn't have to explain herself to Timothy.

'If you'd rung my bell, I could have told you Rex was unavailable. It would have saved you the bother of climbing the stairs.' Timothy smiled, but his tone suggested irritation rather than solicitude.

'It was no bother. I wanted to check that Rex was OK.' *My bell?*

'Why wouldn't he be?' The smile had a fixed quality.

'I was passing.' Freddy bypassed the question and then accidentally, 'I used to take him to Mass.'

'But you don't now.'

'Since getting you for a companion, Rex doesn't need me to take him to Mass.'

'Lucky you.'

'Sorry?'

'I'm not religious. I didn't know light duties included God. I mean, I don't mind in the least.' Timothy drew himself up.

'But if you're missing the trips to church in your fish van, I could have a word with Rex.'

'Better not.' Freddy didn't want to interfere. 'Does he usually have afternoon naps?'

'I've only known him a month, but yes, in that time.' Timothy looked uneasy; perhaps he felt he shouldn't tell Freddy about Rex's habits. She'd overstated the 'friend' thing.

'Have we got a visitor?'

Freddy and Timothy both jumped. Rex was standing in the middle of the hallway. His hair was rumpled, eyes bleary as if he'd just woken up.

'Why, Freddy again. A nice surprise. To what do we owe the honour?'

'I said to Timothy that I was passing by.' Had Rex been on his own, Freddy might have told him about being followed on the lane. But now, in the plush corridor outside Rex's flat, she felt silly. The car driver probably felt nervous of overtaking, a learner driver or a woman being thoughtful.

'Timothy, be a sport, stick the kettle on. There's a box of French fancies in the cupboard.' Rex grinned.

'They're actually mine.' Timothy sounded apologetic, as if to own them was shameful.

'Beg your pardon?' Rex cocked an ear.

'Not a problem.' Timothy was on his way to the kitchen.

'Come out onto the terrace,' Rex urged Freddy.

Mouthing thanks to Timothy as she passed the kitchen, his rueful expression warmed him to her. Timothy had perhaps been looking forward to eating his fancies in the privacy of his room, instead of being on companion duty and having to share them.

An hour passed in a flash. It was like old times as Freddy listened to Rex's stories of what he called 'felons and villains'.

It had been late in the afternoon when Freddy arrived. The lawn below was entirely in shade, the summer house appeared almost luminous through the trees. Dedmans Wood beyond loomed dark and dense. Although Freddy could have settled in for the evening, she was about to make her excuses, keen not to outstay the spontaneous welcome.

'We've got a stiff game of Leela awaiting us tonight. That's snakes and ladders to you and me, Freddy.' Rex rubbed his hands together.

'You're playing snakes and ladders?' Freddy tried to keep the horror out of her voice. Since when did Rex need to play childish games? Was Timothy making him?

'...you'd be shocked by Timothy's true nature – greed, envy, jealousy, avarice...' Rex might have read Freddy's mind. 'Don't be fooled by Timothy's pretty iced cakes, his hidden qualities would freeze your blood.'

Timothy laughed, too heartily, Freddy felt.

Cycling out of Blacklock House's formidable gates, Freddy replayed the scene on the terrace. Rex had said Leela taught you about yourself. He'd joked how, landing on snakes, Timothy had revealed many bad traits. Envy. Jealousy. Had Rex been letting Freddy know he was afraid of his companion?

# 18

*Toni*

Nine o'clock. Monday morning. Two tents had been erected on Dedmans Heath and, some metres into Dedmans Wood, another one. Police tape had been slung from stakes in the ground and wound around tree trunks. Detective Inspector Kemp and Detective Sergeant Lane stood, legs apart, arms folded, noses glistening with the citronella Toni used for mosquitoes. The officers' defensive pose was because the oil was not warding off the smell of decaying flesh that pervaded the hot tent.

'…three bodies, one adult male, one adult female, one is a boy.' DI Toni Kemp considered the picnic rug at her feet. Patches of congealing blood merged with a green tartan rug indicated not a struggle, but where Sally Robinson had been lying, head on a cushion, beside a rucksack, while she read. Her book lay spine up next to her. *Middlemarch*. A novel Toni intended to read one day, but probably never would. Another rug piled with a hamper and a couple of rucksacks lay on another blanket outside the tent. 'The mud on these paths is like fired clay. Please God, may we find a footprint in the woods and DNA on at least one victim.'

It was the third day of a mini-heatwave. It was better than the rain, flash floods and iron-grey skies before that, evidence had a greater chance of surviving. But, as she'd turned up her Jeep's air-con on her way to the crime scene, Toni knew it was all climate change.

'No defence wounds,' Dr Minnie Clovis said. 'We'll check *Middlemarch* for fingerprints, but with no signs of a struggle and a good distance between victims, my guess is the killer caught them by surprise.' She looked pained.

'He picked them off individually,' Malcolm mused.

'This murderer shows skill, most of the cuts are clean.' Minnie Clovis looked as stricken as Toni felt. One reason why Toni had time for the pathologist, she cared.

'Professional hit?' Malcolm's Thomas Cromwell haircut stuck up on one side as if he'd gelled it then slept on it. Toni suspected Malcolm was into Tudor re-enactments, but he'd never said.

'I doubt it.' Toni stifled a sneeze. Citronella wasn't for internal use, but needs must. 'A hitman – or woman – wouldn't waste time on those extra wounds.'

'The killer extinguished life and then inflicted multiple – superfluous – wounds.' Dr Clovis snapped shut her case. 'These others are at different angles.'

'Suggesting the killer got into a frenzy.' Toni breathed. 'The act of killing was perhaps the point.'

'The older man and young boy were killed from behind. This woman was likely attacked reading. The book has blocked the initial escape of blood from her jugular, but there's no way the killer walked away without blood on his clothes.'

'Why did no one notice?' Snapping on gloves, Toni bent and unzipped the rucksack, shining her torch inside. A furled umbrella, tampons, a crushed box of plasters, a penknife, a packet of nappy sacks and a yellow fabric lead patterned like police tape emblazoned *Nervous*.

'*They had a dog,*' Toni exclaimed. 'Find the dog!'

Dialling his phone, Malcolm pushed aside the tent flap and could be heard outside: 'Look out for a loose dog and take care approaching, it's nervous...'

Deciding against her usual judgement to delegate autopsies, Toni would accompany these victims on their closing journey. She thanked Minnie and joined Malcolm outside the tent. She scanned the heath. They had all seen the boy's likeness to the older man. A whole family massacred.

*Dedmans Heath. Dedmans Wood.* A place struck by tragedy made its name a noun. Hungerford, Aberfan, Lockerbie, Dunblane. Saddleworth Moor, where five children had been murdered and buried.

'Did he deliberately choose this area because of the name?' His call ended, Malcolm was echoing her own thoughts. 'Was it a place of execution, like say in the Tudor times?'

'That's more your area of expertise than mine.'

'Not me, gave up history when I was fourteen,' Malcolm said.

'Oh, I thought because of—' Toni would rather discuss Malcolm's hairstyle. 'Dedman is surname, I've seen it in a churchyard.'

'Why stop this killing spree at three? There were plenty of other people on the heath yesterday. Was he, I wonder, after this family specifically?' Malcolm said.

'If he had blood on him from killing the woman, it would

have been difficult to approach people without alarming them.'

'He might have changed his clothes.'

'Which means he came prepared,' Toni said.

'He could have cut through those woods which is why he got the man first.' Malcolm pointed at the wood, where the white of what they were calling the 'father's tent' could be glimpsed through the trees. 'Or it was deliberate, as the man was likely to be harder to subdue.'

'What's beyond the wood?' Toni rolled her shoulders.

'That stately home, Blacklock House, it's flats now.'

'Talk to the residents. Check if it's possible to get to here from the house.'

Toni and Malcolm wended their way along a route dictated by boards and tape between gorse and mauve and purple heathers. High above they heard a skylark.

'Nature goes on, regardless of the senseless act of humans.' Toni squinted upwards, but couldn't see the bird.

'Not really – what about climate change?'

'For two minutes, let me pretend.'

'He could be local.' Malcolm stopped and looked back to the tents. 'Why travel more than, say, half an hour for a picnic? If you live in London you'd head to Sussex for the beach, there's other common land nearer there and Dedmans Heath doesn't look much different to Richmond Park.'

'Good point. The killer seems to have known how to enter and exit unseen,' Toni agreed.

'Even with local knowledge, he was taking a risk.' Flattening his upstanding fringe, Malcolm was again Cromwell. *With a rash*. The red and white blotching on Malcolm's neck was the giveaway that, while cool in a crisis, he felt it. She didn't have a stress indicator, unless you counted glugging Gaviscon like it was mother's milk.

'That slight incline and all these bushes give no sightline to the road or back to the tents.' Toni surveyed the scene. Even in daylight, the heath had an uncanny feel. 'Clovis said they would have died in seconds with no chance to cry for help. Did the killer start with this location and choose victims at random? With these paths and brambles, it's a maze, I'd easily get lost.'

'Or he planned a hiding place and arrived early. Could he carry birdwatching gear, bins or a camera as explanation for crouching in bushes or in that wood?'

'You think he targeted this family?' Toni said.

'Or did he know them? That would explain why they didn't put up a fight,' Malcolm said. 'Did he even know they were a family and not three random people? There was nothing to connect them at that point.'

'Good point. Are we assuming a man?' Toni *was* assuming a man.

'Ninety-five per cent of all murders in the UK are committed by men,' Malcolm reminded her. 'Two in the five per cent being that Aileen Wuornos in the States and that nurse Beverley something.'

'Allitt,' Toni said. 'Surprise trumps strength; add in that she knew her victims and we've got our Five Per Cent Woman.'

'That opens up the field to an older woman too.' Malcolm groaned.

'Let's walk through this. They've eaten. The woman stayed behind to pack up and then get in a bit of peace and quiet with her book. The bloke goes into the woods, maybe for a walk, maybe to find his son since the boy wasn't with him. Who had the dog?'

'Maybe they didn't bring the dog?' Malcolm suggested. 'That lead could have been a spare.'

'True. Or he or she killed the dog.' Despite the building heat, Toni shivered. She had just recalled picnics of her own childhood, her sister staying with their mum while Toni went off exploring with her dad.

'What if one of the parents was having an affair with the killer and the killer, driven by jealousy, kills the other one, but the lover threatens to tell the police so has to die. Or maybe they hoped to liberate their lover but the lover went AWOL so had to die too. Like Thompson and Bywaters in the twenties... actually that's not quite what happened... she was innocent.' Malcolm drifted to a stop.

'It could be that he or she had been dumped and this was revenge.' Toni shook her head. 'Except the boy's murder doesn't fit.'

'He or she could be a peeping Tom who stalks their victims and snatches an opportunity to kill them.'

'Let's go with a man for now.' Toni knew the first stage of a murder case was to set parameters. She hit on another seam of possibility: 'Our killer is lonely, he walks on the heath on a Sunday hoping to strike up conversation with other walkers. He comes across the father, maybe having a pee. Dad is annoyed and is curt, rude even. Killer gets upset and that's that. He comes out onto the heath and the woman sees him. She's a witness. He has to kill her. Maybe he realises the boy is their son and, knowing he'll raise the alarm sooner than the killer wants, he has to go too.'

Horrified by Toni's scenario, they fell silent. Above, the skylark twittered.

'I can't imagine coming here for a picnic. This place has a bad vibe,' Toni said at last.

'We're trained to feel bad vibes,' Malcolm said. 'For normal people, Dedmans Heath is a great choice for a Sunday afternoon picnic.'

'What if the killer came with them? A friend or relation, he gets into an argument and kills them.'

'You might be on to something.' Toni opened a basketwork hamper on a rug a couple of metres from the woman's body. 'Four cups. Four forks. Someone else was here. We need to find their car.' She set off at a pace.

'Not if they lived in Blacklock House,' Malcolm caught up.

'They all live there and took some neighbour dispute out onto Dedmans Heath?'

Nearing the road, the traffic hum became audible and snatches of vehicles flashed between a stand of ash trees at the edge of the heath. Nowhere in Sussex was far from elsewhere.

'There's Sheena.' Malcolm pointed at a woman in a hi-vis anorak stomping towards them.

'Uniform have found a Black Range Rover Defender in a small car park twenty minutes' walk from the crime scene.' Sheena had her notebook. 'Registered to Tristan Robinson of The Laburnums, Barcombe, Lewes. No CCTV on the lanes.'

'A whole family wiped out.' Toni heaved a breath. Hearing the dead man's name was a punch in the stomach.

'Not everyone, boss,' Sheena said.

'What?'

'There's a fifteen-year-old daughter.' It sounded graver in a Lanarkshire accent.

'*You. Are. Kidding.*' The pricking of sweat on Toni's forehead wasn't due to the sun, but to the flashback to when the police officers told her about her dad's murder. Counselling had lessened the fleeting image, but in her job, Toni had plenty of memory aids. 'They had *another* child?'

'How come she hasn't reported her family failed to return yesterday?' Malcolm said quietly.

Toni clamped her hands to her cheeks. 'Please tell me it wasn't called in and we filed it "No further action"?'

'No.' Sheena waved a hand. 'No one has reported it.'

'We need to get there before this girl finds out. What's her name?'

'Too late.' Sheena shook her head. 'Madeleine has seen it on Facebook. The wife, Sally Robinson, has a page and her friends are leaving condolence messages.'

'What kinds of ten-point moron does that? *Hang on...*' Toni couldn't feel much worse. 'How is it these so-called friends *know* Sally is dead when we didn't know her identity until now?'

'Take a guess.' Sheena pointed at the sky as the clatter of propellers obscured traffic sounds. A helicopter swung around and homed in on them. 'There's an uncle, Tristan Robinson's older brother Geoff with her. He and his wife came down from Chiswick, where they live.' Sheena had made it her business to be up to speed. Toni was learning to be grateful she had someone like Sheena snapping at her heels.

'I don't need to be a mind-reader to know you're thinking what I'm thinking.' Toni voiced what had been haunting her since they'd arrived, and she could read the same on Malcolm and Sheena's faces.

'James Ritchie's wife Anna has no fondness for him, but we have no evidence at all that she killed her estranged husband or her son. Jury's out on the Robinsons' daughter or this Tristan's brother,' Malcolm said.

'Same MO,' Sheena added.

'Sheena, I want you to go back in time, look for other spree killings of families, not just in Sussex, go national. Start at twenty years.'

'Wouldn't we remember a man killing families?' Sheena had to kick back. *Good for her*, Toni made herself think.

'We know too well that not every murder whets the media's appetite,' Malcolm reminded her.

'*There it is.*' Toni spotted the lark.

'Where?' Malcolm shaded his eyes from the sun.

'Between the top of that large tree and that cloud shaped like Australia.'

They watched the lark, an intermittent shape in the bright morning glare until, perhaps spying food, it plummeted out of sight behind a sea of bracken.


'Why didn't you go with your mum and dad and Ben on the picnic?' Since Malcolm had what he called a 'stroppy teenaged girl at home', Toni had nominated him to lead.

'It was a stupid idea. All weekend it's been "Ben Ben Ben". I'm fifteen next week, what's going to happen for my birthday now?' Madeleine Robinson glared at Malcolm and then Toni as if she expected an actual answer.

They had arrived in the middle of Madeleine Robinson

painting her nails. Toni recognised that, far from being a sign the girl wasn't bothered by the murder of her family, it was her way of grasping for the normal although, Toni knew, nothing would ever again be normal for Madeleine.

'I'm sure your uncle will...' Malcolm glanced at Geoff Robinson and tailed off. Uncle Geoff didn't look capable of organising a cup of tea let alone the level of birthday celebrations that would satisfy his teenaged niece. Malcolm returned to Maddie. 'You felt Ben's birthday celebrations were over the top?'

'Ben had had enough.' Screwing the top onto the vial, Maddie waved a hand in the air. Not a gesture of dismissal, she was drying her varnished nails. She jutted her chin. 'I'm out tonight, burger with Arnie, Dad said I could.'

Her eyes darted about and Toni guessed it had occurred to Maddie that she could say or do anything, her family wasn't there to stop her.

'Madeleine, put that stuff away, and talk properly to the police. *Christ*, if Tristan saw you dolling yourself up, he—'

'He won't, will he, cos he's *dead*.'

This silenced the three adults. Malcolm recovered first.

'Why did you think it stupid to go to De— the heath?'

'I wanted to see Arnie. I'm old enough to live my own life, I don't have to do what I don't want to do.'

'Lucky you.' Toni gave an encouraging nod. 'I'd be watching daytime telly right now if I'd got my way.'

'Why don't you then?' Maddie wasn't inhibited by a natural respect for the law.

'Mum and Dad only want... *wanted* what's best for you.' Symmetrical good looks, letter-box mouth, square jaw. Add shock and Geoff Robinson could be an avatar. Like Tristan

Robinson, greying designer stubble blended with a waxen complexion, he'd missed out on Tristan's bright blue eyes. His own were a dull brown although, Toni reflected, this was Geoff on a bad-everything day. The key differentiator was that, crumpled across a myriad of tree roots, Tristan had been dead. Geoff was supposed to be alive. Or was the death-mask face down to guilt and exhaustion after committing three murders?

'Only I know what's best for me,' Maddie hissed.

'You never noticed your family hadn't come back?' Geoff thundered.

'Arnie spent the night with you?' Malcolm suggested.

'Might of.'

'What the hell—?'

'Mr Robinson, I'm going to have ask—' Malcolm was firm.

'OK, OK. But look at her, lipstick, nails, sleeping around... Christ, if Tris was here.'

'Sleep around? If Dad was here, you'd never dare say that,' Maddie fumed at Uncle Geoff.

'Maddie, did you wonder where your parents were?' Toni knew how guilty the innocent could act. Murder slices through our best-kept secrets.

'If you must know, I expected they'd taken Ben to the movies, since he couldn't go on Saturday. Dad's trying to keep Mum happy because she knows he's having an affair.'

'That's crap,' Geoff said. Toni watched him – had he known his brother was having an affair and was shocked that Sally Robinson had known, or had Geoff not known this himself?

'Shows what you know? Dad was always saying he had to work.' Maddie blew on her nails.

'Did you worry when they didn't come back last night?' As

if suggestion of an affair was by the by, Malcolm kept to his original line of questioning.

'I was pleased, if you must know. I mean, Mum had stolen my phone, so they couldn't text me. No way was I answering the main line.'

'Did it ring?'

'Might of.'

'Might have or did?' Malcolm barked.

'Didn't.'

No point in doing last number redial, a neighbour had rung to give her condolences and ask if she could do anything. News had travelled faster than fire. They'd need to see the itemised call records.

Toni felt sorry for Geoff and for Maddie. They were poles apart. Maddie's sleeping with her boyfriend might have got her grounded, but it wasn't the capital offence that her parents' death had made it. *Funny what makes you feel lucky.* When her own dad was murdered, Toni had still had her mum, her sister and her home.

'You slept here alone last night, didn't you, Maddie?' Malcolm got Maddie better than poor Uncle Geoff. 'Arnie wasn't here, was he?'

'So what?' Maddie looked deflated. Toni saw that real life was sinking in. 'So, I was asleep, how could I know they weren't in their beds?'

'Maddie, I'm sorry we have to ask you some difficult questions.' Detectives had known who killed Toni's dad from the get-go, but they'd had to build a case. *'Did your dad always go out to fetch the milk?' 'Had your dad had an altercation with the milkman before?'* An altercation. Toni had not known the word. Since then, if she used it – too often in her job – it was a trigger, she was back on her parents' settee listening to the police officers, the early morning sun casting light into the cold grate.

'Have you seen anyone acting strangely, near here or perhaps at your school? A man or a woman lingering across the street or seated in a stationary car?' Toni asked. 'Have you been spoken to by strangers?'

'All the time.' Maddie undid the top on the varnish bottle and did it up again. 'It's the summer, we get tons of strangers. Mum says this is a *quintessential* English village, Americans freakin' love it.'

Toni had not been this rude to the detectives who had descended on her home that terrible day. She'd hardly spoken. Had she seemed remote and sullen to the officers?

'We get people trying to get to the footpath along our drive. It's a Google mess-up, they get sent here. Mum would rush out and tell them, "It's on the other side of the sluice gates."' Maddie's high-pitched posh voice was presumably a parody of Sally Robinson. It made Toni uncomfortable. 'Mum asks them where they've come from – if they were Italians, it was all *prego, grazie, scusi*. So *embarrassing*.'

'I guess she was being friendly,' Malcolm suggested.

'Mum was trying to catch Dad's mistress sneaking a look at his house.' Maddie slammed the varnish bottle onto a table, making the babies tumbling out of a spider plant beside it tremble. Toni loved houseplants, but always killed them.

'Madeleine, your father did not have a mistress.' Geoff looked horrified.

'He wasn't going to tell you,' Maddie spat back. 'Not after you nicked his inheritance.'

'I did what?' Geoff flushed.

'Granny spent all her house money on that extension in your house. What happens when she dies – do we get some of it?' Maddie Robinson's speech sounded borrowed. Had she heard this subject discussed by her parents?

'Leave my mother out of it, young lady.' Giving him his due, Geoff looked on the verge of tears.

'Why do you think your dad was having an affair, Maddie?' Toni asked.

'I heard him and Aunty Lisa in the kitchen.'

'It's wrong to eavesdrop.' Geoff Robinson pulled at his nose with a fist. 'Lisa was just trying work out how this happened, that was all. Like who would harm them.'

'That's our job, Mr Robinson. We are doing our utmost to discover who attacked your family,' Malcolm weighed in.

'Am I in danger?' Gone was the sophistico with the nails and the make-up. The girl huddled on the sofa could have been her dead brother's age.

'No, darling, we'll make sure you're safe.' Toni projected forward twenty years when, she hoped, scarred for ever as Maddy would be by this biographical bombshell, she'd come to love Uncle Geoff and Aunty Lisa as substitute parents. From his agonised expression, Geoff was thinking the same thing.

'I'll get tea.' Toni strode to the door, not to escape the girl's distress, but to catch Aunty Lisa eavesdropping.

Toni shut the kitchen door and indicated one of four stools at an island, a third of which was taken up with a sink and brass taps, in the middle of an open-plan area including a long oak table and two sofas. Above their heads, beams were hung with bunches of dried lavender and thyme. A text book on European history in the interwar years lay face down on a chair beside an Aga. It looked as if Madeleine had been working.

Beyond bifold Crittal-style doors and a stretch of dazzling white gravel was a wild-flower lawn and a wooden structure, a home office from which, Toni knew, Tristan Robinson had run his architectural business.

Presumably responsible for the interior, Tristan had gone for a fusion of industrial and rural. Zinc cladding, wooden counters, blue and green herringbone floor tiles, the suspended foliage and Aga. The cars, the new Range Rover now at the forensics lab, and a smaller BMW parked outside a large house in picture-postcard village, all spelled success. Was it smoke and mirrors, had the Robinsons been expecting a payout on Mrs Robinson senior's demise? Toni would get Sheena onto Companies House to check on the health of Robinson Ecotechture. Plenty of opulent homes and cars were underwritten with fool's gold. Did they owe anyone anything?

'Did you get on with your sister-in-law?' Toni asked Lisa who, caught red-eared at the living room door, was fidgeting about on the high stool.

'She *is* – was – family.' Lisa's emphasis suggested the tense was less a slip than underlining a new state of affairs that may or may not suit her. In jeans and a man's shirt, the flung-on casual style was overtaken by plum-coloured nails and rouge-shaded cheekbones on a canvas of celebrity orange foundation; Lisa Robinson cared how she looked. Perhaps aunt and niece might bond after all.

'I know myself how complicated family can be.' Toni was chummy.

'I met Geoff years after Sally and Tristan had their kids, so Sally was already installed. She'd ruled the roost over the boys and resented me taking Geoff away from her. She told me Geoff had been single so long, she assumed he was gay.' Lisa picked up and put down objects on the counter, a used cafetière, a ceramic salt cellar and a bunch of keys that included a Skoda key. *Not a hefty Range Rover or Beemer.* 'Geoff was head over heels in love with me and anyone could see Tristan had a roving eye. I felt kind of sorry for her.'

*Kind of.*

'So, Geoff isn't gay?' Hopping down from her stool, Toni paraded around the cathedral-like room. Three metal shades, that brought back the dining hall in Toni's convent school, hung over the oak table, each lamp hanging from criss-crossing wires, the effect a giant Newton's cradle. Toni wasn't a fan of the look, only those who'd never worked in a factory were happy to turn their home into one.

'Obviously he's not gay, he's married to me.' Lisa was sharp.

'How often did you see Sally and Tristan?'

'More since Geoff's mother is living with us. Did you hear Madeleine just now?'

Nodding, Toni resisted pointing out that yes, she had heard because, unlike Lisa, she'd been in the same room.

'I mean, why would I want my mother-in law-living with us? *She smokes in bed.*'

The nearest Toni had come to a mother-in-law was Reenie Power when Toni had dated Freddy's younger brother. Had Reenie ever wanted to move in, Toni privately agreed that smoking in bed could be in her top ten of hates.

The digital timer on a slow cooker displayed three hours and thirty-two minutes. In the time since Lisa and Geoff had been in the house, had one of them assembled a casserole? Toni's mother, not usually great on presents, had sent her one for her last birthday. Unlike other presents – usually Buddhist related – the cooker had become Toni's best friend.

'…birthdays, we're supposed to share Sheila at Christmas, she stayed with us last year. Christ, now Sheila will have to be with us for ever. Already she's a sandwich short of a picnic.' Lisa Robinson seemed oblivious to the unfortunate pun.

'It's hard.' Toni could see motivation for murder diminishing with the cooker timer.

'…I read about that family that were stabbed in a seaside town not far from here. Could it be the same killer? Was it? If it was, then it won't be personal. I mean, it can't be Maddie, can it?'

'We are looking into all angles.' Toni gave a stock answer while interested that Lisa Robinson had even had her niece – by marriage – in the frame. 'Could you see Maddie doing this?' Casual question.

'She has these terrible fits. Tristan once sent Geoff a WhatsApp recording where she was screaming that she hated her parents and was going to leave home. Yelling like a banshee. It was really quite shocking.'

'Does Geoff still have the recording?' Nothing should be discounted.

'No. It was toxic. We had to get it off his phone.'

'Teenagers can lose it.'

'I used to say to people, if you are thinking of having a baby just imagine them as a teenager. This does boiling water without a kettle, would you believe.' Lisa was playing with the brass four-in-one mixer tap over the sink. Her tone implied the same outrage as her view of Maddie.

'Are you making something?' Toni indicated the slow cooker.

'Chicken casserole. Maddie was supposed to put it on while they were out, she forgot.' Lisa softened. 'I doubt she has the appetite, but she must eat.'

*Maddie had expected her family to return in time for supper.*

'Do you know if Tristan and Sally were meeting anyone on the heath yesterday afternoon?'

'No idea.' Lisa shrugged. 'Living in Chiswick, we don't mix socially.'

Lisa didn't elaborate on whether the not-mixing was about distance from Barcombe or social grouping.

'It seems Sally was keen for Maddie to go.'

'She was big on family stuff, she was never off Facebook. Sally airbrushed out arguments, sulks and failures as if they led the best life. I knew it was a lie but you still fall for it, don't you?' Lisa lifted the slow-cooker lid and peered at the contents. 'God, it pissed me off.'

'It would me.' For professional reasons Toni didn't use social media, but knew she'd resent reading about her friends' relentlessly happy lives. A perpetual round robin. Money and jealousy and shame were, she'd remind her team, major motives for murder. Admit your own unpalatable traits – jealousy, cruelty, greed – to see the darkness in others. Toni couldn't imagine jealousy leading her to murder but hey, you never knew.

'Sally Robinson was a liar.' Lisa gave the casserole a stir. A chicken leg stuck up above the sauce like Excalibur. Although half-eleven in the morning, having eaten no breakfast, Toni could have tucked in.

Malcolm came into the kitchen. 'You need to see this, Toni.' He held out his phone.

Today the troops are stationed at Dedmans Heath for the last event of the Ben-Fest. What a weekend, phew! Memories have been made! Blue cloudless sky, not a soul about, fabulous to spend quality time with my loved ones. We filled our trusty old Fortnum's hamper with treats, for the kids as well as *Tristan Robinson* and I. Classic Bliss Family Robinson!

'She's tagged in Tristan.' Lisa Robinson had sidled around the island and was looking over Toni's shoulder. In a strangled voice, 'He'll never see it.'

Toni could see that Malcolm was thinking what she was thinking. The photo of Ben and Tristan with Sally, captioned *Maddie the Pap!* was a selfie. Sally had written the post and faked the picture as if about the past and posted in the future.

A future she had never lived and never would.

As she reversed the Jeep in order to turn, Toni looked up at the house. A different design to the Ritchies' house, yet it was also a quintessential storybook family home. The dog, called Teabag, had been found and was returned just as they were leaving. Toni established that it – Teabag was a he – had been checked for hair and fibres – but there had been nothing. It was possible Teabag had run off before either Tristan or Ben Robinson were murdered.

'There's a Ring doorbell. Footage will be stored on their phones.' Malcolm was already on to Sheena asking her to check.

'The red tops will trash Maddie Robinson. She's not the

e-fit of a devastated orphan. More a double of that nightmare daughter in *Mildred Pierce*, with Joan Crawford.'

'After my time.'

'*God*, Mal, it came out in the forties, I'm not that old. It's my mum's favourite, she made us watch it every Christmas.' Toni took a Snickers bar out of the door pocket and waved it at Malcolm. As he always did, he refused.

'Poor kid. You and I can see she's totally messed up by this, but if she gets in front of the camera, she'll crash and burn.'

'You're not thinking of having her at a press conference?' Malcolm looked shocked.

'No. Even if Maddie was Angel of the South, being that cruel would backfire on us.' Toni munched the chocolate. 'But I can see Maddie needing to parade her make-up efforts before a scrum of lenses. Best we keep the remaining Robinsons in purdah.'

'Good point.'

'Is there a way of telling when Sally put up that post? Where she was and indeed if she posted it at all.'

'The language is the same as her others – calling her family "the troops", for instance. That said, anyone could imitate her style.'

'Life after death.' As they drove along meandering country lanes, Toni waved at a man in hi-vis holding a sign turned to GO at roadworks. As a young copper, she'd done time on traffic duty – it was soul-destroying.

'Listen to this post: "Maddie can sleep anywhere!" There's a photo of Maddie with her head resting on a bag. It's the bag Maddie had on the sofa today. Maddie Robinson *did* go on the picnic.'

'That girl is *good*.' Toni felt as though she was plummeting down a lift shaft. No matter how many years in CID, she could be caught out. Maddie Robinson screamed and shouted at her family and had maintained icy hauteur with seasoned detectives. A psychopath, had it been *job done*?

'Maddie knew her mother was a social media freak, she knew there was a picture of her on Facebook, she's been playing us—' Toni reached into the glove compartment, grabbed the flashing beacon and leaned out, clamping the magnet to the Jeep's roof. She hurled the Jeep around, heedless of ditches either side of the lane.

'*Stop*,' Malcolm blurted as they approached the man with the sign now saying *STOP*.

'I'm on it, Mal.' Toni clenched her jaw.

'No, I mean, this doesn't fit.' Malcolm was on his phone. 'Look.'

Toni swerved into the end of a lay-by.

'Maddie is on Dedmans Heath, but the weather's wrong.'

'Wrong how?' If Maddie was a killer, then the remaining members of her family were in danger.

'Not the weather, or rather it's the same, but look how bright it is. The shadows are short. This picture was taken around midday. In her post, Sally talks about arriving later than planned. We know why that was, she was arguing with Maddie.'

'Sally Robinson didn't take this picture of Maddie yesterday.' Her heart racing with adrenalin, arms on the steering wheel, Toni rested her head. 'Good one, Mal.'

'By showing Maddie as being on the heath with them when she wasn't, inadvertently Sally put her daughter in the frame for the murders.'

'Or someone else posted these to make us think that?'

'To be honest, given how quickly we spotted this, I doubt that was the intention. Sally used an earlier picture with Maddie there to make it look like the perfect family outing that, by refusing to take part in, Maddie had spoiled.' Malcolm flapped his Cromwell fringe. 'Maddie said they go there every Sunday, so Sally probably had plenty of outtakes from which to choose.'

Toni studied the photo. 'Ben and Tristan are wearing different shirts in the Maddie picture. That Gunners shirt Ben's wearing in the photo Sally claimed Maddie took was probably a birthday present. We can easily check.' She gave a sigh of relief. 'I think Maddie was telling us the truth.'

Waiting in the roadworks queue, Toni then had a nasty idea. 'James Ritchie had a Facebook account. If we are looking at a serial killer here, is he finding his victims on Facebook?'

'James Ritchie's page is public.' Malcolm was working his phone with his thumbs, a skill that evaded Toni. 'Can't see that the families had mutual friends. Darren can check if it's ten degrees of separation.'

Rounding a bend, Toni braked as they tail-gated a van in front. She pipped her horn.

'They're already doing over fifty,' Malcolm reminded her.

'I'm trying to get her to pull over.'

'Who to pull over?'

Abruptly, the van lurched off the lane through a gap in the hedge. Tyres screeching, Toni swung the Jeep after it. Ahead, a field of corn, a silvery pea-green sea, ears swaying in the summer breeze. The light was so clear it was possible to see individual sheep grazing on the Downs beyond.

'Your offside back light's out, *Ms Fish*.' Toni got out and walked around to the driver's side of the van.

'You idiot.' Freddy was red with fury.

'Joke, OK?' Palms up, Toni backed away.

'I was harassed by a car when I was out on my bike yesterday. It killed my sense of humour.'

'I didn't know, I'm sorry, Freds.' Toni felt dreadful. 'Did you report it?'

'I didn't see the car, so no.' Freddy tipped a hand at Malcolm leaning on the door of the Jeep. 'Guessing you're on these latest murders? Could be there was a connection?'

'These lanes are flipping scary for walkers or cyclists; take care out there, Freddy.' Without Malcolm, Toni would have been more forthcoming, she could trust Freddy.

'Don't I always?' Freddy climbed back in the van.

Watching Freddy leave, Toni reflected she'd looked weary. Toni guessed Freddy was unhappy and, as Toni would paraphrase, you're only as happy as your least happy friend.

'Sheena just spoke to Arnie Beck.' Malcolm broke Toni's thought-train.

'Who's he?' Joining Malcolm in the Jeep, she wished herself lying on one of the haystacks in the field. Bathed in warm afternoon sun...

'Maddie Robinson. That boy she said she was with yesterday and claimed she'd slept with last night. Seems she wasn't with him at all.'

'She lied after all.' Toni's assessment of potential suspects was rarely wrong.

'Yes, but not in the way you're thinking.' Malcolm raked back his choirboy hair. 'She's not going out with Arnie Beck. He's in the sixth form, he has a boyfriend and until he heard about these murders, he'd never heard of Maddie.'

'A crush.' Stuck in a convent school, Toni had been saved from unrequited love. 'Poor love.'

'Maddie has no alibi.'

'Phone?'

'No. When you were making – or not making – tea with Lisa Robinson, Maddie told us her mum nicked her phone thinking it would make Maddie go on the picnic. If we find it, and so far, we haven't, it'll triangulate to Dedmans Heath.'

'We need to rule out Maddie another way or she'll be a distraction.' Toni felt as unhappy as Freddy had looked. 'More likely that James and Wilbur Ritchie's killer has killed again. Is he targeting families?'

'The *Sun* thinks so.' Malcolm read out from his phone. '"Who is the Family Man? Serial Killer on Loose."'

# 19

Barbara Major didn't shop at Waitrose, she drove to the Lidl in Newhaven. That she was pushing a trolley along the tinned soups and pulses aisle on Monday afternoon was not to restock her larder.

Barbara was, as she called it, Keeping Tabs. A euphemistic way of what Garry Haslem had once called *stalking*.

As she tailed subjects through Boots or around Tesco, Barbara imagined what she should have said to Haslem who, as Bunty said, was a spiv. *None of your goddam business, who are you to… I'm researching for my crime writer…* Haslem would be speechless and leave her be.

Barbara's researching (not stalking) took place in public – libraries, supermarkets. Anywhere without an entrance fee, because Barbara didn't have an expense account.

Her job was to light upon a random person and follow them. There were ploys to deflect the prey. She pretended to be on her phone or, like now, she had a shopping list. Both these allowed her to capture detail of clothes, age, idiosyncrasies, hair colour, curly or straight, and mood. Barbara had entered the elderly man she'd spotted scooting his trolley along an empty aisle as *Childish, carefree.* She rubbed out *Nice*, that told you nothing. *Playful.* Barbara kept on the subject until they reached work or their home. If work, she waited until they left and followed them home or to a restaurant. That was awkward because she couldn't go in, spend money and risk them leaving.

Ambushed by Bunty at the fish van one morning, Barbara had told her that her crime writer used a typewriter and made carbon copies; he disapproved of correction fluid. Faced with a typo, he began afresh. Bunty had declared it an absurd conceit and snorted when Barbara had told her she typed the final draft onto her computer. *You're his amanuensis,* Garry had said. Bunty had expressed surprise that Garry knew the word. Barbara could have said that it didn't do to underestimate him.

Dressed unremarkably in shirt and jeans and trainers, long greying hair almost smothering her features, Barbara Major attracted little attention and today was contentedly trailing metres behind a young man in a fitted blue Cassino jacket and deep yellow waistcoat, tape-up gelled hair (Barbara had had to learn words to describe fashion that was like walking on the moon to her). From the back he struck her as shifty. *What does shifty mean?* The crime writer demanded deconstructed descriptions. A hesitancy in his step, he was barely looking at the shelves. He had no basket, but that could be because he thought carrying one would be emasculating.

Concentrating on what it might be that made the man seem shifty, Barbara didn't see she'd gained the attention of the store detective. He had noticed that the dowdy middle-aged woman, pushing her empty trolley, was following a young man around the shop.

There was another young man wandering, apparently aimlessly, around the supermarket that morning.

It was Timothy Mew's first outing without Rex. Rex had said he was going to have a lie-down. Timothy had enjoyed driving the sleek Jaguar into Lewes, but had observed the fishmonger was surprised Rex had a rest in the afternoons. It must be a new thing. Blackstock House was to be Timothy's for ever home, so Rex needed to remain healthy. For the time being.

All the same, wandering around the shop, choosing treats regardless of the list, Timothy felt free.

The store detective had decided that the woman in the torn cotton shirt posed no threat. She had no pockets. Returning to the back of the store, the detective missed the moment when Dowdy Woman met Tall Bearded Bespectacled Man face to face. The convex mirror above the freezer section centred them, making Lowry extras of other shoppers at the edge of the glass.

Timothy Mew and Barbara Major regarded each other with frank dislike.

'You're the *companion*. Sorry, I don't know your name.' The card in Barbara's index file said otherwise.

'Mew. Timothy. You are?' Timothy enquired.

'I live on the second floor opposite Garry Haslem's mezzanine and deafened by the rubbish he plays on his hi-fi.' Barbara dropped her purported list. Timothy got there first.

Glancing at the paper he read, '"Cassino jacket, apricot yellow waistcoat, tape-up gelled hair." You won't find any of this in Waitrose, except perhaps the gel.'

'Caught red-handed.' Barbara danced about on tiny ankles. 'I build characters. You doubtless know I'm a crime writer's researcher.'

'I didn't know.' Timothy looked disbelieving, shifty even, Barbara briefly thought. 'A famous writer?'

'Yes, and so I can't divulge his name.' Barbara looked coy. 'How are you settling in?'

'Rex needs more help than he let on at the interview.'

'A carer's role is thankless.' Barbara put her head on one side like a bird. 'So rewarding though.'

'I'm *not* a carer.' Timothy lifted a tin of chickpeas off the shelf. 'If I was, Rex would be dead.'

'One day we'll all be dead. I'm sure you underestimate yourself.' Barbara rested cold pebble eyes on the man's chest. She hated tall men. 'Does this mean you'll be handing in your notice and leaving our little community?'

'It's my home.' Timothy put back the chickpeas.

'Good. Rex needs company. He lost poor Emily in that senseless accident, no wonder he wants a companion. Although, one neighbour thinks it wasn't an accident.'

'You work for a crime writer, no wonder you imagine you see murder everywhere.'

'Not me, dear.' Clutching her note, Barbara accompanied Timothy to the tills, although neither had any shopping. 'I don't *imagine* it, murder *is* everywhere. Take this latest spate.'

'What latest spate?'

'A family has been wiped out on Dedmans Heath. It's all over the internet. My crime writer is thrilled.'

'That's not very nice,' Timothy said.

'If you don't know those involved it's no different to

reading a novel. When my crime writer heard that an Anderson shelter had been found buried in a back garden, he was sorely disappointed there was no wartime corpse in there.'

'That's horrible.'

'Here you are, see for yourself.' Holding up her phone, Barbara swiped along images of newspaper websites, the *Daily Mirror*, the *Sun*, the *Daily Mail*, the *Star*.

*Horror Picnic, The Family Man Kills Again, Serial Killer Slays Family, Serial Killer on the Loose.*

'Working with a crime writer, you'll have a head start on the culprit.' Timothy was frowning at the screen.

'Hardly,' Barbara purred. 'I do know most murders are committed by people known to the victim. When you get a murder spree hot on the heels of the first, you can't rule out a serial killer. They are difficult to catch. They often kill opportunistically and, contrary to myth, it is the police and press who divine a pattern. We all need to feel in control when the only one in control is the killer. These men chase celebrity status, Shipman and West were exceptions only because no one knew about them until they were caught. Doubtless our man is embracing the tag the press have given him. It may encourage him to concentrate on families when, until now, he killed what he could get.'

'Tristan Robinson.' Timothy stepped back from the phone.

'Goodness, do you know him?'

'Just, it's an unusual name.'

'My writer finds names a nightmare. They've got to fit the character, and to be plausible must hail from the right era – no one in the fifties was called Kylie. Names have got to resonate for the writer or they don't connect with their character. My writer never gives the murderer the same name as a friend. You'd be surprised how people get upset.'

'I'd hate that if it were me.' Timothy stroked his beard.

'Have you a friend who is a writer?'

'No.' Timothy looked horrified at the very idea.

'Then you have nothing to fear. Although I can't speak for our serial killer,' Barbara said. 'I'll see you at the residents' meeting tonight.'

'I said I wasn't going.' Timothy pursed his lips. He hadn't yet found a way to refuse Rex's request.

'Rex will expect you to go. Surely that's the point of a companion.' Barbara gave an icy smile.

## 20

*Toni*

'Yesterday afternoon, Sally and Tristan Robinson took their son Ben to Dedmans Heath on a picnic. It was a birthday treat for Ben who was eight the day before. On Saturday they went to *Stick to Rock*, the indoor climbing place near Worthing with a bunch of Ben's friends.'

Toni was seated between Sussex's Assistant Chief Superintendent Worricker (AKA The Worrier) and Alison Jones, a press officer. At only six o'clock the sun had gone and a strange pinkish-green light was filtering through the windows. Toni looked beyond the TV and fluffy radio microphones – ITV, Channel 4, BBC, the *Sun*, the *Daily Mirror*, *Bild*, *Corriera Della Sera* – ranged in front of the panel. She fixed on a clock at the back of the crowded room. The electric atmosphere was not related to the forecasted storm, the assembled media were pumped up greyhounds in their traps.

'...all three were brutally slain in what we can only describe as an awful and wicked crime. We are appealing for anyone within the vicinity of Dedmans Heath yesterday – Sunday afternoon – or other Sundays recently when the Robinsons picnicked there, to come forward with any observation, however small. Does anyone remember seeing the family on the heath or in Dedmans Wood with their dog? This dog – who answers to the name Teabag – has now been found safe and well.'

Toni ignored the hands shooting up.

'...the Robinsons arrived on Dedmans Heath at around fourteen forty-five yesterday afternoon. We don't as yet have an exact time. Officers will be calling on homes along the route from the Robinsons' house in Barcombe to the heath asking for the video files of members of the public who have a video doorbell and businesses operating CCTV. We do have a sighting of Tristan Robinson at fourteen twenty-five, he fuelled up at the Esso garage. No other vehicle was there. Were you in the vicinity at this time, did you see anything suspicious?'

They would be inundated with shots of postal workers and delivery drivers trotting up paths, kids in the street, cats pooing on flower beds. All of life. Clicking the widget, Toni displayed footage of the black Range Rover Defender outside the petrol station then Tristan Robinson at the till.

'Tristan Robinson fills the car with diesel. Inside the shop, he buys the *Observer* newspaper and a packet of Extra Strong mints. As he leaves, Tristan pauses by the newspapers and makes a call. The cashier believes he left a message rather than had a conversation. Were you the recipient of Tristan Robinson's call yesterday afternoon? If so, please contact us.' Toni looked into the camera, *into the killer's eyes*. 'After this sighting, we have nothing. The Robinsons parked their black Range Rover Defender in a little used space off the heath. I'm asking anyone else who may have used this car park yesterday or on other days to think about who they saw.' Toni clicked the remote and the black car appeared on the screen behind her upside down. Hearing stirring in the audience, Toni turned, swore inwardly and, stretching across Worricker, righted the image.

Toni watched reporters note the torn sticker about badger culling on the car's back windscreen, building a picture of the Robinsons. Well-heeled liberals, politically cool and keen to show it. Toni's job was to excavate the stereotype; people are not always what they want you to think they are.

'...I'd like to thank members of the public, the community and you, the media, for help in raising awareness of this terrible crime. I'll take a few questions.'

Toni must not view the champing reporters as the enemy. Since the dawn of policing, they were the force's conduit to the public. A public who, from a sense of duty, or spite towards a neighbour or enemy, might give the police vital evidence.

'Do you think this is the work of the killer who murdered James and Wilbur Ritchie at Seaford Head last month?'

'It's too soon to say.' Toni picked the woman in a red anorak under the clock. Women were outnumbered and had the worst seats. Her male colleagues – not Malcolm – tended to ignore them. 'Yes?'

'Have you got a suspect?'

'We are following several leads.'

'Is that a no?' The woman prodded the air with her pen. 'Are you waiting for another family to be brutally slain for clues that will lead you to this killer?'

'We never wait, my team is working around the clock to catch whoever is responsible for these terrible crimes.' *Red alert*. That answer would supply the opener, *Police are in the dark while serial killer roams unstopped*.

Some coppers dreamed of catching a high-profile case that would make their name. Toni knew the smallest blunder would make her name mud.

'We are not ruling out the possibility we are looking for a serial killer.' Cutting off a follow-up, 'We are considering several leads.' Toni pointed at a young black man in the front row. His Paul Smith glasses and retro Reebok windcheater marked him as a Londoner.

'To get an understanding of how this man works, are you relying on him killing again?' The journalist's hungry gaze drilled into Toni. Same question, different words.

'We are doing everything possible to ensure there are no more victims.' She walked into the trap.

'What are you doing?'

'Should mums and dads be keeping their kids at home?' This from the *Sydney Morning Herald*. Didn't the Aussies have enough murders of their own? Some insomniacs counted sheep, Toni invented tabloid headlines that taunted her lack of progress. She closed the briefing with the stock response that, being her reason for joining the force, came from the heart:

'Everyone should feel safe to walk our streets, to visit open spaces with loved ones without fear of harassment, stalking or coming to actual harm.'

'Would you agree that not *all* police protect the public?' Toni understood. The murders of Bibaa Henry, Nicole Smallman and Sarah Everard had proved there was more than one bad apple in an orchard.

'Those that don't should *not* be in the police.' Toni had overstepped, but, angry, she didn't care.

'As Detective Inspector Kemp said, it's our job to keep our neighbourhoods safe.' Getting to his feet, Worricker shut down the briefing and, making way for Toni and Alison Jones, ushered them out.

'You just loosened the net below your tightrope, DI Kemp. If I hear any more soapboxing against the police, you're off this case,' Worricker said as soon as they were in the corridor.

'As you wish, sir,' Toni told him.

'OK, so that was rubbish, there isn't a detective this side of Sherlock Holmes I'd swap you for. I'll throw as much as I can at this one for you.' Bless him, Worricker might snipe at the cat, but he could never kick it.

'Thank you, sir.' Toni gripped the poisoned chalice.

'Let me handle those questions next time, DI Kemp.' Alison gave Toni what amounted to a 'sisterly' nod. 'It's my job.'

'Why hasn't that made me feel better?' Toni said to Malcolm when they were alone in the lift.

'It could have made you feel worse.' For the next three floors, Malcolm whistled 'Always Look on the Bright Side of Life'.

'Serial killers love a name.' Shouldering into the Murder Room, Toni could have no idea she was echoing what Barbara Major had told Timothy Mew in the supermarket earlier that afternoon. 'Could be the adults were collateral damage. Calling him the Family Man could cause him to target families.'

'Agree,' Malcolm said.

Toni faced her now twenty-plus team gathered in the Murder Room.

'A loser with no hope of a tennis Golden Slam or Nobel prize or living an ordinary life becomes Murder Cat to Police Mouse aiming at top spot in the serial killers' compendium.'

'He needs numbers.' Sheena did not need to say the next bit. *There would be more murders.*

## 21

*Martha*

A storm was brewing. A slash of black beyond Dedmans Wood bordered skeins of pink-grey streaking the dirty yellow sky. The nineteenth-century painter Atkinson Grimshaw would have needed little invention to portray the sense of foreboding caused by the seeping light. It gave vibrancy to Michaelmas daisies, marigolds and long-thorned roses of blood-red planted in beds edging the lawn. A scent of honeysuckle offered scant compensation for the forsaken summer's night. At this hour, in this light, the long-dead garden designer's penchant for picaresque à la Capability Brown – folly, summer house, rococo fountain – was suffused with nightmare. From the wood a blackbird sang, penetrating notes as if from a loud speaker, a finishing flourish to the dread scene.

The summer house peeped between branches of a beech tree, the scribbled outline of leaves and stems cruelly stripped away marked the stone. Damp leaves, pine cones and twigs lay in the basin of the fountain.

From around the front of the house came the throaty

sputter of a car. Headlights picked out cracks in the rendering as the car crunched to a halt on the gravel. A door slammed. Footsteps.

Martha wasn't due at Blacklock House until nine, but planned a sneaky explore of the grounds before she texted Patrick as arranged. After she had left Dedmans Heath yesterday, she'd phoned Timothy, asking to come and see him. Timothy had said he couldn't talk, Rex had a guest. *So what?* Timothy could have a guest too, Rex had said pop in any time. She had not said that. Next was Tristan, who predictably went to voicemail. She knew exactly where he was. In the end Martha had rung Patrick and told him she would come to his residents' meeting after all.

Expecting to wander about sniffing flowers, listening to birdsong on the idyllic striped lawn, hoping Rex would spot her from his terrace and invite her up, instead Martha was enveloped in premature night. Mauve shot through with moments of pink and yellow when the sun broke through gathering clouds. Devoted to meteorological apps, it had been Timothy who kept Martha abreast of the weather. Not these days. Martha did not know that a storm was blowing in off the English Channel. Vaguely she attributed the drop in temperature to her own creeping unease.

Rex's terrace was empty, the chairs tipped forward against the table. The French doors to his sitting room were closed, the curtains drawn.

A shadow. The faintest click. Martha took a few steps in the direction of the sound. *Text Patrick and cancel.* Martha crept beside the supporting wall of the terrace, her hand on the stone, still warm from the sun.

A scream cut the air.

Properly afraid now, Martha scanned the mingling darkness. Her eye roved over the pale outline of the fountain. Patrick had said it hadn't worked for decades. *Leave.*

A movement, a flutter. *Another scream.* Martha clutched her chest and, to calm herself, laughed out loud. *King Tut.* She had no idea of peacock habits. Where did they sleep? Did they sleep? She'd advise anyone planning to live in a stately home to see it at night. Did Timothy regret his move to Blacklock House? Was Rex Lomax regretting his choice of companion?

Tall, thin larches swayed as a wind got up. Cold, harsh as if from winter. It had been sunny when Martha left Newhaven, a sparkling sea, the beach busy with swimmers and sunbathers. Martha hugged herself as fear and the cold made her shiver.

At the end of the terrace wall was an arch. A black cut-out against the darkening stone. Hardly inviting, but keen to escape the biting wind, Martha ducked inside. She switched on her phone torch and trained it around a fusty damp cavity that stretched off beneath the length of the terrace. The cobwebbed ceiling might have been the set for *Halloween*, deckchairs were stacked against the house wall alongside collapsed parasols resembling dead crows. Martha guessed three shrouded bulks were barbecues. This was where the residents stored garden equipment; dusty and broken, it looked seldom used.

The torch picked out a door. Having convinced herself that the movement and slight sound she had heard earlier was King Tut, now Martha was flooded with adrenalin. Had she seen a person? Had they flitted through the basement door? Or was it an intruder who, unaware she'd seen them, was breaking into the house?

Martha had been unimpressed by security at Blacklock

House. No CCTV, and Freddy the fishmonger said the tradesman's button beside the front door was always in operation. Who else knew that? Yet if they did know, why not enter that way?

At least the door – a hefty wooden affair with brass fittings – was locked fast. Although now, unnerved by the shadowed garden, peacock shrieks and whistling wind, Martha was less concerned with the safety of the residents than in getting inside.

There was something on the oak lintel above the door. A key. Long, with a decorative head, it dated before Banham or Yale and was cold.

Martha was about to insert the key in the lock when the door swung open.

'*What the—*'

'*Arrgh!*' Springing back against one of the barbecues, Martha was pure King Tut.

'Christ, what are you doing down here?' Patrick fell back against the door jamb. 'I could have attacked you.'

'Why in God's name would you do that?' Martha gasped.

'I thought you were a burglar. Or, or with these murders, *worse.*'

'Well, it's me.' Her fear ebbing, caught in the act of snooping, Martha was nevertheless on the back foot.

'I knew you were here. I had to move your car off the drive.'

'Why would you do that? It's as big as a football pitch.'

'Trust me, you don't want to make an enemy of any of my neighbours.'

'I don't care about your neighbours.' Martha took refuge in righteous indignation that Patrick had touched her car. 'How did you do it without the key?'

'You left the key in the ignition. Come on or we'll be late.' Patrick led the way along a flagged tunnel with doors off it at regular intervals and walls the gloss green of old hospitals. 'This is where we store our stuff.'

'Why is there a thermometer on this lock?' Martha stopped by a metal door resembling her idea of an airlock chamber in a submarine.

'That's Garry's wine store. It's worth thousands.' Patrick sounded off-hand.

*How the other half...*

Turning off the passage, Patrick led Martha up a flight of stone steps and pushed on a door of green baize.

They stepped into dazzling light. Martha recognised the entrance hall from that first morning a month ago. Then, it was lit by sunlight filtering through the cupola above which now was a circle of darkness. Illumination came from a chandelier of hundreds of glass droplets which refracted light that bounced off the peeling William Morris wallpaper and revealed the grime on portraits of grim-looking ancestors, faded patches in the carpet and cracks in the plaster. *Not so grand after all.*

'Is the meeting in your flat?'

'Of course not,' Patrick barked. Martha felt her temper flare – how dare he be annoyed when she was doing him a favour? 'We pay through the nose to use the library for parties and meetings like this one. No one has parties, but there are too many meetings.' Cupping her elbow, Patrick guided Martha along a wood-panelled corridor to a door on the ground floor signed 'The Old Library'.

'Everyone, this is Martha.' Patrick raised his voice above the chatter.

Several people seated on straight-backed chairs around an oval table turned as one and regarded Martha. Each face expressed the same disapproval as the framed ancestors hung in the hall and around the old library. Floor-to-ceiling bookcases of leather-bound volumes behind mesh-covered doors, lit by weak electrified gas lamps, seemed ready to topple.

'What are you doing here?' Timothy's tone couldn't have been mistaken for welcome.

'I didn't expect you to be here.' Martha had planned to regale Timothy with the meeting afterwards.

'I *live* here.'

'The more the merrier.' It was Lady something, the elderly woman Martha had met at the fish van.

'This meeting is confidential, Dorothy, we can't invite strangers. Patrick, please ask your... *friend* to leave.' Comb-over Man who, Martha remembered, had presented Freddie the fishmonger with a dud card, jerked his head as if whiplashed. '*Residents* only. We've already made an exception for Rex's... *companion*.'

'He has a name, Martyn.' A woman whose arched eyebrows implied permanent astonishment spoke in a reedy voice.

'Pot, kettle, Martyn mine,' Lady Dorothy tootled.

'What do you mean?' Martyn flushed.

'Sylvia brings *you*.' Lady Dorothy stabbed a bony finger at the retired doctor. She reached into a carpet bag on the table in front of her and hauled out an embroidery frame on which was a fantastically complex pattern of wild flowers. Martha was impressed.

'For heaven's sake, I'm her husband.' Martyn jerked his head again.

'So you say, chummy.' Lady Dorothy aimed her thread wide at her embroidery needle.

'Can we get this meeting over with?' Sylvia, with solid-as-a-rock blonde hair, snatched at spectacles hung from a chain around her neck.

'I can leave.' Martha made a bid for freedom.

'*No*, darling, stay. This mausoleum needs a whiff of air. *Let me entertain you.*' From a common look of bafflement around the table, Martha guessed she was the only one who recognised the faithful Robbie Williams imitation. *Garry Haslem, that was it*. Martha cursed herself for remembering his name. Dim lamplight had ironed out wrinkles and made jewels of his eyes, allowing a glimpse of the Boy Wonder he must once have been. Martha was about sit on one of a couple of chairs against the wall by the door when, his hand still cupping her elbow, Patrick directed her to a chair on the turn of the oval table to Haslem's right. He sat beside her, hemming her in. Damn, not even Tristan took that liberty. *Not true.*

Cold from her wanderings at the back of the house, Martha was grateful for the fire burning beneath the mantelpiece behind her. Smiling at the others around the table, only Bunty smiled back. But, still struggling to thread her needle, it may have been a grimace.

'So, can we minute that now, we bring every Tom, Dick and Harriet to these meetings?' A woman, her black cardigan around her shoulders, folded her arms.

'If your crime writer fancies dropping by,' Garry grinned, 'I could hand him a list of motives for murder and suspects.'

'You assume he's a *he*?' Bunty sucked loudly on the thread and this time poked it through the eye of her needle.

'No lady would fund Miss Marple here to live in the luxury of a stately home.' Garry seemed pleased with his soubriquet.

'Lawks a mussey, the Barrow Boy reads books.' A laugh as loud as canon-fire came from behind Lady Dorothy's embroidery frame.

'Is it a lady-writer, Major Barbara?' Garry leered at the woman in the black cardigan.

Glancing to her right, Martha was surprised to gather the woman who even sitting appeared short, had been in the army, although height wasn't a thing these days. More likely, given her outmoded outfit, she'd been in the Salvation Army.

'And familiar with Bernard Shaw, it would seem,' Lady Dorothy told her embroidery.

Not a reader herself, Martha saw her own puzzlement reflected in Haslem's face.

'None of your business, Haslem.' Perhaps Haslem's assertion about a crime writer had hit home, because two circles of a hectic red appeared on the cheeks of the woman in black, likely called Barbara. Pebble eyes trained on the French doors behind Haslem, which now reflected the room within, she resembled a large Victorian doll propped in her chair. An unsettling image which, despite Haslem's rudeness, diminished any sisterly support Martha might have for his victim.

A spray drummed on the French doors. Everyone turned. The storm had arrived. Large drops of rain hit the glass as if someone outside was hurling gravel. Through the panes, the fountain appeared distorted, almost, it seemed to Martha, as if it was moving, inexorably, towards the house. Although she wasn't now cold – someone must have added more logs to the fire – yet Martha shivered.

'I mixed up dates, then Martha arrived early so I couldn't cancel her,' Patrick lied. 'She can't vote.'

'She can vote with me.' Garry massaged the greying hair escaping from the top of his shirt.

'Simmer down, kids. Let's crack on.' Garry Haslem frowned at his watch, large and gold, enough to cover the price of a dilapidated stately home. Paid for by how many deluded dames? 'Youse have all read my agenda.'

Surreptitiously, Martha consulted her phone. *No text.* She was resisting going on Facebook; it made her so angry. One thing she hated about being Tristan's Not-Mistress was that the Tristan-phone kept her on a short leash. Boring though he was, Patrick was prepared to be seen in public with her. Keeping the Tristan-phone below the table, Martha texted, *I'm around tomorrow morning* and instantly regretted it. Timothy used to say, *'If you must play games, you have to win.'* What did he know? Rex said Timothy kept losing at Lola, or whatever that stupid game Timothy had picked up in the charity shop was called. Maybe Timothy had met his match.

'Garry, excuse me, *Garry.*' The woman who Garry had called Major Barbara got up from her chair – it added little to her height of around five feet – and smoothed down her faded black dress. 'I didn't receive an agenda. *It's the second time this has happened,*' she confided to Sylvia who, ignoring her, told Haslem,

'It's not *your* agenda, Haslem.'

Martha caught Martyn, seated opposite, catch her watching Garry, which meant Martyn had been watching her. *Creep.*

'Nothing personal, *Major* Barbara.' Garry grinned across at Barbara. 'No witch's cat tonight? Here you are, Speedy

Gonzales.' Garry frisbeed an A4 sheet of paper at Barbara. It veered off and landed in Patrick's lap.

Reaching over Martha as if she didn't exist, Patrick passed a copy of the agenda to Barbara. Martha glanced at the sheet as it was passed under her nose, scanning some of the names listed: *Patrick Bell, Treasurer, Barbara Major, Drs Sylvia and Martyn Burnett.* Barbara snatched it off Patrick. Martha felt a twinge of triumph that Patrick got no thanks.

'Can we begin? I don't want to die here.' Lady Dorothy jabbed her needle into one of the bluebells.

'You've lived a thousand years, Bunty, you'll see this meeting out.' Shuffling a wad of papers, Garry said, 'Item one. Repainting the house.'

'Balderdash,' Lady Dorothy remarked, a length of thread dangling from her teeth.

'I agree with Bunty,' Sylvia Burnett said and Martyn the creep nodded as if Sylvia had pressed a lever. 'This is utterly unnecessary.'

'Our contract stipulates the house must be repainted every seven years.'

Everyone, except Haslem who was beaming, looked ready to kill Patrick. Focusing on Patrick's copy of the agenda, Martha recalled that he was the treasurer. No one liked the person who controlled the purse-strings.

'Legally, there is no time-frame for repainting a property. We can vote to push it on until, say next year, and discuss it again.' Rex leaned into the circle of lamplight above the table. Rex hadn't contributed to the volley of insults so Martha had actually forgotten he was there. She felt relief that – apart from herself – there was one sane person amidst this nest of vipers.

'You're *right*, Rex.' Barbara's alacrity was out of proportion. Martha suspected she had a thing for Rex.

'In my day, we never touched the outside.' Bunty twitched her head like a bird spotting a worm. 'This has already sunk to the level of a boarding house. I vote *no*.'

'In *your* day Blacklock House was a ruin, buckets catching drips, rotting carpets, bats terrorising overworked servants.' Garry squared his papers. 'It will revert to that if we don't look after it.'

A flash of white light. The French doors rattled violently. Martha fully expected to see a face at the window. The reflection of the room in the glass had been obscured by water, as if someone was aiming a hose at the panes. There was a distant rumble of thunder.

'Nothing is gained by all this catastrophising.' Sylvia crossed to the French doors and tried the handles, perhaps to confirm they were locked. *Had she too fancied someone was outside?*

'Surely more important than any of this is that a killer is out there.' Barbara pointed at the French doors. 'Or in our midst. We have all had a visit from the police.'

'Who didn't arrest any of us,' Martyn the comb-over reminded her.

'The police are notorious for getting it wrong. Look at that Inspector Lestrade, Sherlock Holmes beats him every time.' Bunty was squinting at her embroidery frame.

'He's a fictional character,' Barbara Major snapped.

'Not to me,' Bunty said.

'For goodness' sake, please can we continue?' Martyn's comb-over was a rat's tail over one ear. Martha would recommend a full shave. Probably mid-fifties, the sickly-looking doctor might be a seventies throw-back.

'I think, since the point has been made, we should establish that we were all ruled out for these recent murders,' Barbara said.

Martha was now confused. What recent murders, and why had the residents of Blacklock House been interviewed in connection with them? She tried to catch Timothy's eye, but writing in a notebook, he didn't look up. Rex must have noticed too, for, leaning over, he tapped the notebook.

'Only record actions, Timothy.'

Timothy was taking the minutes. *Jesus, he'd hate that.* Martha upbraided herself for the stab of satisfaction. She did in fact feel sorry for Timothy – he'd wanted the peace and quiet of the countryside, but this was akin to being in a lion's cage.

'I say, dearest Barbara, you boning up on murder for your crime writer makes you our resident expert.' Bunty broke her thread with her teeth. 'I was grilled by a lovely young man called Darren, it was absolutely topping.'

'Murder is *not* topping.' Barbara's doll-like stature belied her booming voice. '*I warn you all.* If none of us is a murderer, then at the least we are all sitting ducks for whoever is murdering these people.'

'Best not to panic everyone, Barbara.' Rex smiled.

'We must be on high alert. This man planned how to arrive and leave his crime scenes unseen. Did he use a car? Does he live near one of the scenes?' Barbara's voice dropped to a whisper. '*Near here?*'

Martha, for one, was now panicking. She caught Rex's eye. He tilted his head a fraction. *He was reassuring her.*

'Barbara, I really must ask you to dial it down.' Rex reached over and rested a hand on Barbara's arm. This seemed to work.

'Seaford Head is miles away.' Martha couldn't stop herself. Living alone, with no Timothy to call upon, she'd fretted that Newhaven, along the coast from Seaford, was too close for comfort. It was a good five miles from Blacklock House, what was the problem?

'Serial killers have transport. Ted Bundy drove a Volkswagen Beetle, Peter Sutcliffe had a lorry, Steve Wright, the Suffolk Strangler, drove a forklift truck.' Barbara counted off serial killers on her fingers.

'That was for his job, it wasn't his passion wagon.' Garry erupted into gleeful laughter. 'He picked up ladies off the street in his own car. Not a problem when they found DNA of his victims there, he was upfront about seeing prostitutes.'

Fighting panic, Martha struggled to recall something that had puzzled her. Was it something Barbara had said?

*Crash.*

'It's *him.*' Pointing at the French doors, his finger trembling, Martyn Burnett jumped up and retreated to the door.

A draught lifted papers on the table. Martha smelled wax, as if someone had blown out a candle. There were no candles.

On the steps outside a plastic chair tumbled past. Martha was set to rush out of the room. *Patrick had her car keys.*

'...Dedmans Heath, I was showing Timothy the headlines in Waitrose this morning.'

*Recent murders.* Martha went cold. Barbara had said 'recent murders'. Martha was hit with the mad notion that someone had just walked over her grave. The boy and his father were murdered a month ago; she didn't call that recent.

'What has Dedman's Heath got to do with the Seaford

Head murders, Timothy?' Martha practically shouted. Still, Timothy would not meet her eye.

Another crash of thunder. Closer this time.

'We'll vote on repainting next time. Item two. Maintenance payments.' Garry clacked his teeth as if snapping a fly. 'Doctors Burnett, you're several payments in-a-*rears*.'

'Timothy?' Martha persisted.

'It's a mix-up with the bank,' Martyn mumbled.

'*Be quiet*,' his wife hissed.

'Patrick, can I leave this with you?' Garry told Patrick.

*Tap. Tap. Tap.*

'Timothy?'

The tapping was rain overflowing from a gutter onto the patio. *Not a fingernail on the pane.*

'Rex, old mate, you are in credit.' Garry steepled his hands. 'Actually, Dr Sylvia, this meeting is giving me a headache, could I trouble you for a painkiller? A good beefy one?'

'You are a complete and utter *bastard*.' Sylvia, lit by a flash of white light, might have been wrought in silver.

'Hey, guys, cool it.' Rex Lomax raised his voice over the thunder. 'For some minutes now, poor Martha here has been asking Timothy what headlines Barbara so kindly showed him at the supermarket this afternoon. Timothy, be a good man and put Martha out of her misery.'

Another flash of light and all the residents were mannequins arranged around the oval table, their shadows stark against the wood-panelled walls.

'For *God's sake*, if she must know. A serial killer has struck again. This time a whole family on Dedmans Heath. An outsider, you will appreciate the absurdity of wrangling over repainting and maintenance payments when a man is ready to kill us all.' Barbara's voice rose above the thunder, now right on the heels of the lightning.

'Not the *whole* family.' Timothy looked frozen with horror. *Dedmans Heath. Timothy knew what she'd done.*

The French doors flew open. Lightning lit the lawn and the fountain in pure white. The fake gaslight flickered, extinguished and came on again. The next crash rocked the house.

Embroidery frame clutched as a shield, her voice soaring above the cacophony, Lady Dorothy Erskine stopped everyone's hearts, '*The serial killer is here. He will murder us all.*'

# 22

*Toni*

The windows along one side of the Murder Investigation Room gave a panoramic view of concrete, garish cladding, downtrodden Victorian houses and, on days with no sea fret, a glimpse of the English Channel. A bleak, nondescript scene certain to dull the mood of the most optimistic. This evening, drenched deep red by the setting sun, chimneys, rooftops, the abandoned fire station's practice tower, the convent chapel and even the concrete-patched council office took sublime to a new level.

Oblivious to Newhaven's beauty on a summer's evening or that, bathed in rich pink evening light, the tiredness etched in her detectives' faces seemed to vanish, Toni saw only that Malcolm had written nothing new on the board. Time was passing and they were no further forward. Toni couldn't bear to look at the photographs of the boys, Wilbur Ritchie and Ben Robinson. She read their eager grins as reproach. *You have done nothing.*

'This is what has been found on the heath in a half-mile radius of deposition sites for all three bodies.' Darren was screening an image of a table on which objects in plastic bags were arranged. Like a macabre bring and buy sale, Toni caught herself thinking.

'The catchment area includes a mile of the ditches in lanes leading away from the scene.' Darren clicked through a series of close-ups. 'Most is litter, coffee cups, sweet wrappers, condoms, the usual. We did find an engagement ring that matches one reported lost four years ago.'

'We made two people happy.' Toni avoided groaning 'at least'. She must lead from the front, not fling herself down in despair at the back.

'Actually not, ma'am.' Darren held the projector widget out and up as if it were a skipping rope handle. 'They divorced last year. There was one interesting thing, though.'

'Go on,' Toni said. Darren had a habit of finishing sentences as if the opening drum beat of *EastEnders* was playing in his head. 'We found a five-pound note about fifty metres from Ben's body.'

'Interesting because?' Toni said.

*Doof doof, doof doof doof doof-doof-doof-doof...*

'It's a series C note which was launched in 1963 and superseded by series D in 1971.' Darren switched from a close-up of the note encased in an evidence bag to a page off the internet. Toni frowned at the clumsy wording: *the back side depicts a whole-body version of Britannia sat by a heap of coins.* Britannia, in a loose summer dress, grasping what the blurb said was an olive branch, looked less fearsome than Toni, had she been looking for a role model, might have expected. Toni had long ago become her own Britannia.

'If it was lost when it was in circulation, that fiver was worth my granddad's weekly wage back then,' Sheena said.

'Seems more likely it was then,' Malcolm said. 'Why have it on you nowadays?'

'Too much to hope that at some point between the early sixties and seventies it was reported missing or stolen?' Toni said.

'We're on it.' Darren switched back to the actual note and zoomed in. 'This was written on the other side.'

'What is that, a six?' Malcolm was peering up close at a black squiggle on the right of the queen's face on the projector screen.

'It's a nine,' Darren confirmed.

'A bank clerk's marker?' someone said.

'Could be, but usually that includes the batch number, say, three slash fifty.'

'Is it worth much nowadays?' Toni asked.

'Currently on eBay, there's a "crisp" version that's on for twenty-eight quid, so not a fortune.' Darren pulled his memory stick from the laptop and sat down.

'Could be nothing, but get that area combed for any more fivers. Have we missed one?' Toni's urgency had Darren heading for the phone.

'I confirmed Arnie Beck's alibi. His parents did take him to the Croydon IKEA to get stuff for going to uni in the autumn. They're all on CCTV. We can rule him out.' Sheena confirmed what they already assumed.

'But not Maddie?' Malcolm's pen was now hovering over Maddie's name on the board.

'Not Maddie.' Sheena folded her arms.

After Malcolm had reported on their meeting with Maddie and her uncle and aunt, Geoff and Lisa Robinson, he went on, 'Tristan and Geoff's mother claims she was with Lisa and

Geoff all afternoon. A mother as a witness isn't worth a fiver even in today's money, but reading Mrs Robinson senior's statement you get the impression that, had Geoff killed Tristan, this mother would have served her second son up to us on a platter,' Malcolm said.

'We know the Tristan Robinsons didn't reach Dedmans Heath until approximately fourteen forty-five p.m. They ate their picnic so even if they wolfed it, that's three p.m.' Toni walked them through the specifics. 'Journey time from the Geoffrey Robinsons' home in Dale Road, Chiswick to the heath is over an hour and a half, so a minimum of three hours return. Add in the business of murdering the family, which Dr Clovis was willing to put at half an hour max, they'd be back at seventeen thirty.'

'All routes to London were gridlocked due to a crash on the clockwise north-bound M25,' Sheena said. 'So even if Geoff was away by 2.30 p.m. he wouldn't have got back to Chiswick until at least seven.'

'We can scratch them.' Darren swivelled round from his computer. 'Two statements from different neighbours have come in. One says the Robinsons' fifteen-year-old Skoda Octavia was parked in Dale Road all afternoon. The other saw him mowing the lawn mid-afternoon and Lisa Robinson hanging out washing.'

'Good stuff.' Toni had guessed this, but gut feeling was no replacement for hard fact. Especially when gut feeling was maintained by Gaviscon tablets. 'We have two shocking stabbing events that are a month and two miles apart. The press shouting about the Family Man and that a serial killer is out there. We stick to the text books on this and, as we are doing, rule out every suspect pertinent to either the Ritchies or the Robinsons. However, we can't ignore similarities.' Toni bulleted each item on the board as she spoke.

Victims related
Same weapon – a short-bladed knife
Out of doors, broad daylight, potential witnesses in vicinity

Toni turned to the room. The beam of sunlight that had flooded the room with light had dropped below the window frame. The faces before her now looked worn and grey.

'Dr Clovis, the pathologist, reports that, in the case of all five victims, the first or second stab wounds subdued the victim. The considerable number of wounds dealt after these were superfluous.' Toni jotted on her list, *Cool or reckless?*

'In all these murders, the killer got up close without the victim either knowing or feeling the need to defend themselves. Ben was killed from behind; Sally may have been absorbed in her book and by the time she realised what was happening it was over. But why didn't Tristan put up a fight?' Malcolm said.

'Somehow our killer has the ability to gain his victims' trust,' Toni mused. 'Take the Ritchies. He expresses interest in Wilbur and James Ritchie's kite, which probably gained their trust. He attacks James Ritchie first and with James out of the picture, it's easy to get Wilbur.'

'Wilbur Ritchie was also killed from behind.' Sheena was looking at her computer screen. 'Either both boys were trying to run away or were caught unawares.'

'Or the killer didn't want to see their faces while he stabbed them,' Malcolm said. 'They were not his prime target, perhaps the boys were collateral damage.'

Toni had also been avoiding Ben and Wilbur's faces. Now she met their eyes – *We'll get whoever did this to you*. She didn't usually make promises, even to the dead.

'Overkill suggests the actual killing matters.' Malcolm wrote *Important* next to *Overkill*. 'He prolonged each attack beyond what's necessary. That's bold.'

'Could mean he's mentally ill, a terrorist and or a psychopath,' Sheena said.

'Or all three,' Darren said, then, probably worried he'd been flippant, cleared his throat importantly. 'A mentally ill person wouldn't have pulled off what are finely controlled operations. Never mind that most people with mental health problems hurt themselves, not others. A terrorist would have surely done more damage; most expect to be caught or shot, their game plan is unlikely to include killing again. Most serial killers are certified psychopaths. These killings show lack of empathy, poor behaviour control, perhaps impulsivity, but I'm guessing that, given he was carrying a knife, the killer was working to a plan.'

'Should we get in a profiler?' Sheena would know she was pushing the envelope. Toni's core team knew that her opinion of expensive consultants telling them the killer was a dentist or a lorry driver with a dodgy relationship with his mother was on a par with psychics. Toni spared Sheena a rerun of her seminar on how the FBI's case for Quantico, the US profiling centre, had been built on plain wrong statistics.

'We will work with circumstantial evidence. The crime scenes may tell us something about the way our killer operates but they are not windows into his soul. And as for the Family Man, we tread carefully. We don't know this is our killer, we can't divine his inner logic and it's hen's-teeth-rare for a serial killer to work to a pattern. None of us live consciously like that.'

'You're thinking our man's not after families?' Sheena said. 'Isn't there already a profile emerging?'

'Of the media's making, yes,' Toni fired back. 'Peter Sutcliffe wasn't some latter-day street-cleaner targeting prostituted women. He wasn't so switched on that he was operating a Dexter-style code of ethics. He killed women who, whether because they were forced to sell sex or were coming home late, were out after dark on lonely streets. Like Everest, they were there.'

'The family angle may have something, but it's as likely, as Malcolm suggested, the boys were not his intended victims. Did he get satisfaction from killing several victims in one event? On weekends, such groupings are typical and often related.'

'What we can do is know our victims. Read this and get it so these two men, two boys and the woman are your best mates. It will never be the victim's fault that they were murdered, but understanding who they were and how they behaved may help us to know what they may share in common with each other.' Malcolm had a pile of typed sheets beside him on a chair that he now handed around the room.

'James Ritchie, thirty-eight. Good-looking in a beaky sort of way, stubble is less designer than misery. Wife, Anna Petty, was driving their divorce, he wanted back in. Anna says she kicked James out because he saw sex workers, namely a woman going by the name of Belinda. James maintained he only talked with her, but Anna didn't believe him. We know from Belinda that Ritchie was telling the truth.'

Toni questioned the wisdom of asking Anna Petty – whose

rancour hung around her neck like a placard – to provide the unflattering photo. Ritchie's lopsided smile was really a sneer, it was easy to see designer anything didn't come into it. He looked like a man on the edge of a nervous breakdown. They must ask for a happier one for the press. Perhaps harbouring rancour, even after death, somehow kept James alive. Malcolm moved on.

'...Sally Robinson, forty. Posted on Facebook every day. She posted about the picnic as if it had happened, but timings and different outfits in two pictures say otherwise. The nature of the postings and the questionable veracity of previous ones suggest Sally was intent on creating the image of a perfect family. Not in itself odd, no one wants to air their dirty linen in public, yet Sally does air a lot. She was on Facebook several times a day, every day. Was this story she told of an enviable family, gorgeous clever kids, happy outings and expensive holidays a cover? If so, what was it covering? Lisa Robinson and Maddie suggested that Tristan was having an affair. So far, we can find no evidence of this. Keep digging.'

The short bob with a fringe lent Sally a look of naivety. Although Toni suspected the smile was cosmetic, she felt drawn to the woman. A tilt of an eyebrow and a twinkle in the eyes suggested the girl she had once been. Cropped from a family shot, Sally's profile picture was a selfie. All the images of Sally were taken by her and included one or other of her family. It was as if the Facebook narrative didn't work with just Sally herself.

The press had compared Tristan Robinson to Paul Newman, his blue eyes belied that he could possibly be dead. The smile suggested that, unusually for British men in their mid-forties, Tristan had had his teeth done. In one shot, Sally's mouth had been a riot of metal fillings. How much attention had she given herself? There was something on Tristan's neck, in the shadow of his polo shirt collar.

'Wait, what's that?' Toni went up to the picture. 'Look, Tristan's got a hickey. Thank goodness that's not the picture we gave out to the media.'

'Could be a tattoo.'

'The boss is right.' Sheena, nose up close to the board, rarely uttered these words. 'That's a love bite.'

'Why do I doubt Sally gave it to him?' Toni paced the room. 'There were no love bites on his body. How could Sally have failed to see the mark? Or had she seen it and meant others to see it too?'

'Perhaps to show how good things were between them?' Sheena said.

'Or how bad. Did she get him in a clinch and take it?' Toni countered.

'Or someone else gave it to him and, like us until now, Sally hadn't seen it.' Malcolm narrowed his eyes.

'Check telephone numbers again. Are any frequently dialled?' Toni was animated. A love bite didn't rank as a clue, but it was something.

'We could tell the media what we suspect,' Sheena said.

'We need the Robinsons and the Ritchies to continue as squeaky clean in the public's mind, worthy of sympathy and effort. Ben and Wilbur are first-class poster victims, horrible though it is to call them that, but any hint Tristan was playing away or James was seeing sex workers and – serial killer or not – our case could drop off the news radar.' Toni hated having to 'sell' murder but as she'd said before, publicity made the law's long arm longer. Except bad publicity.

'Dr Clovis suggested that, despite the apparent frenzied attacks, the key stabbings were skilled.' Toni wrapped up the briefing. 'These five people were not this killer's first victims. We may not find a pattern, but we will gain more information without more people having to die. For that, we're going back into the past. Sheena, keep trawling the cold cases, we need to gather as much about this man's MO and his preferred geographical area and terrain as we can. I do *not* want to rely on fresh murders.'

'I've got something.' Darren ended a call and above Toni's earworm of the *EastEnders*' theme tune, he said, 'The Robinson's Range Rover Defender was keyed and, from the lack of rust, Forensics say it happened very recently. Likely when it was parked on the heath or wouldn't Sally have put it on Facebook?'

'You're on fire, Chis. Meaning whoever keyed the car, killed the Robinsons.' Sheena high-fived Darren.

Toni liked it when her team got on.

# 23

*Martha*

The figure was framed in the open French doors, arms raised. Above the roar of the wind came a dreadful howl. Lightning flashed. On and off. On and off. Someone might have been playing with the electrical switch. Then the lamp went out altogether.

As if a flash bulb had been fired, white light momentarily flooded the old library, presenting snapshot images of silver and black, one after the other like in a magic lantern. Martyn, teeth bared in apparent agony, bald head gleaming. In the aperture of the French doors, Sylvia, her hair unbending even in lashing wind and rain, gripped Martyn in a headlock. Rigid, his eyes bulging as if in an electric chair, Timothy held something in his hand. *A knife?* Barbara was writing something on a card. Still embroidering, Bunty poised her needle, thread pulled taut. Patrick's jacket hung over his empty chair. There was no sign of Garry either. The crashing wall of sound rivalled the movie *Dunkirk*. Struggling from her chair, Martha teetered as wind howled through the open doors and whirligigged around the room, sweeping each occupant up in its dervish dance.

Between lightning strikes, the last lantern slide, burnt into Martha's retina, guided her to Patrick's jacket. She found her car keys.

As the next cymbal crash threatened to split her ear drums, Martha fled. She blundered along the corridor with no idea at all of where she was going. One corridor led to another. Martha recognised the green baize door. She pushed it and as it swung inwards, she tripped and landed on her knees. The cold stone brought her to her senses. The steps. A square of yawning darkness. Martha knew where she was. Her judgement warned, *Don't go down there.*

Martha found a switch and, descending towards the dirty yellow light, blundered down. Another passage. Martha was back at the metal door which she knew led into the garden. Her inchoate need to get away from Blackstone House had no basis in fact, yet her back tingled as if she was being chased by a deadly enemy.

Residents' voices competed in her head.

'*Whole family murdered…*'

'*Nothing is gained by catastrophising.*'

'*…not the whole family…*'

There was a murderer out there. That was true. *Where?* Martha's brain was fogged, she couldn't arrange her thoughts. Someone had said less than a mile… her memories were chips of glass.

Martha levered the handle up, down, pushed and pulled. Hands scrubbing at her hair, she stepped back. There was a green button to the left of the door. She slammed her palm against it. Click. Stuck in a nineteenth-century nightmare, it hadn't occurred to Martha that the door would operate electronically.

Soaked by sheets of rain, Martha swerved looming shapes. *A shrub? A flower bed?* Her mind knew to dwell on the prosaic. A smash of thunder was some distance away. A fork of lightning cut down beyond dark trees. Trees? Martha didn't remember the trees. Turning the corner of the house she understood she'd come the wrong way. It couldn't matter.

A hand to her forehead to stem the water flooding into her eyes, Martha slowed to walking and dared pause and switch on her phone's torch. The towering wall of the house was on her right, on her left a long wooden structure which, Martha guessed, was what Timothy had pompously referred to as the carriage house, in which was a line of cars. Her car was in the end stall. *How dare Patrick?* Martha stalked furiously toward her car.

A hoot made her jump out of her skin. Less the sound but that it was close. Another hoot. Martha trained her torch upwards towards the trees. The owl was perched on a branch that splayed above a meshed cage, the door swinging back and forth in the wind.

Rex had said one of the residents, Martha believed Lady Bunty, was caring for a baby owl which she would release into the wild when it was ready. The owl, caught in the quivering beam of Martha's torch, feathers blown ragged, eyes wild rather than wise, looked too young to be out. *It had escaped.*

Martha peered inside the cage looking for a morsel with which to lure the bird back inside. The dishes were picked clean. All Martha could do was prop the door open so that the owl – Rex had said her name was Molly – could return if she wished. It wouldn't keep her safe from predators, but was better than nothing.

Martha had expected the latch to be broken, she assumed it had been wrenched free by the wind. She doubted that Lady Dorothy had forgotten to close it, she had struck Martha as having more wits than she let on. The door had a heavy-duty bolt on the inside, with enough space between the mesh to allow it to be locked. The only way it could have opened was if someone had slid it across.

Someone had deliberately released Molly into the wild. That someone had known Molly couldn't possibly survive. Jesus. Flushing hot with a new fury, Martha called, 'Here, *psst psst*, Molly?' Checking she was alone, Martha gave a couple of hoots. Molly continued to fix her with an impassive glare.

'Fancy meeting you here.'

'*What the*—' Martha was shot through with adrenalin. She swung round the torch although she knew the voice. *Garry Haslem.*

'Molly's escaped.' Martha was genuinely concerned about the owl, but her instinct was to distract Garry from... *she dare not think.*

'Who?'

'Lady Erskine's owl. *There.*' Keeping a couple of metres from Haslem, Martha pointed her phone light at the branch above them.

The owl had gone.

'*No*,' Martha wailed. 'Someone unbolted the cage door and she flew out. If she doesn't come back, *she will die.*'

'What happens happens.' Haslem's apparent unconcern didn't surprise Martha.

'Was it you?' Martha forgot they were alone in the dark with thunder, while distant, loud enough to drown out a shout for help. 'You let Molly out.'

'Little ol' me?' Putting his torch under his chin, Haslem grinned.

'*Unbelievable.*' Martha marched around to her car, opened the door and climbed in.

The car wouldn't start. She turned the key back and forth, flooring the accelerator to not only ignite the engine, but mow down Haslem at the same time.

A knock on the driver's window. Martha's veins surged with electricity. She got to the door lock too late.

'*...there's a serial killer on the loose...*'

'Martha, for God's sake, come back inside.' *Patrick.*

Gripped with terror, Martha grappled with the key, but the car was a lump of inert metal. The car door was opened.

'Go *away.*' There was only the crash and roll of far-off thunder.


'I don't have a breakdown service,' Martha said.

Exhausted and soaking wet, she had given in and come up to Patrick's attic flat. Perched on his black leather sofa, she accepted a towel to dry off her hair, but refused the opportunity to borrow dry clothes.

'*...the whole family was murdered...*'

'*...not the whole...*'

'No drama. We'll call a garage in the morning.' The sloping ceiling gave the impression of being on a ship in a storm, Martha felt dizzy.

'I'm calling someone tonight.'

'You won't get anyone tonight. Trees are down, roads are blocked and flooded. No one will come out in this unless you're stranded and in danger.'

*Stranded and in danger.*

Martha became aware that Patrick was busying in his kitchen beyond an oak A-frame. She had followed him blindly back into the house, now she remembered he lived in what he'd called the servants' quarters.

'Martha, are you OK?' Timothy leaned against a timber upright.

'Of course, I am.' Martha was underwater, her vision blurry, sounds distorted.

'Come in, mate.' Patrick gestured with a thumb. 'She's fine, her car is dead and what with Martyn kicking off and Barbara scaring us all with her schtick about killers wandering the grounds, Martha's had a scare.'

'You never get scared.' Timothy sat beside Martha on the sofa.

'I'm not,' Martha told him. In a low voice, 'Garry Haslem let Lady Thing's owl out. She will die.'

'Lady Dorothy?'

'Molly. The owl.'

'You don't know that.'

'Do you?' Martha was swamped by dreadful grief, all-encompassing, for the lost owl. She dropped her voice. 'This family who were… Who were they?'

*Don't answer.*

'I assumed you knew.'

'Knew what?'

*Don't answer.*

'Tristan and Sally and one of their kids. The boy. Well, you know they were going on a picnic yesterday. You told me that. Madeleine, the daughter, stayed at home.'

'I know who Madeleine is,' Martha snapped. 'Madeleine was there. I saw her on Facebook.'

'Did you know the murder victims? The Robinson family murdered on Dedmans Heath?' Patrick put a glass of wine in front of Martha.

'He was a client,' Timothy snapped.

'I'm sorry for your loss.' From deep underwater, Martha sensed Patrick seemed annoyed.

'It's fine.' The response you give when fine is far from what it is. *What happens happens.*

Martha noted her physical surroundings as if hammering in anchoring tent pegs. The counter was crowded with cling-filmed dishes – smoked salmon, cold meats, olives, cheeses, fancy biscuits, an ice bucket. Patrick had intended Martha join him afterwards. *Creep.* OK, unfair, Patrick assumed they were in a relationship. He couldn't know he was leverage for the real deal.

'...I did see how old your car was – anything over fifteen years will conk out at any time. And all that shit they pump out.' Patrick ripped cling film off the plates. 'It's not even safe. I'll look at it tomorrow in the light. If I can't start it, my garage will sort it. Maybe we could go car hunting.'

Patrick talked easily, the solution oven-ready. *I'll look at it tomorrow...* The sofa, a two-seater, was barely big enough for herself and Timothy.

'I have to get home tonight. Or...' She cast Timothy an imploring look.

'I told Rex I wouldn't have visitors. I can't spring it on him now and his third bedroom is a study, I doubt there's a bed in there.' Timothy avoided her look.

'There might be?' Martha persisted. Patrick was virtually a stranger and, although she had slept with Tristan on their first date that was a chemistry thing. She felt nothing for Patrick. Glancing across she saw he was serving food onto two plates.

'*...not the whole family.*'

'Are you sure Tristan didn't stay behind and it was Maddy who...?' *Tristan was in the picture.*

'Madeleine is the sole survivor. I wouldn't rely on Facebook, since when does it tell the truth?' Timothy got up. 'Martha, I wish I could put you up. I'll call tomorrow, see how you are.'

'I'll come out with you, I want things from the car.' Martha resisted pointing out that Timothy could see she was going to be alone with a man powering on with his seduction scene despite knowing that someone Martha knew had been murdered. Had Patrick guessed he was leverage?

'I'll get these.' Patrick moved towards her car keys which Martha must have left on the counter.

'Leave them.' Martha saw Patrick's face stiffen at her reply. *He knew.*

Before Patrick reached the keys Martha grabbed them and pushing in front of Timothy, headed out of the flat and down the stairs.

'Are you really all right, Martha?' On the first floor, pausing by the wall that hid the passage to Rex's flat, Martha was swept back to the sunny morning over a month ago waiting behind Freddy the Fishmonger at Rex's door. She'd liked Freddy, even in about twenty minutes, Martha had known Freddy was a good sort. Since then she'd seen Freddy's van out and about and even considered flagging it down just to say hi.

'It's a mess,' she said now.

'You should tell the police you knew Tristan.' Martha had bent Timothy's ear so many times, Timothy referred to Tristan as if he were a mutual acquaintance.

'What exactly should I tell them, Timothy?' Martha bridled.

'The truth. You and him were having an affair.' Timothy was in stuffy advice mode. 'Have you got an alibi?'

'What are you talking about?'

'Where were you on Sunday afternoon?' Timothy put up a hand. 'Don't tell me, you were up to your old tricks?'

Somewhere in the house a clock chimed ten times. Martha and Timothy waited for it to stop, their gaze on the polished bronze shield at the centre of the two crossed swords.

Martha shut the front door and hurtled down the stone steps. If she could get a signal at the bottom of the drive, she'd call for a taxi.

'Hello again, Martha.' Garry Haslem was leaning on the bonnet of Martha's car. 'Bit of a shit show this evening, hope it hasn't put you off. We're really one big happy family.'

'That's my car. Did you get it started?' Despite only recently having been scared of Haslem, Martha had the urge to hug him.

'I'd like to say it was a tough call.' Garry smacked his hands together and launched off the engine grille before opening the door for Martha to get in. 'But it was a no-brainer.'

'Why, what did you do?'

'I reattached the ignition cable.'

'You need to show me in case it happens again.'

'No need, it won't.'

'But it just—'

'Someone pulled it off.'

'Say again?'

'It was tampered with.'

'Who would do that?'

'Always start with motive. Who benefited from your car being dead?' Garry craned up at the roof where a light glowed from Patrick's attic window.

'That's ridiculous.'

'You should be flattered by the distance our money-man will go to keep you,' Garry said. 'He followed you to your salon and he bollocksed your auto. That's not my style, just saying.'

'Followed me?'

'He went off like a red-arsed fly after you that morning you brought Mr Companion here. Didn't he tell you? Guess you could call it romantic.'

'No. He didn't tell me.' Martha thanked Garry and accelerated away down the drive.

She'd been so concerned to make Tristan jealous she had taken her eye off the ball. When Tristan had called Patrick a creep, he'd got that right. *It took one to know one.*

*Tristan was dead.*

Hunched over the wheel, Martha saw the sign for Dedmans Heath peeping through a hedge. Now the entrance to the car park was blocked by a barrier of police tape. A police car was parked, side-lights on, on the lane.

*If she had left any clues, there was nothing she could do.*

Adopting a neutral expression, Martha drove on by.

Timothy had urged Martha to tell the police where she was yesterday afternoon because he had guessed where she was. It wasn't the first time that Martha had followed Tristan. One time she'd even persuaded Timothy to come with her. They'd sat in her Fiesta near Tristan's house and watched the comings and goings. All it had achieved was to make Martha miserable. Timothy had said Tristan wasn't worth the bother. It had also proved to Timothy that no one had as much reason to hate Tristan's family as Martha.

Martha had not told Timothy that she had been at Dedmans Heath at the precise time the Robinson family had their picnic, but he'd guessed. He had once called her the Bunniest of Bunny Boilers. At the time, after a few glasses of wine, it had been funny.

What Timothy didn't know was, when Martha had circled the Robinson's Range Rover thrilling head to foot with hate, she had prayed with all her heart that every member of the *Bliss Family* Robinson would die. The whole family.

# 24

The moon was snuffed out by clouds. On the drive, the iron-girdled globes of two LED lamps cast a cold halo, in the darkness their glow like distant planets. The ghostly light made a black and grey mosaic of horizontal and vertical planes, the balustrades, the steps to the front door, the iron gate in the yew hedge. Geraniums in terracotta pots, drained of colour, might be forged from the same material as the gate. An artist might represent deep shade with close hatching, brush sweeps for the sky, the grey featureless clouds with smudging.

Hands in his pockets, Garry Haslem watched Martha Merry drive off with only mild regret, she wasn't his type.

'Have you seen Martha?' Patrick Bell held the door open, light from the hall chandelier erasing his features.

'Gone, mate.' Garry swivelled on his heels. 'Couldn't get away fast enough, ask me.'

'Her car wouldn't start.'

'Yeah, so you told her.' Garry grinned. Patrick was the kind of man he despised, a sneak and a coward. 'It started once I plugged in the cable. Sly trick, Bell, mate.'

'That's not—'

'She's not interested in you, Paddy-Whack. Martha bats for the other team.' Garry sucked his teeth. 'Shame.'

'Did you touch her?' Patrick curled his fists.

'Did you?' Garry laughed. 'You going to lamp me? That'll be fun.'

'She has a boyfriend. *Had.*' Patrick backed down. 'She was having an affair with the man who was murdered on Dedmans Heath.'

'Whoa. Rewind.' Garry kicked the gravel. 'She told you this?'

'Martha passed him off as a customer at her salon. But the way that companion Mew told her and that she looked sick as a dog, said it all.' Patrick ran his tongue around his lips. 'I knew anyway.'

'You knew she was seeing this Tristan Robinson *before* he got himself murdered?'

'I see you know his name.' Patrick gave a dry cough. 'I saw her go into the Dedmans Heath car park near the house when I was driving past. I parked further up the lane and went back. I saw Martha keying a black Range Rover. When I saw the news this evening, I recognised the Range Rover as the one in the car park. It belonged to Robinson.'

'OK, and since you're good with numbers you made four from two plus two.' Garry rocked on his heels. '*Interesting.*'

'Leave her, Garry.'

'I don't think that's what you want, is it, Patricia? Or you would have kept your trap shut. Revenge is your dish, ain't it?' Garry sidled up to the taller man. 'Interesting – where I come from, we lick the dish clean.'

'You are *evil.*' Patrick stalked up the front steps into the house. Leaning against the front door, he panted for breath. After some time, he got out his phone. Calling Martha was a quick and easy procedure, he had her on speed dial. *Voicemail.* He texted.

I told Garry. It just came out. He won't forget.

Told him what???

You know what.

Upstairs in his flat, Patrick watched his phone, but Martha didn't reply.

By two o'clock in the morning, the storm had passed. The rain had stopped. The air was cleansed. A rational soul would easily attribute the constant dripping to water dropping from leaves, a creaking to an ancient bough that, battered by the tumult, would soon break. But this was the time when the ghosts roamed the honeysuckle-scented walks, lingered in the arbours and strolled around the fountain. Ghosts of myriad betrayals and cruelties to which the building and ornamental garden bore mute witness. Blacklock House, like those enduring blighted lives, had never been a happy home.

The flesh and blood man currently hunched over his phone in the summer house, a poor imitation of *The Thinker*, was too rational to know he kept company with the long dead. Washed in the gleam of his mobile phone, Garry Haslem's pudgy features were roughly hewn clay. A brutality, once disguised by pretty looks and now by charm, was laid bare.

In the hours since Patrick Bell had confided in him, Garry Haslem had remained in the garden. He was now familiar with the digital footprint of Martha Merry. She was a friend of Sally Robinson on Facebook. Martha's own Facebook was given over to special offers, examples of wedding styles. She described herself as 'in a relationship'. *'Everyone,'* he counselled his fellow residents, *'has something valuable to offer. The trick is to find it.'* The world was a giant playground. And every playground needs a bully.

Garry Haslem got up and stepped out of the shadow of the summer house to stroll over the lawn to the fountain. It had come to life on Sunday evening. He'd called everyone out to see. But by morning, it had died again. The marble basin was brimming, leaves and twigs floating in water from the storm. Used to bending people and objects to his bidding, Garry hated the dodgy fountain. No one would pay to have it mended and his own – amateur – attempts had failed.

Garry was distracted by a sound. *Rusty hinges.* He had advised against oiling the gate in the yew hedge. *It warns of intruders.*

Moving to a bench at the side of the house, Garry narrowly missed a wheelbarrow.

Someone was creeping over the patio outside the tall window of the old chapel now bisected by the mezzanine in Garry's own ground floor apartment. *Pay out the rope.* Garry was disappointed that it had taken Patrick this long.

*Incoming, my darling.* Garry Haslem caught his prey in the act of opening a door that wasn't there.

'Well, I never...'

# 25

*Freddy*

The mid-morning sun brought sharp focus to the scene. Bushes and trees dotting the Downs, the slopes, cut with ancient chalk paths, might be a stone's throw away.

An artist's palette would need greens and purples for Dedmans Wood and the haze of heather and gorse on the heath beyond. The glossy royal blue for the fishmonger's van outside Blacklock House was in contrast to a scruffy Mini parked behind it.

'Two bass fillets, please.'

Freddy hadn't heard the oak door thud or footsteps on the gravel, so was startled by the voice and a shadow casting her display of fish in gloom. *Rex's companion.* Assuming a smile, she swallowed annoyance that, as he now came down for the fish, Freddy hadn't seen the retired lawyer for weeks.

'Not for me.' Stroking his beard – Freddy vaguely saw it had grown in the weeks since the companion arrived – Timothy frowned off towards Dedman's Wood. 'I hate fish.'

'You said.' Freddy made an effort. 'Great that Rex has you.'

'I've found the perfect home.' Timothy flashed a card on

the pay machine. *Rex had trusted him with his bank card.*
'It's kind of coming back full circle. I grew up in a house
like this.'

'Right.' She was surprised by the personal admission; over
the last few weeks Timothy had restricted his speech to saying
he hated fish, telling her what fish Rex wanted – which she
knew – and thanking her. Perhaps he was feeling more at
home. She upped the ante, 'How's your friend Martha?'

'How do you know Martha?' Giving a sharp look, Timothy
brandished a wallet. *Rex's wallet.*

'I don't. I met her on the morning she brought you here.'
Freddy had not expected that response.

'She's fine, as far as I know.'

'*Who was it? Was it you?*'

Freddy vaguely mistook the screech for the peacock and the
sight of Dorothy Erskine, her skirts flapping, hands wringing,
tearing towards them around the side of the house, hardly
disabused the impression.

'Was what me?' Timothy demanded.

'You let Molly out.' Bunty thrust her face up at Timothy.

'Who might Molly be?' Timothy was haughty.

'Has Molly escaped?' To Freddy's mind, Timothy's snooty
expression suggested he was innocent. Although, why be so
calm in the face of a wrongful accusation?

'She has been let *out*.' Bunty shook with noticeable distress.
'It's *murder*.'

'That's awful.' Freddy knew about Molly. While the
baby owl might have preferred dead mice, her diet included
lemon sole.

'Why would I let her out?' Timothy was cross now. 'It's the
peacock who stops me sleeping.'

'Why should someone open her cage?' Trying to soothe Bunty, Freddy saw she'd annoyed Timothy by undermining his point.

'He hates me.' Bunty's lips worked busily.

'You'd better stop right there,' Timothy said coldly.

'Bunty is upset, she doesn't mean it.' Freddy stepped in.

'When I find him, he will be prime for the butcher's.' Bunty flapped back around the house to where Freddy knew she had hung Molly's cage.

'Molly means the world to Bunty—' Freddy began.

'That was libel, you heard,' Timothy said.

'No, actually…' Freddy was saved from falsely claiming to have heard nothing by the arrival of other residents. Or from telling Timothy that, despite living with a top-notch lawyer, he'd used the wrong charge. It was slander.

Gradually, as she fulfilled each of their requests, Freddy became aware that there was no unpleasantness. She tracked the reason. *No Garry Haslem.* The barbs and insults indiscriminately issued over scallops and prawns began with Garry and, like a Mexican wave, spread through the group. Now Barbara Major struck up a conversation with Timothy about favourite smart hotels, on which he appeared to be knowledgeable. Patrick Bell and the two doctors were amicably exchanging impressions of last night's storm, which had disrupted the residents' meeting. They could almost have been mistaken for friends. Had he been there, Garry would have launched his accusations: Martyn Burnett was a drug addict and Sylvia Burnett his supplier; and Barbara, the crime writer's researcher, had blood on her hands. After this morning, Timothy would be a bird-killer and be told, 'Just banter.'

*Bunty would have accused Garry of murdering Molly the owl.*

'Did your friend Martha get home all right last night?' Barbara Major asked Timothy. 'Terrible to think of her driving in that weather.'

'I offered her a bed,' Patrick mumbled.

'I thought Martha stayed with you.' Timothy looked surprised. 'Did you get her car going after all?'

'Yes.' Patrick examined his shoes. Freddy wondered if Martha leaving was because she didn't want to sleep with him. She felt distantly surprised – Timothy had suggested he hadn't seen Martha since his first day at Blacklock House, but she'd been at the house last night. Freddy remembered Bunty and the owl.

'Molly has escaped. Bunty thinks someone let her out.'

'She accused me,' Timothy said.

'Did you let her out?' Barbara rounded on him.

'No.' Timothy sounded livid.

'Martha told us last night.' Patrick nodded at Timothy. *The companion was mixing with the residents.* 'Not much we can do.'

'You already knew her owl was missing?' Freddy couldn't help herself.

'What with the serial killer and the meeting, funnily enough it didn't stick.' Timothy glared at her.

'I have to go.' Patrick peeled off from the group and got into the Mini. The unexpected low purr of the car made Freddy uneasy. *Or did Patrick make her uneasy?*

'He left his fishcakes,' she said.

'I'll give them to him,' Martyn said.

'What's that? *Quiet, ssssh.*' Barbara put a hand to her ear. 'Can you hear that?'

Against the parched hills stretching into the distance, Freddy imagined the sound of running water was an aural mirage.

'A pipe has burst.' Martyn, who unconvincingly posed as a practical guy, was scouring the roof. 'Don't tell Haslem, he'll make us pay through the nose. The little oik.'

'He did say the roof needs mending,' Sylvia said.

'*Sshhh.*' Barbara put a finger to her mouth.

'It's coming from the back,' Freddy said.

'This way.' Leaving Rex's bag of bass fillets on the balustrade, Timothy set off at a trot towards the gate in the yew hedge.

Later, trying to describe the scene to Toni, Freddy couldn't remember who found Garry. Her initial impression was the fountain. It had been a familiar grumble that the fountain didn't work. It had worked twice in the last few weeks, the last time being the Sunday evening. Haslem had told her he planned to fix it. So, when she saw plumes of water shooting upwards, the first thing Freddy had said was, 'Garry's fixed the fountain.'

Water spouted from three stone dolphins high up into the air. Catching the sunlight, rainbow-tinted drops spattered down into the basin and onto the surrounding lawn. Freddy recalled a moist mist cooling her face.

Perhaps spellbound by the intrinsic beauty of the scene, the three women – Freddy, Sylvia and Barbara – stood before the fountain as before an altar. They had been interrupted from their reverie by more peacock screeching.

'*Murder. Murder.*' As if enacting a crude déjà vu, Bunty skirmished from the stable side of the house.

Garry was stuffed in a wheelbarrow, legs and arms dangling. Beside him was a newly planted bed of pinks and marigolds. Garry's suede loafers had GH engraved on the buckles. Whatever colour his shirt and trousers had been, they were now streaked crimson. Blood had oozed from a wound above Haslem's heart.

Freddy tore over the lawn, past the stables, and the empty owl cage, and grabbed her phone from the van. Faced with a dead body, most might dial 999 – Freddy called her best friend.

'Toni, it's me. There's been another murder.'

# 26

*Martha*

Martha was sorting through her hair-styling bag when Patrick walked in. She had opened the door to give the shoe menders next door a delivery and forgotten to lock it.

'Hey, Martha.' He thrust a bunch of roses at her. 'This is for putting you through that terrible meeting last night. I should just have driven you home.'

'You shouldn't have messed with my car is what you mean,' pushing the flowers back against Patrick's chest, 'or stalked me.' Martha kept Patrick the other side of the counter in reception. The café across the street was open, she could shout for help. 'Exactly what kind of a creep are you?' *The sort she should not be alone with.*

'I was desperate.' Patrick flushed. 'OK, it was stupid to follow you, all of it. But the thing is, Martha, I've never loved anyone like I love you. We are meant to be together for ever.'

'We are *not*.' Revolted, Martha backed away.

'You feel the same.' Patrick came closer.

'*I hate you.*' Martha remembered Patrick's text sent in the night. 'What did you tell Garry?'

'I was cross you left me. I shouldn't have said anything.'

'*What* did you tell Garry?' Martha said.

'"Garry", now?' Patrick looked angry. 'I saw you on Sunday, in the car park. I followed you there and saw you vandalise that dead family's car.'

'You couldn't have.' Martha went to jelly. 'I wasn't there.' *I wasn't there. I wasn't there.*

'Did you love him?' Patrick's face hardened, while his smile remained. 'I wasn't a decoy to make Robinson jealous, was I? You'd never do that. You gouged every panel of his car. Did you hate him very much?'

'What are you taking about?' Martha couldn't marshal herself. He was bluffing. There had been no one in the car park, no cameras, no other cars. *No witnesses.*

'For Haslem it was pure gold.' Patrick reached for her hand. 'Martha, do not worry, I've handled *Garry*. I'm here for you.'

'I don't want you to be here.' Martha's voice had no power. *There had been another car.* The old Fiesta. 'What car do you drive?'

'A Skoda, you know you've been in it.' Patrick sounded irritated by the apparent irrelevance.

Her phone rang. Timothy. Martha stepped away from Patrick. She listened to him and then, her voice trembling said, 'Patrick is here. Now. In the salon.'

'I'll call the police,' Timothy said.

'Do it. *Now.*' Martha had cut the line before it occurred to her to keep it open until the police arrived. Seeing Patrick's expectant expression she said, 'Garry Haslem has been murdered.'

'Problem solved, wouldn't you say?' Patrick purred like a cat.

# 27

*Toni*

'How long have you been coming here?' Toni stopped outside a summer house that, she supposed, was mandatory in a country house.

'About a year. Bunty Erskine was my first customer, then the others joined in.'

The summer house resembled a run-down bus shelter, slatted seats and windows coated with mould. Forensics had been over it and hadn't found so much as the murderer's proverbial cigarette butt. Whoever murdered Garry Haslem had not staked out the house from here. Judging by the floor, the most recent visitor was the peacock.

As they walked along a cinder path, through a virtual tunnel of rhododendrons, laurels and dog rose, Freddy told Toni what she knew.

'The oldest resident is Lady Dorothy Erskine. Her nickname is Bunty, but she'll prefer you to use her title.'

'Good tip.' Toni pulled a Snickers bar from her pocket and waved it at Freddy. 'Share?'

'Nope, thanks.'

*How very dare you.* Toni knew Freddy believed the chocolate shoplifted. 'This pile is Lady Dorothy Erskine's family seat, does everyone rent from her?'

'No, Bunty was born here and her father was the last earl but male primogeniture meant Blacklock House went to a cousin in America. Before his death, the cousin drew up a covenant that allows Bunty – as the last surviving member of the family – to live here until she dies. Garry Haslem hated that, he kept asking Bunty when she was going to die.'

'*Whoa.*' Toni nodded. 'Guessing Bunty didn't get on with Haslem?'

Toni and Freddy had reached the iron fence that separated the garden from Dedmans Wood.

'She called him the butcher's boy and ironically, considering where we found his body, the barrow boy, and that in her day Garry would have used the tradesman's entrance and been fed scraps by the cook.' Freddy leaned on the fence. 'Bunty's covenant means she has her flat for life but Garry would threaten to have her sectioned. He boasted he could get Sylvia to certify her.'

'*Phooeey.*' Toni had been feeling vaguely sorry for the victim.

'I forgot.' Freddy pushed off the fence. 'This morning at the van, Bunty accused Timothy of murdering her owl.'

'Say what?' This stately home murder was spiralling into a special kind of craziness.

'Molly is a baby owl that Bunty is rearing. Bunty accused Timothy of releasing her from her cage, she was too young so it's doubtful she's survived.' Freddy looked stricken. Toni got it, she found watching David Attenborough more traumatic than combing an autopsy report. Unless she counted Ben Robinson and Wilbur Ritchie.

'Why did she think Timothy Mew did it?'

'I don't think she did, Bunty was just lashing out. All the same, Timothy said he'd sue her for libel.'

'What did Bunty say to that?'

'She'd gone off to the carriage house where she keeps Molly's cage.' Freddy paused. 'Bunty said something along the lines that when she found him "he'd be ready for the butcher's".'

'Found who?'

'She didn't say, at the time I assumed Garry Haslem.'

'Why?'

'Garry was the resident most likely to have released Molly, he had a cruel streak.' Freddy opened a gate in the fence and led them into Dedmans Wood. 'It can't have been Bunty. Garry was horrible to all the residents. Any one of them could have killed him.'

'Not my problem.' Toni shut the gate after them. 'Thankfully, I'm the advance party until they get in Major Crimes; we're hands full with Operation Foxglove. I'm here to see if there is a connection since it's a stone's throw from the Robinson murders. What was Haslem like with you? Did he complain about the fish?'

'Why would he?' Freddy stopped.

'Keep your scales on, Mermaid, just that I'd expect the bloke you're describing to find fault with anything that cost hard cash.'

'Reckoned he could convert me to men, I needed to meet the right one, blah blah.' Freddy waved a hand.

'Did he try it on?'

'I'm too old. His dolly-birds, as he called them, were pushing twenty – Garry always referred to them as "it". He cultivated the image of a lovable shit.'

Toni could find no words. A murder investigation was fuelled by sympathy, however tenuous, for the victim. She was struggling not to think it no bad thing Garry Haslem had been removed from Earth.

They emerged from the wood onto a landscape dotted with clumps of grass and bushes of gorse and heather.

'*Dedmans Heath.*' Toni stopped. '*Of course*, Blacklock House is the closest house to the Robinsons' crime scene. My guys questioned the residents, did anyone say? Sheena and Darren called it a horror show. Everyone accused everyone else.'

'No one mentioned it to me.' Freddy shook her head. 'The residents bandy insults that could strip paint. Although this morning they were actually polite with each other. I put it down to Garry not being there.'

'All paths lead to Haslem.'

'Is that where the murders were?' Freddy nodded at a taped-off section of heath where duckboards were laid on the springy turf.

'The last one was here, by that tree.' Toni pointed to a tall oak, the girth the size of a car. 'We've just walked the path that, had the killer escaped towards Blacklock House, he would have taken.'

'You think he came from Blacklock House?' Freddy looked shocked.

'It's a possibility. Except all the residents have an alibi,' Toni said.

'Any clues at all?' As discreet as the confessional, Freddy would feel able to ask.

'A black Fiesta that may, or may not, have gone into the car park where the Robinsons' Range Rover Defender was found. Their car had recently been keyed, very likely by the killer, which chucks up the possibility it's personal and not a serial killer. Maddie and her aunt, Lisa Robinson, suspected Tristan of having an affair. So, I think, did Geoff Robinson, but he's not saying. No evidence from Tristan's phone that he was playing away.' Toni skirted a clump of bracken. 'None of this matters, if we have a serial killer.'

'You're sure it is a serial killer?'

'I'm sure of nothing.' Toni trudged across tufts of coarse grass to the oak tree. 'Same MO of stabbing and overkill, outdoor public space for a crime scene, both weekend afternoons, and in each case the killer made a clean getaway.' Toni had been repeating these points like a mantra at night in bed. It beat counting newspaper headlines and explained her ever-present heartburn. 'James Ritchie was seeing a sex worker, but not for sex, he wanted to talk.'

'You OK?' Freddy spoke in a low voice. 'These murders, the violence. That it's kids too. Maddie Robinson is fifteen, only three years older than you were. '

'I have to – dreadful word – compartmentalise. It's awful, but going there won't help me think straight.' Taken aback by Freddy's sympathy, Toni dismissed it, 'I was thirteen.'

'OK.' Freddy's expression suggested she was not about to argue. She cut back to the subject, 'If Robinson was having an affair, he probably had a secret phone.'

'Good point.' Toni's turn to be sympathetic. Freddy's last girlfriend had run a parallel life – on a secret phone – until Freddy found out and ditched her. It baffled Toni that, if you were in a relationship with Freddy – good-looking and the best smile – you'd cheat on her. Freddy had to be a lesbian's poster-woman. 'I know we've checked his bank accounts and found no record of paying for one.'

'Probably had a burner.'

'*You're right.*' Toni slapped her forehead. *Duh.* People having affairs lived like criminals, practised at deception. 'Thank you, Freds.'

Retracing their steps along the path that Toni was increasingly thinking the murderer had taken on Sunday afternoon, they stepped out onto the lawn. The side of the house where Garry Haslem's body was found was now tented. Blacklock House was officially a crime scene.

'Tell me your impressions of this lot,' Toni said. 'We'd ruled them out of the Robinson murders, they had alibis, but given there are no signs of a break-in, we don't yet know if this is an inside job. From what you say, Garry Haslem was everyone's favourite enemy.' Toni saw Malcolm, one foot on the fountain, taking details off an overly smart young man. 'Who's that, for starters?'

'Timothy Mew, he's the companion Rex Lomax employed.'

'He and Rex Lomax alibied each other. What kind of outfit is that, does he think he's lord of the manor?' Toni took in the languid pose and crisp linen suit.

'I suspect he does. He told me he grew up in a stately home,' Freddy said. 'He was decked out expensively on the first morning. I've only seen him a handful of times, when he comes for Rex's fish order and once at Mass, but he obviously cares about clothes.'

'Too much to hope you can put a date on Mr Companion's arrival?'

'I do remember actually because it was the Monday after

that weekend the Ritchies were murdered, everyone was talking about it around the van. I'm usually – like today – here on Tuesdays, but that week I'd swapped.'

'Great stuff, Freds.' Toni was grateful to have Freddy as a key witness, she could trust her to tell her the truth and make salient observations. 'Tell me about Rex – could Timothy Mew be after his cash?' Toni was well aware of predatory marriages – where strangers befriended elderly or vulnerable people, became their spouses, obtained power of attorney over them, convinced them to change their wills to make the predator chief legatee.

'Rex is seventy, no children and he's widowed. His wife Emily was killed in a car crash five years ago, actually on Blacklock Lane near here. Rex tortures himself over it: her car smashed into a tree for no obvious reason. Garry Haslem told me Rex has Parkinson's, Rex has never mentioned it and Garry was not a reliable source. Rex seems fit enough, although at church a few weeks ago I saw him freeze as he went down the aisle, and that is a symptom.' Freddy was suddenly wistful. 'Now Timothy comes down to the van for the fish order, I don't see Rex.'

'Meaning Rex Lomax is cut off from the outside world?' Toni's warning bell clanged in her ear.

'I don't know if he sees other people.'

'Might Garry Haslem have spotted Timothy had gained influence over Rex?'

'I doubt it.' Freddy was adamant. 'No way would Rex Lomax be under anyone's influence. He's handled enough smart criminals to know every tactic.'

Toni wheeled around. 'What? Wait, Rex Lomax, the criminal defence QC?'

'Toni, don't let that put you off him. Rex is not like Sarah.'

*Crap.* Toni had gone on at Freddy, saying that her being influenced by Rex into ferrying him to Mass every Sunday was exploiting her good nature, but she'd never actually asked about him. Far worse that he was a retired defence QC. A man who unpicked the police's strenuously assembled evidence against guilty suspects, allowing them to waltz out of court for a pint with the red tops was on the side of the devil.

'Rex was like a white knight out to protect the criminal justice system from miscarriages.' Freddy looked way too dreamy.

'Is that meant to sell him to me? Why would you choose to work for villains?' Toni didn't add that casting yourself as a horse-riding saviour had to be some kind of medical complex. She caught Freddy's expression. 'OK, for now, Rex Lomax is my new best friend. Tell me about Timothy Mew.'

'Can't tell you much. Rex said Timothy works for Silversage, that charity which supports the elderly. He works on the helpline from home, flexible hours allow him to be a companion. He'd have been vetted for Silversage and Rex said Cuckoo's Nest, the organisation that matched Rex and Timothy, checked Timothy out.'

'We'll vet Timothy.' Toni wasn't letting go of Timothy Mew as a predator. No matter how streetwise a person was – and she had to agree, going by his reputation, Rex Lomax was up there – anyone's better judgement could fall prey to wishes and desires. Had he been keen to sue an elderly woman who had accused him of murdering an owl because, while innocent of that crime, he had murdered Garry Haslem?

'I liked the look of the friend who brought Timothy here.

Martha seemed warm and friendly, shame she's not Rex's companion.'

'Is it now?' Toni raised an eyebrow.

'Stop it.' Freddy swiped Toni's shoulder. 'I only mean Martha was curious, a life and soul sort of person. If she's Timothy's friend that says something; he's rather the opposite, I think.'

'They're not a couple?' Toni knew that the nicest people had friends or partners who were horrors. Take Freddy with Sarah the lawyer. Freddy's judgement could be skewed by her wish and desire for a partner.

'I gathered Martha was seeing Patrick Bell, the accountant who lives in the attic.'

'That was speed dating, since this Martha only appeared here five weeks ago.' Toni had sketched a circle in her notebook with each resident as numbers on a clock. 'Did she already know him? Is Martha Merry the reason why Timothy Mew is Rex Lomax's companion?' Toni's thoughts ran ahead.

'I don't think so. Thinking about it, before we found Garry, Bunty had asked Patrick if he'd mended Martha's car last night. She wanted to know why Martha had been prepared to drive off in the storm. From the shifty way Patrick confirmed he'd fixed it, I wondered if she'd dumped him.'

'Martha was here last night?' Toni hoped Freddy's wondering wasn't just wishful thinking.

'Martha was at their residents' meeting.'

'Sounds like she and Patrick might be serious?' Toni said carefully. 'Like having the key to a bloke's home?'

'Could be.' Freddy's tone gave nothing way.

'So, who else lives here? We have six flats.' Toni flipped a page over on which she had sketched a child's version of the house, divided into six spaces. 'Garry Haslem had the ground floor to the left of the front door with Lady Erskine across the hall. Carry on down the passage past Garry's front door and you reach the Old Library which they use for parties and meetings apparently. Garry's place takes in the side of the first floor with a mezzanine. He showed me once, it's pretty incredible. Rex Lomax and Timothy Mew are opposite also on the first floor above Bunty. The two doctors are on the second floor above Rex opposite Barbara Major who is above Garry. She's always complaining about his music.' Freddy indicated the six squares on the house diagram. 'Patrick Bell is in the attic. He's quiet and polite, if a bit dull.'

'Which one is Patrick?'

'He left just before we found Garry.'

'Convenient. Did he say where he was going?' Toni heard that bell again.

'No, but there's no reason he should have.'

'What about the doctors? Do they buy fish?'

'Yes, although more often than not their card fails – they've racked up quite a tab.' Freddy laughed.

'No fish for them then.' Toni told Freddy.

'They do pay eventually. Martyn Burnett's retired, Garry called him a drug addict, and used to accuse Sylvia of being "The Lady Procurer". She's a GP in Burgess Hill. They don't have kids.'

'Any truth in the drug thing?'

'Martyn looks dreadful most days, so it's possible he's on something. I don't know why he comes down to the van with Sylvia. Perhaps to protect her from Garry's insults, although most Tuesdays it's the other way around. That said, I took what Garry said with a large pinch of the white stuff.'

'You might want to rephrase that.' Toni nudged Freddy. 'So, no love lost between Haslem and the doctors?'

'They *hated* him, he humiliated them every time their card was refused. Garry was chair of the residents' committee and that seemed to give him power over them all. Sometimes I've even suspected they were frightened of him.'

'Do you like any of them?'

'I like Rex, obviously. Bunty's a laugh. Garry could be too. I've got other customers who make the Blacklock House crowd look like angels. Otherwise, there's no one else I'd want a cup of tea with.'

'Who's in this flat?' Toni pointed at a square on the second floor above Garry Haslem's mezzanine.

'Barbara Major. Garry called her Major Barbara.'

'Remember reading that at school? Didn't have him taped as a Bernard Shaw fan,' Toni said.

'Vaguely,' Freddy said. 'It was an army reference, I think. Barbara is single, in her fifties, and does research for a crime writer. She won't say who. Rex said he checked all the famous ones and didn't find her name in the acknowledgements.'

'Would any of them admit they don't do their own research?'

'I don't see why they wouldn't. It's not the same as ghost-writing.'

'What about less famous ones?'

'Whoever it is must sell a lot of books, they paid for Barbara's flat.'

'Must be easy to trace the buyer's name on the deeds.'

'Apparently it's Barbara's name. It drove Garry mad, he hated people getting something for nothing. Although Barbara is always researching something or other so it's hardly nothing.'

'Why wouldn't you have tea with her?' Toni thought that,

with her neighbours, Ms Major was paying through the nose for the flat.

'I don't trust Barbara, she's passive aggressive. She'll say something nice then stick the knife in.' Freddy pulled a face at the phrase. 'Last week she told me she'd loved the scallops, but what a shame two were broken. She didn't care, but was warning me in case I got complaints.'

'*Eeeughh*.' Toni grimaced. 'Tell me you didn't give her a refund.'

'That's the job.' Freddy shrugged.

'Now you know why I don't like defence lawyers.'

The white flapping canvas, green lawn and marble fountain conjured up a wedding scene. *If only*. Meeting Malcolm outside the tent, he told Toni that Forensics had finished and Garry Haslem's body was on its way to the morgue in Eastbourne for the post-mortem. She and Malcolm would head there after they'd seen the residents.

'Timothy Mew, who is companion to Rex Lomax, just told me that when he called his friend Martha to tell her about Garry Haslem, she sounded scared. Patrick Bell, the accountant who lives in the attic, had turned up at her salon.'

'Divert Sheena there now.' Toni and Malcolm had no need of please and thank you.

'Sounds like Bell is trying to get Merry back.' Half listening to Malcolm talking to Sheena, Toni thought out loud to Freddy.

'Sounds like Martha doesn't want that,' Freddy said.

Malcolm was back. 'The murder weapon—' Perhaps recalling Freddy wasn't police, he stopped.

'Call me if you need to know anything else.' Freddy headed away.

'Thanks, mate.' Toni blew Freddy a kiss. She turned to

Malcolm. 'If Tristan Robinson was seeing someone, he was using a burner phone, and we need to find it.'

'Could the killer have taken it?'

'He didn't take Sally's phone so if he did, it could be that it would lead us to him. It could link the two sets of murders. Or it could prove that there is no serial killer after all.'

'It's definitely a serial killer, Toni.' Malcolm passed Toni an evidence bag. 'Forensics found this under Haslem's body.'

Sun beating on her forehead, Toni stared at the contents of the bag. 'Is this—'

'Series C. Like the other one.'

'That means...' Despite the relentless heat, Toni felt cold as ice.

'It means Garry Haslem is the latest victim of the serial killer.' Like the double act they were, Malcolm finished Toni's sentence. He cleared his throat. 'And it gets worse. Like the one we found on the heath, there's a number on the Britannia side of the note.'

'Not a bank teller's tally.' Toni flattened out the plastic bag to see better. 'It's a ten.'

'I'm guessing it's a tally of our man's victims.'

'I'm guessing you're right.' Toni might have been punched in the stomach. She put up a hand to shade her face from the sun and then let her arm drop.

'Sorry to bother you, guv.'

Malcolm and Toni stared at Darren as if he was a stranger.

'...one of them wants to report the murder of her pet owl. Lady Dorothy Erskine. She wouldn't let me take details.'

Close on Darren's heels was a tall, sparrow-thin woman with the patrician face that said she expected the waves to part for her.

'I will only deal with the horse, not the stable-hand.' She bore down on Malcolm.

'I'm the groom.' Malcolm stepped forward.

'I'm the horse.' The discovery of the series C five-pound note like the one they'd recovered from Dedmans Heath pointed to Haslem as the latest of – *Christ, ten?* – victims, which made Lady Bunty, dead owl regardless, an unlikely suspect. However, Toni needed to confirm this for herself. It meant the Crime Squad would not take Haslem off her hands. Garry Haslem was now part of Operation Foxglove.

'It started with Maud.'

'Molly?' Thinking of the baby owl, Toni corrected Bunty.

'Maud is a stuffed tiger, ma'am.' It seemed Darren did a good poker face. But Toni's ability to see the funny side had gone west.

'My father shot her. *Pow.* Clean kill.' Bunty brandished an imaginary rifle. 'Maud belonged in the hall until that scoundrel stole her. Now Haslem has killed Molly, he will *not* get away with it.'

'Bun— Lady Erskine, are you aware that Garry Haslem has been the victim of a fatal crime?' Toni did her worst police officer's voice.

'I'm not batty, Detective Inspector Kemp. Nor am I one iota sorry the rotter is as dead as Maud.' Bunty bashed the wall of the tent. 'I must hold the guttersnipe to account. Take a statement, please.'

Malcolm's pen was poised as Toni got a call from Darren.

'We've got another fiver, boss. In a marshy puddle a good fifty metres from where Sally Robinson was found.'

'And?' Toni held her breath.

'There's a ten written on the back.'

# 28

*Martha*

'...in court. Anything you do say may be given in evidence.'

The police officer, who had announced herself as Detective Constable Sheena Britton, having established Martha was unharmed, was arresting Patrick Bell.

'Martha, tell her,' Patrick urged her.

'Tell who what?' Martha snapped.

'I will remind you, *sir*, that I have arrested you.' Martha thought Britton seriously scary.

'Tell her I haven't killed anyone.'

How can I?' Martha pictured Patrick's smile when she'd told him Garry Haslem was dead. He'd apologised, calling it nerves, but the damage was done. *He had smiled.*

Martha had been relieved when the CID officer arrived. Surprised too, that Timothy had been as good as his word. 'All I know about you is you stalked me and disabled my car.'

'What are you saying, Ms Merry? Is Patrick Bell not a friend?' the Scottish detective constable said.

'No, he is not,' Martha said.

'You're with us, sir.' DC Britton put a hand on Patrick's shoulder.

'Can we go out the back way?' Patrick pleaded. 'I've caused Martha enough trouble without the whole street seeing this.'

'That all right with you, Martha?'

'Take him through the roof for all I care.' Martha escorted them past the wash basins and driers and boxes of products she had yet to unpack to the yard where she parked her car.

'Is this yours?' Sheena had taken scary to a new level.

'Yes.' *Insurance, road tax up to date, no broken lamps.* Martha retreated to the salon door, 'If there's nothing else, I need to—'

'That's a lot of mud on the bumper and the wheels hubs. Been in the countryside recently?' A chatty question.

'No,' Martha snapped, then thought better of it. 'No, I haven't.'

Sheena's phone rang. Answering it, she did a circuit of the Fiesta before returning to say, 'Martha, we're going to need you to come to the station. I've been told you were at a meeting at Blacklock House last night.' All business, Sheena Britton slotted her phone into her holster.

'I left last night.' Martha backed against a dustbin by the shop wall. 'I didn't murder Garry Haslem.'

'Blacklock House.' Examining the mud on the car, Sheena appeared puzzled. 'Hmm, that's in the countryside, isn't it?'

# 29

*Martha*

'You say Mr Haslem mended your car.' The detective tapped her pen on the scuffed table in the interview room. If the sound was meant to irritate Martha, it was working. 'What was wrong with it?'

'I didn't take it in. All I cared about was that he'd got it going.' Martha hesitated. 'He said someone had tampered with it.'

'You mean deliberately?' DC Sheena Britton shifted in her seat. 'Who would do that?'

'Garry said it was Patrick Bell.'

'Why would he do that?'

'Patrick expected me to stay the night. He'd got food and champagne.' Martha had started, she might as well finish. 'He admitted he did follow me to my salon after I dropped Timothy Mew at Blacklock House on his first day. At the time Patrick claimed it was a coincidence that he'd walked into my salon out of the blue. He came back later and suggested a drink. But he planned it all along.'

'Did you go?'

'Yes.' Behind blackened glass at one end of the room and via the wall-mounted camera people would be watching. What were the mannerisms of a guilty person trying to look innocent? What gestures and expressions would get her? Martha kept still. *Dead giveaway.* 'It was only a drink, I saw no harm.'

'You went out more than once. Last night – Monday – you attended a residents' meeting at Blacklock House. I'd see that as significant step in a relationship, it suggests you're a resident. Are you planning to move in with Mr Bell?'

'No.' Martha felt hot. *Don't fidget.* She folded her arms. *Defensive gesture.* 'I said no, then thought that at least I'd see Timothy after the meeting. I hadn't seen him since I took him there.'

'You didn't expect him to be at the meeting?'

'No. He's a companion, not a resident.'

'So, you came to the meeting to see Timothy, not because of Patrick?'

'Both, I suppose.'

'Could Timothy have tampered with your car?'

'He was annoyed I was there, why prevent me from leaving?'

'Why was Mew annoyed you came to the meeting?' DC Britton was relentless.

'Timothy has a fantasy that he's an aristocrat. Whenever we ate out, he'd book a table in the name of Lord Mew. For a laugh, I used to think, but he meant it. Now he's living in a stately home, I'm guessing he is immersed in his world. He wouldn't want me spoiling the image. Also, he hates surprises and me being there was a surprise.' Martha didn't say she'd partly gone to the meeting to annoy Timothy – it did her no favours.

'What happened when Garry Haslem got your car started?'

'I drove away.'

'You said Bell had got food and drink. Once your car was mended, why not eat with him and leave later?'

'He'd ripped out the cable in the first place. I just wanted to get away.'

'Was Garry Haslem alive when you left?'

'I didn't kill him. Why would I, when he'd just sorted my car?'

'Tell me about your car. A black Ford Fiesta. How long have you had it?'

'It was my mum's. She died ten years ago, she left me her salon and the car. She had it from new and looked after it. Until last night it's never broken down.'

'Impressive for a fifteen-year-old car. Indeed, if we believe Garry Haslem, it didn't break down last night, did it? That dent in the back bumper, how did that happen?'

'I don't remember.' Martha hadn't expected this question.

'How strange.' The officer looked puzzled. 'If I prang my car, I'm super clear about how it happened and where it happened. The last time was at the Glasgow Fort, one of those out-of-town places, I scraped a bollard. Eight years ago, but it could have been yesterday.'

'I block out bad things.' Martha's nails dug into her armpits beneath her folded arms. *Could the camera tell?*

'Does that mean you don't recall driving along Dedmans Lane by the Dedmans Heath car park on the afternoon three members of the Robinson family were murdered?'

'Is that what this is about?' Martha's tone was curious, surprised. She hoped. 'Is this why I'm here?'

'I'm asking the questions.'

'I did drive past. It's on the way to Blacklock House.' Martha tapped a vein of truth. 'I decided to pop in on Timothy. As I said, since he became a companion, he hasn't been in touch. I was worried.'

'Why were you worried?'

'It's a big thing, moving to the country to live with a stranger.' Martha had momentum.

'Why not call him?'

'He never picks— It was a surprise.'

'I thought Mew hated surprises.'

'He does, but... Anyway, I never went.'

'Did you key the Robinsons' car?' The question hit her broadside.

'No.' *Think of a lagoon reflecting azure sky. Palm fringes cast spears of shadow. The draw and roll of the sea. Warm sun washing over you.*

'OK, that's it for now.' The officer snatched up her notepad. Martha didn't move. This was the moment when she should tell Sheena about Tristan. *It will be better for you if you tell them now.*

'No more questions?' *Did you know Tristan Robinson? Was he in love with you? Was he going to leave his wife for you?*

'Unless there's anything you want to tell me.' DC Britton waited.

'No.' Martha felt about on the floor for her bag.

'Then you can go.' The officer held the door open. As Martha passed her, she tucked a card into Martha's shirt pocket. An action both intimate and demeaning. 'Just one thing, get that back light fixed.'

Outside, Martha could feel Detective Constable Britton's

eyes on her back as she trotted – innocently – down the steps to the street. She considered phoning Timothy but they might be monitoring her phone. They had no reason to suspect her. *Had they?*

Making her way along the pavement, in sight of the police station windows, Martha affected nonchalance and – *stupidly* – the song 'Walk like an Egyptian' came into her head. It stayed on her mind for the rest of the day.

# 30

'My friend Martha has been arrested,' Timothy told Rex over what Timothy called luncheon.

'Arrested?' Rex paused over the ham salad Timothy had put together. After the discovery of Haslem's body, neither of them had much appetite. 'What on earth can Martha have done?'

'It's to do with Haslem's murder. She says the police have questions about last night.'

'Martha was at our residents' meeting last night, naturally they want to talk to her.' Rex pushed the halved vine tomatoes around his plate. 'They're talking to everyone. They should hurry, you and I might be cooking up a cast-iron alibi for each other.'

'I'm innocent.' Timothy ran his knife through the slice of ham.

'Then so am I.' Rex's eyes twinkled. 'Of more interest is who let Bunty's owl escape.'

'Had to be Haslem.' Timothy felt his new home was being sullied by events and by the other people in the house. Martha being questioned felt too close. When he'd moved, he had wanted to start afresh, but she had followed him. He knew exactly what game she was playing.

'You must be upset about Martha.' Rex supposed the reason for Timothy's stern expression.

'No reason to be. Martha has always been able to look out for herself.'

'If you're seeing her, why not suggest she keeps a wide berth from Patrick Bell? I don't know him well, but instinctively, I don't trust him,' Rex said.

By day, the trees – oaks, dying ash, and larches – of Dedmans Wood, blobs of differing greens appeared less menacing. An artist's eye would have led the viewer beyond the wood to the Downs to where a man, arms clutching two poles, was carved into the chalk.

King Tut strutting around the fountain, fanned feathers dipping and bowing, would claim pride of place in any painting. The fountain had stopped again at some point in the morning.

'They have ruined the garden.' Timothy spoke his thoughts out loud.

'It's seen worse.' Rex didn't expand. 'I have high hopes of Antonia Kemp, although with a serial killer, she's got her work cut out.'

'Who?'

'The SIO on this. Sorry, jargon from my old life. The senior investigating officer. Kemp, is a bit of a star, these murders are on her doorstep, or they'd have got in the Major Crime Team, the specialists. There's no better detective in England.'

'Do you know her?' Timothy began cutting a slice of the baguette with his knife.

'Tim, you'll be all day that way, *give*.' Rex snatched the baguette from Timothy, ripped off a chunk and handed it to him. 'Never had the pleasure, better yet, the misfortune, to defend anyone Kemp has charged. Like a spider with a fly, she wraps her case up good and tight with evidence. I'd have relished the challenge. So, Martha is seeing Patrick Bell? He's way below her pay-grade. Bell is as slippery as one of our Leela snakes. As treasurer of the residents' association, he was effectively Garry's right-hand man, although he claimed to dislike him.'

'Bell's a match to Martha, then.' Timothy didn't fancy the bread after Rex had handled it.

'That's rather harsh about your best friend.'

'Martha isn't my best friend.' Timothy stopped any pretence at eating. 'I don't know Martha that well.'

'You claimed you'd been friends for years.' Rex was sharp.

'I didn't really know her. We got along on a superficial level. I was Martha's listening post, she's good at practical stuff which I'm not. It worked.'

'You are a good listener?' Rex also put down his cutlery.

'I believe I said as such in my Cuckoo's Nest application. In my job on the Silversage helpline, I have to be.'

'You also told me you were practical.' Rex guffawed. 'Tell me a thing? Did Martha know Patrick before she brought you here?'

'No. It was secret, but hardly matters now: Martha was having an affair with Tristan Robinson, the man who was murdered with his wife and daughter on Sunday afternoon.' Timothy waved in the direction of the heath. 'What I meant by Martha being slippery was she was seeing Patrick to make Tristan jealous. Once she heard Tristan was dead

– Martha hadn't heard about the Robinsons until I told her – she wanted to leave, she was furious when her car wouldn't start.'

'I doubt Patrick will like being second best.' Rex shook crumbs off his napkin onto the flagstones.

'Maybe not, he'd gone to the salon this morning. When I rang Martha and told her that Garry had been murdered, she whispered Patrick was there. She sounded scared so I told the police. Could Patrick have murdered Garry?'

'Everyone under this roof could have. But could Martha have murdered the Robinsons? Tristan wasn't leaving his wife and kids, did love switch to hate?' Rex gazed towards the chalk man. 'A fly in the ointment is that according to yesterday afternoon's press conference, the police are hunting a serial killer. Martha had motive for Sunday's killings on the heath but the Seaford Head murders? And don't you think Martha too steady a woman to commit murder like a banal *crime passionnel*?'

'As I said, I don't know what Martha is capable of.' Timothy was thinking that already he'd said too much.

'Did you think the Robinsons looked familiar?' For his part, Rex was thinking he had no idea what Timothy was capable of.

'Familiar?' Timothy wanted to stop talking about the murders. He had hoped for a civilised luncheon on the terrace. 'I haven't looked at the pictures.'

'Look now.' Rex slid his phone across to Timothy. 'Look at the girl.'

'"Madeleine Robinson, orphaned at fifteen."' Timothy read the caption beneath a picture of a girl looking shyly – or was it sulkily – at the camera.

'Isn't she the girl we saw on the heath the week before? The one who dropped her phone?'

'I don't recognise her.' Timothy pushed back the phone.

'I suppose most teenage girls look alike.' Rex sighed. 'I've been glad to be out of the game, but with a serial killer clever enough to evade detection and Antonia Kemp on the case, if he's caught, what I'd give to act in his defence.'

'You are sure it's a man.' Timothy folded his napkin and pushed it through one of the ivory rings he'd suggested they use at mealtimes.

'I am. You can count the number of female serial killers on one hand.' Rex slathered a chunk of bread with a smear of ripe Brie.

'Maybe they'll get in a profiler.' Timothy proffered what little he knew about finding murderers.

'I've heard Kemp is against them. I'm there with her; why pay a fortune to be told to look for a man who used to torture his boyhood teddy bear?' Not having adopted his napkin ring, Rex scrunched up his napkin and tossed it on the table. 'We could offer her Leela. Hey, that's a point, Leela has you nailed as a psychopath.'

'Leela is a game.'

'Joke, Tim.' Rex seemed unaware of his companion's stiff manner. 'Although if you are a psychopath, you'd love games. *Joke again.*'

'Yeah.' Timothy forced a smile. He loathed being called Tim.

'Joking aside, Mr Mew, I advise you compose yourself for your interview with the police.' Rex became serious. 'They are interviewing you about Garry's murder, but what you've just told me puts you in the frame for the Robinsons too. You claim you're not close to Martha, but given how often you land on Bad Company in Leela, might Martha not have inveigled you to do her murders for her? I know enough about how the minds of the police work to know they will be looking for how the killer – likely covered in blood – exited the heath without being observed. In a car? On foot? Perhaps through Dedmans Wood, to Blacklock House. Better to use the lift than the stairs since, given the frequent breakdowns, few of us do.'

'You need evidence to accuse me.' Jumping up, Timothy knocked over his chair. 'You were there all afternoon, you know I didn't leave the house. You are my alibi and I am yours.'

'I was having a nap, we don't actually know each other's movements on Sunday afternoon. I am not accusing you, Tim. I am merely pointing out the relative fragility of our positions. Do not blithely embark upon your chat with Antonia Kemp. Gather your thoughts.'

'I have nothing to hide.'

'That singles you out. I was never interested in a person's innocence, only in convincing the jury of reasonable doubt.' Rex got up and making his way around the table, righted the chair. He grinned at Timothy. 'Freddy told me that you were accused of murder this morning.'

'What do you mean?' Timothy had gone white.

'Molly the owl?' Rex rested against the balustrade, his back to the garden.

'Freddy told me Bunty was lashing out.'

'No doubt.' Rex moved towards the sitting room doors. 'I warn you, we're all in for a rocky time. Folks in Blacklock House will be watching each other like hawks for who killed Garry. Who amongst us is a serial killer? Murder erodes trust, it decimates a community and frankly, this community is already at each other's throats.'

'I never trust people anyway.' Timothy gathered the abandoned meal onto a tray.

'Please excuse me, Tim, I'm going for my nap.' Rex patted the younger man's shoulder as Timothy, carrying the tray, headed for the kitchen. 'After your interview with the police, why not take the afternoon off, lad? And don't waste it, and above all make sure you have witnesses.'

Whatever Rex had meant about Timothy not wasting his afternoon, it cannot have been giving tacit permission that Timothy use his Jaguar. Nor can Rex have sanctioned that, no sooner had he locked his bedroom door, Timothy could remove a twenty-pound note from Rex's wallet on the hall table.

Rex's warning that residents of Blacklock House would watch each other like hawks had been prescient. Concealed by high hedges, branches whipping and snapping at the Jaguar on Dedmans Lane, Timothy supposed he had left Blacklock House unseen.

From her window on the second floor, Barbara Major, the crime writer's researcher, saw Timothy drive away in Rex's car. She was in no hurry, a chance comment made at the fish van that morning meant Barbara knew the companion's destination.

## 31

*Freddy*

Freddy couldn't have said why she had come to the ruined site of her family's fishery. It wasn't to cheer herself up, which, after the morning she'd had since seeing Toni at Blacklock House, was what she needed. Her vague answers to the questions of regulars flocking around the fish van – *'Did you know the victim at Blacklock House?' 'Did you see his body?' 'How was he killed?'* – can't have been worth the price of her fish. The rampant curiosity gave her a sense of what Toni faced from the media. Freddy felt for Toni. Her brave front was just that; underneath, Toni was sensitive. Freddy bet Toni wasn't sleeping. At least she had Malcolm.

Getting out of the van, Freddy pushed through a gap in the fencing and wandered onto the concrete apron where the distribution lorries had parked.

The Power Fisheries sign was buckled and charred. Although the fire had gutted the factory months ago, a keen smell of smoke hung in the air. There was no sign that the new owners planned to redevelop the site.

As if in synchronicity with the bleak cremated ruins, a

canopy of white-grey cloud had obscured the sun and the temperature, muggy all day, was damp and chill. Freddy had been clammy in her Freddy's Fresh Fish overall, now the cold seeping through the fabric was an amorphous foreboding. She glanced around, before deciding she was alone.

Freddy was fretting. Had she given Toni too negative an impression of the Blacklock House residents? None of them would be murderers. Had the man who killed the Robinson family escaped along the path through Dedmans Wood that she'd walked along with Toni? Was Martha involved? Freddy couldn't believe it.

The fishery buildings had been razed. Melted cladding had peeled away from brick posts, the curving aluminium frames and a flame-stained breeze-block wall the only remains of the dawn market where the catches were sold. Instead of lemon sole, bass, huss in primary-coloured boxes hauled from trawlers, there was a mountain of old tyres, the inflammable mass of black rubber as if tempting another noxious conflagration. The gutting shed was a crush of rusted, buckled girders on which rested sheets of crumpled roofing.

Freddy guessed that a chunk of metal the size of a car was the freezing machine. Bought from a frozen-pea company, it had been her dad's pride.

Gone was the busy bustling factory in which Freddy had spent her childhood and which her dad had expected her to run one day.

Freddy's phone jolted her into the present. It was Toni.

'Freds, a favour. Feel free to say no, but *please* don't.'

'No.' Why was it when Toni asked for a favour what came to Freddy's mind was that Toni had been done for shoplifting and wanted Freddy to be a character witness? *Because one day that would be why Toni was calling.*

'You know I told you Sheena arrested Patrick Bell at Martha Merry's salon? Martha who you like?'

'I don't *like* her, I hardly know her.'

'So, the thing is…' Toni dropped her voice. 'As you also know we have fewer leads than an empty pet shop.'

'That's quite good, did you make that up?'

'Yes.' Toni sounded pleased. 'Perhaps we have one lead. When she was at Merry's salon, Sheena spotted that Merry has a black Ford Fiesta. She's matched it to one we had a partial plate for that we spotted on CCTV turning off the A27 onto Dedmans Lane the afternoon the Robinsons were murdered. Martha claims she planned to visit Timothy Mew at Blacklock House, but changed her mind. She has no alibi for that time. With nothing solid, Sheena let her go, but if we are to rule her out, we need eyes on her. Even with a bigger team we don't have the resources for a stakeout.'

'*No.*'

'We have hit a game changer.' Undaunted, Toni chirped on. 'This is special knowledge, we're keeping it back, so afterwards forget I told you. We now know this serial killer leaves messages. A 1960s five-pound note on which he puts what we think is the number of his victims. Haslem is victim ten. We're searching Seaford Head because he must have left a fiver there. We have to hope it hasn't been nicked or we will have to go public.'

'He killed Haslem?' Freddy was looking at the wall with a doorway into what was her dad's, later her brother's, office. No roof, no other walls. Piles of rubble blocked the way in. A discarded Costa cup lay on the step. Freddy felt the visceral memory of putting her boot on the step and opening the door.

'...began killing before the Ritchies, the Robinsons and now, Haslem.'

'Still no.' Freddy crunched over glass and brick, the ground blackened with ash. She peered over the top of the bricks in the doorway. She saw where the desk, the printer and the filing cabinet had been. The air conditioning unit, components warped and melted, was tipped against the wall. Freddy placed a hand on the brick. She felt a tremor. If it wasn't demolished first, the wall would soon collapse.

'...if you go past or, say, blow your horn and pretend to be a mobile fishmonger,' Toni was a dog with a bone, 'maybe Martha would come out and you could chat? No harm done. If she has nothing to hide after all then you two get to know each other and, hopefully, we eliminate her.'

'I *am* a mobile fishmonger.' Freddy meandered across the concrete apron to the wasteland of windblown weeds where Andy, her brother, had installed a township of shipping containers now burnt back to the metal and warped. She had to look away. 'I was there on Sunday afternoon, I dropped in on Rex. Am I a suspect?'

'Yes. Add it to your statement when you come in,' Toni said. 'Seriously, mate, Sheena is sure Martha Merry was keeping something back. Could just be her car insurance has run out or she racked up unpaid tolls from the QE2 bridge, but we have to dig deeper.'

'We? You mean *me*. Why should Martha tell me? Anyway, don't you suspect the killer is a man?'

'People open up to you, Freds. You're the marine equivalent of Father Pete, you could sell fish to the Devil. I do think the killer is a man, serial killers overwhelmingly are, but he might have what we call a disciple.'

'Give me the address.'

Close friends since aged eleven, Toni and Freddy each knew they would move mountains for the other.

No one had died in the fire. It had started when the fishery was unoccupied, after the evening's placement of the next day's orders and distribution lorries arrival at four the following morning. Yet, as Freddy stumbled to the van, she felt chased by death.

# 32

*Toni*

'Do you think Sheena's hunch about Martha Merry holds water?' Malcolm said.

'Sheena's proved herself a decent detective, so yes.' Toni hadn't told Malcolm she'd called Freddy. He would not approve of friends tailing suspects. *Nor did Toni.*

The discovery of the series C five-pound note was, as Toni had told Freddy, a game changer. It confirmed not only what they had already concluded, that the Ritchie and Robinson murders committed over the last five weeks were the work of one man, but that Garry Haslem was his latest victim. If Martha Merry was involved Toni guessed that, like Rose West and Myra Hindley, Martha was his disciple. Despite Freddy's reluctance, Toni had faith that if Merry was hiding something, Freddy would find it out.

It was mid-afternoon by the time Malcolm and Toni were ready to look at Garry Haslem's flat. By this time Forensics had finished so they had the place to themselves.

The hallway caused them both to gasp. Stretching upwards over fifteen feet was an enormous stained-glass window.

Malcolm, who had come armed with a plan of the house from when it was converted into the flats, explained that they were in what had been the family chapel. Toni vaguely remembered seeing from the outside, but with no light behind it, the glass wasn't spectacular.

'Haslem had two floors.' Toni remembered Freddy telling her.

'According to this plan, Haslem's flat is the largest.' Malcolm flapped the photocopy of the damp-stained plan that had been drawn up in the fifties.

'I'd bet that was put in afterwards.' Toni indicated an iron spiral staircase which must lead to the mezzanine.

'The eighth Earl was quite racy, might have been him. Says on Wikipedia that Lord Blacklock's party piece was sliding down the rail singing the National Anthem. One day he lost his grip and hit the tiles headfirst.' Malcolm retreated backwards. 'Whoa, I'd guess he landed right there.'

In a fresher red paint than the staircase a cross had been daubed on a marble tile. 'His skull was smashed to smithereens.'

'*Smithereens?* You've been talking to Bunty.' Toni bet the wiry aristocrat could handle a knife with the accuracy of a surgeon with a ten-blade. Toni had rather taken to the heron-like ladyship with the voice to cut diamonds – could she be a serial killer's disciple? More likely, since she'd threatened Timothy Mew with murder, she was the main woman. 'What's that?'

A woman's voice above the swelling and dipping of orchestral strings, seemed to seep from the walls.

'It's Cilla Black,' Malcolm said.

'She was my dad's favourite. Thankfully he never lived to

see her die. Not that by then he might have been a fan...' Toni batted a hand. 'Who put that on?'

'It's "Alfie". Burt Bacharach, lyrics Hal David. Cher sang it in the film.' Malcolm could go on Radio Two's Pop Master. 'Did you see it?'

'Sadly not.' Toni paced the tiled hall that was big enough to fit both her living room and kitchen. 'Give me a potted history of this dilapidated pile.'

'Lady Dorothy's grandfather died aged a hundred and one in the forties, his son didn't become tenth earl until he was in his sixties, he hit the hall floor three years later in nineteen fifty-three. A long-forgotten American cousin inherited Blacklock House and converted it into flats. He sold it on to a consortium who have owned it ever since.'

'Freddy told me Lady Dorothy can live here until she dies.' Toni led the way through a gold and blue painted doorway beyond the spiral staircase as if into an Egyptian tomb. 'Yowzer. It's like a palace.' Her protective suit crackling, Toni raised her arms. The floor was laid with a disconnecting number of dead-animal skins, and a giant tiger's head appeared to poke out of a wall above a ten-seater sofa. A large window faced the drive. One wall was taken up with glass. They were in what had been the chapel. An enormous photograph of Michael Caine hung over the mantelpiece. Toni murmured, 'No guesses who Haslem thought he was.'

'Oh, my days.' Malcolm gazed at an ornate bowl of red and gold, one of two placed on a sideboard the size of two coffins. 'These come from the Cantagalli workshop in Florence – nineteenth century. There's one like these bowls in the British Museum. I hope Haslem was insured.'

'We need to find out if Haslem himself was insured, never mind a couple of bowls.' Freddy had forgotten that Malcolm's idea of a treat was trailing around museums and antique shops. He could have starred in *Antiques Roadshow*.

Apart from the staircase and the sitting room, the ground floor rooms comprised a kitchen, and a dining room set with fine glassware and screamingly expensive chinaware. Aside from the fancy plates and bowls, the sea of black leather and steel fitted the picture of a rich bachelor. The overwhelming impression that Toni got was of wealth. The beautiful bowls from Italy struck her as out of place. Malcolm agreed.

'Maybe they came with a deal, or he stole them like Bunty maintains he stole Maud the tiger.'

'Can't we stop that song? I am rapidly going off Cilla Black. Did the killer get this going, I wonder?'

'I'd bet that Haslem himself set it on a loop. From the description Freddy gave you, and that picture, Haslem sounded like a Michael Caine tribute act.' Malcolm was pressing his palms on the walls in the hope they concealed cupboards that might contain the sound system. 'It might be upstairs and work off an app. No sign of his phone on his body. It could be in here somewhere.'

'Or the killer has it.' Toni thought back to her conversation with Freddy on Dedmans Heath. If the killer had taken it, again it was because the phone would give him away.

'Let's go upstairs.' Toni gripped the railings at the foot of the spiral staircase.

They emerged in the middle of Haslem's bedroom. The angle of the afternoon sun illuminated the top half of the chapel window. Jesus and his mother Mary sent blue, red and yellow light across an unmade bed large enough to welcome both teams in a five-a-side match. The picture Toni was getting was of a man who intended himself to be larger than life.

'*Yuk.*' Toni wrinkled her nose. 'I don't want to think about when Gazza last changed his sheets.'

'I'll check if he has a cleaner.'

'What's this?' With gloved fingers, Toni peered at a black tin rimmed with gold lines that lay on the tumbled duvet. 'I had a money box like this when I was little. I fitted it with a padlock after Amy, my sister, nicked fifty pence and bought herself a copy of *Jackie*. She had the cheek to offer to lend it to me when she'd finished with it.' Thankfully, Haslem appeared to have no such security issues. With gloved fingers, Toni tipped back the lid.

'There has to be at least five grand.' She gave a whistle.

'Surely not petty cash to pay the fishmonger.' Malcolm peered over her shoulder. 'Is he treasurer of the residents' committee? Bunty said they met up last night. She insisted that's when her owl was released.'

'Even if Haslem was treasurer, why keep five thousand pounds in fifties in a box in his bedroom?'

'Here it is.' Malcolm strode around the bed and, kneeling in front of a smoked glass unit, stopped Cilla asking Alfie what it was all about.

'Could be a rich man's version of a loose change jar.' Toni was ironic. 'Don't you just love forensics for not turning off Cilla? Must have driven them mad.'

'OK, *wow*.' Malcolm was peering at the audio-visual cabinet.

'What?'

'According to this, "Alfie" was on its three-hundredth and eighty-first spin.' Malcolm was checking his phone. 'Spotify puts the song at over two and half minutes, multiply that by the number of spins—'

'Nine-hundred and fifty-two minutes.' Toni had liked maths at the convent. No prayers or prefaces. 'It's now nearly three p.m. so that means it was just under sixteen hours since Haslem put "Alfie" on repeat. Which takes us to around ten thirty last night.'

'Bang on.' Malcolm high-fived their double act. 'Martha Merry told Sheena she left Blacklock House at around then. Patrick Bell and Timothy corroborate that Timothy and Martha left Patrick's flat at about ten fifteen, but of course neither of them saw her drive away. Merry herself told Sheena that Garry got her car going. Patrick Bell has no alibi. Nor of course will anyone else in the house at that time. I look forward to hearing what they tell us.'

'Guv, I've just seen the fingerprint woman.' Darren's head appeared as if resting on the carpet by the spiral staircase. 'She found no prints here.'

'Not even on the hi-fi?' Toni asked.

'Nothing anywhere. Not even the victim's prints.'

'Did someone else set Cilla on repeat?' Toni regarded the player, wishing it could tell her. 'Did someone want us to think that Haslem was alive and crooning at ten thirty? Were Haslem's keys on him?'

'No.' Malcolm reddened although Toni didn't hold him to blame. 'Chis, find his keys.'

'The killer could have returned to Garry's flat, turned on the hi-fi and wiped every surface clean of prints. But, apart from playing silly-buggers with the time-frame, why bother? No one new is implicated by the chance Haslem died early in the morning.'

'It rules out Martha Merry.'

'It's just as likely there is no motive. Serial killers like to play with the police. These five-pound notes are a tease meant to wind us up. Is "Alfie" sending a message?' Toni said.

'How does Garry Haslem fit with the Family Man profile?' Darren's head said from the floor at their feet.

'The media gave him that name, not us. As Toni has said, this killer likely doesn't have a motive. Mostly they don't,' Malcolm said.

'The only apparent consistency in the behaviour of serial killers is the need to feed a warped, unquenchable appetite for power through murder. Each kill provides a high in the moment but, like any drug, the effect wears off. So, he must kill again. Perhaps with greater frequency,' Toni said.

'Perhaps Haslem wasn't even killed for a high, maybe he saw the killer and so he had to die,' Darren said.

'*Darren*,' Toni didn't call the DC by his nickname, 'either come up or go down, your head is creeping me out.' Had they been awash with leads, Toni would have found the sight comic. When Darren joined them at their level she said, '*Good* point. If not for the fiver, we wouldn't connect the murders.'

'Unless the serial killer found Garry Haslem dead and thought it amusing to divert us by planting the money?' Malcolm suggested. 'That is, after all, the net result.'

'I'm wondering if he lives in this house,' Toni said. 'Let's go and meet the neighbours.'

Although Malcolm had switched off the player, Cilla Black sang on in Toni's head. Six murders in three events. *What was it all about?*

# 33

*Toni*

The trees of Dedmans Wood threw premature shadow into a side window in the Burnetts' sitting room. Looking out at it – leaves and branches simplified to a dense mass – Toni thought again how close the house was to Dedmans Wood, where the Robinson family were murdered.

Beyond the mesh-covered radiators and wall and ceiling mouldings, the Burnetts' flat had nothing in common with Garry Haslem's opulent mezzanine. A lack of natural light contributed to the oppressive atmosphere, as did giant black ceramic pots arranged around the room, in which grew science fiction-like cacti. Sylvia signalled they sit on a dark blue velvet sofa that proved unexpectedly unyielding. Sylvia and Martyn planted themselves stiffly in black semicircular armchairs – arms up by their shoulders – which matched the cacti pots.

'Have you lived here long?' Malcolm asked.

'Six years.' Sylvia Burnett's chilly tone said little for her bedside manner. Toni wouldn't take it personally.

'This room must be a haven.' Toni's experience was that

making complimentary noises about witnesses' homes got them on side.

'A haven from what?' said Sylvia. *Or not.*

'You are retired, Dr Burnett?' Malcolm pulled in Martyn Burnett, who so far had been silent.

'What has this to do with Haslem's death?' Sylvia interceded before her husband could respond.

'I'm sure you understand we need to get a picture of the victim's friends and relations.' Malcolm was warmth itself.

'Haslem wasn't a friend.' Martyn Burnett shot a look of malevolence at Toni who again marvelled at how often the middle classes left Mr Manners in a drawer. Her parents would have had something to say if she'd been rude to the police. Surely the Burnetts wanted this killer caught? *Not if they were the killers.*

'You didn't get on?' Malcolm surfed on.

'Haslem was a snake, a reptile. Don't expect crocodile tears from us. I'm not sorry he did himself in.' Martyn burst out of the trap and tore down the track.

'*Shut up, Martyn*,' Sylvia barked from her flower pot.

'You're saying Haslem committed suicide?' Malcolm enquired.

'He wanted to make you suspect us.' Martyn Burnett looked on the verge of tears. 'He killed himself and then made it look like murder.'

'He killed himself and *then* made it look like murder?' Toni echoed the clumsy phrase. Freddy had said Haslem accused Martyn of being on drugs and Sylvia of supplying them. Toni wished it wasn't her job to unravel those already unravelling.

'Ignore him,' Sylvia told Toni. 'Obviously, Haslem didn't kill himself, Martyn is stressed, we all are. Haslem was a neighbour, one has to put up with one's neighbours. One doesn't have to like them. That's what Martyn means.'

'I *hated* him.' Martyn Burnett definitely meant that.

Toni was tempted to think they had found their killer and her disciple, but she knew to keep her powder dry. People can be guilty of hating a victim without having killed them. Mostly, too, the obvious wasn't the answer. She was alert for that black swan event, one so rare or unimaginable as to have escaped possibility but that should still be included in protocol. Harold Shipman being one such buck of the trend. Regardless of murder, Toni was sure there was something the doctors were not saying.

'Doctors try to save lives, even vermin like Haslem.' Sylvia was prim in her plant pot. 'Haslem was a bloodsucking leech. I wouldn't have wasted my liberty by murdering him, but as my husband more crudely put it, we are satisfied that someone has.'

'Who do you think murdered Haslem?' Malcolm used his 'Am I bothered?' tone.

'Those two interlopers. They wormed their way into the meeting last night.'

'Which interlopers?' Toni knew.

'That companion who Rex has – naively – acquired and his girlfriend.'

'Isn't Martha Merry with Patrick Bell?' Toni said.

'Patrick clearly thought so, but anyone with an ounce of nous can see those two are Bonnie and Clyde out to fleece Rex. There, I agreed with Haslem.'

'Garry Haslem suspected Timothy and Martha of planning to con Rex?' Toni was alert. Rude as mincemeat, yet Sylvia struck her as having both eyes on the ball.

'She brought this Timothy character to the house on his first day with Rex. Next minute she's on Bell's arm all lovey-dovey. In my work, we don't hold with coincidence.'

'The girl didn't stay with Patrick last night,' Martyn ventured. 'Did you see Patrick at the fish van this morning? He wasn't one bit pleased she left. Doubtless Haslem was onto them, they had to snuff him out.' It seemed the doctors watched crime dramas.

'What kind of young man chooses to live with an elderly pensioner? Answer, the kind who fancies living in splendour and when Rex dies – sooner rather than later – is sole legatee of Rex's flat.'

'Cuckoo's Nest is a bona fide organisation.' Toni was inclined to go with Sylvia. She would be interviewing Timothy Mew later that afternoon.

'What happened at the meeting?' Malcolm asked.

'Haslem accused us of skipping maintenance payments. Not true, you can see from the accounts and Patrick Bell knew that, but said nothing. Haslem wanted the house painted. Rex saved the day by saying we could wait another two years.'

'You suspect Haslem was embezzling?' Malcolm asked.

'I have no proof because the figures add up. Bell is in Haslem's pocket.' Sylvia went on, 'After that, Barbara brought up the heath murderer, insisting he must be one of us. She works for a crime writer so is obsessed with murder. The meeting descended into wild speculation before someone unlatched the French doors and the storm came crashing in. We took that moment to escape.'

'Are you worried about this serial killer?' Toni wondered why Barbara Major should remain so convinced when police had interviewed the residents without arrest. Was it only Major who was obsessed with murder, or did she know something?

'The prime suspect was murdered last night, so no, I'm not worried,' Sylvia said.

'You are still working.' Toni's mundane statement sent Sylvia off balance.

'I'm a GP in a practice in Burgess Hill, so what?'

'Quite a schlep from here.'

'It's not wise to live near one's patients.'

'Why Blacklock House?'

'For peace and quiet,' Sylvia huffed. 'It's been far from that.'

'It seems peaceful.' Toni indicated the view of Dedmans Wood, the gently swaying branches. Peace and quiet wasn't always a good thing.

'Did you hear anything unusual in the night or this morning?' Malcolm threw in a brass tack.

'Obviously not or we'd have said.' Sylvia looked at Martyn.

'Please could you show us the view from the back of your flat? It will help us get our bearings.' Toni jumped up. With those steeped with entitlement, she could only assume yes for an answer.

Her expression thunderous, Sylvia Burnett reluctantly ushered Toni out. Malcolm remained seated. Toni heard him remarking he'd seen deer in the grounds and hoped the animal opener was the way to Martyn's heart.

A neatly made bed was heaped with a staggering number of cushions fanning out against the headboard. Toni had a theory that cushions on beds stood for cuddly toys never owned or – the fate of her own teddy – tossed out by an empty-nester parent reclaiming their child's bedroom for a yoga studio. Her theory hit a buffer because she could only see Sylvia as having hatched fully-fledged, unpleasant and middle-aged. On the other hand, Martyn might still have a teddy somewhere.

The Burnetts' bedroom looked out onto the fountain on the lawn at the back of the house. It was on the opposite side of the house to where Garry Haslem had been found. The overgrown grass had been battered by the storm last night and further flattened by police vehicles. The casement windows were single-glazed and the wood was rotting. A shout from one of the uniforms on the lawn told Toni that if Haslem had shouted for help in the early hours, the Burnetts would likely have heard. She turned in time to see Sylvia shovelling something into a bedside drawer.

'My meds.' Sylvia realised she'd been spotted. 'I get heartburn.'

'*Me too*,' Toni exclaimed. 'What do you take?'

'Sorry?'

'For heartburn, what do you recommend, doctor?' Toni beamed. 'My weapon of choice is Gaviscon, honestly, I've got more chalk in me than the South Downs.'

'If it persists you should see your GP.' *Bingo*, a smile. 'I use lansoprazole.'

In the hall, Toni asked to visit the loo. An old-as-the-hills ploy that Sylvia should get, but to her surprise Sylvia offered the en-suite which made it a doddle to snoop around the bedroom.

Toni snapped on gloves and swooped on the drawer in the bedside cupboard in which Sylvia had supposedly put her heartburn med. Toni read the label. *Oxycodone*. She photographed it with her phone. The cupboard on the other side of the bed was empty. Toni took pictures of the bedroom then scooted into the en-suite and pulled the chain – literally a chain, the lavatory looked Victorian – and ran the tap. Smacking her hands on her trousers, she breezed back to the sitting room.

'...was one of the group who found Garry Haslem, did you pronounce him dead?' Malcolm was asking.

'It was obvious that life was extinct,' Sylvia said. 'I checked his pulse, although it didn't take a medic to see he'd been dead some time. And no, I didn't touch or move the body.'

'Fabulous stuff.' Toni sounded mad even to herself. 'We'll see ourselves out.'

'Arrested 'em?' White hair, yellow teeth, hawk eyes gleaming, Lady Dorothy Erskine hovered in the door of her apartment.

'Good afternoon, Lady Erskine.' Presuming by the booming timbre that the elderly woman was hard of hearing, Toni raised her voice.

'Come in, officers, put me on your rack and turn the screw.' Lady Dorothy bid them follow her inside.

Tall shutters clamped shut with iron bars cut out the sunlight outside. Dim light from a collection of old-fashioned lamps – Toni hazarded art deco, art nouveau, Victorian – illuminated dark bookcases, tea crates packed with crockery, so many occasional tables the name was ironic; bowls, vases, jugs of different sizes, statuettes of bronze and ivory... Toni wondered briefly if Lady Bunty was running an antique shop from her apartment. As she attuned to the semi-darkness, Toni made out oil paintings on the walls with little or no gap between their frames. The sombre faces of costumed men and women bore no resemblance to Bunty, but Toni presumed they were her ancestors. In the centre of what would be, if it wasn't crammed with stuff, a large room, were three sofas, set in rows. Each faced the fireplace. Groping past fire irons, magazine racks and a vast china vase that would fit even beanpole Malcolm, Toni landed on the front sofa. Malcolm joined her. As if in the stalls of the theatre, Lady Bunty sat behind them.

*This wasn't going to work.*

Toni and Malcolm twisted on their sofa so that they could see Bunty.

'Are you having a clear-out?' Toni said.

'A clear-out of what?' Were it possible, Bunty looked fiercer than Sylvia Burnett.

'You have lovely things.' Malcolm attempted rescue. He hazarded a wave at the walls. 'Wonderful oils.'

'Hideous bunch the lot of them. When Pa died and Hitherto Unknown Cousin inherited, he *allowed* me to keep items that meant something. It all means something. Blacklock House is my home.' Suddenly Lady Bunty appeared defeated.

'Garry Haslem has a bowl like these ones.' Toni spotted three bowls of red and gold ranged on a gigantic marble-topped sideboard. She channelled Malcolm's expertise, 'Nineteenth century, Italian, I believe.'

'Cantagalli, fancy a policeman knowing that.' Lady Dorothy grasped their sofa with, Toni noticed, elegant fingers. 'He *stole* them.'

'Things matter.' Toni passed over 'policeman'. Things did matter, her DVD of *Little Mermaid* evoked her gang of convent schoolfriends, the Mermaids. *Happy days.*

'You weren't actually there when Garry was found dead, were you?' Malcolm said.

'I was looking for Molly. My owl. Haslem let her out. Have you found her?' Lady Dorothy glared at Toni.

'Um… I'm not on that case, we're looking into the mur…' Having forgotten about the owl, Toni floundered. She should not have forgotten, the owl could be important. And she liked owls.

'*Flannel*, officer, your priority is Molly's murderer. Garry deserved to die, he was a monster. He tormented me. On and on about how I was born in his sitting room, had I known Queen Victoria, he called me The Mummy. This is *my* house. Haslem, all of them, are barbarians at the gate. They think Blacklock House as their address makes them better than they are. In my day they were gawping Sunday afternoon sightseers.'

The elderly woman would know the 'barbarians' had breached her barricade of imperial furniture and priceless objets d'art. Maud the tiger, who Lady Dorothy claimed Garry Haslem had stolen from the hall, had not kept the enemy at bay. Toni corrected herself, *someone had kept Garry Haslem at bay.*

'Lady Dorothy, when did you last see Garry Haslem?' Toni asked.

'*Horrors* – Bunty, please.' Bunty tugged at the sleeve of a jacket doubtless a dressmaker's masterpiece, now a mesh of frayed fabric and loose threads. 'At the Gathering of the Ghastlies. I dreaded it, but last night was a terrific hoot. Barbara was in a flap about the chap bumping off families. A disappointment that the girl lacked grit. A full-time murderer, she should have set an example.' In a transport of delight, Bunty darted a hand to her cheek. '*I say*, if Barbara slaughtered the butcher's boy, she's trailed a blaze. Check her cat – it's the devil in disguise.'

'Barbara Major, the crime writer's researcher?' Toni glanced at Malcolm. 'You're suggesting Barbara killed Garry Haslem?'

'She *hated* him. Jolly clever wheeze to plop the barrow boy in a barrow, wish I'd thought of it.'

'What is the name of this crime author?'

'It's hush-hush, Barbara can't say or she'll lose her job. He employs her as a spy. I played spies as a girl – this house is packed with secret places. I'm confined to these quarters now. Although my memory is faulty, so I've forgotten most of them.'

'Barbara spies on people?' Toni perked up; as a girl she too had played spies. She spied and her sister Amy took down what she spied. It would be great fun in a house this size.

'...she stalks bods around Lewes and beyond. She has a card system of portraits of her prey which she sends to Mr Writer for his lurid tales. I have no love for Barbara, she's as trustworthy as an eel in vinegar, but regardless, if I meet her venerable author, I'll have words that he takes credit for Barbara's toil. *Damnable.*' Bunty swung her feet onto the sofa so that Toni and Malcolm had to strain over the back of their sofa to see her. 'Character-building, Haslem said. When his guns were aimed away from oneself, he was a wag. Barbara's man will steal Haslem's murder for his book. A corpse in a wheelbarrow, what a hoot.'

'You seem certain Garry Haslem let Molly out of her cage.' Toni returned to the owl.

'He called me cruel for keeping her in a cage.'

'Timothy Mew told me you accused him of releasing Molly.'

'*I deny it.*' Struggling upright, Bunty bobbed over the top of Toni and Malcolm's sofa. 'That dark horse. Caught him swearing at King Tut when the dear bird was uttering joy at another summer's day. Claimed King Tut was a menace.'

'Did Molly annoy Timothy Mew?' Freddy had expressed disquiet about the young man. A text came in. *Opposite salon. No owl so far.* Pleased with the code name of owl for Martha, Toni whooshed Freddy an emoji: ☺.

'...a clue for you, officers.' Bunty had ignored the question about the companion and the owl. 'Haslem told me that Barbara threatened to kill him.'

'Did you believe him?' Toni needed her suspects to form an orderly queue.

'One could rely on Haslem to tell the truth.' Bunty bashed the top of their sofa, sending up a puff of dust. 'The barrow boy wasn't clever enough to lie.'

# 34

*Freddy*

Toni's reply indicated she appreciated Freddy naming no names.

Freddy sat on a bar seat in the window of a café opposite Martha's salon, a copy of *Sussex Express* propped against the glass. For the last hour she'd made slow work of a latte and a rock cake and skimmed the paper. Head Case was in darkness, as was the window of Martha's flat above. Freddy knew from passing the salon earlier that a sheet of paper stuck on the inside of the door read,

*Closed until next week*

*Why had Martha shut shop?* A sole trader (Garry Haslem thrashed that pun), Freddy knew you didn't easily take a day off. Had her interview with Sheena upset the hairdresser? An interview with the police did that, you felt guilty whatever you'd done or not done. Freddy slugged the last – cold – mouthful of her latte. Freddy had only agreed to stake out Martha Merry because she knew she had done nothing.

The salon door opened and Martha stepped out onto the street. Freddy flew out of the café, leaving the newspaper and the pre-prepared large tip on the counter.

'Hi, Hi, *Hi*.' Freddy hailed Martha like a madwoman.

'Do I know— oh hi.' Martha flushed. Not, Freddy thought, with pleasure. 'What are you doing here?'

'I was passing. Having a coffee, *wow*. Coincidence. Why are *you* here?' Freddy recalled in time that she wasn't supposed to know Martha's salon was a metre from where they stood. *She despised herself.*

'I work here.' Martha pointed at Head Case.

'Oh, brilliant.'

'Not really, crap position, the high street would be better.' Martha began walking. 'Timothy told me you were there when they found Garry Haslem this morning. I didn't like him, although he saved my bacon last night.'

'Last night?'

'I went to this stupid meeting with Patrick.' Picking up pace, Martha seemed to expect Freddy to accompany her. 'The police interviewed me because I was the last person to see him alive.'

'Apart from the killer.'

'Obviously.' Martha gave a dry laugh.

'Because of your car not starting, yes.'

'How did you know that?' Martha came to a stop at the top of Fort Road.

*Toni had told her.*

'A guess.' Wracked with guilt, Freddy had forgotten she had learnt this legitimately from residents around the fish van that morning.

'Did they interview you too?' Martha seemed satisfied with this answer and set off at a pace towards the sea.

'Yes.' If walking around the grounds of Blacklock House with Toni counted.

'...this Scottish detective hauled me over the coals. Why was I there? Did I go to Dedmans Heath? Had I been to Blacklock House?'

'I went to see Rex Lomax.'

'My friend Timothy is Rex's companion, you were there that morning, although I expect you've forgotten.'

'I haven't forgotten.' She had not. 'I didn't know you were a hairdresser.' Freddy knew Toni started interviews with mild friendly stuff to relax the person of interest. Easy, because that was all Freddy wanted to do.

'Why should you? I'm lucky enough to love my job.' It sounded like a phrase that Martha had repeated often. 'Selling fish, you'll see Timothy more often than me now he's Rex's companion.'

'I see him every week. I used to take the fish up to Rex, we'd have a chat.'

'Sounds like you mind.' Martha sounded sympathetic.

'Rex was kind of a friend. Sounds petty, but since Timothy we don't speak.' It sounded pathetic. At least it was the truth and not a ploy to hook information out of Martha.

They reached the end of Fort Road and walked on to what was by way of a promenade above the beach. Through the mist was the ghostly shape of the Transmanche ferry executing the turn towards France.

'Sounds like you mind about Timothy too.' Freddy ventured.

'I did at first, but to be honest, we saw each other out of convenience. Timothy lived nearby. Actually, he was less a friend than a companion. I'd moan about problems and he'd give advice which I ignored. I didn't feel able to ask Timothy about himself, he's very private. I have rung him since he moved, but he's always keen to end the call. He did once complain he felt like an aristocrat who'd been stolen at birth. When he got this gig, he said he was coming home.'

'Is he rather posh then?'

'Nope, he was orphaned and brought up by his grandparents in a council flat. That's one story anyway.'

'There are others?'

'Timothy is a bit of a fantasist.'

They had passed a cheery blue and white café, dwarfed by the chalk cliff behind. Perhaps because of the sea fret, it was closing up. A man fixed boards to the front against sudden gusts of wind, a woman was loading rubbish bags from the back of the shop into a transit van.

At the end of the harbour arm, the lighthouse was a phantom wreathed in mist, dissolving and reasserting itself. Cars and people on foot were heading along the promenade to the exit.

'This fret won't last.' Martha cut down to the beach and, taking a towel from her bag, spread it out and sat down.

'Is it OK to join you?' Freddy felt awkward.

'I think you have.' Unexpectedly, Martha grinned.

Their backs resting against a ledge of shingle, Freddy and Martha sat in silence looking out to sea. Martha's prophecy that the fret would clear was proving right. Beams of sunlight, cutting through grey, hit the beach, the light individuated pebbles. The Dieppe ferry was now a dot no bigger than the buoys floating near to the harbour wall. Fifty metres away, a group of teenagers huddled in a circle, their voices and laughter distinct in the still air.

'Barbara Major said you're seeing Patrick from the attic?'

Freddy steeled herself against Martha telling her to mind her own business.

'That crime writer's researcher? God, I knew she was watching me last night. I took an instant dislike to her. No, I am *not* seeing him, the man's a total creep.' Martha looked livid.

'A creep, how?' Although she'd made Martha lose her temper, Freddy relaxed. *So much for Martha being Timothy Mew or Patrick Bell's disciple.*

'Patrick turned up at my salon the day I met you. He claimed it was a coincidence. Last night Garry Haslem told me Patrick had trailed me and had yanked out a cable in my car so it wouldn't start. He wanted to make me stay the night.' Martha hugged her knees. 'He brought flowers to the salon this morning and told me that it was because he was in love with me. That's exactly what stalkers do.'

'Yes.' *Why wasn't Patrick the number one suspect?* 'Did the police detain him at the station?'

'They let him go.' Martha bit her lower lip. 'Does he buy fish off you? What's your impression?'

'Unremarkable, I guess? He usually gets cheaper cuts, except last Tuesday he spent out on smoked salmon. He said his girlfriend was coming so he bought some to freeze. I suppose he meant you?'

'I'm *not* and *never was* his girlfriend.' Martha shuddered. 'Last Tuesday he hadn't asked me about the stupid residents' meeting. *My god*, he planned it over a week ago.'

'Did you tell the police?'

'I told the woman detective constable he was basically stalking me. The police never do anything about stalkers until you're murdered.' Martha chucked a pebble at the sea, watching it bounce at oblique angles down the slope. 'I'm a suspect for those murders on the heath just because they saw my car in the vicinity.'

'I was in the vicinity too.' Freddy meant it as solidarity, but Toni hadn't sent anyone to spy on her.

'*Did you hear that?*' Martha struggled to her feet.

'No.' Freddy heard only waves crashing on the shore, then the undertow dragging shingle back in its wake. The teenagers had gone. The beach was empty.

'It came from beyond there.' Arms akimbo, Martha began a clumsy wade through loose shingle to the harbour arm.

'That beach is sealed off, it's not possible to get down there.' Freddy followed Martha.

Martha clambered over the low wall between West Beach and the promenade. Tables and chairs outside the line of motorhomes at the end by the harbour mouth were empty.

'*Listen.*' Martha held up a finger.

'*Help.*'

This time they both heard it.

'It's coming from down there.' Freddy peered through the fearsome railings that blocked access to a flight of steps against the supporting wall which descended to a picture-postcard sandy beach. Notices were attached to the railings,

IT IS BOTH DANGEROUS
& FORBIDDEN TO JUMP, DIVE
OR SWIM WITHIN THE
NEWHAVEN HARBOUR LIMITS
OFFENDERS WILL BE PROSECUTED

One, patterned with yellow and black hazard lines, showed a woman jumping down into the sea at high tide. *The water holds hidden dangers.* Another warned of anti-climb paint, another in red, *Strictly No Admittance.* Overhanging semicircular spikes intended to make it impossible to swing around the end of the railings to the steps. The area, once a popular sandy beach now fenced off, had the look of a high security prison.

Above, a seagull wheeled, a cry long and piteous.

'*Help.*'

What Freddy had thought was a buoy vanished then reappeared. *The point about buoys was they floated.* Sharply defined in the brittle sunlight, two arms rose above the waves. Then were gone.

'Someone's drowning,' Martha yelled. 'I can't swim.'

'I can.' Freddy raced towards the harbour arm. A mermaid never followed the rules. She grabbed a huge grey waste bin, checking it for stability.

'Boost me up,' she told Martha.

'What, you—'

'*Now.*'

Martha clasped her hands and grabbing her shoulder Freddy put her foot in the human stirrup. She was caught off balance by the power of Martha's thrust, just landing on the bin without pitching off. Sitting, she pulled off her shirt and struggled out of her jeans, keeping on her boots. In bra and knickers, Freddy bundled up the clothing and laid it over the twirl of spikes topping the gates to the breakwater. The bin took her to a little over a metre closer to the harbour wall, but her way was blocked by another fan of spikes and a sheet of metal rusted brown.

'*Freddy, don't,*' Martha shouted. 'I've called the coastguard.'

'When they get here that person will be dead,' Freddy gasped.

Freddy trawled the drill. One boot on the edge of a spike wheel would give enough purchase. She grabbed the top of the metal barrier, the rusted edge cutting into her fingers. *Ignore the pain.*

Steadying herself, Freddy lunged for the twirl of spikes above the gate where she had bundled her trousers and shirt. Her boot landed full-square on the clothes, below the ball of her foot. *Yesss.*

One, two, *three.* All her weight on her front foot, Freddy pushed herself and as good as stepped over the gate. As she did so she saw one of the notices ...*hidden dangers...*

Against geometrical odds, staggering but keeping balance, Freddy landed on both feet beyond the gate. Some fifteen metres below was the curve of the beach. Freddy ran, then she hopped over metal reinforcement rods sticking out of the eighty-year-old concrete, skirted holes, always avoiding the edge of the narrow walkway. If she looked down, she risked following the direction of her gaze.

'*Help.*'

'I'm coming.'

Freddy came to a teetering stop beneath the lighthouse. Now she dared look down. The sea was green and blue, the swell slow and steady, *caressing.* A dark shape was some thirty metres from the wall. Freddy mentally plotted then memorised a line between the lighthouse and Seaford Head. She heaved a breath and, unable to afford fear, launched off the harbour arm in a perfect dive.

The shock of cold quickly wore off, it was late summer, sun

had warmed the water. Pushing hair out of her eyes, Freddy blinked. Her boots were heavy. Had it been a mistake to keep them on? From above she hadn't seen the dimensions of the swell. Huge waves cut her visibility to a few metres. She could see the lighthouse, but not Seaford Head or the beach. *She couldn't see the person.*

A flicker. An arm. Freddy sucked in air and plunged down in the direction she had seen the arm. *If it was an arm.* Already she felt mesmerised, a dreamlike sensation put everything at a distance. Pushing lower she felt chill envelop her. Blurred shapes, darker patches, lighter ones. Her lungs bursting, Freddy was forced to the surface. She struggled to kick off her boots. The effort caused her to briefly sink. Gasping she swam to the surface.

*There it was.* Freddy swam further from the harbour wall, her only point of reference, pushing a weight of water back with her arms. Where she had seen the figure, the swell was unbroken.

A soft brushing at her ankle. Kindly. *Comforting.*

*A manacled grip.* Freddy's mind worked too fast for sentences. ... *not the sea that gets you... person you're trying to save... fisherman had once told... Save yourself.*

Freddy beat off the creature. Images flashing before her were not of her life, but body parts. *A foot? A hand?* Upper arm. Freddy regained focus. With all her strength she grappled with grappling limbs. She clamped her arm under an armpit then the other. She pushed him, *a young man,* before her and then, swimming on her back, dragged him along. Aware of the lighthouse and then the wall on her left, she aimed for the beach.

At last Freddy scuffed sand beneath her feet. As fatigue enveloped her, the inert body was taken from her.

'*Jesus*, Freddy, you could have drowned.' Martha, up to her knees in water, heaved the boy onto the beach.

Freddy fell onto the shingle. Dazed, she tried to get her bearings. Why was the lighthouse on her left? It took her a moment or two to realise that, *thank God*, she had swum around the harbour arm and come ashore on West Beach.

Martha knelt beside the inert body, elbows straight, strong arms performing CPR. The air swirled. Freddy was deafened by clattering. A red and white helicopter caught the late afternoon sun as it descended to the promenade. *Sirens. Lights. Shouts.* A police car and an ambulance powered along the promenade. People were running towards them.

Spume licked the shingle, creeping closer to Martha and the boy.

The fisherman who had warned eight-year-old Freddy to avoid facing a drowning person had said, *the sea will never be your friend.*

# 35

Below the terrace was a striped lawn, cut with a path to a grand Victorian bandstand, empty and silent on this Tuesday afternoon. A strip of glass-like sea, interrupted by Eastbourne Pier, seemed to shimmer in the heat, the epitome of meditative peace. In the dazzling summer sunshine, the scent of sea salt sharpening the air, seagulls crying. No one relaxing outside the Hydro Hotel would guess Eastbourne's fashionable heyday was long over.

Timothy was one of those taking tea that afternoon. The shadow of a three-tier cake stand slanted across his plate on which lay a strawberry slice decorated with a sprig of mint. He had eaten the sandwiches – ham, salmon and cream cheese, and the obligatory cucumber the last; with no dash of vinegar they had not been on a par with his own.

'It is you,' the woman said.

'Sorry?' Caught in the act of pouring a cup of Lady Grey tea from a silvered teapot, Timothy put up a hand against the sun. It was Barbara Major, the researcher for the anonymous crime novelist. This was his time, he was frosty. 'Hello.'

'I've had worse greetings.' Barbara stood, hands clasped, resting on one hip, blocking Timothy's view of the sea. 'I don't see a place for Rex. Is he not with you?'

'He's asleep. This is my time off.' Timothy added milk from a jug and, little finger crooked, raised the cup and took a sip. No one could mistake Timothy's tone for welcoming.

'I saw Rex's lovely new car outside and knowing you're not allowed to use it without him there too, I stupidly assumed he was here.' Barbara gave a trill of laughter. 'I had no idea you can use it alone – if you are alone?' She did an exaggerated scan of the terrace as if the seeker in a game of hide and seek.

'Rex's home is my home,' Timothy snapped.

'Is Rex in his home by himself?' Barbara sounded pleasantly curious, but from his expression, both of them understood her meaning. *Timothy had gone AWOL with Rex's Jaguar.* 'I ask because after the ghastly business this morning, it's not the time to be alone, is it?'

'Rex sleeps in the afternoon.'

'Does he? That's a new habit. I do hope he's OK.' Barbara looked waspish. 'I was taken for tea here by my lovely writer. He's treated me to one of their delicious high teas. As I see you too have treated yourself to. Goodness, I'd better scoot or the police will think I've done a *runner*.' She did a coy expression.

'I suppose you debriefed your writer on this murder.' Timothy looked sly. 'A murder on your doorstep is too good an opportunity to miss. Were you summoned by your *crime writer*?'

'Have the police talked to you yet?' Barbara addressed the assortment of cakes on the stand with disapproval.

'No.'

'The longer you linger here, the more of a suspect you will seem. What I have learnt from my writer is that these are the police's golden hours when our memories are fresh and any clues not yet expunged. That lady-detective is not my idea of a policeman, but I doubt she'll leave a stone unturned.'

'As it's likely whoever killed Garry killed those on Dedmans Heath and Seaford Head, I'm in the clear.' Timothy didn't want to continue eating with Barbara as audience.

'Who says it's one killer?'

'Why otherwise would the same detective be on all three cases?' Timothy asked hastily. The last thing he wanted to talk about while he took his tea was murder. For good measure he added, 'I have nothing to hide.'

'We all have something to hide, my dear,' Barbara told an éclair. 'I wondered, for instance, your friend, what was her name? The hairdresser who Patrick saw fit to bring along last night.'

'What about her?' Timothy took a fastidious bite of the strawberry slice and as if the action was clandestine, hurriedly wiped clean his fingers on a white cotton napkin.

'She seemed inordinately upset when we were discussing the Robinson murders on Dedmans Heath. Did she know the family?' Barbara Major's beady eyes might have been lasers.

'It was shocking news to her. Me too when you told me.' Timothy's tongue chased vestiges of strawberry out of the far reaches of his cheeks. 'You warning that this serial killer was wandering the grounds got everyone nervous. It caused panic.'

'I didn't see you panicking.' Barbara looked ready to swoop on the éclair. 'And I was spot on, wasn't I? It's a shame that Haslem isn't here to eat humble pie.'

'You didn't say one of us was going to be murdered.'

'But I might have done.' Barbara put a finger to her nose and leaning down grated, 'Enjoy your feast, Timothy, and rest assured, *I won't tell Rex, if you won't.*'

'I don't have to ask Rex—' Timothy shaded his eyes from the sun's glare. Barbara Major had gone. Minutes later, as Timothy was preparing to devour the éclair, his phone beeped. Martha.

Did you tell them?

Timothy had no intention of texting a reply while taking tea on the veranda. He was adding hot water to the teapot when Barbara reappeared.

'Silly me, I was at the bus stop, my feet aching, when I had a premonition. I would not be offered a seat on the bus. Young men don't these days. Not you, Timothy, I have no doubt you're a gentleman. A lord, according to the booking register at the door. I have come to throw myself on Lord Mew's mercy. We know that, were Rex here, he would insist on taking me home.' Hugging her canvas shoulder bag to her chest, Barbara's smile was nothing if not benign.

Timothy paled. He continued eating the éclair. He took a sip of tea and dabbed his lips with his napkin. He folded the napkin.

The reply was almost inaudible. 'My pleasure.'

From their expressions it was clear victory belonged to Barbara.

## 36

*Toni*

'My companion doesn't seem to be here,' Rex Lomax told Toni and Malcolm as he ushered them into the nicest sitting room that Toni had seen so far on their round of interviews with the Blacklock House residents.

Toni met the blank stare of a girl's life-size head carved in jade. More cheering was a painting of Borough Market which, as a constable, had been on Toni's beat and at the end of a shift where she bought treats such as pecan pie or pistachio cake. She recognised the Ravilious print – she presumed it was a print – of an old-fashioned railway carriage, the doors lined with blue and deep red fabric that matched comfy-looking seats. One window gave onto a chalk figure of a horse on a sloping down. Yellow and burnt umber hatching for the wood-lined doors and walls made the painting so realistic that Toni felt able to pull on the leather strap on the far side and lower the window. Or perhaps slide the galvanised door mechanism and step outside.

'We'd like to talk with you too. We can see Mr Mew when he returns.' Toni was vaguely surprised by Timothy Mew's absence – surely the point of his companion was to keep Rex Lomax company.

'Let's hope he does return.' Rex Lomax gave what Toni felt was a nervous laugh.

'Might he not?'

'Who knows? These murders have made us all look at each other with new eyes.' Lomax paused and rested his hands on the back of a velvet sofa. 'He better had return because he's taken my brand-new Jaguar.'

'Where has he taken it?' Toni should have asked the residents to stay put until she and Malcolm had seen everyone. The companion and the Jaguar could be on the ferry to Dieppe by now.

'I expect he's shopping.' Rex pushed off the sofa and continued towards the French doors, already flung wide. The scene might have been another painting. Rex led them out onto the terrace that Toni had seen from the lawn. He asked, 'Any suspects for Haslem's murder?'

'It's early days.' Although she'd been looking forward to meeting him, Toni was steeled for Rex Lomax to grill her as, in his heyday, he turned prosecution witnesses to a crisp.

Apologising that without 'young Timothy' he couldn't offer drinks, Lomax invited them to sit around a wrought-iron table. The cushioned chairs were a similar powder blue to the train painting.

The terrace ended with Rex's flat. To the right, Toni looked down at more French doors which faced a flagged patio. From Malcolm's map, she knew the doors led into the old library where the residents had met the night before. Rex had screened off the end of his terrace with three large pots each with a fig tree.

Rex Lomax looked little older than in pictures Toni had found on the internet when he was saving villains from justice. Still the quintessential silver fox, Lomax was dapperly casual in a blue cotton shirt and jeans. His neatly clipped hair recalled Martha the hairdresser. Now feeling bad for asking, Toni wondered if Freddy had seen Martha. At least if Freddy was unsuccessful, it spared Toni inventing a source for Freddy's intel.

'When did you last see Garry Haslem?' Malcolm asked.

'Last night at the residents' meeting. I rather put a spanner in his plan to have the house painted. I told everyone that contrary to Garry's assertion, repainting wasn't a legal requirement.'

'How do you know Haslem was upset?' Malcolm said.

'He flung me a dirty look.'

'Did that offend you?' Toni sounded concerned.

'If I got so easily offended, Detective Inspector, I'd never have done my job.' Lomax seemed to assume they knew who he was. Which they did.

'Did you like Garry Haslem?' Malcolm said.

'I didn't have a view either way. We have to get on with each other, neighbours do, don't they? Garry was an active chair of the residents' committee. I'm just grateful I don't have to do it.' Rex glanced suddenly at the French doors, perhaps alert for his companion returning. *So was Toni.* 'Haslem could be pretty unpleasant to people. I dislike rudeness in any form.'

'Do you?' Toni was quick to ask.

'I expect that surprises you given how many tough criminals I defended. You'd be surprised how polite – indeed charming – psychopaths can be. Even common or garden bank robbers have manners.'

'Was Haslem unpleasant to you?' Malcolm followed up Lomax's comment.

'Never. Although, after last night I expected a kick-back. Garry hated to be thwarted.'

'How long have you had a companion?' Toni wanted gen on Mew before he appeared – if he did.

'Five weeks yesterday. Poor Timothy arrived the day after the first murders at Seaford Head. I expect you recall the date better than I.'

'You said he goes shopping, what else does Mew do for you?' Toni noticed Lomax wasn't bothered to present his companion in a good light. Perhaps five weeks was enough to spot faults in Mew. *Like taking Rex's car without permission?*

'He has me playing games, snakes and ladders to be specific. I drew the line at jigsaws. I was horrified when he produced the game, but it's proved illuminating. It's a grown-up version of the game, called Lola, Layla, something like that. It's a great way to learn about each other's personalities.'

'You say Timothy Mew brought the game with him?' Malcolm said.

'It was an heirloom, or so he said.'

'You don't believe it was?' Malcolm's shorthand was phenomenal.

'I don't mind saying that recent events – the murders – have unsettled me. The game consistently reveals Timothy as more evil than some of my clients. I've been telling myself – he tells me – that it's only a game. But with these family murders and now Garry, I see everything in a new light.'

'I imagine you do.' Toni nodded. 'Why did you hire a companion? If you don't mind me saying, you seem pretty fit.'

'I'm fit enough. However, Inspector Kemp, it's not only physical deterioration you need to dread, it's loneliness.'

Bunty Erskine had said much the same thing about loneliness. She had also insisted people lived in Blacklock Hall for the fancy address, but Toni didn't feel this true of Rex Lomax.

'You didn't see Garry Haslem after the meeting?' Toni returned to Malcolm's original question.

'I said I last *spoke* to him last night. I saw him later. He was on the drive talking to Martha, Timothy's friend who Patrick Bell had brought to the meeting.'

'What time was this?' Toni got the tingling at the back of her neck which generally meant pretty much nothing. 'Could you hear what they were saying?' Toni knew from Sheena that Martha Merry claimed Haslem mended her car after Patrick Bell had messed with a cable to keep her at Blacklock Hall. So far, Merry hadn't pressed charges.

'Martha thanked Haslem, I didn't at that point know why, then she jumped in her car and drove off. If she had appeared anxious, I would have gone down because, to be honest, Inspector, Haslem couldn't keep his hands off any attractive female. Women's Lib had passed him by.'

'Are you sure that's what happened?' Toni said. Sheena had reported that Patrick Bell, not Garry Haslem had been the problem.

'I do have vivid dreams, a symptom of playing the BBC's World Service all night, it helps me sleep. If you put me on the stand, I'd be a terrible witness. I *am* sorry.' Lomax looked sorry.

'When did you move here?' Malcolm said.

'Five years ago. My wife Emily and I had only been here two months when she was killed in a car crash.'

'That must have been hard.' Toni nodded.

'I considered moving afterwards, but we chose this place as our for ever home and it felt like letting Emily down.'

'Why Blacklock House?'

'We wanted to live off the beaten track with only the sounds of, for example, a combine harvester or the dawn chorus to disturb the peace. Ultimately, as I warned Timothy at our interview, I'm not a people person.' Again, Rex shot a glance at the French doors.

'Yet you were a defence QC?' Toni too wanted to know the whereabouts of Timothy Mew.

'I defended criminals first, *people* second.' Rex cleared his throat. 'Cutting to the chase, detectives, I'll tell you my movements at the time of these killings. I was in bed when Haslem was murdered although I did see him with Martha. I'm sure she'll confirm that, she seemed a nice girl. The biggie is that Timothy and I visited Dedman's Heath the Sunday afternoon a week *before* the murders. Timothy had taken me to Mass in Seaford. We came home for sandwiches and then we visited the heath. We had ice creams. It gets worse.' Rex beamed. 'It's possible we spoke to the Robinsons' daughter that weekend. A family walked past our bench while we were having the ice creams. A teenaged girl dragging her feet had fallen – deliberately I'd guess – behind them. When she realised there was no one around but Timothy and me, she hurried to catch up with her folks and dropped her phone. We – or rather Timothy – retrieved it for her. She complained that she was forced on a family outing to the heath every weekend. Timothy told her that soon enough she'd be grown up and in charge of herself. His tone made me wonder if he knew the feeling.'

'You knew the Robinson family would return the following weekend?'

'Theoretically, but I'd forgotten the encounter until I saw her picture on the news last night. I asked Timothy if she was the same girl; he said she wasn't.'

Toni glanced at Malcolm. They would ask Maddie Robinson. Recalling her own childhood, it was likely that more than one teenager was parentally dragged to Dedmans Heath for fresh air and exercise that afternoon, but Lomax's description of the girl fitted Toni's own impression of Maddie Robinson yesterday.

'I believe the fishmonger called on Sunday afternoon and Timothy told her I was asleep. Sounds dreadful – being caught napping was what I was doing when the Ritchie father and son were murdered too. That time I was napping in the summer house and – thankfully – was spotted by Martyn Burnett. Mind you, were I the defence, I'd rip Martyn's own alibi to shreds.' Rex gave a wry smile. 'Burnett had gone to Seaford Head and seen me when he returned. Sylvia will back him up, every wife does.'

This was too often true, but reading Dr Sylvia's statement, given after the Robinson murders when the Blacklock House residents came into the frame, Toni erred towards believing her claim, that her husband had gone out in their car, but to get eggs from a nearby farm. He had returned five minutes later.

'Does the fishmonger deliver on Sundays?' Toni wanted Rex's view of Freddy.

'Social call.' Rex shrugged. 'Freddy used to ferry me to Mass, now I have Timothy.'

'You see each other socially.'

'Not now. Freddy has her own life.' Rex looked momentarily regretful. Toni was not eliminating him. The murders had required dexterity and surprise, not strength.

'Do you get on with your neighbours?' Toni asked.

'I live cheek by jowl with them, I can't afford not to. I wouldn't choose them as friends.'

'We will need a statement from you.' No one had anything positive to say about the others. Toni got on with all the people in her block although she saw little of them. Had she not, it wouldn't have been so nice to live there.

'I don't need to ask if I'm a suspect. I'm an old hand at this game, Detective Inspector Kemp. I must be in your sights.'

'Until we can rule you out. Yes,' Toni said. 'At least you have access to a good defence lawyer.' *Cheesy.*

'Hah.' Rex sat back in his chair. 'I may never have acted for a serial killer, but I've made a study of them. You and I know that the police rarely catch these men. You will find him when he tires of the game or, lacking intelligence, he makes a slip. My guess is that with all these murders and no clues, this man is clever. But you know that.'

'We have leads.' Toni gave a tight smile and, getting up, followed Lomax back to his sitting room. Again, she appreciated the homely feel. So much nicer than the Burnetts' cold minimalism and Bunty's 'maximalism' and Garry Haslems's hyperbolic opulence. If he did return, Timothy had landed on his feet.

On a card table by the sofa was a board of red and white chequered squares linked by twisting snakes and ladders. The squares had labels such as Bad Company, Happiness Ignorance, Greed…

'Is this the game?' Toni asked.

'One roll of the dice – *die* – can pitch you into hell or send you to heaven. I keep winning. We're using my dice and I'm sure Timothy thinks I'm cheating.' Rex's laugh lacked mirth. *Was he scared of his companion?* Toni doubted Rex Lomax, defender of the indefensible, was scared of anyone.

'Do you have an idea who murdered Haslem? Your companion, for example.' *Leading question.*

'Timothy was vetted to an inch of his life.' Rex sounded complacent. 'Leela is a game. I'm very good at games, Inspector, and at handling losers.'

'Good to know.' Toni gave him her card. 'Nevertheless, if you have any concerns, *please* call.'

'I know you're not a detective who believes they intuit killers then, like Cinderella's sisters, forces facts to fit the foot. Confirmatory bias was my old friend. Nor will you be led by a snake or a ladder, but by evidence.' Rex leaned on the banister as Toni and Malcolm descended one side of the split staircase. 'Thank you for your card, Inspector, but I really can look after myself.'

'I believe it, Mr Lomax.' Toni knew that no one could look after themselves.

# 37

*Tall, six foot, shaved balding hair which undermines efforts to appear refined. Strapping, well-built going to fat, even unremarkable features. No sexuality, boyish, appears benign. Boring.*

Sitting at her bureau, Barbara underlined 'boring' on the index card then reviewed her jottings. Glancing at Rendell, who was watching her from his place by the fire, she crossed out 'boring'; it was judgemental, the reader must decide their view of a character. She had avoided putting 'narcissist', so often a careless soubriquet for vanity. But she was well-versed in a narcissist's qualities: *grandiose, omnipotent, perfectionist* and Timothy Mew – *Lord* – possessed these in abundance. For good measure she also added *germophobe*. Although the latter was rather a cliché for a character. Barbara never failed to feel pleasure at how her filing cards captured a character.

Barbara's card system was populated with living, breathing characters who, given a storyline, would one day walk off the page. Not all those she met merited inclusion in her Rolodex. Garry Haslem was a good example. After the tenth time of him asking to be in her system, she had told him that no one would want to read about him; he was perhaps right for a ticket collector or, as Bunty said, to deliver a meat order. *Or the perfect murder victim.*

Looking out of her window, Barbara sucked her pencil and flipped over the Timothy card. She wrote five points. *Keep it simple.*

Ordered 'cake-stand' tea. Giveaway that a tourist not a lord.
Left no tip.
Dress – smart, fussy.
*Lies.* Not a lord.
*Dishonest.* Took Rex's car without permission.

The last bullet was conjecture and needed confirmation. Would Rex confirm it? Barbara herself had lied about the certainty that Rex would have offered her a lift home. Barbara suspected him of avoiding her. Barbara reached for her Moleskine notebook and, brows furrowed, sketched out a scene. Only an idea, as Barbara often told her neighbours, it wasn't her job to write the novel.

*A man in the car park admires the Jaguar. Timothy tells the man he narrowed down his choice to a Jaguar and a Mercedes. Timothy assumes that from the passenger seat the middle-aged woman who has inveigled him into taking her home can't hear the exchange. As they reach Beachy Head, she suggests they visit. 'The sunset will be glorious.' He can't refuse. As they stand on the edge of the cliff, the woman remarks, 'I was puzzled by what you said to that man in the car park about the Jaguar and the Mercedes. You don't have a car. You are only a companion.' Then what happens?*

As she consigned Timothy Mew to the darkness of her filing cabinet Barbara was startled by a loud knock on the door.

# 38

*Toni*

'What Lomax doesn't know, and what we won't tell anyone, is that, alibi or not, it's looking increasingly likely
that whoever did these murders, lives in or has access to
Blacklock House.' Toni balanced on narrow railings dividing
the turning circle from a meadow of wild flowers many, the
end of summer approaching, brown and wilting. 'I'd like
to avoid the press getting wind that the Haslem murder is
another of this man's victims.'

'A uniform found a woman reporter in the woods behind
the summer house.' Reading his phone, Malcolm exclaimed,
'Forensics have found a strand of hair on the passenger seat
in Martha Merry's car. It's gone to the lab.'

'Can we speed that up?' They needed a break.

'Fast means slow these days.'

'It's a fish to throw to the seagulls at this afternoon's
briefing, which will be a special form of hell.' Jumping off
the fence Toni joined Malcolm who had begun deadheading
geraniums in one of the large tubs of flowers on the drive.
*Bless him.* 'I snapped this in the Burnetts' bedroom. Dr Sylvia

said she took – her word was "used" – lansoprazole for heartburn. Maybe she does, but this ain't it. She tried to shove it in her bedside drawer when my back was turned.'

'Oxycodone. Are we talking opioid use disorder?'

'Could be. Freddy Power told me that Garry Haslem accused Martyn of being an addict and Sylvia of supplying him. He was fatigued and ill-looking, depressed. Sylvia did most of the talking. Wait, there's another packet towards the back of the drawer, Na-something.'

'Naloxone. It's a counter attack for an opioid overdose.' Malcolm's stint on Serious Organised Crime often came in handy. 'Sylvia must keep it at the ready. I'll check if there have been any emergency callouts to Blacklock House.'

'Worth doing, but I doubt there are. I'd expect Sylvia to whisk Martyn to Eastbourne District General herself or more likely treat him at home to avoid a footprint.'

'When you'd both gone out of the room, Martyn blurted out that Haslem was "the devil, now we can stay".' Malcolm did inverted comma fingers. 'When I asked why Haslem's murder meant they didn't have to leave Blacklock House he shut his eyes and complained of a headache.'

'Harold Shipman was addicted to pethidine; he unnecessarily prescribed it to patients, visited to see how they were doing, murdered them and raided the bathroom cabinet and took back the drugs.' Toni paced around geraniums. 'Is Sylvia doing the same? Pops in, tells them they don't need them and kindly saves them the bother of disposing of them. Can you get Darren on that?'

'Did Martyn Burnett retire early to avoid being struck off?' Malcolm was scribbling in his notebook.

'Look at the other bedside cabinet. Anything strike you?' Toni held up her phone.

'Nothing there,' Malcolm said after a moment. 'No book, water glass, specs. The Mandalorian from *Star Wars* takes up most of my bedside cabinet. Martyn and Sylvia don't share a bedroom.'

'Doesn't necessarily reflect the state of their marriage, maybe one of them snores or likes to spread out. Yet they are cold and unpleasant with each other. I'd guess they have little in common beyond their address. And mutual dislike.'

'Garry Haslem had R2-D2.' Malcolm nipped a brown leaf off the plant.

'I didn't notice. Luckily you're specially trained to spot *Star Wars* models.' Toni had seen Malcolm's vitrine of *Star Wars* characters in their unopened boxes. She'd never got the collecting thing and had never seen *Star Wars*. Her concern was that, were he to sell them, Malcolm would retire early.

They were startled by a clang. *Another.* The clock on the roof struck six.

'OK, let's see if Barbara Major is back.' Toni led the way back into the house.

The crime writer's researcher lived on the second floor opposite the Burnetts. They had tried her door before they called on Rex and got no answer. This time, in response to Toni's impatient knock, the door opened almost immediately.

'Good afternoon, officers?' A woman, cheeks pitted with chicken-pox scars undisguised with unsuitable foundation for alabaster pale skin greeted them. 'I do hope you haven't been waiting for me.'

'We have, but you're here now.' Toni was blunt. 'May we ask where you have been?'

'I was having tea at the Hydro Hotel. My writer treats me once at Christmas and once in the summer. I am his right-hand woman.' Barbara indicated a bureau in the furthest corner of a dark wood-panelled sitting room. Piles of books on subjects familiar to Toni – Forensics, the PACE manual, a 1980s murder manual, an encyclopaedia of death and dying – filled bookcases of the same dark wood as the panelling.

This prompted Toni to ask, 'Which ones are your crime writer's books?'

'None. He wants to remain anonymous. I would not be so foolish as to display his works on my shelves.' Barbara looked wrong-footed although Toni supposed that Barbara had been asked by others.

'No signed copies?'

'None,' Barbara said again.

'That's a shame.' Malcolm sounded like it truly was.

'Ghastly business, books are for reading not gloating over. For your information, I wasn't the only murder suspect there today.' Barbara essayed a scribble in the air with a pen. 'I found Lord Timothy.'

'Is Timothy Mew a lord?' Toni's turn to be wrong-footed. Why had no one told them?

'No, but he had booked tea at the hotel as Lord Timothy Mew. It was easy to check there is no such name.' Barbara Major put the flat of her hand under her chin, a strangely self-conscious gesture. 'As I told him, had I known Rex required a companion, I'd have offered. We get on so well.'

'What did Rex say?' Malcolm had ignored Miss Major's invitation to sit in one of two threadbare armchairs and was circling the room, feigning interest in pictures on the panelled walls.

'He said he didn't want to spoil our lovely friendship with mundanity.' Barbara Major looked annoyed. 'It would only have enriched it.'

'You are friends?' Toni said. Rex hadn't mentioned it, rather suggesting the friendship was one-sided.

'We have much in common. Rex being a lawyer and me with my work.' Barbara's pout confirmed to Toni that her friendship with Rex was from her side only. This reminded her of Freddy who missed him as a friend. Having a dead wife gave Rex a special twist.

'Your work sounds fascinating, what does it entail?' Malcolm had finished his perambulations and, all charm, settled in an armchair.

'Much like yours. I follow strangers and note where they live and work. I get their name from the electoral roll, conduct a social media search. Family, friends, connections. Likes and dislikes. I give this to my writer who works them into a fully fledged character.' Barbara darted a look at Toni. 'It's perfectly legal, Inspector.'

'Selling on personal information without the owner's permission is not legal,' Toni said. 'Regardless, if one of them catches you, you could be at risk. I strongly advise you to stop.'

'I don't sell anything,' Barbara said. 'My writer only pays me for proofreading. The character-building is a bonus.'

'Did you know Timothy Mew would be at the Hydro Hotel in Eastbourne?' Unless they proved to be one and the same, Toni wasn't interested in arresting Barbara for stalking, she had a killer to catch.

'No.'

'What is your opinion of Timothy Mew?' Toni didn't think Barbara was telling the truth.

'He's out to fleece Rex.'

'Do you have evidence of that?' Toni had suggested this to Freddy.

'Rex only allows his companion to drive his Jaguar for Rex's trips out and shopping. Today he was having a jolly by the sea.' Barbara looked thunderous. 'Poor Rex couldn't have me for his companion because, you see, I don't drive.'

'Timothy Mew didn't have Rex's permission to use the car?' Toni recalled Rex's anxiety that Mew had not come back.

'He did not.'

'Did you leave Mew at the Hydro?'

'He brought me home. But only because I asked. A real lord would have bent over backwards to offer. He parked at the stables so I had to walk round.'

Toni took that to mean that the companion had stayed.

'I met Timothy in Waitrose yesterday afternoon where, incidentally, he bought nothing. I did notice his perturbation when I showed him the item about the Robinson murders on Dedmans Heath which had arrived on the internet.' Barbara looked pious. 'I got the feeling he was more than taken aback. Almost as if he already knew about them.'

'Perhaps he did. Are you sure he hadn't read it already and was being polite?'

'He doesn't try to be polite, a sulky specimen if you ask me. Inspector Kemp, I know a guilty man when I see one. It's my job.'

Toni couldn't see why it was Barbara Major's job. She suspected that, lonely and ignored, Barbara had embellished a typing job into one of an undercover cop.

'When did you last see Garry Haslem?' Malcolm got back to basics.

'Last night at the meeting. Frightful as usual. I stopped a pointless to and fro about repainting the house and reminded everyone that we have a killer out there.'

'Did you speak to Garry afterwards?'

'I left soon after the storm started and – thankfully – I never saw him again.'

'This window overlooks the front of the house.' Toni took in the turning circle, the winding drive. Dedmans Wood was to her left, the heath beyond that. 'Did you see anyone outside after the meeting last night?'

'I went to bed and as my bedroom is at the back, no, I didn't.' Barbara's reply came too quick.

'Did you hear anything?'

'If you mean Haslem's music starting up in the middle of the night, I did. My bedroom, as he liked to remind me, is directly over his. The sound insulations in these flats are poor, never mind he turned up the volume to annoy me.'

'What time did it start up?' Malcolm kept it casual.

'10.36 on the Monday evening and it went on all night.' Barbara spat the words. 'Nothing unusual there.'

'Could you hear the actual music?' Toni knew her mind was running parallel with Malcolm's. *When Cilla Black began on a loop in his apartment, was Haslem already dead?*

'I thumped on the floor, as per usual he ignored me.'

'Did you go down and knock on his door?' Malcolm was on it.

'That would have been playing into his hands.' Seeming agitated, Barbara paced around her cave-like room. 'He loved to provoke me.'

'Into doing what?' Malcolm murmured as if he wasn't checking out Barbara Major hadn't killed her neighbour and five other victims in the three-mile radius.

'Violence, Sergeant Lane. I longed for him to die, I don't mind telling you. Far better that someone else has his blood on their hands and I reap the benefit.' From her jerk of surprise, it seemed to Toni that this notion had just occurred.

Toni recalled Freddy's broken scallops. Freddy thought Major passive aggressive and untrustworthy. Toni noted books on shelves alongside the bureau: Professor David Wilson, Robert Hare, Janet Malcolm. Fanned out on a table were *Journal of Criminal Psychology*, *European Journal of Criminology* and brightly coloured magazines which could be *Hello!* or *OK!* except the cover faces were not celebrities and soap stars, but dull-eyed murderers. Was Barbara Major expert on psychopathic murder for her crime writer's novels or herself?

*Could the serial killer be a woman?* From his deliberately neutral expression, Toni guessed that Malcolm was thinking the same thing.

'Did you get on with Haslem?' he asked.

'We all hated him. The man was coarse and cruel. Particularly to Bunty as the only authentic one among us.'

'Sorry?' Toni met dull eyes, heard the monotone voice. No blotches. Major – in common with psychopaths – could rein herself in.

'Blacklock House was Bunty's home, now it's a Disney mansion for fantasists to pretend they're top drawer. Not me, my crime writer put me here, and Rex only wants peace in his later years. In your hunt for these people's killer, Inspector Kemp, look no further than within these walls.'

*These people*. Ignoring this – no harm in Major presuming the police dolts – instead Toni feigned surprise.

'You think someone in Blacklock House murdered Garry Haslem?'

'Don't you?' Barbara raised an eyebrow.


'How could Miss Marple know Haslem is a victim of this serial killer? Was that a slip?' Toni said as soon as they were out of earshot on the drive.

'Major struck me as too clever to do that.' Malcolm ruffled his Cromwell mop. 'She could have been fishing to get us to bite. If she is the killer and was playing us.'

'Let's background check her. Plus, we need the identity of her crime writer, I don't want these murders turning up in some best-selling novel.' Toni read a text on her phone. 'Worricker wants us in Newhaven for the press briefing. Fantastic, another chance to tell a herd of rabid reporters we have nada.'

'Mew will know Barbara Major told us she saw him at the Hydro, he might tell Lomax he nicked his car before we do.'

'Given we suspect Rex is nervous of Mew, I certainly don't want him confronting him. When Rex defended Kray-alikes his villains needed him breathing.'

'The uniforms on watch can knock on doors and do a head count.' Malcolm headed over to brief the constable stationed at the front of the house. Toni headed for her Jeep parked by a yew hedge. It would do the companion no harm to stew over night.

'A thought,' Malcolm said when he returned. 'Might Lomax have been gifted a set of weighted dice from one of the casino owners he got off? Not saying he's cheating at Leela, he might not realise.'

'Defence lawyers play dirty as default. Lomax is far from ruled out.'

Blacklock House receding in her rear-view mirror, Toni thought she could do with weighted dice to even their own odds.

# 39

*Freddy*

By the time Freddy had been discharged from the Royal Sussex
County Hospital it was half past seven at night. To avoid local
press wanting interviews with the women who, between them,
had saved the life of a teenaged boy, a nurse had given them
directions through a maze of corridors to an exit far from
Accident and Emergency. They had wandered along streets
until eventually arriving at an Aldi where they called a taxi.

It was Martha who asked the driver to drop them at the
Newhaven McDonald's. Famished, they needed very fast food
indeed. While Martha went over to collect their food from the
counter, Freddy texted Toni.

**Didn't see MM after all. Fxxx**

It felt a betrayal to report on Martha Merry with whom,
over the last hours, Freddy had shared so much. There was
no way Martha, who'd been warm and funny with the taxi
driver and now with a young woman at the counter, murdered
all those people.

Martha suggested they take their quarter-pounders and chips over to the wetlands, a landscaped park between the A259 and the ruins of a Victorian village called Tidemills. Beyond streetlamps and neon signs, the sky was lighter, they easily followed one of the paths to a bench.

'Damn, no signal.' Martha was checking her phone. *Was she hoping for a call?* 'I didn't have one at Blacklock House either.'

'Does that matter?'

'Not now I'm not seeing Patrick Bell.' Martha took a bite of her beefburger. 'Freddy, I never thought you'd get over those railings, but you knew exactly what to do.'

'Me and a friend have swum there since we were kids. The beach was closed in 2008. We worked out how to get over the barricades.' Freddy omitted saying the friend was Toni, not least because Toni was police. 'It's the best beach for miles.'

'Did you go over often?'

'Never.' Lifting the brioche off her beefburger, Freddy layered in chips and replaced it again. 'I remembered the plan as I started climbing.'

'You didn't know if you'd succeed? You could have been impaled on those railings or slipped off the wall.'

'I didn't let myself think that.'

'Christ, Freddy.' Martha took her hand.

'Foolhardy. That boy nearly drowned me, and if you hadn't revived him, he'd have died. We're in this together.' Filled with happiness, Freddy squeezed Martha's fingers.

'It was my fault in the first place.'

'How do you make that out?'

Above the hum of traffic on the road was the rustle of tall reeds by the path. Martha and Freddy were entirely alone.

'I keyed Tristan Robinson's car.' Martha took her hand away.

'Wait, *what?*' Freddy coughed on a slurp of Coke Zero.

'That man murdered on Dedmans Heath, with his wife Sally and their son? I vandalised his brand-new Range Rover.'

'How much damage?' The Coke curdled in her stomach. *Not the question.*

'A grand's worth?' Martha looked too calm. 'Not that he'll have to pay.'

'Why?' Freddy got there.

'To teach him a lesson. I've never done anything like it before.'

Freddy had never keyed a car either, but surely once was enough to make you the kind of person who did.

'Did you know Tristan Robinson?' Toni had not told her about the car so at least Freddy could be genuinely surprised.

'I was going out with him. It drove me mad that Tristan promised to leave his wife, but never did.'

*How mad?*

'How did you know where to find his car?'

'Tristan's wife Sally is a Facebook friend. She posts their every move up there. I knew that's where they'd be. Plus they go every Sunday afternoon. If they weren't there, I'd know he'd lied to me. I found the car and saw red.' Martha chomped on a chip. 'If Tris had accused me, I'd have confessed.'

Freddy's appetite had gone. Was it such a leap from keying a car to killing a family? Both were on the spectrum of hate and revenge.

'This is why the police suspect of you of murder?' *Thanks, Toni.*

'They don't know. I denied going into the car park.'

'You didn't tell them?' Freddy dumped the rest of her beefburger in the cardboard box and crammed shut the lid. Martha was tucking into hers.

'Of course not.' Martha covered her mouth as she chewed. 'They would have arrested me for murder.'

'If you'd admitted it, it points more towards you being innocent. Now they believe you are hiding something.' Freddy no longer cared if Martha asked her how she knew that. 'It's better to tell the truth.'

That afternoon Martha had performed CPR on a drowning boy and, against the odds, saved his life. She couldn't be a murderer. *Could she?*

'It is not. The police charge innocent people all the time. If I told them about the car, I'd have had to say about Tristan. Before I know it, I'd be doing life for murders I didn't commit.'

'I'm not sure that's—'

'*You* think I did it.' Martha was no longer friendly.

'I didn't say...' Now nervous, Freddy sat countering what might well be true. She hadn't noticed the light fade.

*She had Toni on speed dial.*

'The police think both sets of murders were committed by one killer. You didn't know James Ritchie and his son. Patrick Bell sabotaged your car and he stalked you. He lives a stone's throw from Blacklock House.' Seeking to reassure Martha, Freddy did not feel reassured.

The road beyond the wetlands was quiet. From across the marshes was the boom and drag of the sea.

In the darkness, Martha's voice was disembodied. 'I knew all the victims.'

# 40

*Martha*

In the drift of light from the lamp-post outside the café, Martha had been pacing for the half an hour since she'd returned from the wetlands. Every so often she made a pushing motion, grimacing with mimetic effort to push away the five words.

*I knew all the victims.*

*I knew all the victims.*

*I knew all the victims.*

Drunk on the emotion of saving a boy's life, they had sat in the wetlands like old friends. But they were not friends. Martha didn't know Freddy. Freddy had assured Martha she could trust her, but keen to get away, Freddy would have said anything. *Never trust anyone who says you can trust them.*

*I knew all the victims.*

Timothy knew she had been with Tristan. Patrick claimed to have seen her in the car park and he had told Haslem. *Garry wouldn't talk.* Each man knew something, but she had told Freddy everything.

There was someone at the salon window. *Freddy hadn't*

*waited until the morning.* The light behind her, Martha couldn't see her face. She was being given a second chance. She flung open the glass door.

'I promise I won't say anything.' Patrick was inside before Martha could stop him. 'Let me explain.' He pushed aside the chair between them. 'Garry was blackmailing me. He's been taking most of my salary since I moved into Blacklock House ten years ago. The day we got involved, I knew it must stop.' Patrick was pacing the salon as Martha had been minutes earlier.

'We have never been involved.'

'I wanted him gone.' Patrick looked wretched. 'Garry ran a security firm. He had contacts with criminals, many in the police, young coppers moonlighting on jobs because their salaries didn't run to high-end cars. He boasted that he was their real boss.'

'Why are you telling me this?' Martha said coldly.

'...Garry's clients hired him to remove obstacles: ex-wives, business partners, family. He'd bank their secrets or cash in. He took over property, cars. Lives. His motto was that "secrets are more precious than diamonds". He said only idiots underestimated him.'

'What did Haslem have over you?' Martha demanded.

'One of his clients – my friend Marcus – hired his firm to discover who was embezzling his company. Garry got proof and Marcus sacked me. I used the money to buy my flat and Garry realised I was a neighbour.' Patrick's tone was acid. 'He made the most of my accounting skills.'

'Why aren't you in prison?'

'Marcus wouldn't press charges.'

'You robbed a friend?' Timothy had been the nearest person

to a friend. Martha wouldn't have robbed him, although she couldn't say the same about Timothy. Keying Tristan's car was a form of robbery. Tristan would have reported her.

'Marcus had an affair with my girlfriend. He married her.' Patrick's face darkened. *Not so sorry then.*

'People fall out of love,' Martha said. 'Or they never loved that person in the first place.'

'We were meant to be together.'

'Where have I heard that before?' Martha returned to the remark about accounting skills. 'Are you still embezzling?'

'Yes, although I don't benefit.' Patrick looked resentful.

'Garry being murdered works well for you.' Martha felt behind her for her cutting scissors.

'It's not me, you have to believe me.'

'I do *not* have to believe you.' Martha gripped the scissors. *Go for the throat, he'll bleed out quickly.* 'Nor will the police when you tell them.'

'They needn't know. I opened an offshore account under a false name.' Patrick jerked as if he'd been electrocuted. 'Garry has the paperwork.'

'You are *disgusting.*' Patrick had told Garry Haslem she knew Tristan Robinson. Would she have paid for Haslem's silence? 'If you don't tell the police, I will.'

'I'd hate to have to tell them you keyed Tristan's car.' Patrick did sound regretful. 'If you were me, would you go to the police?'

The scissor blades flashed in the lamplight.

'Yes.' *Days ago, this would have been true.*

# 41

*Toni*

**Didn't see MM after all. Fxxx**

Cursing inwardly at Freddy's text, Toni pushed open the door into the Co-op.

'I'll be two minutes, OK?' she told the cashier, a young woman she hadn't seen before, who was looking pissed off to have a customer as she was closing.

In the confectionery aisle, Toni scooped up three Snickers bars then made for the chiller cabinet where she chose a packet of pasta parcels and a tub of carbonara sauce. It wouldn't match her home-made version, but at nearly ten o'clock, after a fourteen-hour day, even heating a pan of boiling water and operating the microwave felt onerous.

She spilled her shopping onto the counter and, waiting as the woman swiped them across the glass, consulted her phone. Self-torture. After that evening's media briefing, headlines would announce the police's – *her own* – failure to find a dangerous killer. Toni paid and, as the news page appeared she thanked the woman, gathered up the two

Snickers, pasta and sauce into her arms, and reading, left the Co-op.

*Heroes of the Sea.* BBC Sussex was leading with a rescue story. The nanosecond of relief was taken over by unutterable incandescence.

'Excuse me. *Stop.*' Toni managed to swerve as the woman lunged at her.

'*Whoa.* That was perilously close to assault.' Toni pulled open the passenger door of the car and rolled her shopping onto the seat. 'What's happening?'

'Don't move, *you're nicked.*'

'Ooh, I think that's my line, madam,' Toni said.

'You stole a Snickers bar. You're not getting away with it.'

'I just paid you, look, here's the docket.'

'I just replaced stock, there's three missing. I'm calling the police.'

'I *am* the police.'

'You're lying.'

'OK so,' Toni checked the badge of the woman's coat, 'Linda, we'll keep it calm. I'm going to reach into my jacket pocket and show you my badge.' She took out a leather wallet and flipped it open.

'Detective Inspector Antonia Kemp.' Linda put her hands to her face. 'Wait, you're the lady I saw on the news earlier.'

'That's me.' Toni sucked her teeth. 'Saying "lady" is too dainty for a hardened cop. *Woman* please.'

'I'm so sorry. I shouldn't have accused you. Me and my mates, we think it's great what you're doing. Keeping us safe.'

'I'm trying.' Not hard enough. 'Listen, Linda, a word to the brave – next time you accuse a customer of shoplifting, don't attempt to restrain them and certainly not on the pavement where you have no jurisdiction. You could be counter-charged for assault.'

'You're arresting me?' Linda gaped.

'No, no. No. Friendly advice, is all.' Toni snapped shut her badge wallet. 'Get off home. You're not paid for standing on the street with me.'

As Toni drove down Fort Road, she lifted a hand off the wheel and shook it. A Snickers bar landed on her lap. She ripped off the wrapping with her teeth and took a bite.

# 42

*Freddy*

'I shouldn't have told you any of that. Have you told the police?' Martha pushed past Freddy and slumped onto her sofa.

'How did you know where I lived?' Freddy remained at the door.

'That detective Antonia Kemp has been on the ten o'clock news appealing for witnesses. If you've told her, she'll arrest me. I had to get out, that wasn't the only reason, Patrick— *Wow*, this is like being underwater.'

Reenie Power had magicked her living room into a grotto. Lava lamps glowed green and blue. Muted illumination from a blue ceiling lampshade mingled with the pink heat-light in an aquarium, the last vestige of Reenie's small animal hotel. A shell-patterned carpet and wallpaper depicting species of fish completed the subterranean effect. The room, reflected in a blue-tinted mirror hung over the fireplace, was Freddy's favourite place in the world and she did not easily invite people to share it. She repeated her question, 'How did you know where I lived?'

'I guessed you lived near your family's old fishery on Beach Road. I started here and there was your van.'

'It's not parked outside my house.' *Freddy should have told Toni.*

'Two doors down from the van was this house, painted blue with a window like the sea, it had to be yours.'

'If you don't tell Toni and she finds out, even if you're innocent, you'll be charged with obstructing a murder investigation.' Freddy bit her lip, she'd said 'Toni'. She too was obstructing Toni's investigation. Christ, why was she protecting Martha Merry from Toni, her oldest friend and the SIO on the biggest murder case in the UK for years?

'You keep fish as well as sell them?' Martha had got up and was peering into the tank. 'Doesn't that feel weird?'

'What feels weird is you're talking about fish instead of reporting in to Detective Inspector Antonia Kemp.' Freddy had dreamed of living in the fish tank, to swoop and dart through the arch, the grottos and bridges, to whisk around the boat of the prince and princess from Disney's *Little Mermaid*, accompanied by Flounder, the princess's – and Freddy's – companion.

'I've done something stupid.'

'I know,' Freddy snapped. 'So have I because, as yet, I haven't rung the police. But you really need to, right now.'

'I've done something stupid. I've let Patrick hide in my flat.' Martha returned to the settee.

'You are kidding.'

'Garry Haslem was blackmailing him. Turns out that Patrick is an embezzler. He and Haslem were ripping off the residents of Blacklock House.'

In the silence that followed, Freddy channelled a Venezuelan cory fish drifting peacefully along the 'seabed'.

'Say something,' Martha said.

'Yeah, that is stupid.' Freddy dragged her gaze away from the tank.

'He asked me and I couldn't refuse. He scared me. All I could think was to find you. I don't have your phone number.'

'So, he killed Garry? That means he could be the serial killer.'

'I think he's innocent. If he'd wanted to kill Garry, why not years ago? I don't think he has it in him. And why would he kill Tristan or that family at Seaford Head? He didn't know them.'

*Freddy wasn't meant to know the police had linked all the killings with an old five-pound note.* She fumbled out, 'If Bell is innocent, why not tell the police?'

'I'm innocent and I haven't.'

'But you're going to?' *Unlike Patrick Bell, Martha had known all the victims.*

Freddy was scared out of her wits by a loud knock on the door.

'Don't answer.' Martha barred the exit.

The next knock was so loud Freddy envisaged the police were battering-ramming the door.

'Get out of the way.' Freddy pushed Martha aside and went out into the hall, flinging open the door.

'You're all over the local news.' *The police bit was right then.*

Her phone in one hand, a half-eaten Snickers in the other, Toni barged into the living room.

'You go and nearly drown saving some teenager who, out of his head on coke, decides to swim to France.'

Toni shoved her phone under Freddy's nose. Freddy stared at a photograph of herself and Martha on the beach.

## Heroes of the Sea

'Did you pay for that?' Looking at the Snickers, the first thing that occurred to Freddy was the last thing she should have said. The second thing that occurred was that Martha was nowhere to be seen.

'"Two friends enjoying an afternoon on the beach became local heroes. When she heard a shout of 'Help' from the sea, Frederica Power didn't hesitate. She dived off Newhaven's harbour wall and, fighting three-metre-high waves, brought fifteen-year-old Nathan Barker, unconscious and not breathing, to shore. Her friend, Newhaven hairdresser Martha Merry, performed CPR and between them they saved his life."' Toni glared at Freddy. 'You didn't think to tell me?'

'I haven't—' *Where was Martha?*

'Not only did you lie in your text and meet Merry, but you're best buddies? *Jesus*, Freddy, I know I shouldn't have asked you to entrap her, but you lied to me.' Toni's voice cracked.

'I needed time to think.' Freddy was back in the real sea – the one she'd been warned not to treat as a friend. *Sinking deeper and deeper.*

'How much time?' Toni aimed her Snickers at Freddy.

'Did you nick that?' Freddy knew Toni got a buzz from the risk. Minimal effort for maximum effect, she used to say.

Freddy also knew Toni only shoplifted when a case was going badly.

'I was this close to this kid doing a citizen's arrest. She tried to knock me down on the pavement.' Toni's humour vanished. 'Did Merry tell you anything useful?'

'Not really.' Freddy hoped that, on the pretend seabed, her blush wouldn't show. 'One day you will be nicked. You'll lose your career all for a chocolate bar.'

'Right now, with too many theories and no evidence, bring it on.' Toni crashed out of the room. Following, Freddy saw her Jeep double-parked, the engine on. Toni hadn't intended to come in. Although she had lied – twice – to her best friend, Freddy felt hurt.

'You rock, by the way.' One foot on the running board, Toni leaned on the open driver's door.

'Why?'

'You saved a life today.' Toni climbed in and as she shut the door added, 'Proud you're my person, Freds.'


'*You stalked me.*' Eyes blazing, Martha appeared from the small kitchen off the living room. 'You made out we met by accident when you're actually a police informer. You're *worse* than Patrick Bell.'

'Since you were listening, you'll know I did not inform Toni. *Twice*,' Freddy stormed. 'I am sorry that I agreed to help Toni and I'm sorry I misled you. It's because I felt we were becoming friends that I haven't told Toni.'

'Misled? You lied to me.'

'So did you.' Freddy lost it. 'I lied by omission and literally to the police so you do *not* get the higher ground.'

'I told you.' Fixed on one of the slowly evolving lava lamps, Martha's voice dropped. 'If I tell them I keyed Tristan's car, that I know all the victims and signed up as Sally Robinson's friend on Facebook, they'll be questioning me until I'm so tired I will confess, it's what they do. You heard that woman, she needs *a solve*.'

'I missed the bit where Toni said she would fit you up.' Freddy was angry on Toni's behalf. 'If you don't go there now, *I* will.'

'I have a better idea.' Martha opened the living room door. 'Why don't you tell your pet detective if she charges me with murder, I'll say I witnessed her confessing she stole chocolate. Let's see how that goes down.' She slammed out of the house.

'What about Patrick Bell?' Freddy followed her out. The street was empty. There was no car and no one was on the pavement.

Freddy returned to the living room where she escaped. *She was basking with the orange cory amongst swaying fronds, neither fish nor mermaid had a care in the world.*

# 43

*Toni*

Light spilled out of the frosted glass pane of the Murder Investigation Room onto the tiled passage. Lit only by a bright yellow anglepoise lamp his wife had bought him for his desk, Malcolm looked even more like Thomas Cromwell labouring over writs and death sentences.

'What bit of "go home to your family" did you miss?' Upset after her confrontation with Freddy, Toni nearly cried when she saw her second favourite person at his desk.

'Right back attcha.' Malcolm was leafing through a thick wad of papers. 'I did snatch supper, while I'm assuming you've only had chocolate.'

'You should be a detective.' Toni couldn't say that narrowly avoiding arrest and badly falling out with her best friend had killed her appetite. 'What you working on?'

'Sheena has pulled up a bunch of colds and solves involving a blitz-type murder going back twenty years.' Malcolm jerked a thumb at a stack of buff files on the table behind him. 'I've drawn blanks so far.'

'It's a long shot. Our killer could have lived abroad until

now, or he is a natural born murderer, or it's beginner's luck.' Toni took half the pile off the table and pushing aside the sheaf of Decision Logs – *crap decisions* – opened the first file.

For an hour neither officer spoke. There was only the rustle and flip of paper as they worked through documents and photographs of murders past and the Exclude piles grew. At last Malcolm said, 'I've got one.'

'Go on.' Although Malcolm's voice betrayed nothing, Toni felt excitement. Malcolm was indeed a good detective.

'Fifteen years ago. Adrian Moon, forty, found murdered on a footpath in the grounds of Reculver Abbey in Kent.' Malcolm swivelled his chair to face Toni. 'Moon's seven-year-old son, Barney, was also stabbed but recovered. Kenneth Todd was charged with the crimes.'

'On what evidence?'

'You may ask. Blood on his coveralls didn't match either victim.' Malcolm rubbed his forehead. 'Nor did it match a human, it was pig's blood. Todd was a keen birdwatcher which explained his being there. He used to go after his shift at an abattoir. Seems the area is rife with birds. Listen to the prosecuting QC's question, '"Was it your habit to hide in the reeds and watch birds?"' Malcolm did a haw-haw voice. 'To which Todd says, "yes". He agrees throughout. Really, the jury had no choice but to find him guilty.'

'Witnesses?'

'A man and a woman had each seen Todd there but neither could confirm it was the day of the murder. A week after the murders, Todd was spotted at the actual site of the attacks. When police arrested him, he claimed he'd seen Adrian and Barney Moon on the day they were attacked.'

'I suppose the line-up clinched it?' Toni groaned. Witness

identifications were either a detective's friend or worst enemy. At least now, witnesses weren't expected to go nose to nose with a potential culprit.

'No, Barney picked out a copper they'd pulled in to help. The clincher was Todd giving special knowledge. He knew the killer had posed Moon's body lying on his back by a reed bed, his son's school bag on his lap. Barney lay a few feet away.'

'How long did he get?' Toni couldn't see why the case had got Malcolm's attention. *Unless*, 'Has Kenneth Todd been released?'

'Yes, after only three years, he got out on appeal and oh *wow*—' Malcolm snatched at a paper, 'His defence lawyer was Rex Lomax.'

'How did he wangle that?' Toni's head was buzzing.

'Todd had learning difficulties. Lomax claimed his confession was motivated by his wanting to impress the police. Todd's possession of special knowledge could have come from leading questions. He fitted their profile of the killer so, consciously or unconsciously, the police wove the evidence around their suspect.'

'That's a stretch,' Toni snorted. 'You've got the transcription there – when was Todd meant to have been led? Cynical ol' me suspects the SIO was up for retirement so he or she kicked the can down the lane. Who was the SIO?'

'Henry Morgan, a chief inspector. I'll check if he's still around.' Malcolm jotted the name in his notebook.

'Let's talk to Lomax again. The murderer could be a relation of the Moons. Barney Moon would be in his early twenties by now. What if he's taunting Lomax, killing ever closer? Is Lomax next? All relatives of victims need a culprit behind bars to properly move on. Lomax blew the Moon case wide open.' Toni should be cheered by the link between Moon and the recent killings. But the link was a defence barrister. Go by that and a good hundred cases in the UK were linked.

'If Todd was the wrong man, why blame Lomax?' Malcolm said.

'Rex Lomax got guilty men off. Maybe Kenneth Todd was guilty. Lomax isn't ruled out. He could be killing in the same pattern to underline he was right to get Todd off. Serial killers have their own logic.'

'Adrian Moon's wife had died of cancer the year before he was murdered. There's an older brother, Charles, who'd be in his sixties now. If he's alive I'll chase him down. Parents were alive for the appeal, but are both dead now.' Malcolm handed Toni a newspaper cutting in a plastic sleeve.

The image was depressingly familiar. Three people, an elderly man and woman with their remaining son – Charles Moon – walking towards court amid a cluster of press dragons, snapping away at them. A smaller photograph showed a grim-faced Henry Morgan, a woman in a mac that matched Morgan's, their collars up, keeping pace. Even if Morgan had done a proper job with the evidence, circumstances, timings, even DNA, could make four look like five.

Arguably an improvement on her own case where disparate facts added up to nothing.

# 44

Nestled in a dip in the Downs, Blacklock House was washed in early morning sunlight. The stark shadow of the – silent – fountain slanted across the neglected lawn on which buttercups and daisies now flourished. The forensic tape and the tent had gone. Only a patrol car parked under trees near the stables remained. The wheelbarrow had been taken away for testing.

The forecast predicted sunny intervals with a 15 per cent chance of rain. In such a sunny interval Rex had suggested he and Timothy breakfast on the terrace, although by the time Timothy brought out the tray laden with a basket of toast, jug of hot milk and other breakfast paraphernalia, the interval was over. A slight chill in the air hinted at autumn.

'How grand, I'll come to this hotel again.' Pronging seashell shapes of butter arranged on a plate and smearing them on his toast, Rex gave no sense that he knew of Timothy's tea at the Hydro Hotel the previous afternoon. 'Are these your napkins?' He held up one corner on which was embroidered *TM*. 'You fit in here better than me.'

'Blacklock House is a perfect fit.' Timothy didn't return Rex's jolly smile. 'I don't go to hotels.'

'On principle?' Rex's fleeting expression would, had she been there, have confirmed Toni Kemp's suspicion that the tough criminal defence lawyer was fearful of his companion.

'I can't afford them.' Timothy took a neat peck of toast.

'I've had my fill of hotels. A downside of my work was travelling, I missed Emily.' Rex's hand shook as he lifted his cup.

'Let me.' Timothy dabbed the plate with his napkin.

'Sorry,' Rex mumbled.

'Have more.' Timothy topped up Rex's coffee from the cafetière.

'Thank you.' Rex didn't attempt to drink. 'Are you prepared for your interview with the police?'

'I don't need to prepare.'

'Leela says this could be your last breakfast of freedom.'

Rex's laugh was perhaps too hearty because Timothy shot him a quizzical look.

'Why should they suspect me?'

'The police suspect everyone until they eliminate them. Garry's murder is too close to home. It's obvious Antonia Kemp is drawing a tight circle of suspicion around this house.' Rex gazed at the fountain where King Tut, the lawn his again, was strutting around the vast basin. 'I had my grilling yesterday afternoon. While you were... out.'

'Rex, about yesterday...' Timothy's tone was smooth. 'I must apologise, I took your car without asking...'

'I'm so *glad* you are able to admit—' Rex visibly brightened.

'...I'd forgotten things from Waitrose on Monday afternoon. I got caught up with Barbara and her crime research and left without buying anything. She told me about Sunday's murders. She seems obsessed, you saw her at the meeting on Monday night. I shouldn't say this, since Barbara Major is your friend, but I don't trust her.'

'These murders have distracted us all.'

'You must be upset,' Timothy exclaimed. 'I barely knew Haslem, but you'd been neighbours for years.'

'It's upsetting when anyone dies,' Rex said. 'Timothy, I wouldn't blame you if you want to leave Blacklock House. You never anticipated being a companion to murder.'

'No one would want to murder me,' Timothy retorted. 'As I said at luncheon yesterday, I've done nothing wrong.'

'I do think you must take this interview with Kemp seriously. Tell her everything you can think of, even if it's apparently irrelevant. For instance, I mentioned that girl we met on Dedmans Heath.'

'How is that relevant or irrelevant? That was the week before the Robinsons were killed.'

'I know we disagreed, but I remain certain that girl was Madeleine Robinson, the daughter who apparently stayed at home last Sunday and thus is alive today, thank god.'

'I know who she is, but compare her picture in the news – the girl we saw looked entirely different.'

'Perhaps.' Seemingly abandoning his breakfast, Rex sat back, his hands clamped under folded arms. 'As for not being a target of this killer, I can tell you that serial killers go for the vulnerable – the elderly, the prostituted, children, trusting young women – I'm in that group and you are not. But they are also opportunistic and we are both, all of us are, like Bunty's owl, essentially caged. Speaking of which, where is that bird?'

'Probably been eaten by a fox.' Frowning with distaste, Timothy folded his coffee-stained napkin.

'Caged and at the mercy of a killer. I urge you to leave.'

'I can look after myself.' Timothy seemed unperturbed. 'And isn't this exactly why you needed a companion? Why don't you leave?'

'I'm not sure any of us will be allowed. Detective Inspector Kemp won't want us fleeing to all corners of Great Britain, we need to be under the nose of those coppers out there.' Rex pointed at the uniformed woman at that moment giving King Tut a wide berth as she walked at the edge of the lawn.

From within the house there came a series of knocks, four in quick succession.

'That's the police.' Although he had claimed the interview was of little consequence, jumping up, Timothy looked aghast. 'They said to meet them at the tennis court, why have they come here?'

It was not the police.

'Martha, what a lovely surprise, sit down.' As she stepped out onto the terrace, Rex struggled up and waved Martha to Timothy's chair. 'Timothy, any chance you can make Martha a fresh pot of coffee?'

'I have to go.' Timothy hurried out.

'It's Rex I need, not you or coffee.' Martha didn't sit down.

'How can I help?' Rex looked concerned.

'Please can you be my lawyer?' Martha said. 'The police think I'm the serial killer.'

# 45

Blackened groynes were exposed by the receding tide. Candy-coloured beach huts were coming to life as occupants, playing Wendy-house, unfolded chairs and tables, set kettles and frying pans of bacon and eggs on stoves and brewed the day's first cup of tea. Beyond, cladded houses with curving balconies perhaps intended to echo the waves had weathered to shabby. And beyond them, a sacred swathe of green was pilgrimaged by men wheeling golf bags.

West Cliff, a one-sided cul-de-sac of Edwardian villas was, before the cladded townhouses, Whitstable's western outpost with only the golf course and the railway line beyond. The ancient town, famous for oyster beds, sat looking across a broad estuary to the Isle of Sheppey and Southend-on-Sea and had, in the last twenty years, morphed from workaday and a few people's secret into the intelligentsia of London's choice of weekend retreat.

A girl pedalling her bicycle in a desultory fashion along West Cliff was either unaware of the Audi crawling behind her or deliberately ignoring it.

Malcolm Lane was a patient man, with daughters, he liked to see girls take the space. After a two-hour drive from Sussex to east Kent, Malcolm was content to crawl at three miles an hour. Having left time for what turned out to be no queues, he was early.

The girl bumped her bike onto the pavement and pushed it in through the gate of the end villa. Malcolm drifted past and parked by a dog wastebin attached to a bollard that blocked a path which, he knew from Street View, led to a railway footbridge in one direction and the sea in the other.

Opposite the bollard was the gate to a large detached stuccoed house. The garden fence, stretching off parallel with the path, was buried under thick clematis and honeysuckle. The entrance was overshadowed by bushes and more climbing plants which, although the sun shone brightly, contributed to an odd air of seclusion and gloom.

Tablet under his arm, Malcolm unlatched the gate and stooped under the arch of foliage to walk up a terracotta brick path to a porch door. A rack of upturned wellington boots was on one side. A milk carrier on the other. Hanging baskets either side of the door and pots of lavender and pinks surprised Malcolm. The sense of gloom had lifted.

The man who answered the door, in polo shirt and chinos with regulation haircut, looked exactly what he was, a retired police detective.

'I keep the outside looking shabby, it discourages the bad guys and hides the CCTV.' Henry Morgan passed Malcolm a coffee and led him into a living room, most of which was taken up with a large bay window giving a panoramic view of a garden easily a contender for horticultural prizes. At the far end, visible behind a trellis, was a trampoline.

'The grandchildren.' Morgan grinned. 'Never got a trampoline for my own two and now neither of them has a garden big enough. Bank of Dad and Mum, eh?'

'They do take up most of the garden,' Malcolm said. 'Trampolines, I mean.'

It was Morgan who brought the affable chat about family and then Malcolm's route to Whitstable from Newhaven to an end.

'That defence lawyer has blood on his hands.'

'Rex Lomax?'

'He knew Todd was guilty. The man confessed, he gave us stuff he could only have known if he'd done it,' Morgan said. 'I'd like to help you, Sergeant Lane, but this is a blind alley. Todd was guilty and since he's dead, he can't be your killer.'

'There are similarities between the murders of Adrian Moon and his son and these cases in Sussex. All were attacks with more wounds inflicted than necessary to extinguish life. The Moons were father and son. Two of our killings were fathers and sons, and a mother.'

'Not the man in the wheelbarrow?' Morgan tweaked the shoulder of his polo shirt.

'Same killer, we think. It's possible Haslem disturbed his killer or knew him.' Malcolm placed his mug on the nearest of variously sized circular tables, each a gradation of blue, dotted about the room like giant mushrooms.

'Or another nutter used the family murders as cover. It's an easy enough MO to imitate.'

'These were found at each of the sites.' Malcolm pulled up the images of the five-pound note on his tablet. 'Ring any bells?'

''Fraid not, but we are talking fifteen years ago.'

'There were no prints on the notes. There are figures that could be the number of victims.'

'Malcolm, I did warn you it would be a wasted journey. We got our man. Lomax discredited our witnesses and portrayed Todd as a vulnerable young man easily suggestible. But Todd held down a job and knew the names of birds. He wasn't stupid.' Morgan grabbed their empty mugs. 'You and your guvnor are chasing a dead man. Kenneth Todd was a vicious murderer who should have ended his days behind bars. May he RIH.'

'RIH?'

'Rot in Hell.'

# 46

*Toni*

'*Get it in the bag before bodies reach double figures.*' Chief Super Worricker's stricture at the media circus the night before rang in Toni's ears as she drove to Blacklock House to meet Rex Lomax's companion. Malcolm had left early for Whitstable in Kent to meet retired Chief Inspector Henry Morgan – 'the Man on the Moon' as Sheena dubbed him, SIO on the Adrian Moon case fifteen years ago.

Toni had arranged to meet Timothy Mew in the tennis court. She wanted him out of the flat and earshot of Lomax, who, despite the affable elderly man image, was firmly in her sights. She found Mew crouched on a bench at the net like an umpire.

'Do you play tennis?' she asked conversationally. Then seeing the parlous state of the court – mildewed net, cracked surface – 'Oh, perhaps not here?'

'I was county champion at school.' Timothy's answer was knee-jerk.

'Impressive.' Toni took the other end of the bench and turned so she was facing Mew. 'I had a demon serve which always took off way over the fence. No aim, was my trouble.'

Timothy had nicked his employer's car for tea in a posh hotel where he'd called himself Lord Mew. Rex had said Timothy kept losing at the creepy snakes and ladders which revealed him as horrible. Not that Toni held much store by any kind of profiling, but at base-line Lomax's companion was dishonest. Freddy thought the same about Toni.

*Freddy.* Toni felt as if punched in the stomach.

'Where were you at school?'

'Eton.'

'So, living in Blacklock House is business as usual.' Toni affected a dry laugh.

'Pretty much.' Timothy didn't expand.

*Check for a Timothy Mew at Eton circa early nineties,* Toni texted Sheena. None of the Blacklock residents had a good word for Mew. Not a great indicator because established groups were often wary of new members, Toni had seen that with her team. No one – Toni included – liked disruption to established dynamics. In Mew's case, Toni had to dismiss her personal bias against a young man holding the dubious role of companion. Again, she wondered what was in it for Mew.

'How long have you been Rex Lomax's companion?'

'Five weeks and two days.' Mew had found a tennis ball under the bench and was tipping it from one hand to the other. 'Or five weeks last Monday.'

'We coppers love specificity. Why did you want the job?'

'It's not a job.' Timothy was quick to correct her. 'My work is training for Silversage, a helpline for lonely elderly people.'

'But you have to do lots of tasks for Rex Lomax. Essentially you're a lodger without benefits.' Toni poked the bear.

'It's *quid pro quo*. I offer my companionship to Rex in return for a room in his flat. I'm *not* a paid employee, the only money that changes hands is my peppercorn rent.' Bouncing the tennis ball, Timothy missed the catch. 'This is my home.'

'You're not put off by these murders? Pretty sure I would be.'

'Murder happens everywhere.'

'Not generally in your own garden.'

'Rex did suggest I leave.'

'You're staying?' Toni noted Lomax had offered his companion an out, it could confirm her suspicion that Rex was nervous of Mew.

'I told him I don't feel in danger. And actually, Rex would still need a companion, someone to take him to Mass and spend his evenings with, do his shopping, make meals. He's lonely.'

'Very noble – that all strikes me as onerous.' Freddy had said she was lonely. Would Freddy let Toni back into her life? Freddy had not told her she had, after all, seen Martha Merry. *Why not?* It didn't take a detective to see Freddy liked Martha. Toni hadn't seen evidence that Freddy had reliable taste in women. She roused herself.

'Who actually found Haslem dead? You were round the fish van on the drive, the wheelbarrow was at the side of the house by the stables.'

'It's called the carriage house. We heard the fountain.' Mew bounced the ball again and again missed it. This time he let it roll away onto the court. *Cackhanded for a tennis champion.*

'All of you, at once?'

'It was the crime writer's researcher Barbara Major, she considers herself observant.'

'Do you think she is?'

'Nosy, I call it. She was following me in the supermarket on Monday afternoon. I'm sure she hates that I got the job of companion.'

'So, it is a job?'

'A turn of phrase.' Mew's face briefly clouded. *The bear was poked.* 'She has a crush on Rex. Classic spinster, I'd guess she's after his money. Her flat apparently comes with the job. If her crime writer decides to get a new researcher, she'd have to leave.'

'Barbara Major told you this?'

'Rex mentioned it one evening.'

'Has Rex Lomax got money?'

'I should think so. He was a top defence lawyer and he owns that flat.'

'Who gets it when he dies? He doesn't have children and his wife is dead.'

'No idea.' Mew's disinterested expression didn't fool Toni. Was Mew hoping – *intending* – it would be him?

'Let's go back to Tuesday morning when you all found Haslem. You seem as observant as Barbara and you're new to the group. How did people react?'

'Lady Dorothy said, "The damn fool was out of his head." Sylvia looked cross and Barbara said something that sounded like "just desserts". No one liked Haslem and I could see why. He was pretty obnoxious. Only the fishmonger was calm. When you arrived, I heard her telling you that you were the first person she thought of calling. Seems she has your private number.'

'I believe she had CID's direct line. I answered.' Toni had forgotten Freddy had rung her direct. Mew *was* observant. *A guilty man would be.* It occurred to her that Freddy had not told her about Martha because Freddy was in love with Martha. If Toni had given Freddy a chance to explain, Freddy would have told her. Feeling marginally better she asked, 'Where did you go yesterday afternoon? Rex seemed not to know.'

'Rex has a rest in the afternoon. I do *not* need his permission to leave the house or to say where I'm going.' Mew reddened. *Not that good a liar.*

'He seemed under the impression you had taken his car.'

'I don't have my own car.'

'That must be inconvenient, living out here in the countryside without transport.'

'I have Rex's car.'

'Rex also seemed to think you only had permission to use his car for shopping or taking him out. Did I get that wrong, I wonder?' Toni's wonderment was wide-eyed.

'It's not like he needed it.' Timothy was stony-faced.

'I'm confused. Barbara Major says she saw you in the Hydro Hotel in Eastbourne.'

Toni tensed – if Mew went for her, passing every fitness test, she was ready.

'As I said, she is a busybody.' Timothy's expression darkened.

'Or observant?'

'She claimed to be there having lunch with her crime writer. She lied – I know she followed me there. She made me bring her back. She is trying to get Rex to sack me.'

'Can he sack you from what is not a job?' Toni got up and retrieved the tennis ball. '*Catch.*'

Timothy put up both hands. The ball sailed past him. *Gotcha.*

'If you're trying to make me admit I murdered Garry Haslem and Tristan Robinson and those others, you won't because I didn't.'

'Rex Lomax is convinced that you and he met Madeleine Robinson on Dedmans Heath the week before.'

'He is wrong.' Timothy shrugged.

'Odd for a defence lawyer,' Toni said. 'In my experience lawyers of any species are observant.' And usually wrong, but she wouldn't develop the argument. She swished through her phone and went over to Timothy on the bench. 'Have another look please.'

'No. Rings no bells.' Timothy gave the picture a cursory glance.

'Take your time, Lord Mew.'

'Still no.' Timothy glared at Toni. 'I signed that in the Hydro Hotel register to wind up Barbara Major.'

'Surely you signed in when you arrived? Ms Major claims she saw you on the terrace eating your ten-storey tea.'

'I saw her going to the Ladies as I was passing through reception, she didn't see me.' *Pants on fire.*

'Why do you think Haslem was a victim of the serial killer?' Toni switched tack.

'Rex said I shouldn't be so certain I wasn't in danger because serial killers usually kill at random.' Timothy Mew ran a hand over his shaved scalp. 'OK, I'm not proud of using Rex's car for the Hydro Hotel, and putting Lord was a joke. I did knock on Rex's bedroom door to ask, he didn't answer.'

'We've all done things we're not proud of,' Toni murmured. 'Over these five weeks and two days, how well had you got to know Garry Haslem?'

'Not at all. The longest I spent with him was Monday evening at this meeting Rex dragged me to and made me take the minutes. I'm doing more than the sixteen hours. I'm more like a slave. If you want to know, that's why I took his stupid car.' Timothy spat out the words. 'As for Haslem, it was obvious everyone hated him, no wonder one of them murdered him.'

'You're saying one of your neighbours murdered Garry Haslem.' This was proving a common idea amongst the residents.

'Rex thinks so and with his background, he should know.'

'Wasn't Martha Merry at the meeting? It seems likely she was the last person to see Haslem alive.' Toni watched Mew's face. '*Apart* from the killer.'

'If you're asking could Martha have killed Mew, I have no idea. I do know Martha is more likely to kill Patrick Bell for stalking her and because Haslem had told her Bell tampered with her car to stop her leaving on Monday. I know he overheard me telling Martha about Tristan Robinson when we were in his flat. Bell didn't look pleased.'

'Why should Bell mind you talking about Robinson?'

'I thought that was why you arrested Martha?' Timothy's surprised expression reminded Toni of Barbara Major letting slip Mew had taken Lomax's car. There were more snakes than ladders in Blacklock House.

'What was?' Toni didn't correct 'arrest'. *Did Mew expect Martha Merry to be arrested?*

'Martha was having an affair with Tristan Robinson.'

# 47

*Freddy*

The sign on the door of Head Case was turned to closed.

'Been shut since yesterday. She swam out and saved a kid from drowning yesterday afternoon, it was all over the news. So like Martha, brave as they come.' A woman, her hair expertly cut, delicate highlights convincing but for the roots, peered through the glass.

'I read about that.' Thinking it churlish to say it was she and not Martha who had risked her life, Freddy was interested that the woman considered Martha brave. *Were serial killers brave?*

'...time like this she needs real friends,' the woman was saying.

'She has you.' Freddy didn't call herself a friend.

'I'm just a cut and colour, love. Never make friends of hairdressers or dentists is my motto – what if you fall out? If Martha doesn't open tomorrow, I'm going to have to go elsewhere.' The woman crossed to what proved to be a Mazda sports car and vroomed noisily away.

*Why didn't Martha have friends?*

It had been a spur of the moment thing to detour to Martha's salon after her round. Fish had featured on *MasterChef* and Freddy had correctly predicted a run on plaice and scallops. Normally this would have left her buoyant, but after her argument with Toni and then with Martha, nothing could dent a mood that was, at best, dismal.

Freddy prayed to God that Martha had, after all, gone to the police.

She drove down to West Quay, paid the two-pound fee to the man in the kiosk and parked by the harbour arm. The beach was crowded with sunbathers, children racing in and out of the sea, people on boards riding waves, a woman floated astride a large inflatable swan. There was no trace of yesterday's drama.

And no Martha. *Was that a good sign?*

Freddy's phone rang.

'Hi, Toni.' Toni wanted to make up. Even when she hadn't started it, at school big-hearted Toni had always been first in to sort things.

'Here's an educated guess. You knew Martha Merry was having an affair with Tristan Robinson, didn't you?'

Freddy nodded.

'*Didn't you?*'

*Ouch.* Freddy moved the phone from her ear.

'I told Martha that if she didn't go to the police today, I would. I thought that's where she was. Her salon is closed.'

'I know that. I'm outside Head-freakin'-Case right now. *Your lovely Martha has done a runner.* Don't move, I've got another call.' Dead air.

Freddy was tempted to chuck the phone into the sea and do a runner herself.

'OK, so Martha Merry has turned up at the police station.' Toni was back. 'Sheena has put her on ice until I get there.'

'Thing is, Toni, I knew Martha wasn't a killer—' *Martha would not have gone to the police if she was guilty.*

'How many innocent people get lawyered-up?'

'What?'

'Martha has hired Rex Lomax as her lawyer.'

'She probably wants Rex as moral…' *Toni had gone.*

At the end of the harbour arm the lighthouse shimmered in the sunshine. The rider of the white swan had come ashore, the swan was deflating to a pool of plastic on the shingle.

# 48

*Martha*

It was the afternoon by the time Martha finished giving her statement and, to her astonishment – she had expected a charge of withholding information at the least – Detective Inspector Kemp had said she was free to go. *For now.*

On Rex's advice – *never good to lie to the police* – Martha told DC Britton she had twice cut James Ritchie's hair so knew him as well as Tristan.

*'Once you knew I'd vandalised Tristan's car and we were in a relationship, you would think I killed them all.'*

*'Did you?'*

*'No.'*

*'Why did you only cut Ritchie's hair twice?'*

*'He didn't come back after that.'*

*'Did that make you cross?'*

*'You win some and lose some. I told you I didn't kill any of them. And I have an alibi for when James Ritchie and his son were murdered.'*

In a break during the two-hour interview, Rex called Timothy and asked him to collect them. Timothy was the last person Martha wanted to see – he'd dobbed her in to the police and robbed her of the chance to get to them first. OK, so Martha knew she should have told the detective yesterday as Freddy had urged her, but it was none of Timothy's business. *Why had he gone out of his way to point the finger at her?* However, Martha had not objected, Rex had come with her even though, retired, he couldn't represent her and he'd said, *'We deserve a treat.'*

As they came out of the police station, Martha was unsurprised to see Timothy – stony-faced – at the wheel of Rex's Jaguar. Martha *was* surprised to find Freddy on the back seat and at how glad she felt to see her. Climbing in, Martha returned Freddy's mumbled greeting.

Rex gave Timothy directions to a hotel in Eastbourne. The merest tip of his head told Martha that Timothy had heard. Martha had spoken honestly when she had told people that, despite being supposed friends with Timothy for ten years, she hardly knew him. However, Martha did know enough to see by his stiff shoulders and grim expression that Timothy was angry.

'Your job is to strip this thing bare. Come on, guys, tuck in.' Rex raised his teacup at a silvered stand filled with cakes including miniature éclairs, lemon curd and meringues, with dainty sandwiches on the lower levels. The last time Martha had had a posh hotel tea was at the Brighton Grand for her mum's seventieth ten years ago, not long before she died.

'It's a long time since I had a tea like this.' Freddy spoke Martha's thoughts. 'Is this a place you know well, Rex?'

'No. I used to go up to London, to the Ritz with Emily. For

wedding anniversaries, and birthdays. Even Christmas when our flat in Blacklock House was being restored. I don't go now since Emily died, it's too painful.' Rex raised his cup. 'You are the perfect company with whom I dare get back in the saddle.'

'Have you been here before, Timothy?' Freddy asked. Martha could not trust herself to look at him. *Tell-tale.*

'No.' Skipping the sandwiches, Timothy lifted an éclair from the top of the stand. 'I've been to many similar hotels though.'

'As I told Martha, we deserve a treat. We've all talked to the police and what with finding Haslem on Tuesday morning, we've had a ghastly twenty-four hours.'

'Rex, I should be treating *you*.' Martha was horrified at her temerity. Rex was eating like a bird. Going to the police had exhausted him. She'd taken advantage of his generosity. *She was worse than Timothy.* 'I shouldn't have asked you.'

'I'm glad you did. It was useful. I collared one of the detectives, a callow chap called Darren. He gave me the impression they are in the dark with this case. Timothy, while I'm sure you meant no harm, pointing them towards Martha distracted them.' Rex smiled at Timothy.

Rex believed her. *In that moment Martha loved Rex.*

'I said you knew the victims because I assumed you'd told them.' Timothy hadn't touched his éclair. 'No problem *if* you didn't murder them.'

'What do you mean "if"?' Martha confronted Timothy. In his cream linen suit, waistcoat and university tie – Timothy hadn't been to university – he was a cut price P. G. Wodehouse.

'I only told Kemp what I knew.' Timothy nibbled his éclair.

'Timothy and I were talking about these murders over

breakfast. Serial murders spread doubt and distrust. It is too easy to suspect our nearest and dearest. The smallest gesture, look, or off-the-cuff comment could indicate something sinister. We will all be relieved when the police find their man.' Rex raised his teacup. 'Time to toast the two heroes in our midst. Guys, don't slough it off. You are life-savers.'

'I'm CPR trained,' Martha said. 'It was Freddy who dived into the sea and got the boy.'

'I didn't have time to think about it or perhaps I might not have.'

Everyone clinked teacups and, for a while, dwelling on the sunny lawn beyond the terrace, no one spoke.

'Timothy, you should probably know that you are not the only one to tell tales.' Rex was all smiles. 'Our resident crime researcher told detectives she saw you here at the hotel yesterday afternoon. Did Detective Inspector Antonia Kemp mention it? I hope you put her straight and, as you have explained, you have never been here before?'

'She is a troublemaker.' Timothy looked horribly pale.

'Barbara is old school, don't knock it. With a murderer on the loose, we need keenly observant neighbours.'

Timothy had been to this hotel yesterday? Martha got why Rex had brought them to the Hydro. *Timothy had been caught getting up to his old tricks.* Her anxiety for Rex increased.

*It never paid to play tricks back.*

# 49

*Toni*

Five o'clock. Newhaven police station. Detective Inspector Toni Kemp and Sergeant Malcolm Lane sat one side of the central table; behind them sat some twenty men and women murmuring into phones and tapping at screens.

'Patrick Bell has taken us back to square one. Garry Haslem was blackmailing *all* the residents of Blacklock House except, it seems, Rex Lomax.' Toni began the debrief of Malcolm and Sheena's interview with Patrick Bell who, ten minutes earlier with no evidence linking him to the crimes, they had let walk out without charge. 'Lomax was a defence lawyer – how come he has no blackmailable secrets?'

'Perhaps Haslem wouldn't go up against a man with likely recourse to an army of villains,' Malcolm said.

'Marcus Rutherford has confirmed Bell's story that Bell ripped him off.' Clasping her phone, Sheena joined Toni and Malcolm at the table. 'He hadn't wanted Bell charged, he still feels guilty that, as he put it, he stole Bell's girlfriend. Not that the woman herself didn't have a say.' Sheena pulled a face. 'Bell ripped off Rutherford because he went off with his girlfriend.' She tipped back in her chair. 'Rutherford hires Haslem's security firm then finds out his oldest mate has embezzled him so can't face bringing charges. Effectively he hands Bell to Haslem. Rutherford is even willing to be a character witness if we charge Bell; he said he'd never murder anyone deliberately.'

'That's all right then,' Toni huffed. 'From what Bell has told us, every single one of the residents had reason to kill Haslem, but the five-pound note says only one of them actually did. We are missing something that is right under our noses. Walk us through it again, Sheena.'

'Bell claims he went downstairs because Martha hadn't returned from the car.' Sheena précised the interview. 'He thought Martha had gone to get her overnight bag, but Martha has told us she made it clear she had no intention of staying. When Bell got outside, Martha had gone because Haslem had mended her car. Bell claims he didn't see Haslem after Martha left Blacklock House so only found out Haslem was dead the next morning when he went – again uninvited – to Martha's salon and she got the call from Timothy Mew. Bell admitted tracking her when she'd brought Mew to Blacklock House and tampering with her car. He said he was in love with her and Merry had led him on. He said he threatened to report that he'd seen her key Robinson's car. However, on Rex Lomax's advice, Merry cut Bell off at the pass by telling us herself.'

'God, this lot are a shower,' Toni groaned. 'We know from Freddy and her customers at the fish van, Bell left Blacklock House just after Freddy arrived and *before* they all found Haslem dead in the wheelbarrow. It confirms Bell's version.'

'Bell collected the blackmail cash from the residents. He

knew all their secrets,' Sheena said. 'Number one, Dr Martyn Burnett resigned from his practice to avoid being struck off for stealing oxycodone to which he is addicted. He said that now Sylvia Burnett supplies her husband. She is Harold Shipman without bodies. She overprescribes the medication or does so incorrectly. She does a house call and retrieves the medicine or the prescription which she will then cash herself. Haslem started off as a private detective in the security firm he ended up running. No sweat for him to dig into Burnett's early retirement and find out his practice had been about to report him. Haslem knew Martyn Burnett had an addiction, he had Sylvia Burnett paying out to keep him sweet.'

Toni whistled. 'Who next?'

'Barbara Major is not a crime writer's researcher.' Malcolm read from his shorthand notes. 'She *is* the crime writer.'

'She uses a pseudonym?' Toni said.

'She's not published under any name. Bell said Major claims she's at the researching stage.'

'A murderer pretending to be working for a crime novelist is a good cover,' Toni said. 'But blackmail material? Who cares?'

'Barbara Major cares. Her neighbours thinking she's vital to a famous crime writer gives her mystique and status. She'd look a fool if the truth came out,' Malcolm said. 'I can get that.'

'She must have money, Blacklock House isn't cheap,' Toni said.

'She won the lottery ten years ago, enough to buy a flat and run it. Haslem has reduced her income to a pittance.' Malcolm had brought up the grid of suspects on his tablet.

'Last, but not least, Lady Dorothy Erskine,' Sheena

continued. 'This is pure *Downton Abbey*. Like Barbara, Lady D – aka Bunty – isn't who she says she is. She was illegitimate.'

'Shock, *horror*.' Toni clasped her cheeks. 'What century am I in?'

'Any century, the reason is the same. Bunty isn't a legitimate relation of the last earl, her father. It was one thing not to inherit because she was a girl but being born on the wrong side of the blanket she has no legal claim even to live in that flat. Instead of kicking her out, Haslem was selling off her treasures. She couldn't argue. Like he did everyone else in the house, Haslem had her on a shoestring.' Sheena finished.

'Why haven't we seen all this in Haslem's papers?' Toni said.

'Haslem played the working-class idiot, but he was clever. If any of the residents had come clean, they would have had no proof Haslem was involved. All trails lead to Patrick Bell.' Malcolm held his pen between two fingers like a tight rope.

'It never fails to amaze me what people are prepared to do to keep a secret. Personally, I'd pay *not* to live in a stately home in the middle of nowhere surrounded by this lot.'

'The lab results on that strand of hair in Martha Merry's car are back.' Darren burst into the room flapping a sheet paper. 'It's Tristan Robinson's. We have a definite link, *we've got her.*'

Cool Darren was so beside himself, he was doing an un-cool jig.

'Martha Merry has told Toni that she and Robinson were having an affair.' Malcolm's tone was intended to let Darren down lightly. 'Sorry, Darren, but even the most incompetent defence lawyer could deactivate that evidence by asserting Robinson had been in Merry's car.'

'Isn't that a motive to kill him?' Darren slumped next to Sheena at the table.

'The day we resort to looking for motives, we'll consider this investigation on life-support,' Toni groaned. 'Leave motive to the media and armchair detectives. We want hard evidence.'

'We're rich in motive.' Sheena caught Darren up on the interviews with Merry and Bell.

'Why can't we charge him?' Darren cried out. 'Who says he's not the murderer? The blackmailing evidence is enough, isn't it? Couldn't Haslem have been the true victim and the others collateral?'

'It would be mighty convenient, but it doesn't work. Yes, if we get irrefutable evidence,' Toni placated Darren.

'Nothing today has changed the theory that the killer lives in or is connected to Blacklock House.' Malcolm looked up from his typing. 'The three series C fivers at two scenes tell us the murders are linked. We're safe in saying, each figure scribbled on the back is a victim number. Probably in the order of killing. It's likely that Haslem, at least, knew his killer. From all accounts, Haslem trusted no one; had a stranger approached him, he would have been ready.'

'Should we go public on the notes?' Darren wondered. 'That might trigger a tip-off.'

'Not yet, it's an ace up our sleeve.' Toni shook her head. 'Our killer will be frustrated there's been no mention of the money in the media. He'll have to push the envelope.'

'Here's the updated suspect list.' Malcolm projected the Excel spreadsheet onto the screen beside the Murder Board.

| Blacklock House Residents and Regular Visitors | | |
|---|---|---|
| Age | Suspects | Ritchie Alibi |
| 52 | Garry Haslem ran dodgy security firm | Met with Lady Dorothy (Bunty) Erskine/Patrick Bell |
| 78 | Lady Dorothy (Bunty) Erskine Born in house. Illegitimate | As above |
| 53 | Barbara Major Crime Writer's Researcher. In fact, BM is writer | No alibi |
| 61 | Dr Sylvia Burnett GP in Chichester | With husband Martyn in flat. Left to walk in garden. Seen by Lomax |
| 57 | Dr Martyn Burnett (retired) | With wife Sylvia in flat |
| 72 | Rex Lomax Defence Lawyer Retired. Wife Emily killed 5 years ago outside Blacklock House. Lonely – got Companion. Afraid of him? | During time frame Lomax in summer house reading/asleep. Seen by Martyn Burnett |
| 35 | Timothy Mew Companion to Lomax | Not resident, not interviewed. At Martha Merry's salon – Head Case |
| 47 | Patrick Bell Accountant, Haslem's accountant/Blacklock House Treasurer. | Meeting with Garry Haslem. Could have murdered |
| 43 | Martha Merry Hairdresser based in Newhaven. | Gave Timothy Mew shave and beard trim and had drink. Said was in salon but Mew was only customer that afternoon. In it together? |
| 45 | Frederica Power Fishmonger lives in Newhaven. There when Haslem found on Tuesday. Swapped day due to van in garage. Rang Toni when body found. | Was with Toni Kemp walking South Downs Way |

| Robinson Alibi | Evidence |
|---|---|
| None except now dead too | Series C £5 notes. Numbered '10' – Victims? |
| No alibi | Hated Haslem |
| No alibi | Hated Haslem. Follows people |
| No alibi | Feeding husband's addition |
| No alibi | Addicted to oxycodone |
| Lomax and Mew on Dedmans Heath in Robinson murder time-frame. Lomax thinks met Maddie Robinson. Mew says it wasn't Maddie. Upstairs when Haslem found. | Maddie Robinson may have told Lomax & Mew that her family on heath every Sunday. Lomax heard Haslem arguing outside house early Tuesday am of murder. |
| Seen by Freddy Power that Sunday afternoon. (NB: Lomax and Mew on Dedmans Heath the Sunday before when Mew disagrees with Lomax that saw Maddie Robinson.) Mew in group that found Haslem's body. (NB Lady Bunty accused Mew of letting out her owl) | Knew of Tristan Robinson. Knows Martha Merry. Took Lomax's car without permission? |
| No alibi. Left before Haslem's body was found. | Martha Merry says Bell followed her and sabotaged her car. Haslem blackmailing Bell over embezzlement |
| No alibi – in vicinity of 2nd Murder. | Knew all victims. Black Fiesta in area. Keyed Robinson's car. Had affair with him. |
| In vicinity that afternoon. Visited Lomax, but Mew informed her Lomax asleep. | Knows Martha Merry? They saved a boy from drowning. Knows all residents. Familiar with area around Newhaven and Lewes. |

'Freddy's your friend, but you said to include her.' Malcolm was apologetic. 'Obviously, she's not a suspect. I did ring the garage to sew it up.'

'Freddy knew Haslem and she met Martha Merry at the fish van when Martha brought Mew to Blacklock House and, as we know, saw Martha yesterday.' Toni swerved her having asked Freddy to get intel on Martha, and now Freddy was *not* her friend.

'That was *brave*,' Sheena breathed. 'How did Freddy get over that barricade? Never mind dive off the harbour wall. I hope she gets a medal.'

'You're Freddy's alibi for the Ritchie murders, ma'am.' Darren was reading the grid. 'Wow, you walked the South Downs Way that day?'

'We did an hour and a half along the ridge from Lewes, bailed out at Rodmell and fell into the Abergavenny Arms for a slap-up lunch. It is true I was with Freddy all day.'

'Freddy is out,' Malcolm greyed out the row.

'Garry Haslem didn't murder himself,' Sheena said.

'Every one of these alibis is provided by another of the suspects,' Darren said.

'Which begs the question, are two of them partnering up?' Malcolm said. 'Rare, but it happens – take the Washington snipers a few years ago. Say, Mew and Merry, Mew and Lomax, the two doctors. Patrick Bell and Lady Bunty were with Haslem for the Ritchie murders, they could have driven to Seaford Head and killed James and Wilbur afterwards. Everyone appears to dislike each other, but for two people it could be an act.'

'Lady Bunty has never had a driving licence and doesn't own a car,' Sheena said.

'I can see Lady B stashing away series C fivers, it was common currency in her heyday.' Toni had a soft spot for the elderly aristocrat. 'I don't see her murdering children.'

'Lady Erskine could have murdered Haslem any time, why Monday night stroke Tuesday morning?' Sheena clearly didn't share the soft spot.

'We can't rule her out.' Malcolm was playing hardball. Toni rolled her eyes.

'Patrick Bell is incompetent, I'm thinking if he murdered the Ritchies, we'd have stopped him before he got to the Robinsons.'

'Possibly, although going by Martha Merry, he's a stalker and they frequently escalate to murder.' Gnashing on her pen, Toni bit off the top. 'The collateral idea has legs. All these people – with the exception of Martha Merry – had reason to want Haslem wiped off the face of the earth.'

'Steve Wright, the Suffolk Strangler, wasn't exactly skilled. He was caught within weeks,' Sheena said.

'Wright was likely killing other women long before 2007,' Toni said. 'It's not just about skill – if at all. Most serial killers murder people who nobody misses or who don't grab headlines. They can move under the radar. That said, this killer using the five-pound notes is left-field.'

'We do know whoever killed Haslem must have known the door code to Blacklock House. They accessed Haslem's flat after they'd killed him and set "Alfie" sung by Cilla Black to repeat,' Malcolm said. 'The number of plays gives us the time frame of from ten thirty on the Monday until about nine on Tuesday morning. Confirmed by Barbara Major, she put the music starting at precisely thirty-six past ten.'

'Ask me, that's too precise,' Sheena said.

'Fair point, although Major strikes me as a woman who leaves nothing undotted or uncrossed. She did say Haslem played music every night, so "Alfie" on repeat was perhaps business as usual,' Toni said.

'The killer wanted us to find the box of cash on Haslem's bed? Or else why didn't he steal it?' Darren said.

'Murdering Garry, or any of the victims, isn't about money?' Malcolm said. 'What we do know is, whoever got in had the door code.'

'*Not true.*' Toni smacked her palms on the table. 'Freddy told me the tradesman's button is always on.'

'So anyone could have got in.' Malcolm's face fell.

'Theoretically, but let's keep it tight to the residents for the moment.' Toni put up a palm. 'Sheena, what have you got?'

'I've pulled up the first interviews me and Chis did after the Robinsons were murdered,' Sheena said. 'No kids or living parents. The Burnetts each have a sister, but haven't seen them for years. Bell doesn't see his family and certainly not Marcus Rutherford. Lady Bunty is the last surviving member of her family. She said her friends are dead. Mew's friend is Martha Merry, but no love lost here. Rex Lomax is widowed, he got a companion because he's lonely. Barbara Major had hoped to be Lomax's companion. As we also know, her crime-writing friend turns out to be imaginary.'

'Toni and I suspected Major had a thing for Lomax. She too seems lonely,' Malcolm said.

'Loneliness is emerging as a theme.'

'So last Monday there's a residents' meeting. At some point that evening someone releases Bunty's owl. What else was different in Horror Hall?' Toni went over trodden ground.

'Martha Merry and Timothy Mew attended.' Malcolm

reminded them that Lomax had invited Mew, and Merry was asked by Bell. 'The Doctors Burnett and Barbara Major wanted them kicked out, but Haslem, Lomax and Bunty said they could stay but not contribute. The meeting broke up early because wind blew open the French doors and there was a brief power cut. Barbara Major announced that the serial killer was in their midst and caused panic.'

'Several residents, the Burnetts, Rex Lomax, told us that the next day,' Toni said. 'As we know, Martha Merry's car wouldn't start, Mew refused to let her stay the night, he didn't want to upset Lomax. A fake excuse since Rex told us he was concerned that Martha had driven home. Bell was angling for her to stay.'

'Timothy Mew had no qualms about nicking Lomax's car,' Sheena said.

'Mew made it clear to me that he had sloughed off his old life when he moved to Blacklock House,' Toni remembered. 'I don't think he planned to see Martha again. All that went out the window when Bell went after her.'

'Martha went to get stuff from her car and found that Garry Haslem had mended it.' Toni re-trod trodden ground. *What had they missed?*

'We only have Merry's word Garry Haslem mended it,' Darren said. 'What if it was never broken?'

'What advantage was there in her being stranded? If she murdered Haslem, it put her in the frame,' Sheena said.

'Merry didn't valet her car after driving out to Blacklock House,' Darren said. 'Could be arrogance, she assumes she's in the clear, or she's innocent.'

'We need to find who Haslem was talking to after Martha had left.' Toni said, 'Sheena, could you get onto Rex Lomax, see if he's remembered anything about who he heard talking to Haslem late on Monday? While you're there, confirm if Rex actually spoke to the girl he believes was Maddie on Dedmans Heath. If he didn't, it makes sense Maddie can't remember him. She's probably oblivious to anyone over forty.'

'Mew and Lomax as a double act?' Darren said while Sheena was dialling Lomax. 'Mew's only been his companion for what, five weeks? From what you've said, they're not singing from the same hymn books.'

'Agreed,' Toni said. 'Malcolm and I picked up that Lomax doesn't trust Mew. Lomax seemed anxious about Mew not being there when we interviewed him.'

'We did.' Malcolm was rubbing the knee which, as a rookie cop trying to be sporty with the hard core, he'd dislocated during a five-a-side. 'Mew had taken the Jag without permission, not for shopping as Lomax believed, but to have tea at the Hydro in Eastbourne where he met Barbara. Lomax joked about this game Leela that Mew brought with him, but it's revealing that Mew is untrustworthy and greedy. A companion like that would make me anxious.'

'Hold up, folks, being nervous of a bloke you beat at snakes and ladders doesn't mean Mew is slitting throats,' Toni warned.

'Mew had opportunity, after Rex Lomax went to bed that night. We know he's used Lomax's car without permission and lied about going shopping. We also know Lomax has naps in the afternoons which means Mew can do what he likes.'

'I rang the Hydro Hotel,' Darren said. 'A Lord Timothy

Mew went for tea there yesterday. That confirms what Barbara Major told you. I also checked out when he was a county tennis champion. Unless Mew used a false name, there's no record of a Timothy Mew at any level.'

'I guessed that. I tossed him a tennis ball and he dropped it.' Again, Toni felt the tingling at the back of her neck that she knew not to trust. This could be another blind alley.

They were interrupted by the phone. Darren answered.

'Murder Investigation Room. DC Mason speaking.' Darren tipped his head as if to better hear the caller. 'He's here, sir.' Hand cupped over the receiver he beckoned Malcolm. 'It's Inspector Morgan, who you saw this morning?'

'I think I just about remember.' Malcolm's sarcasm meant he was as tense as Toni. As he listened to Morgan, Malcolm's shorthand was the speed of light. Frustratingly, his expression gave nothing away.

'That was Henry Morgan.' Toni made a gesture to acknowledge that, yes, they already knew this. 'He said my visit had got to him.'

'You have that effect, Mal,' Toni told him.

'He was niggled by a doubt so has been going through case files in his shed since I left. He found the report of what was retrieved from the scene of Adrian Moon's murder. Sweet wrappings, matchsticks, fag-ends and, as he put it, evidence of sexual activity.' Malcolm took a breath, 'And a series C five-pound note.'

'Bingo.' Toni punched the air. 'Was there a number written on it?'

'Yes.' Malcolm looked sombre. 'Five.'

'No wonder we can't find this man – fifteen years ago, he'd already racked up five victims.' Toni felt winded.

'Four,' Darren corrected her. 'When he left the money, he assumed the boy – Barney – was dead, but he survived.'

'Way to go, Darren.' Toni was pleased to see Darren cheer up.

'The killer must have been worried Barney could describe him. Instead, Barney pointed out Kenneth Todd and we know the rest. It might explain the long gap between the murders, the killer lost his nerve,' Malcolm said.

'I don't think this killer has nerves. However, I think we can rely on the numbered notes we have being accurate.' Toni followed through. 'No luck on the Seaford Head note?'

'Nothing so far.' Sheena had been on that. 'It's likely a member of the public found it and, obviously, they don't know its significance. Is that a reason to put it out there?'

'It is, but I want to hold back, get this man to prod us harder for a reaction.' Toni would once have been irritated by Sheena pushing the point.

'From the fivers we do have it means there were three murders before Adrian Moon and then no more murders until James and Wilbur Ritchie who are likely numbers six and seven,' Malcolm said. 'The notes probably washed into the sea.'

'We have to catch this man before number eleven,' Toni said. 'My question is, who were one, two and three?'

Darren's mobile rang.

'Hey, Marie, OK?' Darren began fussing with his hair as if on a video call. '*You're kidding.* Ahh… OK… OK…' *Fuss, fuss with the hair.* '…that's amazing… I'm seriously imp—Wow… OK, that's so… *wow…*' *More fussing.* 'OK, call if you need me, yeah?'

'You could have been a tad more enthusiastic, Chis,' Sheena teased Darren when he was off the phone.

'Funn-ee.' Darren did a face at Sheena. 'This morning, when I called Marie, the Robinsons' FLO, Maddie had gone into meltdown. It's now sunk in that her family is gone. Maddie had been insisting she'd only do what she likes now her mum and dad aren't on at her. Marie calmed her down and got her to see the counsellor. I don't know how Marie does that job, she's a star.'

'Doing exactly what she wants, that rings a bell.' Malcolm frowned.

'It's what Rex told us Timothy told the girl who Rex believes was Maddie,' Toni said.

'Rex said Timothy reassured Maddie that, one day, she wouldn't have to come to Dedmans Heath every Sunday with her family.' Malcolm slapped the wrong knee and winced. 'Mew knew the Robinson family were on the heath every Sunday.'

'Anyway,' Darren raised his voice to get back everyone's attention, 'when Marie finally got to show Maddie pictures of Lomax and Mew, Maddie said she'd never seen them before.'

'Great.' Toni reached for the Gaviscon bottle.

'The counsellor gets Maddie to describe that last Sunday she did go with her family.' Excitement propelled Darren into the present tense. 'All of a sudden Maddie asks Marie to see the photos again. Maddie still doesn't recognise Lomax, but points at Timothy Mew and says, "*That creep was there.*"

# 50

*Freddy*

A breeze ruffled the umbrellas on the patio. Many of the tables had emptied, staff were clearing tea things on to trays. The afternoon was moving towards cocktail hour. Through the trees, the sea glittered like gold.

Freddy saw her alarm when Rex handed over his AMEX card to Timothy for him to pay for the slap-up tea reflected in Martha's expression.

'I asked Timothy to pay because I need to get you girls on your own.' Rex clasped his hands and leaned forward at the table. 'I believe Timothy is stealing from me.'

'Stealing?' Freddy gasped. Rex had said what was uppermost in her mind right then.

'I can't prove it and maybe I'm daft old bugger.' Tapping Freddy's hand, Rex stopped her protest. 'He came here yesterday in my car and – I can't prove this – paid for a tea with cash from my wallet. Now, I'm not proud of this, but I left the wallet out as a test and I am sorry to say, Timothy failed it.'

'Why did you think he would steal from your wallet? What

else has happened?' Freddy was set to punch Timothy when he returned. It had been unreasonable to resent the companion because he took Rex to Mass and her fighting the feeling had caused her to take her eye off the ball and miss that Timothy Mew's presence fulfilled her fears for Rex. Not at any point had Freddy wanted to be right.

'At first I put it down to me. Emily teased me for losing things, forgetting where I'd put something, it often made us late. She was responsible for my appearing so efficient at work. *"Phone, reading glasses, wallet..."* She'd call out a checklist as I was leaving, I'd always forgotten some vital item.' Rex looked sad then roused himself. 'I wanted to think I was wrong about Timothy. I had wanted a companion, someone to talk to, share ideas with, simply have in my home. The relationship has to be based on trust or it doesn't work.'

'You have to sack him,' Martha said.

'I have no proof.' Rex's voice sounded frailer than ever.

Freddy's fists curled. *Toni would tell her not to be her father's daughter.* Fred Power smacked her brother at the drop of a hat. It had been Freddy's job to protect him. It was her job now.

'...if he's innocent? I'm ruining his chances of finding another position with Cuckoo's Nest.'

'Stupid name,' Martha said. 'A cuckoo takes the food out of the mouths of the baby birds whose nest it has infiltrated.'

'You're right, Martha.' Rex laughed. 'I should have guessed.'

'This isn't your fault,' Freddy said. 'I hate to ask this, Rex, but do you suspect Timothy might have... might have killed Garry?'

'Goodness no. I don't think he's a serial killer. I do wonder if he thinks he can hoodwink me and take over my property. There are safeguards, but these people are clever. I should know, I've represented a few of them.' Rex got up and leaning over the table looked severe. '*Please*, let's keep in our minds Timothy may *not* have stolen anything, he may not be a con-artist after my money and he's certainly not a murderer. Neither of you suffers fools, I am relying on your judgements.'

'I never see Timothy now he's moved in with you,' Martha mumbled.

'I see him once a week when he collects your fish, that's about three minutes' worth of interaction. I used to bring the fish upstairs.' Freddy just snatched back resentment that it was Rex who had stopped them meeting.

'This is a big ask, but please, I need you both to attend our extraordinary residents' meeting this evening.'

'Absolutely,' Freddy agreed.

'If I don't have to sit anywhere near Patrick Bell.' Martha nodded.

'I will make damn sure of that. I have one question.' Rex darted an anxious glance at the door into the hotel. 'Martha, you've known Timothy a long time, if superficially. Have you seen evidence of dishonesty... or, er... worse?'

'Never,' said Martha.

# 51

*Freddy*

A car space was heaped with flowers, cellophane rattled in the breeze, labels flapped and twisted. The bouquets were laid in rows, stems facing out. Some flowers had been crushed by the tyres of cars. The little used car park on the far side of Dedmans Heath had recently become popular.

An elderly man in a thick anorak despite the summer's day turned away from the display with open disgust.

'It's not a crematorium.' He glared at Freddy and Martha as if they were responsible for the mountain of dying flora. Climbing stiffly into his car, he reversed over gladioli as he left.

'People hate death.' Martha clutched the chrysanthemums she had bought in the Lewes Tesco earlier. She bent to read one of the labels.

*My darling Tris, I will never forget you. My shining star!*
*Txxx*

'Christ, that's over the top.'

'T may have been a friend.' Freddy was careful, Martha lurched from being furious with Tristan Robinson to grief. She followed Martha, who held the chrysanthemums high to avoid thorny branches along a path narrowed by brambles.

Dedmans Heath betrayed the beginnings of autumn. Here and there, bracken leaves had browned, beech leaves were tipped with gold. Circumventing cowpats and clumps of soft rush, Martha and Freddy headed along a sward of grass cropped by cattle, sprinkled with yellow tormentil and bordered by gorse and creeping thistles.

'I can't remember where it was.' Freddy scoured Dedmans Heath. In one direction a church spire peeped above trees. In the other was a dense line of trees. Dedmans Wood. She had walked from Blacklock House through the wood; Toni had pointed to an area to their left. 'I think it's over there.'

'See the police tape?' Martha stomped over to a blackberry bush, the fruit pecked and shrivelled where, with the rapidity of a humming bird's wings, a snag of plastic whirred in the breeze.

'Are you sure about doing this?' *Maybe a bit late to ask.*

'No, I'm not, but we're here now.' Martha plunged down one of myriad paths forged by animals as well as humans within the bracken. Thistle burrs clung to their shirts, Freddy stumbled on a bramble tripwire and then they were in the wood. Stopping and facing out to the heath, Freddy got her bearings. It seemed another lifetime ago that she had stood there with Toni.

'I read Tristan was found last.' Martha followed the faint outline of a track.

'Yes.' Freddy knew that. *Had Toni told her?*

Away from the breeze, in the gloom of thickly overarching trees, the silence was as of bated breath. Bulbous fungi, ugly in the gloom, grew between giant tree roots. The rotted and picked-over corpse of a rabbit lying nearby might be nature's reminder of the banality of death.

'Tristan would have come here to ring me without Sally hearing.' Martha ripped the cellophane off the flowers and with a perfunctory, 'Rest in Peace,' propped them against the oak tree. 'I left my Tristan phone at home to spite him.'

'Shame,' Freddy said. 'It would have been around when he was murdered, it gives it a time parameter.'

'"Time parameter." What, you're a detective now? I wanted him to suffer radio silence. He did it to me all the time.' Martha looked weary. 'It's weird, Tristan's been dead four days, and although I'm shocked that he's dead and definitely by how he died, I don't miss him.'

'Regardless of where you left this burner phone, it will show a missed call. Did you tell the police?' Freddy rested a hand on the oak tree as truth dawned. 'Please tell me you gave Toni the secret phone.'

'There's nothing on it.' *No, then.*

'It'll say what time he called you and *it'll show when Tristan was still alive.*' Freddy wiped a hand down her face. '*Jesus*, Martha, the police think you told them everything. *So. Did. I.* What time was Tristan's missed call? He must have rung minutes, seconds, before he was murdered. Did he leave a message?' Freddy ran out of breath.

'No.'

'No what?' Freddy demanded.

'Tristan did not leave a message and there was no missed call. He never called.' Martha bent down and examined the ground. She stirred dead needles from a nearby pine and picked up a pine cone, tossing it back and forth between her hands. 'Tristan can't have taken the Martha phone to the heath or the police would have traced it to me long before Timothy dobbed me in.' Martha's words appeared to startle her, as if she hadn't thought this before.

'Or the killer took his phone before he had a chance to call you.' Freddy heard herself trying to make Martha feel better while feeling progressively annoyed by the concept of Martha and Tristan phones.

'Don't try to make me feel better,' Martha said. 'It's likely that he didn't take it. I've been having an affair with Tristan for over three years and still he hadn't left Sally. To be honest, I was more taken with making him leave than considering that if he did, what would happen next. Tristan was a narcissist, he also liked being at the centre of his family. He would never have left.'

'Nice that you left flowers.' Freddy quelled excitement. *Martha didn't care enough about Tristan Robinson to murder him.*

'He hated chrysanthemums.'

Somewhere deeper in the wood was a snap, a twig perhaps. Rustling. A squirrel leapt and bounded from branch to branch above their heads.

'These woods border the grounds of Blacklock House,' Freddy whispered. 'I came here with Toni after we found Garry. It would have been easy for someone there to leave Blacklock House last Sunday, kill the Robinsons and return unnoticed by residents or anyone else out here. Dedmans Heath would have been busy last weekend, these bushes and the bracken are thick here. From that path we came in on, we'd only see the tops of trees in Dedmans Wood. That's why no one witnessed the murders.'

'The killer would have known he could work unseen,' Martha said.

'It's a local.' Freddy led them to a grassy circle edged by bracken. Private, with birds tweeting, it was a perfect picnic spot. Tyre marks and flattened foliage were a reminder that the perfect picnic spot was ideal for the perfect murder.

'I lied.'

'*God*,' Freddy groaned. 'What now?'

'Timothy stole money from my purse and from the till at the salon. Only tenners, so the first time I thought I'd spent the money and made a mistake cashing up. Then, when we were out at a pub, I left Timothy with my bag while I nipped to the loo. When I returned, he'd bought us drinks. Later I knew for sure that he'd paid for them with my last twenty.'

'Did you confront him?'

'Like Rex, I didn't want to believe it. Since then, I've watched him like a hawk. Like an idiot, I caught myself offering my sofa because I knew instinctively this companion thing was a mistake. Lucky for me, Timothy would never stoop to staying in a flat over a salon. Not lucky for Rex.'

'Why did you lie to Rex?' Freddy was confounded. She had just become certain that Martha had nothing to do with the murders and now this.

'Rex didn't sound sure. Like he said, you have to really think before you trash a reputation.' Martha didn't sound convinced. Nor was she *convincing*. 'My suspicions about Timothy are based on flimsy stuff and my imagination.'

'What flimsy stuff?' Freddy was having trouble keeping it

together. It seemed Martha was incapable of telling the truth. There was always another lie.

'Things he said or was interested in. He had papers at his flat on getting Power of Attorney, changing a will. I teased him about it at the time and he snatched up the documents and shoved them in a drawer. Soon after that his landlords told him they were moving in with their daughter and gave him notice. I didn't think any more of it until he told me he had applied to be a companion for this company called Cuckoo's Nest.' It was Martha's turn not to breathe. 'I worried that Timothy planned to inveigle himself into Rex's life, get possession of his flat and persuade him to change his will.'

'You didn't think to tell Rex this?'

'Tell him what? I have no evidence.'

'Timothy told Rex he went to Waitrose yesterday afternoon when he'd booked himself in as Lord Mew at the Hydro Hotel. Rex took us to give Timothy a chance to own up. I think that was a mistake. No one likes to be shamed. Rex doesn't think Timothy could murder anyone, but what if he's wrong?'

'Rex is familiar with people who think nothing of committing crimes. I looked him up. He's defended some high-profile criminals. One of them was a serial killer. He will know better than us who is a danger.'

'He does know. He wants us at this friggin' meeting tonight because he thinks he's in danger.' Freddy was losing it. 'Timothy stole from your till – what if he's seen a list of your customers and is working his way through them?'

'But why?'

'Maybe Garry saw what Timothy was up to.' Freddy was less making it up as she went along as building the picture.

'Garry threatens to blackmail Timothy like he was Patrick Bell and ruin Timothy's plan. He has to kill Garry.'

'Timothy had no reason to kill the Robinsons or the Ritchies.'

'If Timothy planned to kill Rex, he had to distract attention from himself and towards someone else,' Freddy said.

In the silence, birds tweeting, far off the roar of a tractor engine, both women knew that they actually had no idea what Timothy Mew might do.

# 52

The breeze that had rustled the bracken and gorse on Dedmans Heath when Martha and Freddy had visited the crime scene earlier in the afternoon was building to a strong wind. King Tut, feathers tucked in, uttered his blood-curdling scream as he strutted around past the empty bird cage swinging in the wind. Although the sun hadn't quite dipped behind Dedmans Wood, stars twinkled in the pink-grey sky.

Weather warnings had been issued; the wind heralded another storm. It was not an evening to be gardening.

Yet, bending over a flower bed at the opposite side of the house from where the peacock was pecking about, gardening was what Barbara Major was doing. Snip-snap went her secateurs as she deadheaded the pinks she had planted in the spring. Gardening, as Barbara would have reported to her imaginary crime writer, was a marvellous way to keep an eye on things. A glance here, a peep there while you dug in compost or cut back the peonies. This evening she had stationed herself at the corner of Blacklock House where she had a view of the lawn and the summer house in the far corner, and was not immediately obvious to anyone using the path from the yew hedge or cutting through the woods from Dedmans Heath. Barbara prided herself on being prepared.

Rex had set the extraordinary residents' meeting for eight o'clock. That gave her ten minutes. Everyone had been annoyed at having another meeting only two days after the last ghastly shindig, as Bunty had put it. For once, Barbara was looking forward to it. She had her own ideas for Any Other Business. She hummed as she snipped. Some thought gardening was about encouraging new life, but for that to happen there had to be death. Barbara stopped humming – she should capture that nugget. No, she would remember it. She whispered another such nugget, planned as the first line of her novel.

'Even the most intelligent make mistakes. *You made a mistake.* The cat chases the mouse. *Who catches the cat?*'

The sun set. The moon rose above the trees. Silvery light defined the fountain and glinted on the new wheelbarrow in which were scattered Barbara's deadheads. Were Barbara to write her story from the point of view of the woman gardening, she must consider that, facing the other way, her character would not see the gate in the yew hedge opening or a shape gliding towards her. Nor due to distant thunder might the character hear the creak of gate that Garry Haslem had advised against oiling to warn of intruders. Later, Barbara might forget that, setting her scene in the dark, only the narrator could describe the bloodstains on the secateurs.

# 53

*Martha*

Martha gave up waiting for Freddy when the first drops of rain began to fall. She had texted but, presumably because Freddy was already on the road, got no reply. Martha hoped Freddy wasn't bailing on her. Apart from having then to face the meeting on her own, Martha was looking forward to seeing her.

The front door was ajar. She crept into the hallway. The chandelier was off, the only light came from the landing above. Martha found the switch and flicked it. Nothing. She didn't envy whoever would have to get up there and replace the bulbs. Martha was tempted to leave, but would feel bad if Freddy arrived after all. She girded herself and padded carefully along the carpeted corridor to the door at the end. The old library.

Martha dumped her bag on one of several chairs set against the wood-panelled wall opposite the French doors. This time she would not sit at the oval table. She wanted to support Rex – she planned to tell him her suspicions – but if she was there as an observer, she must be able to observe. She wandered over to the window and, blinkering her face with her hands, peered through the glass out into the darkness.

The library looked out onto the lawn and the fountain, but with no lamp-post at the back and low electric light suspended over the table, Martha could only see herself reflected.

Wind drove raindrops against the glass. Martha retreated. The French doors shook. The light flickered. A body in a cupboard would complete the picture. *We've had the body.* Was this going to be a repeat of Monday's horror show? She should have waited in her car for Freddy. *She should have refused to come to the meeting.* Rex had helped her at the police station, she owed him. But better offering him a return match at the Hydro Hotel, not another night in Murder Paradise.

'What is a murder suspect doing here?' Dr Sylvia Burnett stopped in the doorway.

'Until you arrived, there was no murder suspect here. As you will remember, on Monday we established we can invite guests.' Rex breezed past Sylvia and sat where Garry Haslem had sat on Monday evening, at the head of the table. In crisp suit and tie, he looked ready for court. Dr Burnett, in a black dress with a skimpy woollen jacket, had made an effort. Martha had not changed out of the jeans and shirt she'd worn to the crime scene with Freddy. She felt like a slob.

'I repeat, why is she here?' Sylvia said.

'Is this your new companion?' Martyn Burnett took his seat.

'Where is the companion?' Sylvia switched tack. 'There were no murders until he arrived.'

'He arrived *after* that poor dear family were found mutilated on Dedmans Heath, Sylvia dear.' Lady Dorothy settled herself in the carver at the other end of the table, facing the French doors. 'Timothy's a sweetie Always polite and a spit of cousin Charlie. Now *there* was a rascal. Dead now.'

Martha almost wished Garry Haslem was there to fill the ensuing awkward silence with a well-aimed insult. Out of nowhere it occurred to her that had Haslem not mended her car he might have returned to his flat and not been murdered. *Had those extra minutes cost him his life?*

'Sorry I'm late.' Patrick hurried in and took his seat at what had been Garry Haslem's right, but was now next to Rex. He looked astonished, then, she was sure, angry, to see Martha. He nodded a curt greeting. Martha let her eye rove over him. *Dead to me.*

'Without Haslem, we can wrap this up quickly.' Martyn Burnett had cut himself shaving. At least he had shaved, but Martha doubted he'd recently washed. His comb-over was stuck to his scalp, his eyes were bleary pinholes. Sylvia Burnett caught Martha seeing this and berated her husband, 'Shut up, Martyn. I told you not to come.'

'I'm not staying upstairs alone. If someone else meets a sticky end, I'd have no alibi.'

'For once I agree with the "doctor".' Dorothy tapped the side of her nose and sniffed, perhaps to suggest Martyn wasn't a doctor. Which, since he'd retired, Martha supposed he wasn't. Were she not fretting about Freddy, Martha suspected that, even without Garry's jibes, she might enjoy herself.

At that moment Timothy walked in and any idea of enjoyment turned to ash. Timothy was typically smart although his linen suit looked a bit tired.

'Timothy, dear, plant yourself beside me,' Lady Dorothy cooed from across the room.

'He can't sit at the table,' Dr Sylvia said.

'Timothy, please sit over there.' Without looking up, Rex waved to where Martha sat by the wall. When Timothy saw her, his expression was eloquent. *Hate.*

'We're missing Barbara.' Patrick cleared his throat. 'She'll be cross if we start without her.'

'Then she should get here on time.' Nudged by his wife Martyn subsided into silence.

'Barbara said to start without her,' Timothy said. Martha was surprised that, after Barbara had dobbed him in about the hotel, Timothy was speaking to her. Suddenly she didn't believe him. *Where was Barbara?*

'We shall begin with a game.' Rex leaned into his bag and fished out a box which he laid on the table. 'This heirloom belonged to Timothy's grandfather. He and I have been having fun with it since he came to Blacklock House. I'd like to share it with everyone.'

It was the game Timothy had bought in the charity shop on their way to Blacklock House that first day. Timothy had once told her his granddad hadn't been further than Butlins at Bognor Regis. Timothy looked very unhappy. After the Hydro Hotel tea, Martha should have warned Rex not to trap Timothy. Too late, now Rex was literally playing a game with him.

Martha failed to concentrate as Rex explained the rules.

'...we learn each other's secrets, foibles and faults...'

No, Leela was not boring old Snakes and Ladders, he told Martyn Burnett, this game of knowledge would enable everyone to discover strengths, it weeded out the weak and gave direction.

Martha was relieved when Rex instructed her and Timothy

to sit it out. If he planned another humiliation for Timothy, it was not with Leela.

*Where was Freddy?*

'As Timothy knows, we each play with a counter that has significance to ourselves. A talisman, if you will.' Rex had to raise his voice above the rising moan of wind.

*If Freddy was driving in this...* Martha clasped her hands between her knees. Please God that Freddy had decided not to come. Surreptitiously Martha checked her mobile in case Freddy had texted. No messages. Then she froze. *She had accidentally picked up the Tristan-phone.*

'...in my version of the game I choose your talisman. I know you well enough to understand you. Each object will represent you on the board.'

Martha watched with amorphous dread as, one by one, Rex passed each player their object.

'Martyn, yours is a blister pack ⟵ used, before you check. Sylvia, accept this gambling chip all the way from Las Vegas. Patrick, you get an eraser.' He leaned across Patrick. 'Dorothy, my dear, for you a lump of fool's gold, gorgeous just like you.'

'What does—' Patrick scowled at the rubber Rex had given him.

'Bear with me, Bell.' Rex held up a hand.

Gusts of wind buffeted the French doors and rain lashed the panes. Martha caught herself thinking Rex had orchestrated the weather too.

'My counter will be this signet ring which belonged to someone who holds particular significance to me. I did have a sacred medallion, but I've mislaid it.'

'*Liar*,' Timothy hissed. Martha's horrible feeling increased. Rex's other game had only two players.

Each resident threw the *die* – Timothy had told Martha the correct word. Getting a six, Martyn Burnett counted along the board to the fourth square.

'Greed.' Rex looked at Martyn. 'That doesn't describe you, does it? Me, I look up to doctors. They heal the sick. They administer medicines which, if not offering a cure, have a palliative effect. But you, Dr Burnett, you squandered everything for drugs. Now look at you, no more than a pusillanimous dribbling wreck reliant on *Mummy* for your next fix.'

'This is terrible.' Martyn was actually crying. Martha could see that no one around the table was happy. Were they concerned for Martyn Burnett or for themselves? Rex was the only one enjoying himself.

Rex sounded so soothing as he described how Martyn Burnett swindled his partners, stole drugs from his practice and cared nothing for his patients that it took Martha some moments to realise what Rex had said could strip paint.

'You bastard.' Martyn staggered to his feet.

A clap of thunder shocked him into slumping down again. In a faithful repeat of Monday night, the French doors burst open, the curtains billowed. A dark shape appeared to come through the starkly outlined doorway, but Martha knew she'd imagined it.

Rex, seated closest to the blast of cold air seething around the room, enquired politely, 'How much did you pay Haslem each week for his silence?'

'It's none of—'

'How much were you paying?'

'A thousand pounds a month.' Sylvia's voice cut through the whistle of the wind like a shard of glass.

'Haslem was being kind, I'd want double that.' Fists on the table, Rex pushed up to standing and moving behind his chair, fastened the French doors.

Rex hadn't locked them. Martha fought the urge to cross the room and do it herself. But Rex had asked her to watch Timothy, she couldn't leave her post.

Martha felt keen disappointment when Patrick landed on Delusion and Rex said nothing. He said no more until everyone had taken one turn.

Something hit her sandal and rolled under her chair. Timothy made a grab for it, but Martha got there first.

*Follow the footprints of the Lord. They will lead you through troubled times and brighten your life.*

'Give it back,' Timothy mouthed.

'...is a crude attempt at blackmail. I'm calling the police. I could sue you for defamation.' Sylvia's voice rang out.

'Dear Sylvia, harsh words. Defamation of character only works if the accusation is *untrue*. You supply drugs to what is left of Martyn and you obtained them for Haslem to sell on. Our Garry wasn't stupid enough to use anything himself. He kept his wits sharp.' Rex was genial. 'Bunty darling, your turn.'

'Where did you get it?' Martha mouthed to Timothy.

'He gave it me.' Timothy nodded at Rex sitting beyond the circle of light.

Lady Dorothy threw a six which took her to Sorrow, a neutral square without a snake or a ladder.

'Liar.' Martha fired Timothy's insult back at him. 'You stole it from Rex.'

'...that is how I'm sure we all feel at saying farewell to you, *dear Bunty.*'

'Where are you going?' Martyn sat up in his chair.

'I'm not going anywhere,' Bunty said. 'Who told you this?'

'Leela told me, *Ms* Erskine.' Rex smiled kindly at the elderly woman. Forgetting Timothy for a moment, Martha was appalled to see that Bunty looked very frightened indeed.

Across the sky behind Rex, she saw a jagged fork of lightning. Thunder rocked the room. The light went on and off. One by one, Rex was unmasking the residents. As she had on Monday, Martha wanted to rush out of the old library. Get as far as possible from Blacklock House.

'If you tell Rex, I will give him proof you murdered the Robinsons.' Timothy spoke into her ear.

'You have no proof,' Martha was sibilant. How could you know someone for ten years and not know them at all? Martha had said this to the police, and Freddy; now she realised the man she had known was a figment of her imagination.

'You wouldn't dare,' she told him.

'...Bunty was not, as she loved to tell Garry, born in his sitting room. She was born in a run-down cottage – now a commuter's palace – on the estate, to a scullery maid that the last Earl Blacklock took a fancy to and then had sacked. With no heir and lonely after his wife died in childbirth, he adopted the baby and brought her up as his own.'

'That's nothing to be ashamed of,' Sylvia said.

'Oh, believe me. I have proof.' Timothy's eyes seemed to look through her.

'You are right, Dr Sylvia.' Rex grinned. 'Unfortunately, the law is less understanding. Bunty lives *gratis* in her flat for the duration of her life because she is the earl's only daughter and her American cousin felt for her. Garry Haslem knew the difference between nine-carat gold and the fools' kind. It was a doddle to get Bunty's DNA and compare it with that lock of the earl's hair in the – genuine – gold locket she hawks about the house like it's a holy shroud. Not a match. Dorothy is the spawn of a humble farmhand. Haslem found relatives living in the village and, Leela tells me, threatened to introduce you, didn't he, Bunty?'

'He could have evicted her. It can't be true,' Sylvia persisted.

'If Garry had unmasked Bunty, those worldly goods she has stashed in her flat would go to the consortium that owns everything apart from our personal belongings and our leases. The nice cousin had said Bunty could keep what meant something to her. Haslem kept Bunty's secret and, bit by bit, relieved her of priceless Italian pottery, paintings, jewellery, furniture. Some he kept, most he sold.' Rex sighed. 'Garry was smarter than any of my clients; he never got caught.'

On the throw of the die, Rex reiterated that Sylvia Burnett supplied her husband with his drugs and were this to come out, she would be struck off. Martha already knew Patrick had embezzled his friend's money. She did not know he'd been Garry Haslem's gofer. She knew it was Patrick, rather than Leela, who had told Rex everyone's secrets.

'Barbara is *not* a crime writer's researcher.' This time it was Timothy. 'Barbara claimed her mystery crime writer treated her to tea at the Hydro Hotel. I know she went there to find me. There is no writer.' Martha could see that Timothy hated Barbara Major for betraying him to Rex and to the police. *Where was she?*

'Very good, Timothy, but you are wrong.' Rex looked

annoyed that Timothy had spoken. The clock was ticking, Rex planned to unmask Timothy. She needed to go.

The six figures seated stiffly around the oak table might be in a painting. Rex at the head was a blurred shape against the French doors. Every few seconds, lightning flooded the lawn in silver and washed over the dark panelled walls.

'Had Barbara deigned to appear, I'd expect her to land on Darkness, square sixty-three. Timothy, how often have you slithered down that scaly body all the way to two? Illusion.' Rex smiled at his companion.

'It's only—' Timothy began.

'A game?' Rex stopped smiling. 'But it isn't, is it?'

'What did Barbara say to you?' Martha rounded on Timothy. 'Why isn't she here?'

'Stop.' Sylvia banged the table. 'Rex, if you want to drag us all through the mud then yes, Haslem was blackmailing Martyn and me, and it seems all of us. He got another spineless snake to collect the cash. Bell, I'll give you the benefit of the doubt and guess you too were being blackmailed. Rex, if this is leading to you carrying on where Haslem left off, forget it.' Sylvia took the blister pack and the gambling chip off the Leela board and slid them across to Rex. 'We are not playing your game.'

'Stay exactly where you are,' Rex told Sylvia. 'It's time for my story. Five years tomorrow was the last time I saw Emily. When your loved one leaves a room, it never occurs to you that you will never see them again. Emily was going to the village hall, my fault, I persuaded her to stand as chair of the Women's Institute. I said she'd win hands down. I hadn't legislated for how much Barbara also prized the role and would stop at nothing to keep it. *Including murder.*'

'Bell, did you know this?' Sylvia said.

'Garry never told me what any of you had done,' Patrick said. Against every bone in her body, Martha believed him. *Would Freddy believe her if Timothy provided evidence that would implicate her in murder?*

'Of all of us, Barbara is the most steeped in methods of murder and evasion. She has spent years concocting the perfect murder. All she did was wait on Blacklock Lane and when she saw Emily's car coming, step out.'

As if the weather was there for orchestration Rex's speech ended with a deafening crash of thunder and the French doors blew open again. This time, Rex didn't move to shut them. No one did.

'Barbara found the car and rang the emergency services. She tried to get—' Sylvia was an actor who had forgotten her lines.

'Barbara told me she held Emily until she died. The police returned a Waitrose shopping receipt on which Barbara wrote Emily's dying message to me: "Love you, Rex, and always will."'

'Sorry.' With a sob, Bunty flapped her hands uselessly. 'You must take comfort from that.'

'That's when I knew Barbara was lying.'

'You must believe Barbara or Emily's death will torture you for ever,' Bunty instructed Rex.

'Emily didn't love me.' Rex threw the die and ascended a ladder to Happiness. Got that wrong, Leela. Martha would have laughed if she wasn't dizzy with fear. 'She stopped loving me, fifteen years ago.'

'People speak the truth when they die,' Sylvia said.

'People lie when they cover up murder,' Rex replied.

'Timothy, would you like to tell the assembled company your secret?'

A whirring. Something brushed past Martha's face. A bolt of lightning flooded the library with cold light. The something swooped onto Martha's shoulder. *Molly the owl had returned.*

The air was rent with a scream.

'*You killed them all.*'

The French doors swung violently back, smashing against the wall, a pane of glass fell out. Water spouted from the gargoyles and spattered onto the flagstones like sharp stones. Someone lunged across the room. A flash of steel. A chair was tipped over. As if the dead were talking, the table rocked. Everyone leapt to their feet. Only Rex remained motionless.

The light went out and stayed out.

Martha ran. Head down, hands cupped to her chest. Pelting rain stung her scalp, her sodden clothes hampered her. She felt a hand on her shoulder. With every ounce of strength, she forced herself forward, slipping and slithering on the soggy lawn. A fork of lightning crazed down ahead of her. Distantly, Martha knew she was going to die.

She tripped and rolled to her side to avoid crushing the owl. She hit the side of carriage house wall. The light fluttering against her palms brought her back. No one was following her.

Levering herself to her feet, Martha leaned against the wall. Cars had long ago replaced horses. Rex's Jaguar gleamed in the faint light of the storm. The Burnetts drove an old Rover besides which was Patrick's ten-year-old Mini. Haslem's Aston Martin was covered by tarpaulin, his electric Fiat was charging. The cars spoke for their owners. Haslem had the residents on a shoestring while he lived in luxury.

Martha crept out of the stables and around to the cage. She deposited Molly inside and secured the door.

'You're safe, little one.' Momentarily, Martha felt a strange calm.

Martha heard ringing. She had a phone signal. Patting herself down, Martha found her phone in her back pocket. The screen said Swiss T, her code for Tristan's number. The voice on the end of the line was not Tristan.

'Timothy?'

# 54

*Freddy*

It was a quarter to eight. Although still summer, the dusk was
due to dark grey clouds that seemed to weigh down the spire
of Our Lady of Sorrows.

Freddy hastened through the gates. A storm was coming.
There was electricity in the air. The church was shut, the
stained-glass windows, protected by grilles, were dark.
Freddy was relieved, she did not want to run into Father
Pete and have to explain why she was there. She barely
knew herself.

Rex had told them he had deliberately left his wallet where
Timothy would see it. He had set a trap for his companion. He
had taken refuge in his own doubt that he might be mistaken
about Timothy. Martha had admitted that Rex's suspicions
matched her own. Freddy had been impatient with Martha: if
you suspect something, say something.

Freddy had ignored her own suspicion. An idea born of
something she had seen, but barely registered.

After she and Martha had been to Dedmans Heath that
afternoon, they had arranged to reconvene at Blacklock

House that evening for the extraordinary residents' meeting. Neither of them wanted to go, but at least they'd be there together. Freddy went home, fed the fish, but, still full from the hotel tea, decided against the scallops with ginger and garlic she had lined up for supper. Gazing into the aquarium, dreaming herself among the fish, ducking beneath the grotto, over the bridge, Freddy saw instead Mary's Garden at Our Lady of Sorrows. The pale statue, Mary's face sublime, the face of those Freddy had ever truly loved or would love.

*'I needed a bit of peace. Silence.'*

As Freddy imagined herself curled up in the prince's boat, just with the princess, the picture gained focus.

The first Sunday Freddy had attended Mass since Rex had his companion. Feeling rejected and annoyed too that the companion had not actually attended Mass but stayed outside jingling Rex's keys, she had slipped past Rex and retreated to Mary's Garden.

'...do penance, to sin... avoid whatever leads... Our Saviour Jesus Christ suffered and died for us, in his name, my God, have mercy—'

Rex was praying by the statue. Freddy had tried to help him up but, smacking grass clippings off his trousers, he had batted her away.

'What are you doing here?'

'I was—' Freddy couldn't say she was hiding from Rex and his companion. 'What about you?'

'I wanted company, but there's always a price to pay.' Unless you were looking for clues, you could miss them.

A rumble of thunder. She must leave, she was already going to be late.

Rex had not been praying at Mary's statue. He'd been

behind it. He was concealing something. Who from? *The companion.*

The rain began, huge drops splashed on the paving, bowing down the leaves of the laurel bushes. Freddy began clawing the damp earth behind the statue. At last, she felt something. Blinking away rainwater she directed her phone-torch down. A tin. She wiped off a smear of wet soil. A Virginia tobacco tin, her dad had used one for screws after he'd smoked the tobacco. Kneeling in the mushy soil, Freddy prised off the lid.

# 55

*Toni*

'It's rare for an officer to go looking for evidence that could blow a hole through their own solve.' Toni dabbed up a scrap of pizza crust from the box with a damp finger and popped it in her mouth.

'Morgan struck me as a decent bloke,' Malcolm said.

'Strange they didn't give it more attention at the time of the Moon murder.' Darren was doodling, horses and riders leaping at a jump. Rather good, Toni noticed.

'They did fingerprints and got nothing. It wasn't found at the murder site, it might have been dropped by anyone.' Malcolm gathered up the pizza boxes and began distributing them among wastebins by one of the now empty desks.

The buzz from Morgan's news had given way to exhaustion. Officers were trawling solved and unsolved murders before the Moon murder for the three earlier victims of the serial killer. A search on cases featuring five-pound notes had brought up nothing.

Toni's core team had ignored her order for everyone to go

get some sleep. The four detectives remained seated at the table in front of the Murder Board.

Darren's phone startled them all. Abandoning his horses, he flew to answer it.

'You are *kidding*. Mate, that's *way* cool...' No hairtitivating this time. 'Wow, you went the extra mile, more than one beer in that for you. *What a star.*'

'Who is a star this time?' Sheena wasn't being sarcastic.

'Joe Blaker, him and me go way back, we were at school together.' Not that 'way back'; Toni could tell twenty-eight-year-old Darren his 'way back' was like yesterday to her. 'Joe's in the planning department at Lewes Council.' Darren did his jig again. 'It was a punt, but I asked him if there had been any alterations to Blacklock House since planning began.'

'Haslem punched a hole into his ceiling for the spiral staircase,' Sheena said.

'That was the eighth Earl Blacklock when you didn't need permission.' Darren sat down again. 'He slid down that spiral staircase and broke open his head, remember? Haslem marked the spot with an X. But Joe said there was a relatively recent permission, not an alteration; it was to restore what had been there.'

'Which was?' Toni's neck was tingling again. *Bad sign.* She dared not hope.

'When Blacklock House was converted into flats in the 1950s they sealed up the servants' staircase. Five years ago, a resident was granted the right to remove a wall and unbrick a door. Joe is pinging over a scan.'

'Which flat was it?' Toni was on her feet before Darren replied.

★ ★ ★

In the empty Murder Room, the photographs of seven murder victims – Adrian Moon, James and Wilbur Ritchie, Sally, Tristan and Ben Robinson, and a smirking Garry Haslem – were for ever fixed. Receding footsteps died away. Car doors slammed, engines fired and accelerated away.

Then silence.

# 56

*Freddy*

Freddy flung the van around the turning circle outside Blacklock House and skidded to a stop at the steps. She grabbed the tobacco tin from the passenger seat and, leaving the van door open, sodden sneakers squelching, stumbled up the steps. She pressed the tradesman's bell first. The door didn't open. Then Bunty, her favourite customer at Blacklock House. Then every bell until she realised there was no light on the panel. It was disconnected.

*Martha.* Freddy nearly fell down the steps as she prodded about her phone for *Martha Mob* in contacts. At last, she pressed the green receiver icon. No answer.

A crack of thunder was followed swiftly by a fork of lightning that, it seemed to Freddy, hit the meadow beyond the railings. Freddy guessed the meeting was in the room they all paid for. Although she'd delivered fish to Rex, she'd only ever gone upstairs to his flat. Martha had said that at the last meeting, the French doors had opened. That put the meeting on the ground floor. No lights were on at the front.

Freddy hurtled down the steps to the gate in the yew hedge

she had gone through when they found Garry Haslem in the wheelbarrow. *It was locked.* She tugged at the padlock then, desperate, in the same fugue state as when she had climbed the railings at Newhaven Harbour, flung herself at the hedge. She bounced off. The branches were dense and pliable. Another go. A branch scored her cheek, the pain barely registering. Freddy felt along the hedge and found the long-ago break between two plants. The weakest link. Facing backwards, she pushed and shoved. She felt her shirt rip, branches tore her skin. Suddenly there was no resistance and Freddy toppled through and was hit by something sharp.

'*Ouch.*' Freddy was on her feet, hand up to ward the next blow. None came. She shone her phone on a pair of secateurs lying on the grass beside a bundle of clothes. Freddy had no time to register relief. From the back of the house came a terrible scream, long and shrill and heart-stopping.

'*Martha.*' Clutching the tin, Freddy raced towards the sound.

## 57

*Toni*

'*That's Freddy's van.*'

Toni braked the Jeep in a spray of gravel. The four officers flung themselves out and, as Freddy had done minutes earlier, belted up the steps and tried the tradesman's bell. An enormous crash of thunder directly overhead caused them to huddle for a split second.

'It's dead. Try the back.' Toni led the way to the garden gate. Like Freddy, she rattled furiously at the solid padlock.

It was Sheena who spotted smashed branches in the hedge a couple of metres along from the gate and, head down, charged it like a bull.

In the criss-crossing beams of torches, the officers saw the bundle of clothes immediately. Unlike Freddy, who had been distracted, they saw that the clothes were on a body.

'It's Barbara Major, the crime writer. We're too late.' In anguish, Toni fell onto her knees. She put a finger to the woman's neck. 'There's a pulse.'

A screech.

'It's from over there.' Darren was off.

'It's the peacock,' Malcolm called after him.

Another scream. No mistaking that for a bird.

'Sheena, call for backup.' Toni stopped Sheena from going after Darren. 'Stay with the victim, this is no time for heroes.'

It was a time for reckless officers. Toni and Malcolm raced across Haslem's patio and around the corner of the house.

'*Shit.*' Malcolm never swore. 'Ma'am, stay back.'

'*No.*' Toni saw why.

Freddy lay in a slant of light across the grass from the library. Martha was cradling Freddy's head in her lap, Freddy's eyes were closed. Sylvia Burnett was tying a tourniquet around Freddy's arm.

'Is she…'

'Luckily, Timothy only nicked her with the blade. Although she'll need stitches.' Sylvia was matter-of-fact.

'Toni, I know who—'

'Freddy, don't move,' Sylvia told Freddy.

'Timothy has the Tristan-phone, I should have—'

'Toni, don't blame Mar—'

'Don't try to speak.' Toni hadn't expected Freddy to be there, let alone get herself hurt. Stupid, it was pure Freddy.

'The serial killer stabbed Rex,' Patrick Bell bleated from the library steps where he sat, Martyn Burnett beside him, his head between his legs.

'You OK there?' Toni asked Martyn.

'He needs a fix.' Sylvia might have been remarking that her husband had skipped dinner.

'Except for an utter lack of moral and physical courage, there's nothing wrong with these two.' Bunty wandered out of the library and onto the lawn.

'Toni... my pocket...' Freddy grimaced from obvious pain.

'Dr Burnett, when you're done with Freddy, we've found Barbara Major in a critical condition.' Pointing to the side of the house, Toni tried to stop Bunty. 'Lady Dorothy, *please* stay here.'

'When the fountain plays, death is nigh,' Bunty warned.

'Barbara? *No.*' Sylvia grabbed her doctor's bag and ran to the side garden. 'Barbara has hurt no one.'

'Toni, there's a tin—'

Following Bunty's finger, Toni saw the fountain was working. *When the fountain plays, death is nigh.* The fountain had worked the morning Garry Haslem died. Someone had said in their statement that when the Robinsons... Toni yelled, 'Where is Timothy Mew?' The wood-panelled library was empty. Patrick's words echoed in her head, *'The serial killer stabbed Rex.'*

'Toni.' Freddy was wild-eyed, her other arm flailing. 'My pocket. Tin.'

Toni bent down and pulled an old tobacco tin from the back pocket of Freddy's trousers.

'...that gorgeous policeman who interviewed me followed them...'

Toni opened the tin. Staring at the contents, she got the import of Bunty's words. Darren.

*'Bunty, stay where you are.'*

Blood thudding in her ears, rain streaming down her face, Toni was further drenched as wind blew spray from the fountain into her path. Everywhere was water.

*'Not Darren. Not Darren,'* Toni pleaded to Freddy's god. *Do not hurt that keen, intelligent man.* Absurdly, Darren's sketches of horses and riders popped into her mind.

'Put down the knife, mate, yeah? It's over now. It's over.' Darren was cajoling someone in the summer house.

Peering from behind a tree, Toni made out two figures. Darren was in shadow, shining his torch at a man with a knife. If Darren tried to cut and run, he'd get no further than the doorway. He was up against a ruthless man who was not open to negotiation.

'Bend down, lay the knife at your feet. Give it a kick towards me, yeah?'

'*Darren.*' Toni could not wait for backup. She barrelled at the man with the knife, knocking it out of his hand. She would be disciplined for it. No officer should take a risk more likely to end in the death of themselves and their colleague.

Darren Mason had Timothy Mew up against the wall. Timothy began sobbing, over and over. 'He was going to kill me. He was going to kill me. He was...'

'If he's not hurt, take him to the station,' Toni gasped. 'Good work, DC Mason.'

'He's bleeding out.' Handcuffing Mew, Darren gestured at a prone figure slumped in the corner. 'Mew wouldn't let me near him.'

'Paramedics are on their way.' Crouching beside Rex Lomax, in the light of her torch, Toni saw that, whenever the ambulance arrived, it would be too late.

'When did you know?' Rex's speech was clogged with blood. Toni jammed tissues from her pocket against a deep wound in the lawyer's throat.

'The secret staircase clinched it.' The tissues were soaked with blood. 'Afternoon naps in your bedroom. You represented Kenneth Todd at his appeal and got him out. Perhaps you would have anyway, you were a smart defence lawyer, but how much easier to build a case when you'd done the murder yourself.'

'Any evidence, Toni? I may call you Toni, may I?' Rex coughed up blood.

'Until tonight, if you'd defended yourself, you would have walked.' Toni flashed the torch around the summer house. The tobacco tin had skittered under a sofa along the back wall when she'd dropped it to disarm Timothy. 'We have a tin of five-pound notes. Series C which, I needn't tell you, were superseded in 1971. Was it a rainy-day stash you forgot until it was too late to spend it or did you specifically save them as messages for us?'

'Nice try, Toni Kemp, but you have nothing to connect them to me.' Lomax's eyes gleamed.

'We have a witness.' Toni had no idea how Freddy had come by the tin. She stared at a number on the uppermost note. *Eleven*. It would be Barbara Major if she died from her injuries. 'We didn't find the ones at the Ritchie murder scene.'

'I forgot.' *A confession.*

'You are *kidding*.' No wonder Toni could feel her job was impossible. She had to start with the principle that perpetrators kept to their own rules. Serial killers didn't have rules.

'Did you try to kill Timothy Mew?'

'Mew was going to steal my flat. He forged my will and tried to frame Martha for the murders.' Rex's voice was weak, Toni bent closer. '*Met. My. Match.*'

'That was chivalrous, you hardly know Martha.'

'I resent someone getting credit for my actions.' Rex began to shiver. Toni grabbed a blanket from the couch and carefully covered him with it. 'Martha would have stolen my glory.'

'I don't think she'd have seen it that way.' Toni had tumbled, like Alice into Wonderland, into the crazed logic of a cold-blooded murderer. 'Do you have proof Timothy Mew planned to con you?'

'In his wardrobe, papers... forged... signature.' A gout of blood shot out of Rex's mouth. *'Pol-gise tonia Kemmm... under par.'*

'Why no murders after Adrian Moon until now?' Toni was racing against death.

'You want an explanation, Antonia Kemp?' Rex capitalised on a burst of strength. 'I had more faith in you. You know serial killers don't have reasons. Nor do we tell the truth.' Another cough. 'I kill when I'm lonely. Will that do?'

'Not if it's a lie.' Lomax's faith in her was well-placed; Toni had known looking for motive would get them nowhere.

'Is that why you hired a companion?' Toni kept trying. 'Because you were lonely?'

*'My luck... hissss's con-man.'* Almost inaudible with the ghost of a smile.

'I'm thinking maybe Karma?'

Rex Lomax was past hearing. Toni raised the blanket up over the dead man's face and, getting up, left the summer house.

# 58

## Six Weeks Later

Martha didn't believe in God and recently her faith in people had also taken a knock. Nevertheless, she'd offered to attend Mass at Our Lady of Sorrows with Freddy. Her finger held the page in the missal – a tatty volume which apparently Freddy had owned since a child – headed, *Twenty-Eighth Sunday in Ordinary Time*. Martha was trying, for Freddy's sake, to understand the meaning of the text. No joy, so far...

Ordinary Time. Since the morning, two and half months ago, when Martha had driven Timothy to Blacklock House, nothing had been ordinary. The man she had been having a secret affair with had been murdered. Freddy had told her that Toni Kemp had traced the 'lovey-dovey' message on the bunch of roses they'd seen amongst the tributes left on the heath to the hairdresser to which Tristan had switched after he and Martha got together. He'd said it was to avoid a slip-up. By then Martha didn't care.

Tomorrow she was opening her salon again. Freddy's conviction that Martha's customers were loyal was right, Martha was booked up for weeks. *Hurrah for Ordinary Time*.

'...you take away the sins of the world, have mercy on us;
you take away the sins of the world...'

The congregation were reciting the words. *Panic*. Martha had lost her place in the missal.

'You don't have to join in.' When Mass had begun, Freddy had tried to discourage Martha from standing up, it was enough that she'd come. But Martha had been determined to *do it all*. Hurriedly, she found the place and reading – loudly – she completed the Gloria without taking a breath.

'...are the most High Jesus Christ in the Holy Spirit in
the glory of God the Father. *Amen.*'

'Let us pray,' said the priest who Freddy called Father Pete. 'Oh God, by whom we are redeemed...'

Two of the residents of Blacklock House were dead. After the night of the storm a month ago – *the second freaking storm* – no day was ordinary.

Timothy was on remand in Wormwood Scrubs, charged with Rex Lomax's murder and with attempting to defraud him.

'...I loved her more than health or beauty, preferred her to the light, since her radiance never sleeps. In her company all good things came to me, at her hands riches not to be numbered...'

The reading from the book of Wisdom filled Martha with joy. Wisdom had taught her that her rubbish relationships with men were because they weren't Freddy Power.

★ ★ ★

Newhaven Cemetery was carved out of the Downs in the latter part of the nineteenth century. Despite the hundreds of grave markers dotting the grassy slopes, it only accentuated the majestic sweep of the hills.

Framed in the arched aperture joining two chapels stood the bronze statue of a boy, hands clasping a holy cross above his head. Behind him, a metalled track tapered away to the crest of the hill.

Toni bent over a tap affixed to the wall of one of the chapels and, laying down the bouquet of dahlias, ran her wrists under cold water. Although it was autumn, the day was warm. She pulled a plastic jug from her bag and filled it. Had she not been wearing one of her best shirts, she'd have tipped water over her head. Instead, dahlias in one hand, jug in the other, she took a meandering route across the cemetery to where a beech tree, the leaves golden brown, shaded a grave,

icholas Kemp 1948–1991

257
Forever in  ur hearts
Safe with  esus

Rereading the epitaph on the flaking headstone – her mum's words – Toni reflected, as she had many times, that in another thirty more years, the words would be worn to nothing. One day no one would know who lay buried beneath. She stared at the headstone and did a rapid calculation. Freddy had said Toni was twelve in 1991. Toni maintained she was thirteen. She hadn't said that she should know how old she was when her dad was murdered. But she was twelve. How could she have got it wrong?

Toni arranged the dahlias. This ritual, as close as Toni – an atheist who didn't expect to be safe with Jesus – got to a votive offering. She knew why. She had wanted her dad with her longer and, subconsciously, she had given him another year. *She had given herself another year.*

On the morning Nicholas Kemp had been murdered, he had discovered slugs had reduced his dahlias to blunted stems. Toni's dahlias were by way of compensation. She didn't come on anniversaries, Christmas, nor his birth and death days.

Toni came when she would have come were her dad alive. On a Sunday or after work. She told her dad about her latest cases, the problems, the successes. That she, like him, got heartburn when she was stressed. She didn't mention the shoplifting.

Now Toni sat on the bench she had paid for herself when she returned to Newhaven after years in the Met. She told Nicky Kemp about the Cut-Price Killer. Rex Lomax would have hated the name the media had given him, but these days a fiver was worth nothing.

'I can't claim credit, Dad. One of my younger officers discovered Rex Lomax had reinstated a back staircase with access to the garden. Garry Haslem must have seen him coming out, perhaps to commit another murder, and guessed what he was doing. Rex said Haslem was clever, but not clever enough for Rex Lomax.' Toni looked across the cemetery.

Two figures, sketchy from a distance, were weaving between graves towards Toni. Freddy and Martha stopped holding hands as they got closer.

'Thought you'd be here,' Freddy called.

'Spur of the moment.' Toni had intended to come and Freddy would know that. Toni didn't feel comfortable around Martha, she'd lied to the police... *and she knew Toni's secret.* Freddy had told Toni that Martha had been in the kitchen when they had rowed about her stealing Snickers. If Freddy and Martha ever broke up, Toni just hoped it was amicable.

'Martha came to Mass then we had coffee in that shack on the river which does brilliant bacon butties.' Freddy kissed her fingers and touched Nicholas Kemp's headstone. Crossing herself, she whispered, 'In the name of the Father and of the Son and of the Holy Spirit. Amen.' Nicky Kemp had been a better father to Freddy than Fred Power senior.

Glancing at Martha, Toni returned her tentative smile. If Martha had looked embarrassed by the Catholic thing, Toni would have tossed her over the fence.

'I went to Blacklock House on Friday.' Freddy moved away from the grave. 'Patrick Bell's signed his flat over to that friend he swindled and moved out. Sylvia Burnett has got Martyn into rehab.'

'Good for Sylvia.' Toni knew that Sylvia had been wrong to feed her husband's drug habit, but Haslem had kept it going. She recalled Sylvia's cry of anguish that Barbara Major was seriously injured. Sylvia had feelings after all. 'It's Bunty I feel for. Horrible she has to leave her home.'

'I was going to tell you.' Freddy was excited. 'Bunty is staying at Blacklock House. Garry Haslem bequeathed her his flat and the contents.'

'*Wow.*' Toni was a tad fed up with being caught by surprise. 'Why? I understood he hated her.'

'Garry put in his will that him being a barrow boy and Bunty a farmhand's daughter they had something in common.

Before you get misty-eyed,' Freddy joined Toni on the bench, 'Bunty pointed out that Haslem expected to outlive her so it was meaningless. Garry didn't reckon on mild-mannered Rex Lomax slitting his throat. Bunty will pass the flat onto the local hospice one day, she says.'

'That's nice.' Although summer was nearly over, Toni imagined the green shoots of spring. There was good in some of the residents of Blacklock House.

'I am sorry for not telling you sooner,' Martha blurted out what she'd said many times over the last month.

'Enough with that.' Toni didn't want to hear it. 'At least Timothy never got to frame you.'

Toni thought that, but for Rex stepping in, Martha was doing a good job of framing herself. *Black Ford Fiesta, keyed Range Rover, failure to tell the police that she'd known all the victims and lastly, retaining important evidence in the form of what she'd called the Tristan-phone.* They had found the 'Martha-phone' in Rex's jacket. He had rung Martha after she had escaped from the library with Molly the owl. It was Sheena who found the untaxed black Ford Fiesta in a lock-up that Rex owned. The car he had used to get to and from Seaford Head, and, it seemed from CCTV, to drive much further afield. The lock-up was a grim museum of victims' trophies that led them to the first murders. When they'd gone public about the currency, a retired constable from Gloucestershire Police had recalled a five-pound note. It was found in their evidence stores without a tag. A member of the public came forward with one more. The third one never materialised. Malcolm said it had probably been sold on to a collector. The murders of Jack Menzies, Stephen Bryant and Matthew Jeffreys had begun with Menzies thirty years ago when Lomax had just had his first case. All the men were fathers of young boys, one murdered walking a dog, and the other two jogging in green spaces. Lomax's wife Emily had temporarily left him in the period when he killed Bryant. He had had a cancer scare when he murdered Jeffreys. So many patterns. No pattern.

Bunty had shown them the talisman that Rex had used to reveal their secrets while putting them through Leela, the game of knowledge. Rex had used a signet ring he had taken from Jack Menzies. Lomax had told the group that the ring's owner, had meant a lot to him. Why had Menzies meant a lot to Lomax? Because he was the first victim? There were no links between Lomax and his victims. Lomax had chosen them at random. Martha had said Rex claimed he'd lost a medallion he'd got at mass. She told Toni that Timothy had stolen it from Rex. He hadn't said Freddy had given it to him. Freddy confessed to Toni she'd found it under her pew and felt guilty, because she suspected the medallion had been Rex's all along.

'I suppose we can't ask if you're charging Barbara with Emily Lomax's murder?' Freddy was tentative.

'We have no proof Barbara caused Emily's crash.' Toni gazed out at the band of glittering sea beyond Newhaven. 'Possibly she stepped into the lane without seeing Emily Lomax's car and, feeling guilty, couldn't admit it.'

Toni shifted her gaze to the hills. A ribbon crossing a patchwork of fields, the Ouse, a tidal river, wended down from Lower Beeding, a village in the west of the county. Even on dull days, this was a view Toni Kemp loved.

'What mattered more to Major was that her neighbours never knew she was trying to write crime fiction. Just shows that the weight of a secret is calculated by how important it is to the keeper,' Freddy said. 'Who honestly cares if Barbara is trying to write a novel?'

'She doesn't dare put pen to paper, or fingers to keys.' Toni rested a hand on her dad's headstone. 'Shame, because she has terrific powers of observation. She was on to Rex before us. We thought Barbara had a crush on Rex, but all the time she had noticed discrepancies in what he told people and what she had observed. Barbara had wanted to be Rex's companion to get closer to him and confirm her suspicions. She had seen Rex in his black Ford Fiesta. She had also noticed his hand only shook when people were watching. Rex's doctor confirmed that he was as fit as a fiddle. He did not, as Garry claimed and Rex let you all think, have Parkinson's Disease.'

'He lied to us all.' Freddy hadn't got over that Rex was as horrible as her father. *Worse.* Fred Power senior had not been a serial killer.

'Barbara saw Rex take the path out of the garden to Dedmans Heath that afternoon. She was stopped from following him by Bunty wanting to talk about her owl. But later she saw Rex talking to Haslem outside the house. She decided to confront him the night of the extraordinary residents' meeting. Barbara underestimated Rex. She's got Sylvia's doctoring skills to thank that she's alive.'

'Remember that time you followed me into that field?' Freddy was animated. 'I was followed by a car, the sun was blinding so I couldn't tell the colour. I was sure the driver was trying to intimidate me, if you hadn't come along when you did. What if it was Rex?'

'Why would he want to hurt you?' To give her her due, Martha looked very worried.

'Maybe he thought you'd seen him in his car,' Toni said. 'Later, perhaps, he realised you knew nothing so he spared you.'

'The day the Robinsons were murdered, I called on Rex,' Freddy said. 'Perhaps he saw me. Timothy said Rex was having a nap, but you've established that he was never in his bedroom. He sneaked out down the secret staircase.'

'Did you find who let Molly the owl out?' Martha asked.

'I put equal odds on Lomax, Haslem or Mew.' Toni removed a weed from Nicky Kemp's grave.

'The papers are saying that he killed because he was lonely. Like Dennis Nilsen.'

'That's what Lomax told me, but he was playing me. We'll never know why he killed. I'm not convinced he knew himself.'

'If we did know, would it help?' Martha wondered.

'It might give the families peace of mind, but not much.' Toni spoke from experience. It had not helped her to know her dad's murderer was going through a divorce and lost his temper over a pint of gold top.

'We found a cable from the fountain to the hidden stairs in Rex's flat ending at a switch. He turned it on when he'd committed a murder,' Toni told Freddy. 'Rex's nod to Patrick Hamilton's *Gaslight*.'

Toni's phone rang. 'Hey, Mal.'

'There's been a robbery at the Co-op, a man with a knife has taken the contents of the till and, er, um, loads of confectionery. The Worrier wants his "dream team on the scene". Any chance you could meet me there?'

'Every chance.' Toni turned to Freddy and Martha, 'Guys, I've got to go, there's—'

'I heard.' Freddy raised her eyebrows. 'Did Malcolm say how many Snickers were missing?'

'You're *funny*.' Toni swiped Freddy on the shoulder. It would have tied loose ends to know why Rex Lomax had murdered ten people, but what mattered more than anything was Toni had got her best friend back.

# Acknowledgements

When I'm teaching creative writing, I suggest that students write the novel they want to read. Me, I love to curl up with a country-house murder story, so I decided to write one.

My heartfelt thanks to Dr Charlie Skinner for showing me around the country house in which he has a flat. A brave decision since Charlie knew I've been known to stick a murder in my own sitting room...

I read many books on serial killers for this story. I was particularly inspired by *Signs of Murder* by Professor David Wilson. It tapped into my long-held interest in psycho-geography. After that I devoured everything by David Wilson I could find.

As always, friends and my family have given me stalwart encouragement. My cousins Tasmin Barnett and Katherine Nelson are my readers too, and I've valued their lovely comments. Thank you both.

Such thanks to Juliet Eve for being my back-up proof-reader as well as a supportive friend.

I'd also like to acknowledge Lisa Holloway who is a true friend.

Sunrise walks on the Downs with the Horseradishes (named after our foraging exploits), Tina Ross, Gill Hamer and Joann Weedon have been precious.

No novel gets written without the support and comradeship of fellow crime writers, Domenica de Rosa and William Shaw. You two are the best. I have given Domenica's lightning sketches of horses heading for a jump to DC Darren Mason. Domenica's horses grace my pinboard as I write.

Big thanks to fab emeritus profs Jenny Bourne Taylor and Flis Henwood, and to Vikasini (aka Marianne Dixon) and Candida Lacey. I am ever grateful to retired Chief Superintendent Stephen Cassidy for valuable advice over the years and to Shirley Cassidy for being such a supportive reader.

Always *such* a thank you to my agent George, at Georgina Capel.

The story owes much to my editor Laura Palmer who is pure gold. And there would be no actual book on a shelf without the fabulous Head of Zeus team. Starting with Peyton Stableford, Laura's right-hand woman who has been so helpful. Thank you to Liz Hatherell for another sterling copyedit. I am chuffed to have Jon Appleton on proofreading. I'm thrilled that Sophie Ransom (legend) has handled PR. When this isn't a book, it's an audio and is read beautifully by the chocolate-voiced actor Richard Attlee. I love the cover of *The Companion*, so thank you to Emma Rogers.

My partner Melanie Lockett is my first reader, on paper then when the book is published. I couldn't wish for more love and support. It's returned in spades.

I can't say enough how I appreciate the support of readers and of our fabulous libraries and bookshops who have got behind my novels. One reader is Dorothy, sadly no longer with us. Lady Dorothy is named in her memory. Big thanks also to actor Jeremy Preston.

*The Companion* is dedicated to Philippa Brewster. Philippa published my first novel, *Seven Miles From Sydney*, in 1987 when she was founding boss of Pandora Press and has always been in my corner both professionally and as a friend.

Lesley Thomson
Sussex, 1st February 2022

# About the Author

LESLEY THOMSON grew up in West London.
Her first novel, *A Kind of Vanishing*, won the
People's Book Prize in 2010. Her second novel,
*The Detective's Daughter*, was a #1 bestseller and the
resulting series has sold over 750,000 copies. Lesley
divides her time between Sussex and Gloucestershire.
She lives with her partner and her dog.
Visit her website at lesleythomson.co.uk